a borrowed boyfriend

ANGELA CASELLA

Babes of Brewing

Best Served Cold

Worst Nanny Ever

Unlucky in Love

The Love Fixers

The Love Bandits

The Love Losers

The Love Destroyers

The Thief Who Saved Christmas

Finding You

You're so Extra

You're so Bad

You're so Basic

You're so Vain

Fairy Godmother Agency

A Borrowed Boyfriend

A Stolen Suit

A Brooding Bodyguard

A Reluctant Roommate

Bringing Down the House (Nicole and Damien's story)

Highland Hills

(co-written with Denise Grover Swank)

Matchmaking a Billionaire

Matchmaking a Single Dad

Matchmaking a Grump

Matchmaking a Roommate

Bad Luck Club

(co-written with Denise Grover Swank)

Love at First Hate

Jingle Bell Hell

Fraudulently Ever After

Matchmaking Mischief

Asheville Brewing

(co-written with Denise Grover Swank)

Any Luck at All

Better Luck Next Time

Getting Lucky

Bad Luck Club

Luck of the Draw (novella)

All the Luck You Need (prequel novella) by Angela Casella

To my English teachers, some of whom probably regret everything they ever taught me.

one

MARNIE

IS *that guy checking me out?*

I feel a prickle of self-consciousness that has everything to do with the fact that I'm wearing an old Star Wars T-shirt I sleep in more often than I should admit, including last night, and that I ignored Andy's not-so-subtle advice to put on some makeup for once. Yeah, no, he's *definitely* not interested in me. He's gorgeous enough to make angels weep. Which means he's staring for the same reason everyone stares at me lately.

"Nice shirt," Angel Guy says with a nod.

"Um. Thanks," I reply, gritting my teeth against what I know is coming next. I should probably just walk away, but I really need that drink.

I send a desperate glance at the bartender, who's already passed me over twice for women who, unlike me, probably spent more than two minutes getting ready. Lo and behold, the bartender notices me. Our gazes meet for an instant. His eyes are the color of the whiskey I'd like to drink. I feel the warmth of his gaze down to my toes.

I guess I must really want that drink. The bartender takes a step toward me, which is a promising development.

"It's you, isn't it? Sinclair Jones's sister," Angel Guy says, pulling my attention away. "You look different without"—he motions around his head as if to suggest the hours I'd spent being primped and polished on the morning of my wedding. Or, I should say, the morning of what was *supposed* to be my wedding. "Well, you know, you look different now, but you're the woman from that meme. Can I buy you a drink?"

"Nope. No can do." I can feel the bartender watching me, taking in the situation, and I flush with embarrassment. "You understand. I have important Force-related business." I give him the Star Wars hand signal, then turn and start walking away before he can object . . . or start snapping pictures. Let's be honest, I know what he really wants—a selfie with the woman who became a meme.

God save me from this lookie-loo. I've had more than enough embarrassment to last three lifetimes, thank you very much. I don't need to add any more line items to that list.

I hear a soft laugh behind me, and someone asks, "Isn't that the Vulcan hand gesture from Star Trek?"

Whatever. It's my brother's shirt. Drew's a bit of a nerd, obsessed with his space operas. I love him, but he can keep his intergalactic dramas to himself. Why am I wearing his shirt? Because we live together, and he skipped doing his laundry for several weeks in a row. I finally broke down and did it myself, but in retaliation I stole his most comfortable shirt.

When I slide into the booth across from my friends, Andy and Grace, they cut off their conversation so quickly it's obvious they've been talking about me.

Andy eyes my empty hands, and I avoid the urge to cover my bare ring finger. It's the lack of a drink she cares about.

"I thought the point of getting a drink was to get a drink," she says.

"I changed my mind," I say. "Maybe I'll do a sober January thing."

Grace gives me a dubious look, and fine, she has a point. If ever there were a January to not be sober, it's this one.

"Or not," I amend. "Anyway, aren't we here to talk about the book? You dragged me out tonight on the pretext of having a book club meeting."

"Did you read the book?" Andy asks.

"No," I admit.

Andy shoots a quizzical look at Grace, who develops a sudden interest in the scratched-up tabletop in front of her. A sudden flash of light reflects off her glasses, and I flinch, but then I realize it's a reflection of whatever's on the TV across from her, not a camera.

"Come *on*," Andy says. "Marnie gets a pass, but you had a whole month. I read *Outlander* when you asked us to. That was a very long book."

"There was a lot of sex in it," Grace says with a twinkle in her eyes. "Hot Scottish Guy sex. Admit you enjoyed it. We *all* did."

"Never."

"Anyway," Grace says, "the book is immaterial—"

"Says the person who didn't pick it," Andy mutters, sweeping her long black curls over her shoulder.

I'd take part in the conversation, except I honestly don't remember what we were supposed to read. Don't get me wrong, I love reading . . . I'm just not in the right headspace. Every time a guy in a book does something stupid, I want to hit him over the head with a rolled-up newspaper. Every time a woman trusts someone she shouldn't, I want to . . . well, honestly the newspaper approach still sounds pretty good. It makes reading stressful.

"We could talk about *Outlander*," I suggest. "I just rewatched the first episode."

Grace gives Andy a knowing look.

"These looks you're giving each other . . . do they have anything to do with whatever you were talking about when I went up to the bar?" I ask.

It does not soothe me when Grace slides her glass of white wine across the table to me, and not just because I would have preferred Andy's bourbon. Still, I have a feeling I'm going to need some bolstering, so I don't push it back.

"What did you do?" I ask.

"We're worried about you," Grace says, which isn't an answer. I know they're worried about me. *I'm* worried about me.

"You have plenty of reasons for that," I concede.

After all, it's not every day a woman is left at the altar. It would've been easier to get over the whole thing if one of our guests hadn't caught it all on tape, including me tripping over the aisle runner and falling flat on my face. It became a viral gif *and* a meme, and my image is now all over the internet.

Spend fifteen minutes poking around, and you can find stills of my face registering horror before I run—followed by an image of me after I fell face-first on the carpet—accompanied by messages like: *When I remembered* Sisters of Sin *is releasing today. When you find out he likes pineapple on pizza.* Or, a personal favorite, *When he realizes your sister is Sinclair Jones and that he was about to settle for second best.*

Touché.

Sometimes people get fancy and include the whole video. Or use it as a tongue-in-cheek response to other people's posts online.

I write my own takes on the meme when I'm feeling punch-drunk, or particularly sorry for myself.

"You should sue," Andy says.

I sigh. "We've been over this. I don't know who got the footage. At this point, I'd have to sue thousands upon thousands of people to get it to go away. It's not worth it. It would make it look like I care."

"You *do* care," Grace points out. From the look on her face, she cares too, which I appreciate. The thing is, there's a very good chance that the jerk who recorded that video and released it was someone close to me. Not one of these two, obviously, because I trust them down to my soul, but someone else.

That knowledge keeps me up some nights.

"It doesn't help that your asshole sister keeps talking about it to the press," Andy says.

"Hey," I say, lifting my hands, feeling a prickle of defensiveness. "This isn't her fault."

"Well, it would help if she'd shut the fuck up."

"Yes," I admit, "it would help."

It would also help if she'd stop texting me little uplifting messages, often accompanied by selfies of her perfectly made-up face. Or if she would stop trying to FaceTime me at odd hours, working around the shooting schedule of her show, *Sisters of Sin*. Or if my sister, who's older by two years, weren't playing a character who's eight years younger than me.

Sinclair's pitying looks aren't exactly boosting my self-esteem, is what I'm saying. Yes, my house looks like someone unleashed a pet tornado in it, and I've definitely looked better, but I need a little time to wallow, don't I?

Wallowing is normal. Wallowing is healthy. I went to one appointment with a therapist, and she told me so, which I took as permission to never go back.

I tell my friends as much. "I know this whole thing will blow over eventually," I add. "I'll be fine. Perfectly fine."

They exchange another look, which is frankly annoying, and then Andy points out, "It's been three months, Marnie."

Which pisses me off more. "I'm well aware of how long it's been, Andy. I'm the one who designed the invitations."

I take a sip of the donated wine.

Andy clears her throat. "It's just. Chet has been doing some work for Tilton Expeditions."

"What?" I nearly drop the wine glass. "Why didn't you say anything?"

Tilton Expeditions is Brock's business, Brock being the man who whispered, *Sorry, Marnie, I can't go through with this*, to me at the altar three months ago after making a proposal that was so over the top and frankly embarrassing that people would still be talking about it . . . if they weren't instead talking about the fallout. Chet is Andy's current boyfriend, a position no one has ever held for very long. I think it's because she tends to date men who are hotter than they are smart, but I'm not in a situation to judge or offer advice.

Andy tilts her head and gives me a look.

"Fine. I get why you didn't say anything."

"Anyway," she says slowly, "Brock asked your boss for a meeting next week. He's going to hire your team for a new project, and he specifically said he wants *you* to be involved."

"Fuck," I bark out.

A blond woman in the booth next to ours pops her head over the back and gives me a dirty look, like a pissed-off groundhog. "Excuse me. I have a *child* over here," she says fiercely. "This is the second time you've spoken a foul word. You should be ashamed of yourself."

"Maybe you shouldn't have brought your kid to a bar on a Saturday night, lady," Andy says, swiveling her head and looking up. "You're lucky we're not having a passion party."

The woman huffs but drops back down into her booth. I'd like to pretend it has something to do with the glare I gave her, but I'm no fool.

Andy isn't the kind of person you'd want to pick a fight with. She's muscular and toned, and she's got these *I don't take shit from anyone* eyes that are so deep brown they're almost black. It's a superpower that's not wasted on her gig as a daycare teacher, regardless of what her parents tell her.

Grace smiles at Andy. I smile at Andy. The two of us lack that natural ability to intimidate. If Andy's a predator, then we're more like prey. Give me fifteen minutes and a word processor, and I could put together a message that'll really mess up someone's day. Or a card that'll make them feel excellent, horrible, or amused. But in real life it's a bit difficult to excuse yourself for fifteen minutes in the middle of a tense moment. Lucky for me, and for Grace, we have Andy, the rare bobcat who befriends a couple of bunnies.

The thought's almost enough to make me smile . . . and then I think of Brock hiring Val's Visions.

"Why would he do that?" I whisper-hiss.

Grace does this half-shrug, half-head-tilt thing and says, "Maybe he feels guilty and wants to make sure you're okay."

Andy snorts. "Or he knows you're the best graphic designer in town, and he wants you to do his work for him while also proving there are no hard feelings so he can stop looking like the bad guy. Sounds like he's about to land a big deal with Edgar James."

If I'd had a drink, I would have spat it out. "*Seriously?*"

Edgar James is a famous survivalist type. He had his own show for a while on the Discovery Channel, and now he runs an extreme camping business with several locations across North Carolina. Brock has always been borderline obsessed with him. A few months back, Edgar nearly drowned on a white water rafting trip, and Brock, no joke, spent five hours trying to choose an appropriate *sorry you almost drowned* gift to send him. They'd only met once, at a conference, so my thoroughly ignored vote was no gift, but apparently sucking up pays off.

"No. I said it for shits and giggles," Andy deadpans.

"I guess good things really do happen to bad people," I say with a sigh.

"My point is that you're going to have to see him, and you'll be around other people who'll be watching your every reaction," Andy says. "Are you prepared for that?"

My smile slips, and I can feel my heart pounding too fast in my chest. I mean, I knew it would only be a matter of time before we ran into each other. Asheville's hardly a huge city. I was just hoping it would be more like four years, or preferably ten. And that I'd be happily married to some nondescript handsome guy who I could wave in front of myself like a flag. *See? You publicly humiliated me, but I did just fine.*

"Sure," I say, pouring an admirable amount of bravado into it, if I do say so myself. "I'm not the one who did a fucked-up thing."

"No, but . . ." Grace looks to Andy for help.

"You don't want him to think he broke you."

"Ouch," I say, rubbing my chest. "I . . ."

"Look at yourself," Andy says in that tough love voice I've heard a lot of recently. "You've probably been wearing that shirt for forty-eight hours."

"Twenty-four," I say sullenly. "I dress professionally for work. How I dress in my free time should be no one's concern. The only thing I did today—other than this amazing outing, obviously—is visit my aunt."

Andy raises her eyebrows as if to say I'm only proving her point.

"Aunt Helen is awesome. We had a wonderful afternoon." I might be exaggerating slightly, since we spent the morning cleansing crystals, and she eventually made me leave because I had, and I quote, "dark energy," but what can you do?

Grace and Andy are still giving me dubious looks, so I ask, "Why should I care what Brock thinks of me, anyway?"

"You shouldn't," Andy says. "But you *do*. You have a perfectly natural desire to see him suffer. So do I, honestly."

Grace leans across the table a little. "Yeah, don't you want revenge? That—" She peeks at the booth back behind her, and Andy rolls her eyes. "That jerk did something unforgivable. Wouldn't it be nice to flaunt how well you're doing without him?"

She's one to talk. Still, she's not wrong.

"Yes," I say with a sigh, "but as you've both kindly pointed out, I'm not doing well."

Truthfully, I don't miss Brock. What I miss is my self-confidence, which has been shattered into a million little pieces that have been tumbled to the consistency of sand. What I miss is the temporary Band-Aid our relationship, which felt exciting right up until it didn't, spread over my other problems. I'd told the therapist as much on that one session we had, and she said I had "a remarkably mature perspective."

See? No reason to go back.

"We want you to do something about that," Andy says resolutely.

"Yes, well, I'd also like to not be a loser wearing a dirty shirt stanning a TV show I never watch."

"Movie," Andy says, shaking her head sadly. "*The Empire Strikes Back* is a movie. It's been out for, like, forty years."

"I don't need to feel worse about myself," I mutter, picking idly at my sleeve. "Besides, I didn't think this place would be so crowded." Andy chose the bar, because that's our deal—the person who selects the book also selects the meeting place. Summer Nights is a bit of a dive, with low lighting and a halfhearted attempt at beachside décor that's not displeasing but it's an odd choice for a mountain town in North Carolina.

Grace, who's apparently voted herself good cop, slides a card across the table to me.

I look at it before I speak, mostly because I was expecting a different approach. I figured they'd ask me to go see that therapist again, or bribe me to throw away the most offensive items in my wardrobe, many of which have been stolen from Drew. Maybe I'd even let them.

I pick up the card, taking a moment to appreciate the design before I absorb what's written on it. "The Fairy Godmother Agency? Is this some kind of a joke?"

But I can't lie, my mind is summoning an image of a pleasantly plump woman in a shimmery dress with a star-tipped wand. She looks a little like somebody's mother, and she has an air of *I'm going to make everything all right.* I have a thing for mother figures, I guess.

I have to admit, it would be nice to hand my problems over to someone else.

"This is no joke," Andy says. "They helped someone I know."

"Did they make her a pumpkin carriage? Because I don't know where I'd park something like that. Finding street parking gives me hives."

"No," Andy says, giving me a pointed look. "Her husband left her. They helped her get even."

MARNIE

I CONSIDER Andy's comment for a full second before I burst out laughing. "You want me to hire a fairy godmother to fuck with Brock?"

There's a beleaguered sigh from the next booth, but Andy must have really freaked out Momma Groundhog, because she doesn't pop back up.

"They're private investigators," Andy says. "A husband-and-wife team. But their focus is on helping women who've been wronged."

"Sounds like a country and western song."

"I think they're just called country songs," Grace pipes up. "Why don't you give it a try, Marnie? What do you have to lose?"

I don't want to admit that she's right, although I struggle to believe anyone can glue those grains of sand back together to restore my self-respect. Not when my face is on the internet thousands of times over. My mother's always insisted there's no such thing as bad press or negative attention, but she's not the one who's become a meme.

"They only take jobs by referral," Andy says. "My friend and I told them your story, and they're interested. They want to help."

I could be angry. I could remind her that it's my story to tell—or not—but let's be honest, so many people know about what happened to me that it hardly matters if she's confided in two more.

"I'll take it under advisement," I say instead, slipping the card into my pocket. I take another sip of the gifted wine. "Now, how about that book we didn't read?"

My friends exchange another look, then Andy says, "It was *The Alchemist*. I thought it might be inspirational for you."

"I feel inspired already," I say. "Give us the CliffsNotes version."

They must know I'm done talking about Brock, the video, and everything, because Andy complies with my request and summarizes the book for us, and then Grace launches into an entertaining story about her boss's latest antics.

She works for Vera Valence, a dragon lady who happens to be one of the most famous living romance authors. The woman insists on typing every novel on a typewriter rather than a word processor, and one of Grace's jobs is to transcribe them. She has many other jobs, including running a vast array of personal errands for Vera, everything from bringing Vera's dog to a groomer who charges more than any hairstylist I've ever visited, to driving all the way to the Raleigh airport to check lost and found for a coat her boss thought she left there. (She didn't.) But Grace is a prey animal, like me, and she takes it. Besides, *The Wind in Her Hair* was her favorite romance novel, and she's convinced Vera will be her mentor someday, when she finally finishes her own book. Andy and I have our doubts. We used to be fans too, but now I can't separate the woman who uses my friend without any apparent appreciation and the artist who authored the books I enjoy. It's another example of reality not living up to the fantasy, although Grace would never admit it. She'll loudly proclaim she's happy as she drops off Vera's dry-cleaning and, at her bidding, explains the sources of the stains in depth.

It's a mostly pleasant evening now that we've gotten the intervention behind us. I'm not at all upset with my friends as I bid them goodbye and head out to meet my Uber.

I jolt a little when someone shouts at me from behind, "Hey, Star Wars."

I whirl around to see the bartender from earlier staring at me, leaning over the bar with his hands resting on the varnished wood. With his arms played out like they are, I can see how muscular they are beneath that shirt. Some deeply buried part of me purrs . . . until I notice the intensity of his whiskey stare.

Is he pissed that I didn't tip him?

Wait. He never gave me a drink. If anyone should be pissed in this situation it's me.

I try to rev up some righteous indignation, but I feel like a fly in a spider's web. Now that he's not standing by Angel Guy, I can see he's a dangerously good-looking man, with dark brown hair and a barely there beard that might just be the result of an aversion to shaving. I say dangerous because he's more my type than Angel Guy. There's an edge to him that reminds me of one of the extras in Sinclair's show. They always telegraph which of the male costars are bad boys by putting them in leather jackets, as if they're part of the same motorcycle crew. Grace calls them the leathers. While the bartender's not in leather, he has on a black Henley shirt, the sleeve of which is hiked up enough to show half an inch of a tattoo. The leathers are the kind of men you lust after but not the kind you bring home . . . or at least that's the moral of Sinclair's show.

Then again, it's not exactly the kind of thing you'd watch for the plot. She's been on it for seven years, and her character still hasn't graduated college.

"What?" I finally reply, realizing the bartender is still looking at me.

"Can you flash me the Vulcan symbol again?" he asks, one side of his mouth hitching up.

"So you're the one who has a thing for Vulcans."

"Yeah, I guess I am." His grin spreads, transforming his face from attractive but slightly threatening to radiant, and it only stretches wider when I flash him the bird instead.

He laughs. "Looks a bit different than I remember it. Can you come closer and show me?"

I want to, dammit. It feels like we're flirting, although I can't forget who I am. I'm the woman from the meme, the loser in the oversized shirt, the normal sister of a celebrity.

Odds are this handsome man is just teasing me.

"What happened just now?" he asks, his smile fading. He looks almost worried.

"What?" I ask in alarm. Did my face go slack? Did a murderer enter the bar behind me?

"You were smiling, and now you're not."

Oh, that.

"I remembered I'm a punchline, and everyone but me is in on the joke."

The look in his eyes surprises me. It's soulful, and he opens his mouth like he's about to say something deep, or maybe refer me to a new therapist, but I suddenly can't bear to be here. I turn and leave, feeling his gaze burning into my back, and if there are some residual shivers, like my body's not quite done reacting to him, no one needs to know but me.

By the time I Uber home to the house I share with my brother, I can add regret to my list of grievances, because it's hard to banish the image of the sexy bartender. At least Drew is away for his yearly camping trip with his friends, so no one is around to try to convince me not to make a drink that's seventy percent alcohol.

A little while later, I'm sitting on the couch with my drink, my mind pleasantly hazy, studying that card—*Fairy Godmother Agency* —when my phone rings with a FaceTime call from my sister.

Sighing, I set the card down on the coffee table and answer.

Sinclair's flawless face is immediately sympathetic. She regards me the way someone might look at a bedraggled cat at their front door. Her gold-kissed brown hair falls in effortless waves around her face, although I know from experience that she probably spent at least an hour in a makeup chair to get the effect. Still, I hate seeing myself in that little rectangle above her image on the screen. We've always looked a little alike, only I'm the watered-down version. I'm a single ray of her blinding sunshine.

"Oh, Marnie," she says. "What am I going to do with you?"

"I'm fine," I insist, aware of my stiffening jaw.

"Honey, you're not fine. You're wearing that shirt again."

I avoid the urge to lift a hand to hide it. "It's three hours later on the East Coast. I'm about to go to bed."

She bites her lip, looking unconvinced. "I'm worried about you. You're staying out there all alone, with only Drew to look after you."

"Drew's great," I insist, feeling an old need to defend him.

"But he's a man, Marnie. You need a woman to take care of you."

I have two, but there's no point in saying so. Show business is cutthroat, and Sinclair doesn't have many female friends. I suspect my mother is partially responsible for that. She sees every fresh face on the show as someone who could supersede Sinclair, every new starlet in the tabloids as competition.

"I'm going to send Mom to stay with you for a few weeks."

The prospect of having my mother around for three weeks is enough to scare me stupid. She's always found me lacking, and right now, I don't need anyone to open my eyes to my faults. Besides, she'd definitely regard being sent to Asheville to spend time with me as some sort of punishment—and she'd make damn sure I knew it.

Just like that, I find myself blurting out, "You know, I actually just started seeing someone, Clair. I didn't want to say anything because it's new, but I really, really like him, and I don't want it to get weird if Mom's hanging around."

Sinclair gives me a pitying look. "Oh, Marnie. You don't need to pretend you have a boyfriend again."

My jaw tenses. I did that once, in junior year of high school, two years after Mom and Sinclair left for Los Angeles, and my sister will never let me forget it. I mean, obviously, yes, I *am* lying again, but is it that difficult to believe that someone would want to date me? I'm gainfully employed, run a small and fairly successful side hustle, and own half this house. Even in crappy clothes, I'm not horrible to look at.

Of course, I'm no Sinclair Jones.

She's still giving me this sad *Oh, Marnie* look, which must be the reason I snap, "I *am* dating someone. If you don't believe me, you can meet him. On FaceTime, obviously."

"How about tomorrow?" she says cheerfully. She's testing me, and I can practically see Andy rolling her eyes. There's no lost love between those two.

When it takes me a moment to answer, Sinclair tilts her head, giving me that *you poor homeless cat* look, and says, "It's okay, Marnie. I won't think less of you if you're lying. I understand. You've been through hell."

"I'm not," I huff. "Tomorrow's great. What time?"

Her gaze narrows. "Eleven your time. We'll have brunch together."

"No way. Brunch would take too long. We can't go more than five minutes without putting our hands all over each other."

She smiles at me. "Then I'll have quite the view. What's his name, anyway?"

Panicking, I glance across the room, as if hoping to find my imaginary boyfriend's name magically written on the wall. My gaze lands on a framed photo of Mount Mitchell.

"Mitchell," I say triumphantly. It's a perfectly reasonable name, a *nice* name.

"Mitchell what?"

My mind feels like a sandcastle blasted by a wave. "Mount—" I start, then panic, and finish, "Mountainbottom."

If it were a voice call, I'd be smacking myself in the head right about now, but I keep the phone remarkably steady.

"Mitchell . . . Mountainbottom?" she repeats.

Her confusion is understandable.

"It's French."

"Uh-huh," she says, her eyes glimmering. "I can't *wait* to meet him. I look forward to seeing you and Mitchell tomorrow, Marnie."

She hangs up, and for a moment I just stare at my phone.

Shit. I have thirteen hours to find a man named Mitchell Mountainbottom.

I mean, obviously I can't find a man named Mitchell Mountainbottom. There probably isn't a single man in the whole world with that name, but can I find one who'll play pretend?

I won't lie, I want to shock my sister. I want to prove to her that I'm not predictable little Marnie. Still, I *am* predictable little Marnie. And even if I find a stand-in boyfriend to wipe that smug look off her face, she'll find out the truth eventually, and then she'll *really* think I'm pathetic.

I pull up my group chat with Grace and Andy. I send, *I just told Sinclair that me and my boyfriend, Mitchell Mountainbottom, would have brunch with her over Facetime tomorrow. On a scale from one to ten, how screwed am I?*

Grace sends back a frowny face emoji. *No offense, but that's one of the worst made-up names I've ever heard. It's almost as bad as Thurston Thrusterton in Vera's worst book.*

I panicked, I explain. *She threatened to send Mom for a visit.*

Yikes. Would any of your brother's friends be willing to help?

I consider this for a beat, then respond, *Drew's on his camping trip with, like, all three of them.*

Andy finally pipes in, but only to say, *Call the Fairy Godmother Agency. TONIGHT. THIS IS NOT A DRILL.*

Laughter tears out of me.

What, are they going to turn a rat into a real boy?

Maybe, she responds. *You'll never know unless you ask.* ;-) *Seriously, you suck at asking for help. You need help asking for help.* TAKE THE HELP, MARNIE.

Her words are true and resound in a way that slides in deep and settles.

My gaze lands on the card on the table. I grab my drink and finish it. Then I pour myself another. It's only then that I pick up the card and dial the number.

A woman answers on the first ring. "It's about time you called, Marnie."

"Are you psych—" my mind supplies "psycho" before settling on, "—psychic?"

"No, but it doesn't take a psychic to read *you* like a book."

Good God. I haven't even met this woman. I say as much, and she laughs.

"I'm the one who told you not to say *foul words* in a fucking bar. And you and your other friend listened. That's definitely a problem. It's also a problem that you let Griff keep passing you over at the bar. Oh, and you refused to let my husband buy you a drink. My husband is the most attractive man on the planet."

Angel Guy.

For some reason my mind latches on to that detail. "You wanted me to hit on your *husband?*"

"I wouldn't have enjoyed it, no," she scoffs, "but it would have indicated you were in good mental health. And don't get me started on your shirt. While I won't deny that *Empire Strikes Back* is the best Star Wars movie, the shirt's at least two sizes too large for you. Maybe three. It looks like it belongs to a man."

"Wait a minute," I say, my mind finally catching up. "You were all watching me earlier? Tonight was a setup?"

"More like a test," she says.

"Did I pass?" It comes out more like *pash.*

"Yes," she says. I experience a moment of stupid satisfaction before she finishes, "Although, to be honest, this is the kind of test you want to fail."

Sounds about right.

I should be pissed at Andy for her role in all of this, and eventually I will be, but there's a pleasant hum inside of me from the drink, and honestly, at least all of this is interesting and different. All the same, I can't deny that the woman on the other end of this call doesn't sound jolly and apple-cheeked, the way any halfway decent fairy godmother should. Actually, she's kind of abrasive and bossy.

"What happens now?" I ask.

"A makeover is obviously on our punch list," the woman says. "And we'll need to conduct a full interview before we form a plan of action. Are you drunk?"

"A little."

"Fun! Well, we'll do it tomorrow afternoon."

Panic claws at me at the mention of tomorrow, and I exclaim, "But I need Mitchell Mountainbottom."

"*Excuse* me?" she says.

My brain, which suddenly feels like it's enveloped in candy floss, tries to craft an explanation. "My sister wants to have brunch with me tomorrow. Well, she lives in Los Angeles, but she wants to have brunch over FaceTime."

"Is there a point to this?"

"I . . . she was sort of pushing my buttons, and she threatened to send my mother to Asheville for three weeks. My mother and I don't get along. So I told Sinclair I have a boyfriend. Named . . ." I pause and take a deep breath before continuing. "Mitchell Mountainbottom. I promised he'd be on the brunch call."

The woman starts laughing as if I cracked a hilarious joke. "Oh, that's good," she says. "We can work with that."

"We can?" I ask in shock.

"You're going to borrow a boyfriend, Marnie. That'll be step one."

"A boyfriend?" I stammer. "Whose boyfriend?" It's not like they grow on trees, after all.

"Yours, for now. What time does he need to show up?"

"Eleven. I can text you the address."

She's quiet for a moment, hopefully because she's writing it down so she can send me a . . . what? A male prostitute? A man of the night?

Then she says, "Marnie, we're going to turn your life around."

Maybe I should be more alarmed by this whole thing, but my first response is a feeling of relief. Because even if she's not the motherly figure I was hoping for, she sounds like she means business.

"I'll be in touch tomorrow," she says, and it occurs to me that I don't even know my mystery benefactress's name.

"What's your name?" I blurt out.

"Nicole, but I'll also answer to Fairy Godmother."

three

GRIFFIN

"WE CAN GET Matt to do it," Nicole suggests, taking a sip from Damien's beer. If anyone else tried to take something from Damien, he'd have words for them, or a look so crushing they'd turn to applesauce, but he smiles at her. That's Nicole and Damien for you, soft only for each other. And, yes, they'd twist that into a sex joke if I said it aloud. They're the only ones left at the bar. Even Reggie, the retiree who might as well live at Summer Nights, has gone home. "He's single now. He's kind of a shit actor, but he's really pretty. We need someone pretty."

Damien laughs, putting a hand on her thigh. "You know he hates it when you call him pretty."

"Well, he's obviously not as pretty as you."

"What are you talking about?" I ask. "Other than rating your male friends. I'm a ten, aren't I?"

"Eight and a half," Nicole says. The blond wig she had on earlier is sitting on the bar, and her hair, always dyed some shade of pink, is a bright pop of color under the bar lights. "Damien's the only ten."

He kisses her knuckles, and I roll my eyes. They ignore me.

I was cleaning up in back, so I missed the first part of their conversation. In all likelihood, they're discussing Marnie. She's their

21

next "sad case," as Nicole calls their Fairy Godmother Agency clients, although I don't think the term fits. Marnie's sad for certain, with eyes so big you could drown in them, but she has a metal backbone. I saw it earlier, when she turned Damien down, and again when she gave me the finger. The spark in her eye could have lit a fire.

I don't want to show too much interest, so I pick up a rag and start rubbing the already clean bar.

"We're talking about our girl," Nicole confirms. "She needs a fake boyfriend. We're thinking Matt will do nicely."

"Since he's so pretty and all," Damien says with an indulgent grin, hiking his hand up a little higher on her leg. "Nicole has exacting standards."

"Damn straight." She gives him a wicked glance. "Just look at you, you beautiful bastard."

"Oh, come on," I complain without any heat. "I just cleaned up. You're going to make me throw up, and then I'll have to clean up again. It'll be a vicious cycle."

Truthfully though, my mind's not on their PDA, which is always over the top. It's on Marnie. Before she left, I was thinking I might like to take her home, even though I knew what Nicole and Damien were planning.

I typically don't mess with their machinations. While Nicole named the bar Summer Nights and insisted on the beach theme, an homage to her irrational love for *Grease*, she and Damien mostly let me do as I please with it. I'm one-third owner because they gave—as in *literally* gave—me a stake in the place. I'm paying them for my share slowly, at my insistence, but I'm very aware of all they've done for me. I'm not the kind of dog who's going to bite the hand that feeds him. Without them and my stepbrother, Gary, I don't know where I'd be, but it wouldn't be anywhere good. Still, there's something about Marnie that makes me want to forget my own rules.

Maybe it's because she's bent but not broken.

She's stronger than she thinks, and I'd like to be the man who helps her see that.

Hell, maybe I'm not nearly that noble, and I'd just like to fuck her.

"Why does she need a fake boyfriend?" I ask, going for casual. "I thought you were helping her with that video."

"She was sort of drunk when she called me," Nicole says nonchalantly, "but it had something to do with her sister. I guess the sister threatened to send their mother to Asheville to check on her, so Marnie panicked and made up a boyfriend. Happens to the best of us."

Marnie's sister is a starlet. Nicole played an episode of her show in the bar last night after closing, and Damien and I took turns groaning.

"Matt wouldn't impress Sinclair," I say.

I've met him before, and "douchebag" is putting it mildly. The man once got so drunk at Summer Nights that he pissed in the broom closet, thinking it was a bathroom. The thought of him hamming it up with Marnie, putting his arm around her and making innuendos with a shit-eating grin on his face, makes me fist my hands. He hasn't even met her or heard her name, and I already want to punch him.

I'm not sure what's wrong with me, but there's definitely something going on, because I hear myself add, "What the hell. I'll do it."

Nicole looks me up and down. "Excuse me?"

"You heard me," I say. "I might not be an actor, but I'm a bartender. It's my job to charm people."

"Yes, you're extremely fucking charming," she says, "but you've never agreed to do this kind of thing before. Why now?"

She has a point. The bar is my baby. I help Nicole and Damien out with certain things, including setting up their little meet-cutes for potential agency clients and occasional information-gathering missions, but I've always refused to pose as a fake boyfriend or fake date.

The thing is, I might be good at playing pretend—I've gotten far more than the requisite ten thousand hours of practice that Malcolm Gladwell talks about in that book—but I don't like it. It's an unfortunate side effect of having grown up with the kind of father who couldn't have gotten his shit together if he'd had two dozen instruction manuals.

All that practice came at great personal cost, and I don't want to get stuck with another expense sheet.

Except here I am, basically begging Nicole and Damien to *pick me, pick me.* What is it about this woman that made me volunteer for something like this? Maybe I'd explain myself to them if I knew the answer.

"I never thought this day would come," Damien says as a slow smile spreads across his face. "Nicole, FaceTime Gary. He needs to see this shit."

She's already pulling out her phone.

"Oh, come on, guys," I say, slapping the rag down. "No need for the theatrics."

Theatrics are their thing, though, and I already know they're not going to give this up for anything.

"I resent this," I say. "For the record."

"No one's making a record," Damien says, smirking.

Nicole nudges him. "Speak for yourself."

"Hello?" Gary asks, picking up the call.

Nicole swings the phone's screen toward me. "Take a look at your brother," she says.

"Yes," Gary replies. "I'm familiar with what he looks like. Hey, Griff."

I greet him with a salute. "Aren't you supposed to be swimming at the pool tonight?"

"He has a point," Damien says with a frown. The results of

Gary's last physical were alarming, and the doctor told him he needed to take precautionary measures to lower his blood pressure and avoid diabetes, two conditions that run in his family, so Damien and I teamed up to design a health regimen for him. We do a lot of the workouts with him to keep him honest, and his wife Liza has embraced the diabetic, heart-healthy-diet side of the equation.

"It's my wild card night," he says, his tone a little sullen. "I decided it was too cold to go to the pool. I don't feel like walking around with wet hair."

"You're still supposed to do cardio," I object, grateful for anything that takes the focus off me.

"Who says he didn't?" Damien says, giving Nicole a wicked look.

She heaves a long-suffering sigh. "Oh goody, it's another *Gary's boning my mom* joke."

That's how I met this pair of maniacs: Gary is married to Nicole's mother. When I left Asheville as a teenager, Gary was in his mid-twenties, a bachelor focused on his career. When I came back after a ten-year absence, he was engaged to a woman I'd never met. Those are years I can't get back with him.

"Anyway, we didn't call because you're not swimming like you should be," Nicole says. "We're not the pool police. We called because your brother has a *crush* on someone. This is not his usual *let's go to pound town* attraction, he genuinely has a crush on this woman. You should have seen him scoping her out when he thought no one was looking."

"Was not," I say, instantly transformed into a second-grader.

Gary's face lights up. "Holy shit. This is awesome! Liza!" he calls out, Liza being his wife.

"Oh, for God's sake," I groan, glaring at Nicole. "I offered to help you out. You don't have to make it a whole thing."

"But it *is* a thing," Nicole says victoriously. "You have never, ever agreed to be anyone's fake squeeze before."

"We've asked you before," Damien comments blandly.

"We've begged you," Nicole adds. "Didn't we beg him when we were helping that one lady whose boyfriend ran off with her boss?"

"*Begged* him," Damien agrees.

"But no go," Nicole continues.

In the meantime, Liza has joined Gary on the screen. She gives us a bright smile, but there's a shuttered look in her eyes that I'm not sure anyone else notices.

I don't think Liza quite likes me, or at least she hasn't forgiven me for the shit I've put Gary through. Weirdly, I like her more because of it. If I were in her shoes, I'd feel the same way.

Gary and his mom are the best people I know—they're the lifeline I grabbed even though I knew I shouldn't—and he deserves someone who loves him enough to resent me.

"To be fair," I say, "I help you with a lot of things. The day that woman you mentioned came into the bar for your test, she started stroking my arm and quoting a poem about griffins. I'm pretty sure she would have sexually assaulted me if I'd shown up at her house."

"So you wouldn't mind if Marnie sexually assaulted you?" Nicole asks, accusatory.

"I don't want anyone to sexually assault me," I say, lifting my hands. "I'd think that would be a given."

"What's going on?" Liza asks softly.

"Oh, how the mighty have fallen," Nicole says, her eyes sparkling. "Griffin has fallen prey to cupid's arrows . . . he's . . ."

"Very funny." I'm tempted to revoke my offer, but when I open my mouth to say the words, I see Marnie's big eyes—teasing one moment, devastated the next. I've never met anyone else whose emotions were so evident in a single look. Even now, even with my sort-of family giving me grief, I don't want to take it back. I might not fully understand why I want this, but there's no denying that I do.

"You know what? Enjoy it," I say. "I'm glad to be your amusement for the evening."

"It's refreshing for it to be someone else for a change," Gary says, although there's plenty of humor in his voice. We do give him grief occasionally, but it's because we all love him. We know, without having actually discussed it, that he's the best of us, to be protected under all circumstances. Hence the health regimen. Damien, Nicole, and I are probably as desperate to keep him around for a long, long time as Liza is. His mother, who still insists I call her "Ma" even though she and my father divorced fourteen years ago and his ashes are floating in the Pacific Ocean, feels the same way. She's a chronic food pusher, though, so she's still adjusting to his new health regimen. I guess pushing sliced carrots on people just isn't as satisfying.

"We'll pass along information as it becomes available," Nicole tells them, acting like she's a reporter in a war zone.

I give a beleaguered sigh as she hangs up the phone and sets it on the bar.

When she looks up at me, she seems intensely pleased with herself. Damien does too, but maybe that's because his hand is practically up to her underwear by now.

"Okay," Nicole says. "The job is yours."

"Thank you?"

I should be consumed with regret because they're absolutely not going to let me live this down. Not even a little. But the only thing I feel is anticipation.

I'm going to see Marnie tomorrow.

"Oh, I forgot to tell you the best part, Griff," Nicole says. "Your new name is Mitchell Mountainbottom."

four

MARNIE

GROANING, I open my eyes. Light is filtering in through the shades, and someone is banging on the door. Actually, they're probably knocking at a perfectly reasonable volume, but it feels like my head is splitting open.

It also feels like a creature that lived at the bottom of my bourbon bottle died in my mouth.

I glance at the clock on the wall and bolt upright.

10:52.

The knock lands again, and I remember my call with Nicole last night. She said she'd be sending someone, a man, over.

Shit, shit, shit.

Is this a persistent sales call, or is it Mitchell Mountainbottom?

I'm still wearing the Star Wars T-shirt, and I'm pretty sure there's an imprint of my brother's novelty robot throw pillow on my face. Not a great look.

The clock ticks over to 10:53, and I groan and force myself out of bed—er, couch.

The last thing I want to do is meet my borrowed boyfriend looking and feeling like this. Then again, he *is* a fake boyfriend. He doesn't have to find me appealing.

I make my way to the door, which feels like a much greater distance than the twenty or so feet it actually is, and open it. What's waiting on the other side makes me gasp, and not just from the frigid air that wafts in.

Holy shit. Nicole sent *him*?

It's the hot bartender from last night, the leather, and he's holding a bouquet of flowers and a reusable shopping bag. For a second I just look at him, taking in his dark brown hair and lighter eyes, his firm jaw covered in stubble, and the slight crookedness of his nose, as if it's been broken before. He's wearing a worn-looking leather jacket, which is on point, and his arms look firm in a way that might be intimidating if not for the flowers. In fact—

"Nicole and Damien sent me over. Will you let me in?"

I frown. "Who's Damien?"

"The guy who offered to buy you a drink at the bar last night. He's Nicole's husband."

Which means he's my other fairy godmother, I guess.

My visitor gives me a once-over, not bothering to be subtle about it. "You should have accepted. I save my heavy pours for people who wear Star Wars shirts but haven't actually seen the movie. I was going to offer you one on the house, but you left before I could."

"Aren't you going to introduce yourself?"

One side of his mouth hitches up, and I feel an unwanted stirring inside of me, as if my body is warming up after a few months in deep freeze. "I'm Mitchell Mountainbottom, obviously. Don't you recognize your own boyfriend? I'm here for your call with your sister."

He makes a good point. I step aside and nod for him to enter.

He does, and as soon as I close the door behind him, the house instantly feels smaller, like it's folding in to embrace him. Stupid house.

I take the flowers he's holding out to me, suddenly feeling a rush of self-consciousness. A very large stranger is in my house, looking at my things, his gaze skimming across the mantel to the corner of the living room and the Christmas tree I still haven't packed up. I have the inane impulse to explain that Drew's supposed to do it when he gets home.

Instead, I carry the flowers into the kitchen and stuff them into a mason jar filled with water before returning to the living area.

Mitchell's gaze swivels to me and lingers.

I wrap my hands around my chest as if I can hide the T-shirt. "I fell asleep on the couch."

He nods slightly, and there's a twinkle in his eyes that makes me want to lean in close. I resent that twinkle. "I can see the pillow imprint on your face."

"How do you know Nicole, anyway?" I ask, wanting to turn the spotlight on him.

"She's my business partner."

"So you work at the . . . agency?" It feels weird to say it, like I'm in some cloak-and-dagger movie. Actually, it's kind of a fun thought, and I find I don't hate it.

"Sometimes," he demurs, "but that's not what I meant. She and Damien own the bar with me. I'm the manager."

I frown. "They own a bar *and* a detective agency. Who are these people? I mean, my friend told me a little about them, obviously, but there are lots of question marks and red flags. Tons of red flags."

There's a slight twist to his mouth as if he's amused with himself, or maybe with me. "Nicole's my niece."

"Your niece? Is she a *teenager*?"

He laughs with genuine amusement. I wish I were in on the joke. "No, my stepbrother is a lot older than me, and he married Nicole's mom, who had her really young."

A family tree swirls to life in my head, the branches a twisted mess. I shake it away. "It's much too early for this sort of thing."

"Had a late night watching Star Wars?" he asks mischievously, lifting his brows.

"Very funny," I mutter.

"I thought so."

"You know who she is, right? Sinclair?"

"Your sister," he says slowly, like I may be deficient in understanding.

"I mean, you know that she's famous, right?" I feel like an idiot, but he needs to know if he doesn't. Better for him to be forewarned than starstruck.

"Nicole and Damien mentioned something along those lines, yes."

A quick glance at the clock tells me it's 10:58.

I'm still wearing that damn shirt.

As if he can read my thoughts, "Mitchell" pulls a box from the bag he's holding, then hands the bag over. I take it on reflex. "Nicole thought you might need a change of clothes."

"It's like Nicole really is a fairy godmother," I say under my breath. A fairy godmother with a bad attitude and a controlling personality.

I lift the garment out of the bag.

"I can't wear this!" I shake the skimpy silk nightgown. "It's winter, for God's sake. I'll freeze!"

More to the point, I can't wear this thing in front of *him*.

He just looks at the Star Wars shirt, and I have to admit he makes a good case.

"Where are your plates?" he asks. "I brought breakfast too, in case you wanted props. I'll get everything ready while you're getting changed."

I'm annoyed by his presumption, but we're supposed to call Sinclair in two minutes. I've already committed to this insane scenario, might as well see it through. At least this embarrassment won't have been in vain. So I show him to the cabinet and then hustle into the bathroom and change into the purple nightgown.

I'd be more self-conscious about the skimpiness of the nighty, but I'm still barely awake, my mind a muddle of Mitchell and fairy godmothers and my sister. So I just tug it on, surprisingly unfazed, and do a cursory brushing of my teeth so I don't fumigate Mitchell.

It's only then I realize I forgot to ask for his real name.

When I leave the bathroom, he's already sitting at the table, a perfect croissant on the plate in front of him, plus another on the plate beside him. The mason jar of red and yellow flowers sits between them. He's taken his leather coat off, and beneath it he has on a long-sleeved, form-fitting blue thermal shirt. His arms are more sculpted than I'd realized, and he almost looks too big perched on one of my puny chairs. A few swirls of colorful ink peek out from under the right sleeve of his shirt.

For a second, the scene takes my breath away.

It's just the look of it that's perfect. A set designer might as well have staged it.

Mitchell gives me a once-over that heightens my awareness of the soft silk brushing against my skin and the way the nighty ends at my upper thighs. He seems almost . . . appreciative.

Maybe he's one of those method actors who never turns a character off. Maybe he'll spend the next however long eating, sleeping, and breathing Mitchell Mountainbottom.

Maybe he can method-act right into your bedroom.

I cough. Apparently, I'm hornier than I realized, or my mind hasn't quite relinquished the idea it had last night, looking at this man under the low lighting of the bar. In which case, my subconscious mind needs to shut the hell up.

"Nicole's always right," he murmurs.

I'm struck by the realization that this man has a lovely voice, like the audio equivalent of toast covered in melted butter and honey.

"I look forward to meeting her," I say, not entirely sure that I mean it.

Ignoring the urge to cover my chest like a chaste Victorian, I get out my iPad and prop it up, preparing to call Sinclair.

Before I do, I turn to Mitchell, taking him in. He's nothing like the men I usually date. Despite his casual charm, he gives off this primal energy, like he's one of the alpha werewolf shifters in those books Grace likes to read. Then again, maybe I only think so because of his broken nose.

Despite myself, I wonder how it broke. I can't imagine a scenario that doesn't involve someone's fists.

"What's your real name?"

His lips twist into a smile, but he gives a little shake of his head. "You have to remember to call me Mitchell."

I want to ask him dozens of other questions, like why he's doing this and how he knows Nicole and whether she's a psychopath. Actually, I should ask him whether *he's* a psychopath. But if he is, I've already made the mistake of letting him inside, and it's two minutes past eleven. I settle for dialing Sinclair.

I'm leaning forward when she picks up, so she gets an eyeful of my chest in the purple nighty.

Oops.

Her eyes fly wide as I adjust the screen to show both of us, me and Mitchell, our plates like something out of Instagram. Despite having suggested this brunch farce, my sister has no food.

"Hi, Clair," I say brightly, glancing at the big man to my left. "This is Mitchell. Mitchell, Sinclair."

Sinclair looks like someone just force-fed her trans fats in the days before a photo shoot, but my gaze doesn't stick on her. I find myself studying Mitchell. Most people stare at Sinclair as impulsively and uncontrollably as squirrels collect shiny things. Including most of my ex-boyfriends. But he regards her with nothing but muted interest. "Nice to meet you. Marnie's told me a lot about you."

He's acting like her only significance is as my sister, and I feel a weird warmth in the pit of my stomach, even though he's a complete stranger who means nothing to me, and vice versa.

"To be honest, I didn't think you existed," my sister says with a brittle laugh. "I thought Marnie had made you up."

I grit my teeth together, because that would have been a super shitty comment if she weren't one hundred percent correct.

Mitchell raises his brows. "What an odd thing to say. Why would she do a thing like that?"

"But . . . your name," Sinclair sputters. "Mitchell Mountainbottom . . . it's . . . you have to admit it's an unusual name."

"It's my stage name," he says. "I'm an exotic dancer."

Sinclair smiles at him. She clearly thinks he's joking.

Wait a second. He *is* joking, right? My mind conjures an image of him writhing around onstage, and I take a big bite of croissant to cast the image back to the mind pit where it belongs.

Oh my God, it's good. It's filled with that almond paste with a fancy name I can never remember. I take another bite and then another.

"My name's German," he says as I finish the croissant.

Sinclair frowns, then seems to remember frown lines, and her expression returns to stoic. "But I thought it was French."

"My family's Swiss, technically," he says smoothly. "From the area in between the German and French parts. Our name got the Ellis Island treatment."

It's actually a feasible explanation. Go, Fake Mitchell.

He gives me a little bump with his shoulder, flashing me that dangerously charming grin. "You must have gotten it mixed up, honey."

"Yeah, guess so."

Sinclair grins at him. "So what do you actually do, Mitchell?"

"I told you," he teases. I think. "What do *you* do?"

She gives that tinkling laugh men have always loved. "You *know* what I do."

Mitchell cocks his head. "I don't believe Marnie's mentioned it, no."

My sister's gaze darts to me, almost accusatory. "You didn't tell him?"

Didn't I? I asked him if he knew she was famous, and he said yes. Then again, I guess she could have been famous for owning the largest private collection of bouncy balls. "She's the star of *Sisters of Sin.* You know, that Netflix show everyone's always talking about."

"Oh," he says, sounding unimpressed, "the one where the cast is ten years older than the people they're pretending to be and they're all sleeping with each other?" He tears into his croissant as if the topic of our conversation weren't engaging enough to distract him from his food. "Not my kind of thing."

Sinclair wheezes as if someone punched her in the lung. "But dating heartbroken women *is* your thing? Doesn't it bother you that Marnie is on the rebound?"

I can't contain the hurt gasp that flies out of me. Sinclair must see my expression, because she turns to me and says, "I just don't want you to be taken advantage of again. That awful man put you through enough."

Something dark flickers across Mitchell's face. "We all have baggage." He takes my hand, and even though I know it's just for the camera, I feel a weird shiver of heat where his fingers are touching me. "Hers is part of who she is, but it doesn't define her. I'm lucky Marnie believes I'm worthy of her time."

I should be looking at Sinclair, but my gaze is on his tawny eyes. He's acting, obviously, but it's hard to look away.

None of my ex-boyfriends have ever said anything nearly as charming.

"Aw, you two are staring into each other's eyes like you're teenagers," Sinclair says, slicing her way into the moment. I shift my attention to her. The words are sweet, but my sister is obviously not appeased. To be fair, she's spoken to me nearly every day for the last month, and I've been feeling down for a while. Now I'm suddenly in a relationship with a man who looks like *this*, wearing a nighty that could have been stolen from the set of her show. She probably has whiplash.

Then again, maybe she thinks I could never find a man like this without bribing him. It stings, even more so because she's right.

"What can I say? Mitchell makes me feel like I'm a teenager again," I tell her, my tone tight.

"The same age you were when you pretended you had a boyfriend?" She grins at Mitchell, that thousand-dollar grin that's on dozens of posters. "See? I have my reasons for suspicion."

Old hurt wells up inside of me. My sister was a beautiful TV star, and I was an awkward teenager who couldn't attract a second glance from a guy unless he was teasing me. So, yes, when she asked if I had a date to prom, I claimed I did. Rupert Wrightman.

Shit. I'm really bad at coming up with fake names off-the-cuff.

I look down, but suddenly strong fingers are touching my jaw, tipping my face up. Then I'm looking into Mitchell's eyes, which look hot, like caramel starting to boil, and he shocks me by leaning in for a soft kiss. It would have lasted for only a few seconds, just long enough for me to register his soft but firm lips, the brush of his short beard, and his spicy scent, but my mouth parts in surprise, and then I find myself pressing into him, electricity arcing between us and gluing us together. He's the one who pulls back, a slight smile on his face as he lifts his hand to my jaw and softly traces it.

"Seems to me there must've been plenty of guys half in love with her," he says, still looking at me, and my pulse is galloping in my chest, so alarmingly fast I think I might actually die. "If she did pretend to have a boyfriend, it was probably because she wanted to let them down easy." He lifts a hand to my jaw again, tracing it. "She's thoughtful like that."

I'm at a loss for words. Actually, I can't do anything but gape at him. Should I be pissed at him? Probably. Maybe I would be if I could form a single coherent thought.

It's for the best when Sinclair takes over. "You guys are too cute." There's a bit of an edge to her voice. She's still suspicious, although I'll bet she's no longer altogether sure *why* she's suspicious.

"Yes, we are," Mitchell says with a smirk, our gazes still locked.

I'm the one who finally breaks the stare. Glancing back at my sister, I clear my throat. "We have to go. Talk to you later?"

"Where do you have to go?" she asks. "You haven't even finished your breakfast."

Mitchell gives her a suggestive grin. "Isn't it obvious? It was nice meeting you, Scarlett."

Then he reaches over and ends the call.

MARNIE

I LOOK at Mitchell in shock, and maybe a little awe. "You hung up on my sister. You called her Scarlett."

I silently add, *you kissed me*.

He quirks his brow. "Isn't that her name?"

"You know her name," I insist.

"I know her name," he confirms, pushing his plate away. Then he looks up at me, meeting my eyes. "Your sister's a bully. I didn't like the way she was talking to you."

I'm torn between a strange feeling of protectiveness for my sister and a rush of . . . gratitude? People don't usually stand up to Sinclair. Most people are too eager to impress her to risk pissing her off.

"In all fairness, I'm a bit of a mess," I say, getting up. I don't actually have a destination, but now that the call is over, it feels weird to sit this close to him, heat passing between our bodies. I take a couple of steps away and lean against the wall. "She probably figures I'd have acted differently if . . ."

I trail off, not sure how to end the sentence.

"If you were having regular orgasms," he suggests with a twinkle in his eyes.

I feel myself blushing and scowl to counteract it. "You wish.

38

Besides, a woman doesn't need a man for that. There's a reason nearly eighty percent of women over the age of eighteen own a vibrator."

He tilts his head to the side, a corner of his mouth twitching up, and good God, my sex drive has come roaring back to life like a bear coming out of hibernation, still tired but hungry as hell.

I remind myself this man has been *paid* to be here. He might as well be an escort.

"You aren't really an exotic dancer, are you?" I blurt, then swallow.

"Says who?" he asks.

I must be doing a terrible job of controlling my reaction, because he immediately laughs.

"No," he concedes, "but if I were, I'd seriously consider using Mitchell Mountainbottom as my stage name. It has a certain ring to it."

"So why wouldn't you tell her what you do?"

"I didn't want to tell her in case you'd already said something," he says, rising from his chair. "It was obvious she wanted to trip you up. Besides, I doubt your sister would be impressed with a bar manager."

He's good at this. It makes me wonder if it's something he does frequently.

I have no reason to dislike the thought, but there's no denying I do.

"Give me your phone," he says.

"Why?" I ask, immediately suspicious, although I'm not sure what of. It's not like he's going to find another super embarrassing video on there to spread around the internet.

"Sinclair wasn't satisfied," he says. "I could see it in her eyes. She's going to push. Besides—" he grins at me, "—I like being Mitchell Mountainbottom. Maybe I should have my name changed."

He's right. Sinclair's been calling nearly every day. It'll seem fishy if Mitchell Mountainbottom disappears too suddenly. If this guy's willing to help, he can put in a few more appearances to tide her over. Of course, that's dependent on how much his fake-boyfriend services cost, but it would feel awkward to ask him now that he's already played his part, like asking a prostitute for a quote after you've had your third orgasm.

Oh, God. I must have drunk more than I realized last night, because my brain is creating dangerous images of Mitchell in my bed.

Maybe he notices and is—rightfully—afraid, because he says, "I should go. Nicole wants you to meet her at the bar at two."

I almost ask him where he's going before I remember it's none of my business. There's an unexpected urgency pulsing through my veins, though. It's probably because he did me a massive favor, and I haven't done anything in return. Admittedly, I'm probably going to end up paying for this . . . literally . . . but even so. He didn't need to stand up for me.

He didn't have to kiss you either.

I tell the voice in my head to shut up, then step over to the mantel to grab one of the prototype thank-you cards I've been working on.

"Here," I say, thrusting it at him.

He looks down in confusion. "Is this a card someone else gave you?"

"No, it's one of mine."

His eyes twinkle again, like he's amused by me. "Seems like you just denied regifting that card and then copped to it."

"No," I insist, embarrassed now. "This is my side hustle. I make greeting cards and chore wheels." I gesture toward the one on the fridge, which is turned to *Clean the fridge. It smells like something died inside.* Thankfully, that'll also be Drew's chore when he gets home. Guess he'll be pretty busy. "Stuff like that."

"So you're a small business owner."

"Not really," I say, shifting uncomfortably on my feet. "A couple of local stores carry my stuff, but my sales are mostly through Etsy."

"Don't sell yourself short. Sounds to me like you're a business owner."

"I guess I am," I hedge, trying to avoid swallowing my own tongue. When has any man ever spoken like this to me? Brock thought my business, Sweet Nothings, was "cute." The guy I dated before him suggested it was a waste of time. "But I also have a shitty job."

He laughs, a sound that sends tingles through me. "That's you and most people."

"But not you?"

He smiles. "Nah. I work with my friends, and I get to meet interesting people sometimes." The glimmer in his eyes suggests I'm one of them. "Tell me about your day job."

"It's seriously nothing special. I design graphics and logos for businesses, sometimes terrible businesses, and my boss, Val, is a misogynistic asshole who talks as slowly as Marlon Brando in *The Godfather*. He also just agreed to work on another ad campaign for my ex-fiancé."

He flinches. "Ouch."

"Right? Brock and I met through work in the first place, so the people I work with know *everything*. They're going to be watching us every second we're around each other. My boss hasn't broken the news to me yet, but my friend Andy found out."

He holds his hand out for the card, and it strikes me that I've been blabbering like an idiot, talking about Brock of all things.

I thrust it into his hand and step back.

He looks it over, his mouth working a little, like he wants to smile again but doesn't want me to think he's poking fun at me.

"*I'm one thankful fucker.*" He taps it against his chest. "Thank *you*, Marnie. This is going up behind the bar."

"You don't have to do that," I demur.

"Obviously," he says. "But you gave it to me, so it's mine to do with as I like."

I'm not sure whether he's teasing me, or really what I should say, so I settle for saying nothing. I find myself looking at the slightly crooked bridge of his nose, wanting to run my finger down it.

His gaze scans the mantel, pausing on the hand-turned wooden container in the middle. "Did you make that too?" he asks, nodding to it. The spindle that rises up from the middle has always reminded me of the one that sent Sleeping Beauty into her slumber.

"Um. No," I say, blushing again for some ungodly reason. "That's my dad."

He almost physically recoils, so either he thinks my father shapeshifted into a vase or he gets what I meant and probably thinks his fake girlfriend shouldn't be throwing him emotional grenades. "Shit," he says. "How long ago did it happen?"

I rub my chest, then remember it's practically naked and cross my arms over it instead. "Ten months ago."

"Oh, Marnie, I'm sorry," he says, and tugs me to him, pressing me to his very firm, very warm chest and nestling my head under his chin.

Shock curls around me, turning to something more seductive. Which is beyond messed up since he's trying to comfort me about losing my dad. The thought should spill a pitcher of ice water over my libido, but it doesn't. To be honest, it's been a while since I got any action from my vibrator, and I'm not quite as satisfied by Felix as I suggested. (Yes, I named my vibrator. I mean, I'm getting intimate with him . . . I should at least know his name.)

Mitchell releases me and steps back, but he's still close enough that I can feel him, as if he radiates a force field of energy. "I'm so goddamn sorry," he repeats. "I didn't realize."

"You didn't kill him," I say.

He doesn't laugh because it's not funny, and I realize I've probably made him uncomfortable. Scratch that. *More* uncomfortable.

"I mean . . . no one did," I stammer. "It was a heart attack."

"That doesn't make me any less sorry," he says. "It's a real mind-fuck to lose someone. Were you close?"

"We were," I say, feeling a twisting sensation in my chest, as if my own heart is considering giving out. "He and my brother and me. We all lived here together, actually. Ever since my mom and my sister moved out."

What am I doing? I don't know this man, and I'm standing half naked in my freezing great room in front of my father's urn. I should be ushering him out the door, not telling him my life story.

"When did that happen?" he asks, seeming genuinely interested.

"When I was a freshman in high school. My mother said I could go to LA with them, but she didn't really want me to. She and Sinclair were like their own little team. My dad disapproved of the way they excluded me as I got older."

Maybe that's why I'm telling him all of this. Because Mitchell stood up for me, even if I didn't ask for it or necessarily want it.

The memory of his lips brushing against mine makes me admit to myself that last part is a lie. There's apparently a cavewoman living inside me, dormant for all these years, and she'd like nothing better than to drag him into the bedroom and slam the door behind us both.

He looks at me for a long moment, his eyes at once tawny and intense. "Family is complicated, but you have no reason to regret who you are or the path you chose. In fact, I think you should send *them* thank-you cards."

"Why?" I ask, baffled.

"So you can thank them for excluding you. If they hadn't, you might have become a conceited—"

"Be careful how you finish that sentence," I say, bristling. "You're talking about my sister."

He lifts his hands, the card fluttering in one of them. "Sorry, you're right. I wouldn't let anyone talk about my stepbrother that way."

I'm tempted to ask him about his stepbrother, but truthfully this interaction has gone on for long enough. My space feels crowded. It's as if the whole house has become drunk on him.

"I really should go," he says. "I'll see you at the bar later."

He starts moving toward the door, and I blurt out, "Aren't you going to finish your croissant?"

Glancing back over his shoulder, he smiles. "You finish it. I liked the sound you made when you tried it."

I should definitely say something. I should tell him he's arrogant, or say that I have no intention whatsoever of eating his leftovers, but I can't seem to find any words. All I can do is watch his retreating back.

It's only after he's left, when I have a mouthful of his croissant in my mouth, because *of course* I had to eat it, that I realize he never told me his real name.

six

GRIFFIN

MY MIND IS in knots over Marnie. Despite everything she's been through, despite her tough spine, there's something beautifully open about her. She wears her heart on her sleeve for everyone to see. She's—

A pretzel hits me in the middle of my forehead, and I whip my head around. Nicole's high-fiving Damien, leaving me in the dark as to which of them did it.

No, it was definitely Nicole. She's got a mischievous glint in her eyes. Then again, she almost always looks like that. I think her face was made that way.

"Very funny," I say. "We're going to come off as a real professional outfit when Marnie gets here."

"You made me do it, Griffin. You were getting all broody, and I had to repeat my question."

"You know she hates repeating herself," Damien says, wrapping an arm around her waist. She nestles into him.

They're sitting on two stools in front of the bar while I prep for opening.

Marnie should be here in a few minutes.

Assuming she isn't having second thoughts about this arrangement after I kissed her.

I shouldn't have done that. I didn't *mean* to.

It's just . . . her sister was taking immense pleasure in tearing her down. Marnie has those expressive Bambi eyes, and I hated the look Sinclair put in them. It was a look of acceptance, like things had always been this way between them, and she's learned to live with it. Like she didn't even notice it was screwed up. I know a thing or two about growing roots in a bad situation, and no good can come from it.

You're no saint, Griff. You don't need to play pretend with yourself.

No, I suppose I don't. I also kissed her because I felt like it. She was cute last night and this morning, the kind of girl a guy would want to bring home to his parents if his parents were the type to give a shit, but that purple nightgown clung to her body in ways that fired up my imagination, transforming her soft, sweet prettiness into something sensual. She's funny and a little unusual, and nothing like the women I usually take upstairs to my apartment. True to my word, I hung up the card she gave me behind the counter, next to a photograph of the original owner, Leo Switzer, sent from his new beach house in Boca Raton.

Another pretzel strikes my head. "You're doing it again," Nicole says.

I shake it off. "What was your question?"

"I wanted your gut feeling. Is she going to be receptive?"

I think of the soft brush of her lips. Of the little throaty sound of pleasure she made when she tried that croissant. She looked up at me as she did it, that silky nightgown barely covering her breasts.

"Yeah," I say, gripping the side of the bar and trying to make my voice something other than a rasp. "I think she'll be receptive."

Nicole's eyes widen in glee. "Have you guys already banged? That was quick work."

"Oh, for fuck's sake," I groan.

"Not yet," Damien says, scrutinizing me. "But it's going to happen."

"You guys need to take it easy," I say, glancing at the door. "She's going to be here any minute. Besides, even if I was interested, and I'm not saying I am, she's hung up on her ex. That's the whole reason she needed this intervention, right?"

Except it's possible she's not cut up over her ex at all. Marnie just lost her father, and grief is like the one-night stand you want to forget who won't stop texting and calling you. Just when you start thinking she finally lost your digits, she slides in one last DM.

"Not the vibe I got," Nicole says. "I think this is more about the public embarrassment than the pencil dick who left her. Besides, the best way to get over someone is to get under someone." She and Damien exchange another of their pointed looks. I'd attempt to dissuade them, but they'll do whatever they want regardless of what I say—it's kind of their thing. I'd be annoyed except their habit of pushing people in directions of their choosing has helped me more than it has hurt me.

"Did you learn anything else about the video?" Damien asks.

I'd intended to. But the call with Sinclair hadn't gone down the way I'd thought it would, and after we hung up—correction, after *I* hung up—I felt the need to get out of there quickly before I did something stupid.

Stupider. The word is stupider.

Of course, if I told them that, it would only convince them they're right about where this is all going.

Is it wrong that I want them to be right?

"He's mooning again," Nicole says. "You wanted to help, Griff, so *help*."

"No new intel on the video," I say, "but it sounds like her sister and her mother are real pieces of work."

Damien nods. "I'll look into them. You know, the sister paid for the whole wedding. Not a small bill."

"Sinclair was even involved in the proposal," Nicole says, popping one of those pretzels into her mouth.

"What do you mean?" I ask, although there's an uncomfortable prickle on the back of my neck, like I've turned into a territorial dog.

"Brock got the sister to do it for him on a national talk show," she says through a mouthful of pretzel. "And he brought Marnie to Buchanan Brewery to watch it on their new flat-screen in front of a crowd of people. He even paid a cameraman to livestream her reaction."

"Shit," I say. I might not know Marnie well, but that's the worst fucking way he could have proposed to her. Her sister has always been the center of attention, and Brock found a way to make her the center of his proposal too. "What a dick."

"Right? I'm thinking he's packing something pretty small," she says conversationally, "because that was definitely a compensatory move. I'll bet he wanted some good press for his business . . . and for a while he was getting it. Marnie designed his new logo too, which only adds to his little story."

"Until he screwed her over and it went viral," Damien says with an eyebrow quirk.

"Sinclair got good press through all of this," I say. "I have trouble believing she helped with the proposal and wedding because she thought Brock was perfect for Marnie." Obviously, I can't be sure of that after only a short conversation, but there was something mean-spirited about Sinclair on the phone call today, like she was disappointed she hadn't found Marnie alone in her apartment, eating cereal out of the box and wearing their brother's old shirt. If she wanted her to marry Brock, it wasn't because she thought Brock would make her happy—it was because Sinclair thought it would work to her own advantage.

"I have some contacts in LA," Damien says. "I'll get them to ask around about Sinclair. Maybe she had some bad PR she wanted patched up."

"Marnie won't want you doing that," I warn them. "She seems protective of her sister."

We don't have time to say anything else, because there's a gentle knock on the door. Through the window next to it, I can see Marnie, wearing an oversized coat.

Nicole's eyes light up. "How long do you think she'll knock before she tries opening it?"

Another test.

Feeling a twinge of sympathy for Marnie, I give her a slight nod through the glass, and she pushes the door open.

"Spoilsport," Nicole says, throwing another pretzel at me.

I catch this one in my mouth.

I'm still chewing when Marnie approaches us, nervous. Her eyes land on me, a silent request for introductions. I'm about to follow through when she exclaims, "What's your real name, Mitchell?"

Nicole laughs. "You didn't even make it through introductions?"

"We were busy," Marnie says.

Nicole and Damien both start laughing. At least they didn't try to FaceTime Gary again.

Rolling my eyes, I tell Marnie, "You'll get used to them. I'm Griffin. This is Nicole, and this guy, who inexplicably agreed to love her for all eternity, is Damien."

"*You* love me," Nicole says, leaning forward to rap my knuckles.

"You're my favorite niece," I agree. "I'll give you that."

Marnie looks like she's wondering whether she stumbled into a nightmare, but she takes off the enormous coat and lowers onto the stool in front of me. She's wearing that Star Wars shirt again, and I can't help but grin. She obviously did it to fuck with Nicole. I appreciate the message. She may be down but she's not out.

"Is that thing glued to you?" Nicole asks, lifting her eyebrows skeptically.

"Superglued." Marnie's gaze flits to me before settling back on them. "Now, excuse me for being blunt, but who are you people?"

"Didn't Griffin just tell you our names?" Damien asks with a flat expression.

Her eyes widen, and her lips part, but Nicole's already laughing. She leans over and kisses Damien, taking her time, then turns to Marnie, whose cheeks have gone pink. "We're your fairy godmothers."

"You'll have to do better than that. I stopped believing in fairy tales when I was a little girl."

Nicole reaches over and bops her on the nose. "That, Cinderella, is exactly what we want to cure you of."

"What exactly do you mean by that?"

"We're going to find out who filmed and dispersed that video. Ideally, we'll also get you some sweet, sweet revenge while we're at it. Among other perks." She winks at me.

"And what do you charge?" Marnie asks, eyeing her dubiously.

"We don't," Damien says firmly. "Not for our . . ." he sighs before repeating the name Nicole chose, ". . . fairy godmother clients."

Marnie gapes at him for a moment before recovering. "Nothing's free."

"Your freedom will be," Nicole says. "All you have to do is find our next fairy godmother client, like DeeDee's friend found you. It's a pay-it-forward kind of thing. We work with one person at a time, for however long it takes."

Marnie frowns. "DeeDee?"

"Your friend." Nicole makes an emphatic hand gesture. "The one who brought you here last night. Don't you know her name?" She eyes me quizzically. "I got the impression you were close."

"Andy. Her name is Andy. I've known her since high school."

Nicole shrugs. "I got one syllable right."

Marnie worries the ends of her hair, her eyes flicking to me. I hold her gaze until she looks away. "But why? Why would you do something like this for free?"

"Damien came into a large inheritance a couple of years ago. We decided to use it to help women who've been dicked over by men. It's what you might called a shared interest of ours."

Damien's expression is stoic, but Nicole reaches for his hand and squeezes it. She's always been good at seeing through his bullshit. Damien's grandmother was the only person from his childhood who really cared about him, just like Gary and Ma are for me. Becoming a many-times-over millionaire is nice, I'm sure, but he'd prefer to have her back. To her credit, Nicole feels the same way. It's a rare person who loves you more than they love what you can do for them.

"But why?" Marnie insists, frowning.

"Part of it is that both of our fathers are assholes," Nicole offers.

Damien straightens on his stool. "And my grandmother was a strong, independent woman who never took any shit from anyone. We're honoring her legacy by helping other women become more like her."

"But Griffin says you also own the bar," Marnie says, her forehead wrinkling in confusion. "Did you buy this place just to scope out potential clients?"

Nicole laughs with genuine amusement.

"No," Damien answers, giving her a squeeze. "It has sentimental value. It used to be a really run-down place with shitty food and drinks. Worse service."

"Nicole saw something here when no one else did," I add.

She's good at that, Nicole. I'd know. She saw something in me too.

"We needed to give Griff a reason to stick around, so we made the former owner an offer he couldn't refuse," Nicole says. She's teasing, sort of, but I think she also means it. They did it for me, because I needed an anchor, and also partly for Gary, because he needed me to be anchored *here*.

Marnie's eyes have that Bambi look again. She glances around as if worried she'll be overheard and whispers, "You *threatened* him?"

Nicole laughs as if she made a hilarious joke. "Only a little. We mostly threw money at him. He wasn't really making any. The floor was always sticky back then, and the food came from the microwave. Griff is much better."

"I didn't know you offered food here."

"Pretzel?" I ask, smiling as I pushed the bowl toward her. "I wouldn't recommend you have any after we open, though. That famous TV special about urine content in bar snacks is probably a bit of an underestimate, actually."

She doesn't smile back. I suspect she's hung up on the "we only threatened him a little" assertion. Turning to Nicole, she says, "So, you run a bar, and you investigate the people who have wronged your clients?"

"Among other things," Nicole replies. "We don't like putting ourselves into boxes."

A smile plays on Damien's lips. "We do some other P.I. work, plus we both have hobbies."

Marnie licks her lips, her gaze drifting to me and then to the card taped behind the bar. I don't want the slight upturn of her lips to affect me, but if you know how to stop yourself from wanting something, I'd like to hear how.

"And you also have a boyfriend loaner program," she says softly.

"Sometimes," Nicole says.

"You've been a fake boyfriend before," Marnie guesses, tipping her head and studying me. Something flickers in Marnie's eyes. Maybe it's disappointment. Maybe it's judgment.

"Griff does a little bit of this, a little bit of that," Nicole says, surprising me. I figured she'd probably revel in the opportunity to put me on the spot. But maybe she realizes I'll come off as weird if she tells Marnie I'm helping her on a volunteer basis, because no, I don't do that often.

Turning back to Nicole and Damien, she asks, "What comes next?"

Rustling through her shoulder bag, Nicole pulls out a wrinkled document. Damien looks like he's on the verge of laughter as he watches her. "You need to sign this engagement letter. Griffin's step-brother, Gary, is the one who makes us deal with the documents. He's a stickler for details, our Gary. An old friend drew up the papers for us." Her gaze settles on Marnie. "The same friend who'll hand out takedown notices like they're Halloween candy . . . after we're done. Because we don't want the person who did this to you to know we're looking for them."

Marnie accepts the document silently, flips through it, then looks up at them uncertainly. "You really don't charge?"

"Not for this," Damien repeats.

Marnie starts flipping through the document again. Her nose wrinkles. She glances up. "So basically I can't sue you if you make my life worse, unintentionally or otherwise?"

"Correct," Damien says.

For a second, I think Marnie is going to say no. I think she'll turn and leave the bar, and the sight of her shapely ass in those leggings, mostly but not entirely covered by the large coat, will be the last I'll see of Marnie Jones. I shouldn't care about that, but I do. I tell myself it's because she needs Nicole and Damien, not because I want to spend more time with her.

Like most people, I tell myself a lot of things that aren't true.

"You should do it," I blurt. "They've helped a lot of people."

"Yeah?" she asks, perking up.

"Yeah. And those memes . . . I've seen them."

She pulls a face. "Everyone in the continental United States has seen them."

"Don't undersell yourself," Nicole pipes in. "They're also very popular in Latvia."

I shrug her comment off, my eyes on Marnie. Her dark hair

frames her face, making her lips look pinker and more inviting. I barely brushed them earlier, but they were soft and sweet from the pastry. The curves of her cheeks make me want to touch them.

Marnie could be dangerous to me, but I want her to heal more than I want to stay away from her—and that's only partially because I don't want to stay away from her at all.

"You deserve to know who did this, Marnie," I say. "If it's someone in your life and they have bad intentions, you're better off knowing. If you don't deal with it, this sort of thing could happen again. People don't change. Especially when you don't give them a reason to."

If I'm a hypocrite, so be it. I truly believe the sentiment, but sometimes life isn't as straightforward as we'd like it to be.

"You have no reason to hide, not from them or from anyone. Why don't you show them who you really are?"

She holds my gaze for a long moment, long enough for me to see the specks of gold clustered around her pupils, then she swallows, her elegant throat contracting. I feel something stir inside of me. "What if they don't like what they see?"

"Then fuck them," I say, my voice coming out husky.

Still holding my gaze, she says, "Do you have a pen?"

I hand her one over the bar, our fingers brushing, and she signs the document without another moment's hesitation.

She tucks a lock of long dark hair behind her ear. "Why do I feel like I just made a deal with the devil?" There's a slight smile on her face, like maybe she wouldn't mind. Like maybe she's the kind of Red Riding Hood who wouldn't mind inviting the wolf home, if only for one night.

"Because you're smarter than you look," Nicole responds.

Marnie startles a little, as if she'd forgotten Nicole was there. I'd forgotten too. "What happens now?" she asks.

Nicole gives me a significant look, which Damien follows up with a slight nod. He doesn't find all of this nearly as amusing as

Nicole, but he'd do anything for her. I suppose maybe we both would.

Sighing, I press play on the music Nicole cued up on my iPad—"I'm Coming Up."

"Now," Nicole says, "it's time for your makeover."

I pour Marnie a drink.

True to my word, I make it a heavy pour.

seven

MARNIE

I PROBABLY SHOULDN'T HAVE SIGNED that contract.

I probably wouldn't have if Griffin hadn't stared deeply into my eyes and given me advice.

He was right.

I'm used to being overlooked, to *hiding*, and that's what I've been doing since the would-be wedding. I've been burying my head in the sand in the hopes that this will go away. I hesitate to admit this, because I don't like the way it makes me sound, but it had never occurred to me to be *angry*.

But in that moment, with Griffin staring into my eyes, pouring courage into me like a drink he might serve at the bar, I *was* angry y —partly at myself because I'd let this shit happen without snapping back, and partly at whoever did this to me.

So I signed the document.

If I'd thought my day couldn't get any stranger, I was suffering from a limited imagination.

Twenty-four hours ago, I didn't know Nicole existed. Now I'm sitting in her mother's living room while her mom, Liza, cuts my hair.

56

A video of my wedding is playing on the TV, streaming from my phone.

The videographer, who had a no-cancellation policy, sent me what he'd filmed. At the time, it seemed like he was throwing a bag of small-batch, curated pink sea salt (he's an *expensive* videographer) into my open wound, but there may be some use for it after all. Nicole and Damien are studying it with the avid interest of crime scene pathologists, comparing it to the angle in the video that was released online. They think they can figure out who took the original video, or at least narrow it down to a few people.

I avert my eyes from the screen, not wanting to see a close-up of Brock's face as he watches me nervously, preparing to break the news.

To think. I'd thought he was nervous because we were about to get *married*.

Truthfully, although I haven't told many people this part, I was nervous too. The night before the wedding, my brother had pulled me aside to tell me it wasn't too late. A woman who was madly and deeply in love probably would have gotten pissed off for many reasons, particularly the timing. But I'd felt a peculiar lifting sensation, as if I'd been playing a months-long game of hide-and-seek, and someone had finally peeked behind a curtain I'd been hiding behind and found me.

It's too much, too soon, Marnie, Drew had said. *Especially after everything we've been through this year. Like most things Mom and Sinclair touch, it's all gotten out of control. If you really love this guy, you'll love him just as much six months from now. You can elope. You don't need all of this. It's not you.*

He was right about all of it, and I must have hugged him for two minutes, crying, before I told him I'd think about it and we'd talk in the morning. I *did* think about it. In fact, I stayed up all night thinking about it. But Sinclair had already paid for the *whole* wedding, and it was at the Biltmore, the largest private home in the United States.

I could think of no acceptable excuse to hesitate.

Brock was everything I'd always thought I wanted: handsome and put-together, capable of steamrolling through life, whereas I've always tended to roll along as if I'm a passenger, commenting wryly but not taking control of anything.

Other people had told me I was lucky, and for most of our short relationship, I'd *felt* lucky. I was used to being overlooked, but Brock had insisted I was the only woman for him, within weeks of meeting me. He'd appeared to mean it. Grace had told me our romance was like something straight out of a romance novel, and she'd know.

Anyway, the bottom line was that I'd gone through with it, only to be publicly humiliated—on tape, no less.

I guess Drew could say I told you so, but he's a good brother, so he's held back. For now, at least. I definitely foresee plenty of smugness coming my way a few years down the line.

My gaze snags on the fireplace mantel, pulling me back to the present, as Liza snips more hair. There are various photographs, including one of Damien and Nicole in outfits straight out of *Grease*, but my gaze is drawn to a lone frame toward the end. It's Griffin. *Young* Griffin, probably only a teenager. He's standing next to a much shorter man whom I recognize from the other photos as Gary.

Griffin isn't here with us. Before we left, he called out, "Hey, Star Wars." When I turned to look at him, trying to seem annoyed, he said, "Don't let them change too much, okay?"

"Is this goodbye?" I asked.

He shook his head slowly, smiling at me. "No, I'll be seeing you. It's not that easy to get rid of a Mountainbottom."

I hope he meant it. I mean, he *was* right about Sinclair. She'd get suspicious if I don't send her occasional updates.

My attention circles back to the photo on the mantel.

Young Griffin has that angsty look, down to a leather jacket that's much too large for him. It looks the same as the one he had on earlier, although his body has grown to fit it. The photo Griffin has the same light brown eyes and shock of dark hair he has now, but his nose hadn't been broken yet.

"What was Griffin like as a teenager?" I wonder aloud.

"Shhh," Nicole says, pressing a finger to her lips. She and Damien are snuggled up on the sectional couch as if they're watching a rom-com, Nicole half on his lap. They have the gif up on their phones while they watch the video on the screen. There's a bowl of Chex Mix on the coffee table. It's a real party. "You can moon over Griff later. We're getting to the good part."

I roll my eyes. The "good part," I take it, is my tumble down the aisle.

"Thanks a lot."

Liza clucks her tongue as she circles around and cuts more hair. There's an alarming amount of it on the floor, but I agreed to let her do her thing, so I hold my tongue.

"None of us knew Griffin back then," Liza tells me in an undertone. "His daddy moved him away when he was sixteen, and he didn't come back for ten years. Gary was beside himself. His mother too."

"They didn't keep in touch?"

She bit her lip. "No, Griff might as well have fallen off the face of the earth. Then he showed up five years ago, right before Gary and I got engaged. He hasn't left yet." She looks around wildly, making me worry for my hair—did she accidentally cut a chunk off because we were talking?—before reaching over and knocking her fist on the wooden coffee table. It looks like it's made from pallets, arranged in a zigzag pattern.

"Oh, he's not going anywhere," Nicole says, munching some Chex Mix. "We're much too good to him."

Liza doesn't seem convinced. Then again, it's her husband who spent ten years missing him.

I find myself looking at that photo again, thinking of teenage Griffin plucked from his roots and his family. That could have been me if I'd gone to Los Angeles with my mother and Sinclair. At least I was given a choice.

I want to ask Griffin about it, although it's none of my business.

My fingers skate over my pocket, feeling the ridge of my phone. I'm tempted to pull it out. He saved his number as Mitchell Mountainbottom, which made me laugh when I noticed it. Later, at the bar, I saw that he really *had* hung up my card. It was actually the only thing on the wall behind the bar other than a framed photo of an older man in a Hawaiian shirt.

"This is almost too easy," Nicole says, breaking into my thoughts.

Her mother takes another snip of my hair. "It *is* coming along well," she says. "It's been a while since someone let me take their shoulder-length hair down to a short bob."

"*What?*" I cry.

She jolts a little, and my gaze flies to the scissors in her hand, making me quick to temper my reaction.

"Didn't you know?" she asks, her brow furrowing with worry.

"I didn't know it was going to be that short, no, but I'm sure it'll be . . ." I trail off, because I'm not sure what to say next. I've never had a bob.

She pats my shoulder. "It looks fantastic. It's the right style for the shape of your face and your eyes. You look just like Winona Ryder."

"The lady from *Stranger Things*? Doesn't she have a shag haircut?"

Liza laughs. "I'm showing my age."

Honestly, she looks like she's *my* age, but there's no feasible way a twenty-nine-year-old could have given birth to Nicole. She must just have one of those faces.

"I'm not talking about her hair," Nicole says, rolling her eyes, then gives me a once-over and does a nod-shrug combo. "It's a definite improvement though. She looks less like a poorly cared-for coma patient."

"Your compliments could use work," I say, lifting my fingertips to my hair. It's true that I haven't had it cut for some time. Brock prefers women with long hair, and I cared about what he thought for a hot minute, so I'd let it grow.

"You're not the first person to have told me that," Nicole says flippantly, "and you almost certainly won't be the last. But you have every reason to be happy with me right now. I've already narrowed down the pool of people who could have filmed this video. We're looking at three contenders."

She's preening as she says it, the fire of victory in her light brown eyes, and Damien's watching her with a bemused smile. He tends to look at her like that, like she's where his eyes naturally want to rest. I'd think it was sweet if I weren't so anxious.

It's in this moment that I realize I was hoping they wouldn't be able to find out. If someone I trust is actively scheming against me, I don't actually want to know. It's a foolish thought, though, because Griffin is right. If someone did this to me intentionally, I have to know so I can protect myself. Ignorance won't serve me—it'll only serve whoever's screwing with me.

"Who?" I say, my voice tight.

Nicole points to the paused image on the TV screen. "Her, her, and him."

Just as I feared, they're all sitting on my side of the chapel.

Grace.

Aunt Helen.

My *brother*.

"How can you be so sure?" I ask, my voice shaky. My stomach feels like it's been transformed into the contents of an hourglass.

"From the angle of the gif, the video must have been taken in the first row on your side of the chapel, and they're the only ones who have their phones out."

"I don't believe any of them would have done it," I say. "In fact, I'm sure they wouldn't have."

Grace is, well, Grace. And I'm not totally convinced Aunt Helen knows what the internet is, let alone a meme. She's a decade older than my father, who was, according to my aunt, a "blessed" surprise to their parents, and if she had her way, she'd probably live in a yurt somewhere. She's settled for a green retirement community called Green Oasis, however, and doesn't possess a computer. The smartphone is a concession she made to help us get a hold of her when we have the need. As for my brother . . .

No way. He never liked Brock, so I could see him trying to interrupt the wedding, but he'd never willingly humiliate me. He knows how hard it was for me to grow up as Sinclair's little sister. Being her big brother wasn't always easy either. They've never been close, but he's still protective of her, and he doesn't take kindly to the sort of remarks men make so freely about famous women. It's not quite the same as what I've gone through—Drew never felt the strain of being compared to a woman who is widely considered to be perfect—but he understands the impact the experience has had on me. Even before the meme, my photo made its way onto a few websites in those roundups about the "normal" family members of beautiful people.

Gee, thanks, US Weekly. I realize I wasn't wearing makeup when I bought that tomato, but I figured the tomato wouldn't mind.

I relate all of this to Nicole and Damien (minus the tomato thing) while Liza makes a "few finishing touches" on my hair. By the time she's done, I'll be lucky to have any hair left.

"One of them took the video," Damien insists, giving me a level look. His eyes are flinty and unblinking. "But that doesn't mean that they willingly or even knowingly dispersed it."

The words are like Pepto for my stomach. "You mean, someone could have taken it from their phone?"

"Exactly. There was a lot of excitement after you left the chapel.

Say one of them set their phone down for a minute. Another person could have easily grabbed it up and sent themselves that video. Try to think of anyone who might have held a grudge against you."

I've thought of little else for months.

It's hard to imagine anyone dislikes me enough to see such an opportunity and take it, but I'd prefer to imagine that than a vindictive Aunt Helen. What would it be in retaliation for? That time Drew and I used her henna to draw pictures on the wall of her old house, which had to be painted over?

Nicole stares me down, her pink hair almost painfully bright. "Or you could be wrong about these people," she says. "There's always that."

"No," I object. "None of them would willingly hurt me like that. I'd stake my life on it."

I half expect her to argue, but her slow nod suggests she's glad to see I have a backbone, even if it's made of toothpicks. "Well, all right. The next step is to figure out whose phone it came from. We'll work from there."

"I'll talk to them," I say, getting up from the chair. Hair clippings cascade off me.

"Will they show you their phones?" Nicole asks.

"Yes," I say without hesitation. "All of them. Shouldn't I be able to tell pretty easily if the video was sent to someone else?"

"Not necessarily." Damien rubs his jaw. "They could have texted it and deleted the text. Or emailed it and done the same. That would make it hard to tell."

"The best way is to get them to play the video they took and see if it matches," Nicole says.

Fantastic. I'll get to watch my embarrassment from three different angles. Maybe it'll be like exposure therapy and I'll eventually stop caring.

"No time like the present." I make it one step toward the door before Nicole's laughter stops me.

"Oh, we're not done with you," she says. "We haven't even looked at your wardrobe."

Well, shit.

Something tells me she's going to say the vast majority of my clothes are sad . . . or at least the things I've been wearing down to their threads for the last several months.

I wrap my arms around my Star Wars shirt. "You'll throw this away over my dead body."

Nicole smirks. "That can be arranged."

My hair is short.

Very short.

Nicole's mother is a legit genius, though, because it looks good, sexy and saucy, as if I'm some French ingenue and not a bored graphic designer.

Nicole has already said *I told you so*, twice in fact.

Even so, that doesn't mean I'm going to let her get everything she wants.

I manage to save the Star Wars shirt by quickly changing and hiding it while Nicole is reviewing the guest list for my wedding on the desktop computer in my bedroom. Damien catches me doing it, but his eyes scrunch with amusement, and he mimes zipping his mouth. To my surprise, he tells her he knows where it is but refrains from sharing the secret, even when she threatens him with bodily harm. Actually, they both seem suspiciously into the whole argument. There's a strange energy that zips back and forth between the two of them, like they might run off at any second and have sex in the bathroom. I feel weirdly jealous of it. I don't think I've ever had that kind of chemistry with anyone. Despite owning an expedition company, Brock only ever wanted to have sex in a bed. Andy had nicknamed him the poster boy for false advertising.

At Nicole and Damien's recommendation, I decide to text my brother to ask him for his version of the video. He'll soon be out of range of any cell phone towers, but I can probably catch him now, early on in his trip.

Of course, the minute I get my phone out, I see I have almost a dozen missed texts. Sinclair sent a suspiciously bubbly text about "Mitchell" that includes at least five exclamation marks, but my gaze slides to a text from "Mitchell" himself.

I can't deny my heart starts thumping a little louder in my chest. *Checking in to make sure you haven't murdered Nicole. I am grudgingly fond of her.*

There's another one after the first, sent ten minutes later, asking for the name of my Etsy shop.

I answer: *Sweet Nothings.*

Hardly nothing. Your card's already gotten a dozen compliments.

A glow forms inside of me, and I'm slightly surprised my fingers don't start giving off light. It's for the best that they haven't, really, since I do not want Nicole to know what I'm doing.

I answer him, then send a selfie photo showing my new haircut. *It's . . . short.*

While I'm waiting for him to answer, I check my other messages —one from my mother asking me to call her (no, thanks), several update requests from Andy and Grace, and a photo from Drew of a bear from what thankfully appears to be a safe distance. Ignoring the other messages, I text my brother and ask him to send me his video of the wedding-that-wasn't.

When I finally look up from the phone, Nicole has abandoned the computer and is sifting through my wardrobe.

"All of these need to go," she says, gesturing to the collection of turtlenecks I acquired this winter.

"They're all new!"

"It's time to stop hiding," she says, and it's so similar to what Griff told me at the bar that I feel like she slapped me.

Was that what I was doing? Honestly, the reason I'm so fond of the turtlenecks is because they're comfortable. They make me feel like a hibernating turtle. Only turtles aren't exactly confrontational creatures, so that's probably not a strong defense.

"They're comfortable," I say.

"So are Snuggies, but you wouldn't wear one to work."

Sighing, I check my phone again, and see Drew responded.

Marnie, I don't think it's healthy to fixate. Brock's an asshole. It's time to move on. Do you want me to set you up with one of my friends?

I roll my eyes, mostly because he has only three friends that I know of, and I know them all well enough that they might as well be my brothers too.

Gross, I reply. *Danny will forever be the kid who peed in my princess pool, and despite what we've told Shane, I will never forget the time he got drunk and sprained his ankle doing an interpretive dance. Burke is just Burke. Besides, I'm TRYING to move on. I hired a couple of P.I.s who are going to figure out how the video got out.*

That's great! he writes. Then the three dots of doom show up. *Wait. Do you think I did it?*

Obviously not, dum-dum. But it might have come from your phone.

No, he responds instantly. *I stopped filming the second you tripped. I remember it distinctly. I filmed up until then because I thought it might be empowering for you to have footage of when you walked away from the worst almost-mistake of your life.*

Thanks for that, I say. I'm about to type something about the bear when a new text from Griffin pops up.

You're beautiful. I keep trying to think of something else to say, something that's better, but that's what I keep circling back to. You're beautiful, Marnie. I'm glad Liza could help you see it.

I remind myself that he has to say things like that, that even if I'm not paying him to spend time with me, Nicole almost certainly is, but it doesn't do anything to cap the fizzy feeling inside of me.

Thank you, I say. *You're the best fake boyfriend I've ever had.*

I glance up and see Nicole's throwing all of my turtlenecks into an enormous trash bag Damien's holding open.

"It's for your own good," she says firmly.

"The video didn't come from my brother's phone," I report. "He stopped filming the moment I tripped."

She tosses another turtleneck into the bag, my favorite, but I decide to allow it. I got to keep my Star Wars shirt, and I will absolutely be wearing it around her again to remind her of my victory.

"Well, that's a wrap," Nicole says as Damien ties up the bag. She seems entirely too satisfied with herself.

"We're done here?"

She laughs. "*He's* done here."

"Where are you going?" I ask him.

"I have stuff to do," he says, knotting the bag, "but first I'm going to Mountain Valley to donate this." He lifts the stuffed trash bag.

"Wait," I say, turning to Nicole, "they're not okay for me to wear, but other people can wear them?"

"It's a retirement home, Marnie," she says. "Everyone who lives there is above the age of sixty-five. Many of them have good reasons to hide their necks. You do not."

I could sulk more, but I suspect it wouldn't do much good. Worse, I realize there's a chance she might be right.

"Fine. You said Damien's the only one who's leaving. What are we doing?"

"You and I are going shopping. Where does your aunt live?"

"Green Oasis."

"It's settled. We're going shopping *and* we're going to see Aunt Helen."

And we do. Damien goes off to donate my clothes after kissing Nicole thoroughly enough to make me turn away, and then she and I go shopping downtown. It's a very long trip, filled with arguments. Although Nicole flashes a platinum credit card at the cash register of the first store, I insist on paying for my new and improved wardrobe . . . well, everything I like. Nicole pushes several things on me that I refuse to try on let alone buy.

After we finish up, I leave the store wearing one of my new outfits, a black sweater dress with knee-high boots and a two-tone peacoat.

"Do you feel like Pretty Woman?" Nicole asks with a smirk as I drive us toward my aunt's retirement home.

"No, I don't feel like a prostitute, thank you very much." All the same, I find myself smiling back. "But I do feel pretty damn good."

"That's what I like to hear."

She lifts her hand for a high five, and I give it to her.

"Now, tell me about Brock."

I sneak a quick glance at her. "You don't want to hear about Aunt Helen?"

"Not unless she's secretly a bad bitch who screwed you over."

The thought of my aunt screwing over anyone is hilarious. She's such a pacifist that she used to read poems to the spiders and other bugs in her house, hoping to lull them into peaceful cohabitation.

"No, she's not."

She waves a hand in a go-on gesture. "So tell me about Brock."

I think for a moment. "Well, I guess he's going to hire my firm to put together another campaign for him. Andy's hookup has been working there, and he overheard Brock talking about it. I guess he wants me to be involved in the campaign. Which means I'll probably have to see him soon."

"Okay," she says. "That's good."

"Good?" I ask, unconvinced. "I fail to see how it's good."

"To give you the full fairy godmother treatment, we have to at least mess with him a little. If he's around, then we have access. Tell me more about him."

I suspect she's already looked him up. Actually, based on what I'm learning about her, she probably knows his social security number. "He owns Tilton Expeditions. They lead rafting trips. Hiking. Camping. That kind of thing."

She wrinkles her nose. "So you like really outdoorsy guys? The kind who wear flannel shirts and smell bad?"

"He's not like that, really," I say. "He runs the business, but he employs guides who go on the actual expeditions. He's a big-picture kind of guy, obsessed with figuring out a way to take things to the next level." Hence his obsession with Edgar James, whose profile is much bigger than his.

"Then he's the kind of guy who gets other people to do his dirty work," she says knowingly.

It's on the tip of my tongue to object, but there's a ring of truth to her assessment that has me hesitating. Despite owning a business that encourages digging in the dirt, I don't think I ever saw him with a speck of it on his clothing, and I know for a fact that he pays his employees practically nothing. Andy's sort-of boyfriend confirmed it. "Yeah, I guess maybe he is."

"What's he look like?" she asks.

"He's handsome. He's tall and slim and has blond hair." I dart a quick glance at her in confusion. "Wait a second . . . you just watched him in that video. Several times."

"And he's just that forgettable. Is that really what you like?" she asks contemptuously. "A man who looks like he's dying of consumption in a Victorian novel and could be blown away in a stiff wind? A man who gives other people his work and takes the credit for it?"

Laughter spills out of me. "I see what you're doing here. You're trying to make me feel better."

"No, I'm trying to make you realize that unless you *do* want those things, it was his loss."

"No, of course I don't." My brain must be pretty stupid because it conjures up someone else—Griffin in that thermal shirt, the fabric sleeves nearly bursting from trying to contain his arms. *Griffin* wouldn't leave the hard work for someone else. He'd do other people's hard work *and* his own.

"He didn't always seem bad," I say, trying to force my mind down a more sensible pathway. "He was really sweet to me in the beginning, and it helped keep me distracted."

"Because your dad died," Nicole finishes, the words landing like a kick to the solar plexus.

She must see it, because she lifts a hand. "Sorry, that was blunt. Your friend mentioned it. I get it. Or at least I sort of do. My father was a piece of shit, but Damien and I were close to his grandmother. Losing her sucked."

"Sorry," I say, because that seems like the kind of thing you should apologize for.

"Eh, my life would have been worse if he'd stayed. You met my mom. She's the best." She gives me an appraising look. "I don't know if Griff told you, but his father died a few years ago. They were close."

"What?" I blurt out. It's just . . . why didn't he say so when I told him about *my* dad? It would have made our conversation at least fifty percent less awkward.

He didn't say so because he's not your real boyfriend. He didn't want to make things overly personal.

Only it had felt pretty damn personal. Maybe he's good at pretending. He probably does that a lot. For all I know, he had to run off to make a fake lunch date.

I can feel Nicole's gaze burning into me. "Why are you so surprised? People die all the time. A hundred and twenty of them a minute."

"That's a morbid statistic."

"And a true one. Anyway, Griffin's dad was a piece of shit. He was worse than my dad, and considering my father pulled a runner when I was seven, that's saying something."

"How was he worse?" I ask.

"You're gonna have to ask Griffin."

Except I can't, obviously. If he'd wanted me to know, he would have told me himself.

We arrive at Green Oasis, which is neither green nor an oasis, and sign in at the desk before heading up to Aunt Helen's unit.

I'm arriving unannounced, but Aunt Helen is nothing like my mother, who has a stick firmly lodged up her ass and will gladly take any excuse you give her to be unpleasant. My aunt waves us into her apartment, patting her white curls, and then offers us a plate of cookies that look like they've been in her pantry for long enough to have expired twice. The décor of her apartment is warm and earthy, with terra-cotta accent walls, and a couch that both looks and feels comfortable—an important distinction. There's too much clutter, with stacks of books and pretty boxes holding God knows what, but it's a pleasant kind of clutter.

On the way to the couch, I "accidentally" spill the plate of questionable cookies—frankly, I didn't want my aunt to eat any of them either. As if we'd choreographed it, Nicole immediately steps in and gathers them up, spiriting them away to the trash can.

"Oh, no," I say, my concern falling a little flat. "I'm so sorry."

"That's quite all right," Aunt Helen says, patting me on the back. "They were probably past their prime, but you know how I hate to waste things. It doesn't seem right for someone to make a cookie and then not eat it."

It does if the cookie's going to give them food poisoning. But I suppose she's made it through seventy-five years living life her way. It's gotten her this far.

Nicole and I sink into the couch, Aunt Helen taking the chair across from us.

It doesn't take long for me to explain what we need. It takes much longer for me to explain what's been happening with the memes, something I've concealed from her, but when she finally gets it, she develops the dejected look of a child who's learned the truth about Christmas . . . or an aging sunshine girl who's finally learned how shitty people are on the internet.

"Oh dear," Helen says. "*Of course* your friend can look at my phone."

She hands it over, and Nicole pulls up the video app.

"Holy shit," Nicole says, but she sounds more delighted than horrified.

I peer over her shoulder and jolt. She's watching a home video of Aunt Helen getting it on with some older guy. A very graphic video.

"Oh *my* God," I say, looking away in shock. I mean, I knew Aunt Helen used to be a swinger, but I had no idea she was still in the filming-herself-mid-coitus stage of her life.

Nicole watches for what I consider way too long before scrolling to the next video.

"Nope, it's another one," she says, looking up with shining eyes. "With a different dude." A grin stretches across her face, revealing sharp white teeth. "Go, Aunt Helen."

"Why?" my aunt says in confusion. "What are you looking at?"

Nicole lifts up the phone, which is playing a video of my aunt giving a blow job to an older guy who probably has enormous feet.

"Drat," Aunt Helen says, a little annoyed but unconcerned, as if a dog just peed on her mailbox. "I forgot those were on there. Never mind. There should only be three or four of them before the video I took at the chapel."

"Three or four?" I repeat, choking on my own spit.

My aunt is officially having three or four times more sex than I am. No, that's not true. Three or four times zero would still be zero.

"There's nothing wrong with sex, Marnie," she chides. "It's cleansing for the body *and* soul."

"As long as you use protection," Nicole comments.

Aunt Helen clucks her tongue and waves to a colorful display on a nearby shelf. "Oh, my crystals provide me with plenty of protection."

My mouth gapes open.

"Here we go!" Nicole says. I glance over warily, half expecting to see my aunt in a compromising position, but it's a video of me at the altar.

I can already tell it's not the right one. The camera isn't steady enough, and the angle isn't quite right. Nicole looks up and gives me a slight nod.

My heart starts racing.

This means the video originated from Grace's phone.

"Nope. Didn't come from here," Nicole says, giving the phone a little tap before she hands it back. "But you should password-protect this sucker. And your vagina. Crystals don't care about sexually transmitted diseases, and if some asshole steals your phone, they won't care about sex being a cleansing experience. They could use those videos to blackmail you, and even if you don't care whether they're released, I'll bet your famous niece would. I've seen it happen before."

Aunt Helen looks slightly taken aback, but I nod fervently. "What she said. Please be careful."

She gives my arm a fond little pat, then bustles over to the refrigerator. Before she lets us out the door, she shoves Tupperware containers full of leftovers at both of us. It's hard to tell from a cursory glance, but I'm fairly sure there's mold inside of mine. I fully intend to throw it away when I get home.

Or maybe I'll save it for Drew's return since he's on fridge duty.

Nicole's either shifty about telling me where she lives or eager for a drink after spending all day with me, because she tells me to drop her off at the bar. I feel a little twinge as I pull up outside of it.

I want to see Griffin.

But he's working, and I need to be realistic. Spending time with me would be one more job for him. Sure, he may not mind some back-and-forth texting, but that doesn't mean he wants to spend quality time together.

Nicole gives me a sly look. "There's a space just ahead. Why don't you park and come in? I bet Griff would like to see you."

Can she actually read minds?

"Why would he?" I ask. "I mean . . . I get that he's your friend, but he's being paid to hang out with me. He probably doesn't feel like doing two jobs at once."

Her expression hasn't changed, though, and I slide the car into the spot and park. I'm not getting out, I tell myself. I'm just giving us a chance to talk.

She cocks her head. "He didn't tell you?"

"This is getting tedious," I say. "Why don't you just say what you want to say?"

She tucks a lock of vivid pink hair behind her ear. "Because it's less fun that way."

"For you," I mutter.

"For me," she agrees. "We're not *paying* Griffin, Marnie. He helps out with the agency now and then as a favor, because we hooked him up with the bar. We haven't ordered him to do anything. When he heard you needed help, he *volunteered*." She waggles her eyebrows up and down. "I guess he must have liked the look of you at the bar last night."

Oh. My spirits bob a little, because there were a few moments earlier when it felt like I wasn't just a moony teenager lusting after someone unreachable, but an adult attracted to another adult. At the very least, I'm relieved that he didn't help me because he was paid to. If he's doing it because he feels sorry for me, then so be it.

"Thank you for telling me," I say. Part of me still wants to go in, to talk to Griffin, but he's working, and I'm on edge. "But I think I need to go home right now. It's been a long day."

She shrugs, as if to say *your funeral*. "Text me after you talk to Grace," she says. "And I want to know exactly what happens with

Brock. After your boss breaks the news to you, we'll figure out our next steps. We might have to think of a way to reunite all the key players from the wedding." Her eyes twinkling, she says, "It'll be like a human game of Clue."

That sounds like a whole lot of nope, but I have a feeling it won't be easy to dissuade her, so I concede, and we part ways.

It's late by then, after seven, and even though I definitely need to talk to Grace, all I want to do is take a bubble bath and eat a pint of ice cream for dinner.

That's self-care, isn't it?

I get home and unload my new clothes from the trunk, only to find that Nicole somehow one-upped me. She apparently bought a bunch of the shit I refused to try on and stuffed it into the trunk while I was distracted. She probably knows that I'll feel guilty enough to actually wear it.

Sighing, half annoyed and half grateful, I carry the bags upstairs, more than ready for my night of self-care.

Andy and Grace are waiting for me in the living room.

eight

MARNIE

"YOUR HAIR!" Andy shouts. She and Grace are both gaping at me, and Grace nearly drops her glass of red wine onto my couch.

"Is that a good *your hair* or a bad one?" I say self-consciously, lowering my shopping bags.

They set their wine glasses down and flock toward me.

"It's definitely good," Andy says, ruffling the back of my hair.

"And your outfit," Grace says. "Not that you don't always look nice, but . . . you look especially nice."

She's not wrong. What I have on is absolutely an upgrade from my new normal.

Nicole made sure to tell me she wouldn't wear ninety percent of the items she'd helped me choose, but I guess she's a better fairy godmother than I thought, because she helped me pick out stuff that suits me.

"You haven't answered any of our texts," Andy accuses, "so we had to use your super-secret key."

Which obviously isn't super secret since at least two people know about it. It resides on our front porch in a poly-resin key holder designed to look like a rock.

"Can one of you pour me some wine?" I ask, pulling off the coat and then the boots. I hang the coat on the back of one of the kitchen chairs, and it strikes me viscerally that this is where Griffin sat, the hulk of him nestled in the chair. I'm surprised it didn't break.

Grace pours me a drink, and we all sit on the sectional couch. I should probably start by asking Grace about the video, but I find myself telling them about Mitchell Mountainbottom and my call with Sinclair.

"Ho—ly shit," Andy says. "I sincerely wish I were there. She probably instantly got a zit after he said *Sisters of Sin* wasn't his thing."

"No," I say. "She still looked immaculate."

"Of course she did," Grace says. "And you said he was the bartender from last night? I remember him. He's hot. Like one of the guys Vera would bribe to be on her book covers."

"Yeah," I say, peering into my wine. "He's pretty good-looking."

My mind naturally skips back to his text. *You're beautiful.*

He's beautiful. He's like one of those cakes you don't want to dig into because it's too nice to be eaten.

No, that's not quite true. I'd like to take a big bite out of him.

I can feel Andy's dark eyes boring into me, intense as always. "It's nice to see you noticing."

It occurs to me that all of this, every crazy and fun and interesting thing that's happened in the last twenty-four hours, is down to Andy.

"I reserve the right to take this back later," I say, "but thank you for referring me to Nicole and Damien. I think I needed . . . something."

"A swift kick in the ass," Andy says, but she's smiling. "You know I got you, boo."

"There's something else," I say.

"Oh my God," Grace says, rapt, leaning over so far her glasses almost fall off her face. She adjusts them, her eyes on me, and says, "Did you have *sex* with Mitchell Mountainbottom?"

"Griffin?" I choke out. "No!"

"Well, that's a disappointment," Andy says. "You might want to work on that."

I snort. "He's not actually interested in me. If anything, he likes teasing me."

My friends exchange a look. "You know, it's not just little kids who do that when they like a girl," Andy says. "Although I see it all the time on the playground. Those little suckers could give telenovelas a run for their money."

"I've had enough teasing to last at least three lifetimes, thank you very much."

"That's what the woman on *Mareas Locas* said, but the third time they brought her back to life she totally hooked up with the guy who'd been on her case since the first episode."

A smile sneaks out of me. Mostly because I'm imagining Andy watching telenovelas with her grandmother.

"Griffin's just doing his job," I say, because even if he's not getting paid for it, it's still sort of true. We probably never would have talked again, after our little Star Wars back-and-forth, if Nicole and Damien weren't helping me. "You're not supposed to flirt with someone while they're working. It's sexual harassment."

"Speaking of work," Grace says, biting her lip, "we didn't make a new book club selection last night."

"You're not selling it by calling it work," Andy says. "Why don't we just choose *The Alchemist* again? I'm the only one who read it."

I'm about to say I'm good with that, but there's a subtle pucker to Grace's mouth.

"What is it?" I ask. "Do you have an objection to *The Alchemist*?"

"It's not that," she says. "It's just . . ." Her eyes light up, the pretty gold bits near her pupils practically glowing with whatever she's about to tell us. "I thought you guys might want to read *my* book instead."

"You finished?" Andy says, leaping up off the couch. "No way."

"Yes way," Grace says, smiling softly. She's embarrassed, I can tell, but also proud of herself.

Andy grabs her and pulls her up and into a bear hug, and I join them, making it a threefer. This is big. No, it deserves a weightier word than that. It's *momentous*. Grace has been working on her first novel since the end of business school, six years ago. Andy and I met her just after she moved to Asheville to work for Vera, at a Meetup book club started by Grace. We were the only people who showed, and we spent the majority of the meeting interrogating her about what it's like to work for Vera. The three of us have been best friends ever since. She hasn't let us read any of her book until now, though she's shared bits and pieces about it over the years. It's a romance about two people who hate each other, right up until they don't. Andy and I are convinced it was inspired by a relationship from Grace's past, with Enoch, the guy who screwed her over in business school, but I haven't pressed. It went down a long time ago, but it never scabbed over the way most wounds do. Maybe this book is her way of letting the past go.

I hope it is. Grace doesn't date much, and when she does, it's always with an abundance of caution that leads her to the kind of men who wouldn't raise anyone's blood pressure. She deserves a real romance, the kind that sweeps her off her feet, but she'll never get it with her current limitations.

"And we really get to read it for book club?" I ask. "If so, I'm definitely going to read the book this time."

"I mean, only if you want," she says. "I don't want to force it on you. The ending is not quite right, so even though I'm done, I wouldn't say I'm *done*." She fiddles with her sleeve. "Actually, I was hoping you guys could help me figure that part out."

"Obviously we want to read it!" Andy says. "Champagne, let's have all the champagne!"

"We're already drinking wine," Grace says, laughing.

"Not good enough!"

"It *is* a Sunday night," I say. "Don't you have young minds to shape in the morning?"

Andy grabs a pillow off the sofa, which she proceeds to throw at me. "Spoilsport."

We sit back down, and Andy and I gather around as Grace sends the manuscript to our e-readers. It feels like the historic occasion it is. Only . . . seeing her phone reminds me of something else.

When Grace sets it down, I say, "Grace, there's something I need to tell you. There's a good chance the video of me came from your phone. Nicole and Damien watched the videographer's footage from the wedding, and they told me you're one of three people who could have taken it. We've eliminated the other two as possibilities."

Hurt flashes through her eyes, and her spine straightens. "I would never do that to you. *Never.* I know what it feels like to be betrayed. You *know* I do."

"That's not what I meant," I say. The last thing I want is for her to think I'm equating her with the asshole who hurt her. "They think someone might have taken it from your phone. You know, if you left your clutch on your chair or something."

Grace wilts. "Thank God. I mean, that's awful, obviously, and I hope it's not true, but it's better than you thinking . . ."

"I would never," I say, meaning it. "*Never.*" Grace has been through enough. Although I don't know all of the details, she and Enoch viewed each other as rivals until they got drunk together one night. She spilled her soul to him. She thought they were starting something; he, however, used her secrets to secure a coveted internship with her estranged father. Damage done. I only hope it ends differently in her book. No one wants to read a romance that ends in disillusionment.

"Now that we've both established that you'd never have done it on purpose and Marnie wasn't accusing you of it," Andy says, pulling her hair up into a ponytail using a hairband she had on her wrist, "let's check if they're right." She flashes her phone, which has *the* gif.

Pulling out her phone, Grace scrolls through her photos, which include several glamour shots of her boss, Vera. I guffaw at a photo of Vera wearing a diaphanous peacock-colored silk dress, petting a baby goat.

"Is she doing *Blue Steel*?"

Grace's lips firm. "Yes, but I didn't tell her."

She runs Vera's Instagram account. For someone who doesn't believe in Instagram, as if it were the sort of thing a person could believe into or out of existence, Vera certainly takes an interest in the photos that go up there.

Finally, with shaking hands, Grace lifts up the phone for us to compare the video she took with the gif on Andy's phone. I can tell from the look in her eyes that she already knows.

My stomach twists as I register that the footage is the same.

"Shit," Andy barks.

I agree. Because the person who did this probably used Grace's phone on purpose. Either to drive the knife in a little deeper or because they knew I wouldn't press the issue if the person most likely to get in trouble was one of my best friends.

Griffin was right.

"Whoever did this to me hates me," I say in a small voice.

I half expect them to disagree with me, but neither of them do.

They don't stay for long after that, and I kind of feel like a dick for ruining the celebratory atmosphere after Grace agreed to show us her book.

I decide I'll make up for it by staying up way too late reading, but before I pick up my kindle, I catch sight of my phone.

Usually, I'd spend several minutes kvetching over whether it's wise to reach out to him.

But I remember what Griffin said to me earlier. *If they don't like what they see, fuck them.*

Maybe it's time to start embracing that attitude, even if it's with him.

Today was the weirdest day of my life, I text him, pressing the send button before I can chicken out. *Thank you for being a part of it.*

Two minutes later, my phone rings.

It's Griffin.

I fumble my phone as I answer. "Griffin?"

"I was going to ask Nicole for proof of life earlier," he says. "She didn't scar you too much?"

"No," I respond, surprised by how much I mean it. "If anything, I think my aunt Helen might have scarred her."

I didn't intend to tell him everything, but once I start, it's hard to stop.

"She said the crystals would protect her from STDs?" he says once his laughter dies down.

"I'm pretty sure she meant it too," I say. "I guess my grandparents didn't believe in sex education."

"I don't know. Sounds like she learned everything else well enough. Maybe they just really had a thing for crystals."

"Don't," I say with a groan. "Do not. I do not want to relive those videos. No one wants to see one of their relatives *in the act*. Nicole actually dealt with the whole thing like a champ."

"Don't tell her that," he says, sounding amused. "It'll go straight to her head."

"I don't think she needs anyone to compliment or humble her. I think she knows who she is, and she's good with it." Only as I say it do I realize that's what I want for myself. I still have a ways to go. Today felt like a good first step though.

"Don't tell her that either," he says, but there's something different in his voice, like maybe my words meant something to him too.

"I've been thinking about what you said, Griffin."

"Which piece of brilliance?"

"About the person who did this to me," I say. "Spreading the video, I mean. I think you're right. They must really hate me to have done something like that."

"I know everyone talks about turning the other cheek, but from my experience, that's a good way to get another slap. I don't want that for you."

"Are you off work?" I ask, trying to imagine what he's doing and where he is. Too late, I realize what it probably sounds like I'm asking . . . "I mean . . . I didn't . . ."

"Yeah, Marnie," he says softly. "I'm not closing down tonight. I was about to sit down and read when you texted me, but I'd prefer to keep talking to you."

So he likes to read? Griffin's so personable, I figured he'd be out drinking with friends or watching a game with buddies or doing whatever people who have irregular hours do on a Sunday night. But I prefer this image, Griffin sitting on his couch with a beer, reading a book. I'd like to sit with him, reading mine. There's something companionable about reading with someone, something sweet.

"You know, my friend wrote a book," I say. "One of the friends who was with me last night. She's going to let me read it."

"Really?" he asks, sounding genuinely interested.

"It's a romance, though. I know how men are about romance."

He laughs. "I've always thought that was stupid. If you want to please your woman, you should find out which romance books she loves. It's all right there, written down for you."

"I think you're honestly the only man on earth who sees it that way," I say. I'm torn between thinking he's brilliant and feeling put out by the thought of him reading romances as manuals to help him please other women.

Then again, I'm the one he called, aren't I? That has to mean something.

Maybe he just feels sorry for you.

It's the same badgering voice that's been tearing me down for months.

"What's *your* favorite romance novel, Marnie?" he asks, his voice as smooth and sinful as melted chocolate. "I'd like to read it."

Good grief. It's like he's asking how I'd like him to fuck me, and my mind takes a break from psyching me out to produce dozens of images of Griffin naked.

"*Beauty and the Bar* by Ivy Anders," I squeak out. "What are you reading, anyway?"

"*The Alchemist.*"

"Oh! I was supposed to read that for book club," I say. "Is it any good?"

He pauses for a moment, considering, and I imagine him in his house, or apartment, or wherever, sitting on a couch. Shirtless, because my imagination doesn't care that it's winter. "I don't know if I agree with the message."

"What's the message?"

"Aren't you worried about me spoiling it?" he asks, his voice teasing.

"To be honest, there was a slim chance of me picking it up any time soon. I've acquired a fake boyfriend and a couple of fairy godmothers who are being *very* demanding on my time."

He laughs, but when he speaks again, his voice is serious. "The message is that if you want something badly enough, the universe will conspire to help you get it."

"And you don't believe that?"

"No, Marnie, I don't."

Our conversation moves on to different books, followed by stories about Nicole and Damien that seem too ludicrous to be true, but my mind keeps returning to the weight of his voice when he spoke about the universe.

What happened to Griffin?

GRIFFIN

I TALKED to Marnie for two hours last night. Two hours.

I'm used to talking to people. It's as much a part of my job as slinging drinks, but those conversations are usually superficial, forgotten minutes after they've ended. It's not like that with Marnie.

She texts me on Monday to say her boss is a dick, and I respond with a cartoon drawing of a windup dick and promise to upsell the hell out of her Etsy business to anyone who walks into the bar.

Truth is, her business is a bigger deal than she led me to believe. She's had thousands of sales, and her reviews are mostly five stars, with enough lower ratings thrown in to suggest the others weren't written by a sea of bots. Her merch is funny, and a little fierce in a way that suggests I haven't read her wrong. She might think she's the beta to her sister's alpha, but she's selling herself short. If someone threw her in the deep end to sink or swim, she'd pull a Katie Ledecky.

Or maybe she's so used to people underestimating her and taking her for granted that she expects it of everyone, including herself. Secretly, I wonder why she doesn't take the plunge and quit the job she dislikes. From a few things she's said, I gather that her dad left her and her brother the house, and also some money. The timing seems to be in her favor. But I doubt she'd thank an almost-stranger for unsolicited life advice, however well intentioned.

We continue to exchange messages over the next two days.

I tell her about a couple who loudly break up at the bar because of a disagreement about the best brand of sandwich cookies, which somehow led to a larger philosophical debate about capitalism.

She tells me about the boxed lunch that's been in her office's break room refrigerator for so long that everyone has stopped using it.

On Wednesday, she sends me an SOS text.

Sinclair is asking for cute photographs of us. Help a girl out?

A smile spreads across my face.

Yes, I reply. *Helping is the Mountainbottom way. It'll be easier the earlier you can get here.*

It's only a Wednesday, but sometimes we get a good happy hour showing, and Leah, our other bartender, doesn't come in on Wednesdays.

An excuse to leave work early? she replies. *Why yes, thank you. I'll take it. I'll be right there.*

It's early afternoon, and I just opened. The only patron present is Reggie, the seventy-something regular who has basically retired at the bar. He looks like a red-cheeked Santa Claus, enough so that a kid whose parents brought him to the bar before Christmas asked him for an autograph. To his credit, he gave him one. Of course, he signed his name Reggie, which probably led to some uncomfortable questions.

"Hey, Reggie," I call out. "Want to take some pictures of me and my girl? There's a free beer in it for you."

He straightens and looks around, as if he expects to find another Reggie present. Actually, maybe he's looking for the girl in question.

"You've got a girlfriend?" he asks. "Since when? I've been coming here for years, and I've never seen you with the same girl twice."

It's an exaggeration. But I'd rather he didn't spout off to Marnie about it. I don't care to examine my reasons.

"Maybe don't lead with that, friend. She's on her way."

He mimes zipping his lips, although it's not altogether comforting. He's been known to make exactly the wrong comment at exactly the wrong time. Nicole insists it's part of his charm.

Marnie shows up a few minutes later, her cheeks slightly pink from the cold. She's lovely, and I feel something warm unfurl inside of my chest. If I didn't know better, I'd think I'd missed her.

"This her?" Reggie asks.

"It is," I say, grinning at her. Maybe I'm an asshole, but she *did* want a pretend boyfriend, so I round the bar and take her into my arms.

She leans into my embrace at first, and it feels better than it should, right up until she whisper-hisses, "What are you doing?"

"Taking liberties," I admit. "Reggie over there is going to take pictures of me and my girlfriend."

She gives me a perplexed look. If she's wondering why the hell I told him about our fake relationship when we could have just taken some selfies, it would be a fair point. But I don't mind the ruse.

I help her take the coat off, and she turns to Reggie, smiling like the leader of a Girl Scout troop. "Thanks for agreeing to help us. I'm Marnie."

"Reggie," he says, patting his considerable girth. "You know, I've never known Griffin here to have a girlfriend."

Fuck. I knew the zipped-lips promise was a lie.

"People change," I say. "And Marnie's special."

She raises her eyebrows and stares me down as if to say she sees through my game, but I'm not being disingenuous.

"Well, what are you waiting for?" Reggie says, growing impatient. He holds out two hands and scoots them together. "You don't want couple photos where you're standing three feet apart. You want to set a real mood."

Jesus. He has a lot of opinions suddenly, not that I mind. I hand over my phone, and he takes it, grumbling because "it's no real camera."

"It takes photos," I say. "That's real enough for me."

We scootch in closer, but it's apparently not enough because Reggie scoffs and says, "Put your arms around her, you idiot."

So I do. I hold her in front of me, my arms clasped around her, and I hope to hell that my buzzing awareness of her curves and soft skin doesn't send too much of my blood flow south. The last thing I want is to scare her off with a hard-on.

"I'm sorry," she says in an undertone. "This is awkward. You don't have to do this."

"I told you," I say, tightening my hold on her. "I like being Mitchell Mountainbottom, and touching you is no hardship."

She flushes, and Reggie says, "Beautiful, beautiful. That's the stuff."

He's right. Being around her after the talking we've been doing . . . . I can't deny I feel a pull toward her. An *interest*.

"Kiss her," Reggie presses. "We need a money shot."

"Um, that's not the kind of photo shoot we're looking for, bud," I say. But I won't lie, I'm kind of hoping Marnie will go for it. I'm kind of hoping she'll grab my collar and pull me down for a kiss.

I've been thinking about that kiss the other day, about her soft lips.

She doesn't, though. She gets a little pinker, a little more blood flows to my dick, and she steps away, which is probably for the best. "I think we got enough. Thank you, Reggie."

"Not a problem, not a problem," he says. "You've made an old man very happy." He returns my phone and claps me on the back. I'm not sure if he's talking about his role in cataloguing our supposed happiness or the free beer I promised him as a thank-you.

"Thanks," I say, scrolling through the pictures. There's an unusual warmth in my chest at the sight of Marnie and me together, or maybe it's from the way she's leaning over my arm to look at the photos. "You did a great job."

He didn't. Most of them were out of focus or cut off the top of my head, but at least he tried. Plus, I like the pictures even if they aren't any good. I send the best ones to Marnie, including a little message made entirely of emojis. Hearts, heart eyes, and an eggplant just to fuck with her.

Or maybe to test her . . . to see if I'm the only one having thoughts.

"I used to be a photographer," Reggie says proudly.

No shit. I can see why he retired.

I've asked Reggie why he comes here so often, but the only reason he's ever given me is that it's habit, and he's reached an age where he doesn't care to form new ones. I can respect that. I'm a man of my habits too. Despite all of the people who come in and out of the bar, my life has a small footprint. I don't cause trouble. I don't take part in any drama. Or at least that's the way it's been for the last several years.

"You think these will satisfy your sister?" I ask, turning to Marnie, who's studying her phone with an unreadable look on her face.

I have to ask my question again, and she gives herself a full-body shake and replies, "Yeah. For now."

"What's she going to ask for next, a video of the two of us drinking each other's blood?"

Marnie gives me a look like she understands what I'm saying and doesn't particularly appreciate it, and I remind myself that her sister, however conceited, is her sister.

"Okay, fine," I say, "but we'll have to use pomegranate juice."

"You have a plan for how we can fake-drink each other's blood?" she asks, laughing.

I smirk at her. "You seem like the kind of woman who believes in being prepared."

Her eyes alight, she adds, "We'd have to get special vials."

"I guess you'd better get on that."

A couple of people come through the door, and she bites her lip, eyeing it. "I should probably go."

I'm not sure what possesses me, but suddenly it seems important for her to stick around. "Stay awhile," I say. "I'll make you a drink. I'll even give you some untainted pretzels."

"What's wrong with the pretzels?" Reggie asks gruffly.

"Urine," I say, leaving it at that. He shrugs as if to say he doesn't see what the big deal is and returns to his silent contemplation of the television. When he comes in early, which is always, I let him pick what to watch. It's usually something like the *Andy Griffith Show*.

Marnie looks like she thinks it's a bad idea to stick around, and she's most likely right, but then she shrugs. "I've got a book in my bag." Her expression turns almost sly, and she pulls out a slender copy of *The Alchemist*.

"Oh, gonna give it the old college try, huh?" I ask.

"I thought I would, yes. I'm reading Gracie's book too, but something prompted me to pick this up this morning."

"The universe?" I ask, lifting my eyebrows.

"You're teasing me."

"Yes. I've formed an appreciation for teasing you."

And for making her laugh. I like the things it does to her face, and since I'm being honest, I'll add that I like watching her breasts bob with it.

She stays for a long time. Reading at the bar. Talking to me when I have downtime. It's an easy conversation, like it was the other night, but that doesn't mean it's meaningless. She tells me more about her dad, who sounds like he was the sort of father who could have gotten an honorable mention on *The Brady Bunch*.

I *don't* tell her about mine. Most of my stories aren't the kind you'd share on a first date.

The thought catches me off guard, because that's not what this is . . .

But it's kind of what it feels like.

We do talk a little about Damien and Nicole, and I tell her stories that make her question her sanity in handing her problems over to them.

"You're in good hands," I assure her. "They usually get results."

They haven't gotten any for her yet, admittedly, but I suspect they're in no hurry. Nicole thinks I'm interested in Marnie, and it's hard to dissuade her from any of her beliefs. In this case, I'm not sure I'm inclined to try.

Usually, she and Damien show up at the bar every night, or near enough, but they're a no-show tonight. I wonder if they know Marnie is here somehow. If so, they didn't learn it from me.

"I think I like this book, you know," Marnie says, lifting the paperback.

"Uh-oh," I say, "does this mean we're having our first argument?"

She smiles at me, and the way it fills her eyes gives me the stupid urge to kiss her. I stuff it down, but it doesn't die an easy death.

"Yeah, I guess maybe it does," she says. "It's about hope. Hope's never a bad thing, *Mitchell*."

"Dare I *hope* that you're going to come in tomorrow so we can drink each other's blood?"

One of the other patrons, sitting close to Marnie, gives me a weird look, and I have to laugh, which probably only further convinces him we're psychopaths. She follows my gaze, picking up on the joke, and smiles.

"I think maybe I will," she says.

And, fuck, she really does.

She comes in not long after opening, and if something like happiness fills my chest at the sight of her, no one needs to know. Grinning at me, her cheeks pink, she pulls a couple of small crystal vials out of the pocket of her coat.

"Oh, it's on," I say.

"Yes. Where's the blood?"

I laugh, a bit delighted, to be honest. "Look at you, going straight for the jugular."

She shrugs off her coat and sits on the same stool she claimed yesterday. It feels like *her* stool, in the same way Reggie's stool belongs to him, which is a dumb thought given she's only sat in it once.

I grab a bottle of pomegranate juice from the fridge beneath the counter and fill up the little vials.

"Hey, Reggie," I say, because of course he's here as always. "We require your filming services."

"Hi, Marnie," he says, perking up as if he was hoping she'd show up as much as I was. Hell, maybe he was. He's got to be sick of me by now. Then again, he's still watching Andy Griffith after all these years. "What're you doing?" he asks with interest.

"We've decided to drink each other's blood to honor our love for each other," I say, looking into Marnie's eyes.

They crinkle slightly at the corners.

"Oh, I read about this on the internet."

I should probably tell him it's fake, but he seems so tickled by the idea that I don't want to break the illusion. Marnie must have the same thought because she stays silent.

Like before, I hand over my phone, and Reggie does the honors.

I lift up my crystal vial to Marnie, and she does the same.

"Cheers," I say, winking at her, and we both down the juice.

"What did it taste like?" Reggie says, still filming.

"Everlasting love and devotion," I say, and this time Marnie can't help but laugh. "And for you, sweetheart?" I ask her. "What did it taste like for you?"

"Copper pennies," she says with a wicked look.

I stifle a laugh as Reggie hands back my phone. I pronounce the video perfect, even though there's a definite wobble, and he heads back to enjoy his show.

"Should we tell him?" Marnie asks in an undertone, her eyes twinkling.

"Nah, we'll let him believe the illusion. He seemed into it."

"I'm not actually going to send it to her, am I?" she asks.

"That depends. How much has she been badgering you for details about our relationship?"

Her face scrunches. "I get a check-in text or call at least once a day."

Seems like a lot for a busy celebrity, but I don't say so. Maybe Marnie likes getting the calls.

"Send it to her the next time she annoys you."

She grins. "Should we make a stock of videos of us doing weird relationship shit? This could bring me a long way."

"Like what?" I ask, wanting to see what she has in her arsenal.

She thinks for a moment, then brightens. "We could pretend to get couples tattoos! That'd really freak her out."

I have to laugh because her notion of "weird relationship shit" is frankly tame. "Your wish is my command, Marnie Jones."

Just like last night, she stays for a while. I mix her another drink, and she hangs out with her kindle while the after-work crowd trickles in. It seems she finished *The Alchemist*, because I get the impression she's reading Grace's book. The looks she gives me while she reads it send awareness coursing through me. Is she reading something sexy? Is she thinking about me while she does?

After she finishes her drink, she tucks her kindle away, and I head over to her, my stomach sinking since she's obviously preparing to leave.

"Was it something I said?" I ask.

She grins at me. "No, I'm going to go bring my aunt Helen some dinner. I try to do that a couple of times a week so she's not stuck with her own moldy leftovers."

"Why are they always moldy?"

"She makes too much food and then forgets about it," she says with a slight smile. "Which is no different from most people, but she refuses to do the logical thing and throw it away."

"So you're bringing her more food that will eventually go bad," I tease.

She's told me a bit about her aunt. It sounds like she takes care of her, even though Helen has a daughter of her own who is perfectly capable. It sounds like Marnie takes care of her brother too, or at least they take care of each other, sharing chores at the house. Still, I would have selfishly preferred if she'd stuck around longer. The whole place is brighter when she's here. It's like there's a glow inside of her, one that's growing stronger.

"Absolutely. There's nothing I like so much as contributing to a problem." She gestures between us. "I mean, look at us. I've been doubling down on this lie like a champ."

I must've been taking a lot of stupid pills lately, because I don't like to hear her calling our supposed relationship a lie.

"I like that you've been coming here," I say. "I hope you'll come back. Maybe you can bring your friends by this weekend."

She studies me for a second, her gaze unwavering, and then says, "Maybe I will."

Then she leaves, and even though there are at least two people trying to flag me down, I watch her as she walks out the door.

Fuck. This probably isn't good.

After I serve the people I've been ignoring, Reggie summons me to his corner with a hand gesture. "I'm going to give you a piece of advice, young friend," he says.

"Shoot."

"Don't fuck this up."

A surprised laugh escapes me. "Duly noted."

"I mean it," he says, tapping the bar for emphasis. "Take it from an old man who's lost everything more than once. If you let this one go, you'll regret it. She's a sharp knife in a drawer full of butter spreaders. The women you usually spend time with don't measure up."

"You had a woman like her?"

"Yes, and I let her go. Now I spend my days here with you. That paint a clear enough picture?"

As I pour and mix drinks, I find myself thinking on what he said. Marnie and I aren't actually dating—she reminded me of that tonight —but at the same time . . . he isn't wrong. There's something about her that has slid under my skin, but if I want to pursue something real with her, there are obvious obstacles. For one thing, her sister thinks my name is Mitchell Mountainbottom. For another, Reggie wasn't wrong about me. I've never in my life been in a meaningful relationship. For most of my life, I've run from them. Then there's the real problem.

Marnie would probably run straightaway from me if she knew about my past.

I wouldn't blame her if she did.

ten

MARNIE

"HE'S LOOKING AT YOU AGAIN," Grace coos.

"Oh, please," Andy scoffs. "That's hardly news. He's barely looked away from her all night."

"That's not true," I say, though I can't deny it pleases me to believe it.

I have it bad.

I mean, I started lusting after Griffin the instant I saw him.

Then he sparked my interest by handling the call with my sister so well, and spending time with him this last week has lit a spark inside me that has all the marks of becoming a destructive forest fire. I didn't want my friends to realize the intensity of my attachment, but I must be doing a poor job of hiding it.

When Griff sent us a round of pomegranate cocktails earlier, I burst out laughing . . . so I had to share the joke about the pomegranate juice. I'd kept it to myself for some reason, maybe the same reason that I'd watched our video five times. I can't deny that I have zero inclination to send it to my sister. Filming it had been a slender excuse to see him again.

Then there's the way I beamed at him when he introduced me to his co-bartender, Leah, as his girlfriend. There's no reason for him to carry on the pretense with the people in his life, so the fact that he's told at least two people must mean something, right?

I'm choosing to ignore the shock on Leah's face, as well as Reggie's comment that he's never known Griffin to have a girlfriend.

"It's all part of his Mitchell Mountainbottom act," I tell my friends, even though I don't really believe it. There's a certain energy that arcs between us when we're together. I don't think you can feel that sort of thing unless the other person does too, just like a single battery won't power a device programmed to use more. Besides, while I haven't talked to Griffin about this, Nicole said he volunteered to help me. No one is forcing him or paying him. He's spending time with me because he wants to, right?

Or because he feels bad for you, a little voice supplies.

"Uh-huh, sure," Andy says. "You go on telling yourself those things you don't believe. Have the P.I.s uncovered anything else?"

"Not really," I say. "I get the sense Nicole's waiting for Val to pop the news about Brock. Val's been less insufferable than usual, so I get the sense he's trying to butter me up."

My boss, Val, has also been giving me plenty of significant looks, which suggest Nicole's not the only one who's been biding her time. Admittedly, *everyone* in the office has been giving me significant looks. On Monday, no less than five of my male coworkers commented on my appearance, one of them asking if it was time for him to shoot his shot, or if my makeover meant I was already getting laid by someone else.

I would have reminded him of our HR policy, but it would have been a moot point. He wrote it.

"Your job is the worst," Andy says, drawing out the last word.

She's one to talk. Apparently she was projectile-vomited on by two different kids yesterday.

"Yeah, it's not great," I admit. "And it'll be even less great once Brock's involved again."

I glance at Griffin, and feel a shiver pass through me when I find he's watching me too. He grins and gives me a suggestive look that does nothing to cure me of my attachment to him.

Sighing, I look away and take a swig of the drink.

"Look at you downing that blood," Andy says joyfully.

To change the topic, and also because I've really been wanting to talk to her about it, I say to Grace, "We need to talk about your book. You're a genius. It's at least as good as Vera's big book. Maybe better."

"You finished it already?" she asks, looking alarmed.

"Is that what you've been doing all week?" Andy asks, which makes me blush.

"Yes," I fib. It's sort of true. They don't need to know that I read a good portion of it at this bar the other night.

Andy shrugs and says, "I finished it too, and she's right."

"No," Grace says, already shaking her head. "Nothing's as good as *The Wind in Her Hair*. I mean. The ending of my book sucks. Any thoughts on fixing it?"

The ending *was* the weakest part. She doesn't give the couple a happily ever after but instead leaves a thread of hope that they'll end up together. There's beauty to be found in subtlety, I guess, but not in a romance novel. Or at least I don't think so. I read them when I need an escape, and no one wants to escape to a world that ends up feeling as uncertain as their own.

"I'm not going to lie," I say. "I wanted the Happily Ever After."

Andy purses her lips and nods. "Yes. Unless you're planning a second book."

Grace sighs. "You're right. I know you're right. I was going to give them one, but something about it felt wrong and trite. I'm going to keep working on it."

"Are you going to show it to Vera?" I ask. All this time, Grace has been doing her dirty work—and I mean this literally—because Vera promised to help her get her first novel published. Grace, somehow still her fan despite having laundered cloth diapers for Vera's dog, has been counting on her to follow through. "Maybe she'll have some ideas."

Grace nods resolutely. "Yes. She promised she'd help, didn't she? I'm going to ask her to read it next."

Andy gives her a skeptical look. "I don't know, Grace. She's not exactly a woman of her word. I mean, she promised a cover to that one guy she was screwing, and look what happened there."

What happened was that she made Grace break up with him for her—and also break the news that he wouldn't be her cover model.

"That's different," Grace objects, although we all probably realize it's not so different.

Still, I can tell Grace needs this. However much she loves us, and however much we love her books, she needs the assurance of someone who's a professional to believe her efforts are worthy. Part of it, I know, stems from what she went through with Enoch in business school. It made her hesitant to trust her gut.

If I could give her one thing, it would be the ability to believe in herself. Because she has good instincts, whether she realizes it or not. Well, maybe with the exception of trusting Vera, but I suspect the only reason she hasn't seen the light there is because she, like me, has mommy issues.

While my mother always found me wanting, hers passed away when she was a young girl. I had my dad and my brother, though, and Grace didn't have much of anyone. Her father was cold and withholding and *busy*, and her nanny disappeared from her life once she wasn't paid to be there anymore.

"Oh, shit," Andy says, and I jolt a little, yanked from my thoughts. She's staring at the bar, so my gaze skates there too.

My stomach sinks. A woman is leaning across the bar toward Griffin, her perky breasts practically spilling out of a shirt that is much too revealing to be weather appropriate. I watch her run her hand up and down his arm as if she owns him. There are two shots on the bar between them, and they clink glasses and then drink, the woman eyeing him as if she'd like to be sucking him down instead.

No, that's not what bothers me. There's something in the casual intimacy of the moment, of her gaze, that tells me she already has.

I'm an idiot.

Griffin works in a bar. He must constantly have beautiful women hitting on him and asking him to go home with them. There's probably a line outside his door.

"Marnie," Grace says, her voice concerned, shaking my arm.

"I'm going to head home, guys," I say. "I need to eat a pint of ice cream. Instantly. A transfusion of it would be preferable."

"Grace, I don't think he's—" Andy starts, but I'm already pulling on my coat and lifting out of my chair, in a haze as I push my way to the door.

Someone calls my name, but I don't turn back.

I hear my name again after I exit the bar, and then a warm hand lands on my arm, large and slightly commanding, turning me.

"I have pepper spray," I call out as I'm whirling around, but then I see *him*.

Griffin doesn't have a coat on. There's a look of concern on his face—his brow's knit with it.

"I believe you," he says. "You've always struck me as a dangerous woman." He pauses, seeming uncertain of himself. "Marnie, why'd you leave like that? Is this . . . is this about Gwen? She's just a friend."

"But not in the way that I'm just a friend, right?" I say, unable to stop myself. "You've slept with her."

It's a ridiculous thing to say, but it's too late to take it back. I'm not even sure I want to.

He rubs his nose, looks away. "Yes," he says. "But not for a long time. We're just friends."

"I guess you have a lot of *friends*," I say, pissed without fully understanding why.

He takes my hands, his touch shocking my system, and stares

into my eyes. There's something deep and intense in his gaze, something that goes beyond his usual teasing. It occurs to me that it's a busy night, a full bar, and his co-bartender can't handle the crowd by herself. Still, he left to talk to me. That has to mean something, doesn't it?

"I've had plenty of *friends* before, I guess," he says, "but none of them are like you."

There's something thick about the moment, something heated. I think maybe he's going to kiss me, I *hope* he is, so it's another shock to the system when he steps back.

"I need to get back inside, Marnie. We'll talk?"

I nod slightly, trying not to feel rejected.

Trying not to think about Gwen at the bar, waiting for him to return.

eleven

GRIFFIN

IT'S WEDNESDAY NOW, and I haven't seen Marnie in person since Saturday night. I've thought about her, though. A lot. Many of those thoughts have to do with how much I fucked up on Saturday.

I shouldn't have poured that shot for Gwen, obviously. I'm not interested in her. I never was, really, although we did spend one night together last fall. It was casual, easy, something with no potential to pull either of us in deep.

I should have kissed Marnie. I wanted to, and from the way she tipped her head up to me, looking into my eyes, I thought maybe she wanted the same thing. But something held me back. Maybe because I feel a different kind of current with her, one that *could* pull me under if I'm not careful.

I've texted her since then, telling her about funny things Reggie's done around the bar, plus a woman who brought in a "service" dog that had to weigh two hundred pounds and ate all of our pretzels. She's responded, but her answers are restrained. She doesn't offer stories in return the way she would have last week.

There's a difference in her, and it's my fault.

Because I'm a masochist, I read her favorite romance novel last night, and thought about Marnie touching herself, using that vibrator she mentioned, when I read the sex scenes.

That's not the sort of thing you imagine about a girl who's just a friend. I'm not enough of a fool not to realize it suggests a deeper kind of interest. But I feel like I'm wading into water that could easily engulf my head and drown me.

I shake off the thought, focusing on the sidewalk beneath my feet and the relatively mild January day.

Running. I'm supposed to be running. The bar is closed for the night, and Damien and I are out on a run with my stepbrother, part of our *let's keep Gary honest* campaign. It's a good day for it. Working out usually helps me relax and forget the things that are troubling me, but my mind's a mess today, no clearer now than when we began. We're moving at an easy pace, slow enough for talking, and I ask Damien, "Any progress with finding out who spread the video of Marnie? What else can we do?"

Oddly, I haven't seen Damien in several days, so if something has happened with their investigation, I'm unaware of it.

I mean, it's obviously not on me to solve this mystery—while I may help them with their work from time to time, I'm not the P.I.— but I'm invested in this. In *her*. If she doesn't want to talk to me, at least I can help her in my own way.

If Damien's surprised by my interest, he doesn't let it show. Then again, I'm not convinced he and Nicole don't have some insider knowledge of what's been going on between Marnie and me. He's also an accomplished actor who used to spend a good portion of his free time at a local theater. If he wants to keep something to himself, he does.

"Her friend Grace loses her phone all the time. Either the person who did it got lucky, or they purposefully used her friend's device to play mind games with Marnie. Neither scenario helps us figure out who orchestrated this."

"Shit," I say.

"Shit," he agrees. "But there are some other developments. Marnie says Brock's assistant always seemed to have a thing for him. We looked her up, and it turns out she recently quit. She's been staying with family in Virginia, but she gets back later this week, and she agreed to talk to us. Could be helpful. As far as I know, Marnie's boss still hasn't spoken to her about Brock." He pauses, giving me some side-eye as if he expects me to have more information for him. I don't, and once again I reflect that I have no one but myself to blame.

"Nicole also has a plan to get everyone from Marnie's side of the wedding back together again, all in the same location," he adds. "She thinks it's our best chance for finding the perp."

"Why's she so sure it's someone from Marnie's side?"

"She's not. But Marnie didn't know the guy's family well. They'd only been dating a few months before they got engaged, and the engagement was short."

"So his family might've wanted to break them up, but it seems less likely they'd care about embarrassing her, especially at the cost of making Brock look bad."

He gives a slight nod of agreement. "Nicole and I think it was a spur-of-the-moment thing. They saw her filming, and when she set down her phone, they checked the footage and sent it to themselves. Posted it on the internet later. That would mean the perp was sitting toward the front, likely on Marnie's side. But we're going to talk to Brock's people too."

"What about Marnie's sister?" I ask. "Have you heard anything from your contact?"

"It sounds like she hasn't been getting along with the new director for her show. Maybe she was trying to make herself a sweetheart in the public eye to counter any bad press he might throw her way. I guess he has a reputation for sinking the careers of people he doesn't like." He shoots me a pointed look.

"Women who reject him, you mean," I say, feeling a surge of

indignation. I hadn't expected to feel any sympathy for Marnie's sister, but if what he's implying is true, it's a bunch of bullshit.

"Exactly. We're hoping to interview her in person."

I angle my head to look at him. "You going to LA?"

"I will if I have to," he says. "But with any luck, she's coming here."

"Which brings us back to Nicole's grand plan. What is it, exactly?"

It occurs to me that Gary's not with us anymore, and maybe hasn't been for a while. I glance over my shoulder and see he's a full block behind us. His face is slightly pink and sweaty, and I wouldn't be surprised if his glasses slid clear off his face. Shit. I was so caught up in our conversation I must have sped up without realizing it.

I gesture for Damien to slow down, and we settle into a walk, giving Gary a chance to catch up.

"I'll let Nicole tell you what she's thinking," Damien says.

"I don't like the sound of that."

"Wha—" Gary starts as he catches up with us, then cuts himself off abruptly, lifting a hand and hanging his head for a second as he pants. When he looks up, he says, "Walking. The rest of this . . . is going to be a walk. No objections. No telling Liza. You two . . . going to kill me. How . . . you talking?"

Damien claps him on the back, then grimaces and looks at his damp palm.

"You walked right into that one, buddy," I say.

Gary rolls his eyes at us. "What . . . don't you . . . like . . . sound of?" he manages through a series of huffs.

"Nicole has a grand plan she wants to run by me."

Gary laughs, then groans. "Why does it . . . hurt to laugh? I thought getting into shape was supposed to make me feel better, not worse."

"It'll make you feel worse before it makes you feel better," I say, because I don't like lying to Gary if I can help it.

"Why ... do ... people do this?" Gary pants.

"So they can enjoy quality time with their friends," Damien quips as we resume walking.

"So they can soak in the great outdoors," I add, gesturing to the overdeveloped street, every house within feet of its neighbor.

"Let's go back to the house," he says, shaking his head. "Mom and Liza said they were making lasagna for dinner. Enough for everyone."

Damien and I exchange a look. They were bustling around the kitchen when we left the house, but this plan is news to me. Liza's the one who's gone all in with Gary's health regimen. Why is she suddenly making him lasagna?

"What'd you have to do to get her to make you lasagna?" Damien asks.

Gary sighs defeatedly. "It's not that type of lasagna. It's vegan lasagna made with ground-up cashews, zucchini, and whole wheat noodles."

"No can do," Damien says without missing a beat. "I have dinner plans with Nicole."

"Traitor," Gary tells him without any heat, then turns to me. "Griff?"

I give the nod of a man who's been sentenced to eat vegan lasagna for dinner. Not because I like vegan lasagna, or at least whatever version of it Liza, who is self-admittedly an unskilled cook, will make. I just can't say no to Gary or Ma.

My mother left my father and me when I was still a baby, and even though my dad didn't have it in him to properly care for a hamster, he kept me instead of turning me over to child services. Maybe that was a good decision, and maybe it wasn't—all I know is that's the decision he made. He married Ma when I was eleven, and for five years, I had an almost normal childhood. Ma made us dinner every night, she asked me about school, and even though I rebelled against her every way I knew how, she stubbornly insisted on loving me.

Now that I'm back home, the least I can do is show her how much I appreciated that.

Even if it means eating some damn vegan lasagna.

"Liza's taken this whole exercise and diet thing too far," Gary grumbles. "My blood pressure is a little high, and suddenly she's convinced she's going to outlive me if she doesn't take my health in hand."

I laugh. "Good. I'm glad I didn't have to be the one to handcuff you to the StairMaster."

"That's a waste of some good handcuffs," Damien says with a wicked smirk.

Gary gives a long-suffering sigh. "Why do you always insist on being yourself?"

Damien's smile stretches wider, and he must have forgotten the soaked state of Gary's shirt, because he claps him on the back again. "You married Nicole's mother. You're stuck with me."

twelve

GRIFFIN

IT TURNS out Damien is stuck with us too, because when we walk back into Gary's bungalow, Nicole's in the kitchen, popping chips from a bag while she watches Liza take the vegan lasagna out of the oven.

Gary reaches for Nicole's chips and gets a swat.

"You're the one who's responsible for this atrocity," she accuses, waving the chip bag at the lasagna.

"No," he says miserably, "my poor genetics are to blame." His gaze shifts to Ma, who's pulling a stack of plates out of the cupboard. The kitchen has wallpaper covered in flowers and a tile backsplash that I helped Gary put up after he and Liza moved in a few years back. "I mean, obviously not because of you, Ma. I think we can all comfortably agree that Dad is at fault."

His father was an asshole too. I guess she has a type.

Ma waves his comment off. "We all know my blood pressure isn't what it could be."

"The lasagna's going to be good," Liza insists. "Your mother helped me, and it *smells* divine."

Far be it from me to disagree with Gary's wife, but the kitchen smells like tofu that's been left out for a week.

"We found the recipe online," Ma says. "It got three stars."

"Three stars is nice-people speak for it sucks," Nicole says, crunching on a chip.

I stifle a laugh with a cough.

"You were supposed to be my excuse for leaving before dinner," Damien grunts as he stoops to kiss her.

She gives him a small smile. "I brought us takeout."

"That's my girl."

I'm tempted to ask if there's enough for three, but I already know the answer.

"I'll set the table," I offer, and Ma comes over to hand me the plates. I take them from her, and she gets on her toes and kisses me on the cheek. "Nicole tells me you met a girl."

I give Nicole some side-eye. "That's inaccurate information. Don't trust anything she says."

"Oh," Ma says, wilting a little. "I keep hoping you'll find a nice girl and settle down like Gary did."

It's sort of laughable that she still refers to Liza, who's almost fifty, as a girl, but I'm not about to correct her for the fiftieth time. All of us have tried, and certain things are just hardwired into her brain. It's the one thing she had in common with my dad.

"I don't need a girlfriend," I say. "If I had one, I wouldn't have so much time to spend with my dysfunctional family."

"Is that a promise?" Nicole jokes.

At least I'm reasonably sure she's joking.

"So there's no girl?" Ma asks in confusion.

My mind darts to Marnie. To her Bambi eyes and hard spine. To her sense of humor and the lush softness of her lips. To her determination to make the world better for everyone but herself.

To the way she looked at me on Saturday night . . .

"Oh, there's a girl, all right," Liza says, beaming, "and she's lovely. I cut her hair just the other day. You know, she asked about you, Griffin."

"What'd she say?" I ask before I have the sense to shut the hell up. I can feel someone staring at me. Actually, maybe it's four someones.

"She wanted to know about that picture on the mantel."

I don't have to ask which one she means. It's of Gary and me, right before our shared lives were blown to smithereens.

I asked Gary to take the picture down, but he dug his heels in.

To him, it's probably a good memory of the calm before the storm.

To me, it's a reminder that I'm the one who planted the grenade, and the only other person who knew is dead.

Gary and Ma have accepted my official story about what went down back then: Dad got sick of playing the family game and convinced me to leave with him. He got me to cut ties with Gary and Ma by saying Ma had been working on him to send me to military school after I was caught drinking behind the high school a second time. The story goes that I didn't realize it was a lie until years later, after it felt too late to mend bridges. Then I came back to Asheville after my father died because it was the only place that had ever felt like home.

That last bit is true at least. The rest? A fabrication to hide a darker truth.

I strongly suspect Damien and Nicole know my story is bullshit, but they haven't pushed me on it.

"This girl," Ma says, giving my arm a little shove. "Why didn't you say anything?"

"She's just someone Nicole and Damien are helping for the agency," I say, unnerved to feel my ears burning. "I'm doing her a favor, is all. We're not actually dating."

I see her face again, tipped up toward me.

"Well, why the heck not?" Ma says. "You haven't brought a woman home to meet me since you were sixteen." Her brow furrows. "If you don't like girls, you can tell me, Griff. I saw an old episode of

Sally Jesse Raphael about boys who were afraid to tell their parents they loved other boys, but I wouldn't hold it against you. You could bring a boy home to meet me, and I'd greet him with open arms and be grateful."

Nicole bursts out laughing. "He's not gay. You should see all the women he's picked up at the bar."

I wish I had a pretzel to throw at her, but the only thing I'm likely to find in this house is one of the gluten-free, salt-free crackers from the family-size box in the pantry.

"Oh," Ma says softly, and I know what she's thinking.

The apple doesn't fall far from the tree.

"It's not like that," I blurt. "And it happens much less often than she's implying. I just . . . prefer to keep things casual. It's easier that way."

Liza glares at me. She doesn't have to say what's on her mind. She thinks I might melt away into the night, and even though I have no intention of leaving, she's right: I still live parts of my life like I might. It's a deep-seated reflex, one I've had to work continually to shed. Obviously I still haven't succeeded.

Ma pats my hand. "Maybe you should think about spending more time with this girl."

"I agree," Nicole says, grabbing a random assortment of silverware from a drawer. "In fact, I have a proposal for you." I'm certain she doesn't have the slightest interest in helping me set the table, which means this is a ruse to get me alone. What does her big plan entail? I'm suddenly more curious than wary, and I know why.

Her plan obviously involves Marnie.

Ma studies me for a moment. "There's more to this than you're saying."

"Not really," I say, which is true.

"Except that he wants to f-u-c-k her in a tree," Nicole says. "He put up a card she gave him behind the bar. A greeting card. And he's been bragging about it to people. Does Griff seem like the kind of guy who keeps greeting cards and *talks* about them?"

"I obviously keep all of the ones you give me," I tell Ma.

Nicole waves the handful of silverware at me. "Let's go. This table isn't going to set itself."

I have a sinking feeling she's not going to help me set it either.

My stepmother looks like she has more to say about the whole Marnie situation, and I'm very aware that everyone in the kitchen is watching us, with the possible exception of Gary, who is trying to sneak something out of the cupboard without being seen. I catch a flash of the bag: pretzel goldfish. He's supposed to stay away from extra salt, but an addict will do anything to get a fix.

"I see you, Gary," I say.

He straightens as if someone poked him with a cattle prod, and Liza swoops in and discards the goldfish. "Where have you been hiding these?" she asks, infuriated.

It takes all of five second for her to discover he's been hiding them in the hollowed-out box that used to contain gluten-free, salt-free crackers. Huh. Smart. He glowers at me as she throws them in the trash, saying, "It's for your own good, sweetheart."

"Narc," he mouths at me.

I salute him. While I partially did it to draw the attention off myself, I also love my stepbrother too much to watch him destroy himself.

Even if it's only with pretzel goldfish.

"I'm going to go take a shower," he announces sullenly. I need to change my clothes too, but I decide it can wait until after the table is set.

I follow Nicole into the dining room, wood-paneled when they moved in but now painted a soothing gray, and start distributing the dishes around the dining room table. I can feel her watching me as she sorts through the random bunch of forks, knives, and spoons. We're not eating anything that requires spoons, I don't think, but then again, I don't know what variety of deliciousness she brought for herself and Damien that the rest of us will be salivating over.

"So what's this big plan Damien mentioned?" I say, trying to sound the right degree of disinterested. I should have never hung that card up behind the bar—it was too big of a tell—but I like it too much to regret it.

"You know, on second thought, I think maybe we'll wait until dessert," she says, her eyes sparkling. "I'd prefer to give it a bigger buildup."

Fantastic. The last thing I need is for Ma to get the news, whatever it is, at the same time I do.

"So what did you want to talk to me about? Because I wasn't born yesterday. There's no way in hell you have a genuine interest in setting the table."

My phone starts ringing in my pocket, and since everyone in my inner circle is in this house, I pull it out to check the number.

It's her.

I glance up at Nicole. "It's Marnie."

"So answer it, jackass," she says.

She looks like she's in no hurry to give me privacy, so I abandon the table setup and bring the phone into the attached living room.

"Marnie," I say, answering. "What's up?"

"I'm sorry," she blurts.

"What are you sorry for?" I ask. I'm the one who's sorry, but I can't outright say it, because if I do, I'll have to tell her what I'm sorry for. I don't know which I should apologize for, not kissing her or lusting after her even though I know this "relationship" isn't real. "I think you're supposed to apologize *after* you've told me what it's for."

"You know how people say it's better to ask for forgiveness than permission?"

My gaze lifts to the mantel, to that photo of Gary and me. I look away and start pacing around the couch, needing to release some energy. "That's just something people tell themselves so they'll feel better about doing what they want."

It's always been one of my justifications, after all.

"Okay, fair point," she says. "I'm just going to come out and say it. I told you that my boss agreed to work with Brock again, right? Well, apparently Brock invited the whole office over to his house for happy hour on Friday. It's going to be this whole to-do, I guess."

"And you're expected to go," I say, pissed on her behalf. Her boss really is a piece of work. Maybe I'll send him a bag of gummy dicks. Nicole has a candy shop hookup who'll do it anonymously.

"Yeah, and I kind of told my boss that my boyfriend was coming with me."

It feels like someone popped a bottle of champagne and handed me a glass. I've been worried she was angry at me, that whatever we were doing was over, and now she's invited me to spend an evening with her. "So I get to see you *and* moonlight as my alter ego? I thought you said this was bad news."

"Don't you have to work on Friday? It occurred to me after the fact that it's probably the worst day for you to take time off."

"It's not a problem. I'll arrange for someone else to fill in. Leah's working anyway, and if she had to hold down the fort alone for a while, she could."

Leah's the stalwart type, as tall as I am and more than capable of standing up for herself if anyone gets mouthy with her.

"Are you sure?" she asks. I imagine her biting her lip, her teeth white against the plump flesh.

"I'm sure."

"Thank you, Griffin."

"Did I just earn another of your cards?" I ask with a grin. I stop pacing and prop a hand on the back of the couch. If I had to offer up just one word to describe my mood, it would be *relieved*.

"I think maybe you earned two of them," she says. "I've noticed an uptick in my sales over the last week. You really have been giving people the hard sell, haven't you? Even though—"

She pauses as if she's not sure how to complete that sentence, and I don't offer to finish it for her. I wouldn't know how. I still don't fully understand my intentions toward her, or what any of this means.

"It might've been Reggie," I tease. "He has a real thing for you."

"I hope he's not the only one," she says, and then sucks in a breath as if she wishes she could swallow the words. Something warms within me, like a space heater flicked on in my chest.

"I heard it. You can't take it back." Then, because I can't seem to help myself, I say, "If we're doing this for a whole evening, we should probably meet up first. Have dinner or a drink. We'll want to make sure we answer people's questions the same way, that sort of thing. Maybe we can even have a little check-in call with your sister."

She's quiet for a long moment, and I'm sure she'll say no. We haven't even discussed my agreement with Nicole and Damien. For all she knows, I have half a dozen fake girlfriends and two dozen real ones. Neither is true, but I haven't assured her of that fact, and she obviously sensed the history between Gwen and me. I could have settled her mind, but I suppose I kept silent on purpose, to preserve some distance between us.

My gaze lifts to the mantel again, to that picture of Gary and me.

Maybe I'm being stupid again, keeping one foot out the door like Liza's always silently accusing me of doing. Maybe it's time to take a chance.

"When?" she asks softly. "I work during the day, and you work at night. We're like Romeo and Juliet." She's silent for another second, then says, "Oh God, forget I said that. Anyway, yeah, presuming you're not desperate to get away from the crazy lady now, when do you want to do it?"

I glance into the dining room, where my entire sort-of family is now watching me with interest. The vegan lasagna is sitting on the table, looking as unappealing now as it did fifteen minutes ago. Maybe more, because someone sprinkled it with fake cheese, and it looks like it has a bad case of dandruff. I'm not saying all vegan food is unappetizing, mind you—I've lived in this town of countless vegetarians and vegans for long enough to know that's not true—but *this* vegan food is vile enough to turn someone off food in general.

Don't fool yourself. You're looking for excuses to see her again. You've missed her.

I'm self-aware enough to realize it's true, but I still find myself saying, "The bar was closed for its monthly deep clean today, so I'm off work. You free now?"

"Oh . . . sure," she says. "Where would you like to meet?"

"Why not come out to the bar?" I suggest. "They'll be done by now. I can make us some drinks, and we can have a pizza delivered. No one will be around to bother us. Not even Reggie. As an added bonus, it'll be clean."

"You really want to go there on your night off?" she asks, sounding surprised.

No, not particularly. But if I suggested meeting at her place, it would be harder to show restraint. The bar is safer.

"I live there," I joke.

"*Ohhh*," she says slowly. "You didn't say. I had no idea."

"I'm kidding. Well, sort of. I live in the apartment over Summer Nights."

Before now, she'd never asked, and I'd never offered.

"Thank God," she gushes. "I was having these awful images of you having to sleep on the ground behind the bar. It looks very narrow back there, so you'd probably only have room for a sad little pillow. I was going to have to offer you the guest room in our house, and my brother would *not* be happy to discover a new roommate when he gets back from his camping trip on Sunday."

I laugh, because dammit, she's funny, and there's a strange feeling of lightness inside of me as I imagine the evening ahead.

We set a time, then I hang up and break the news to the others.

Nicole is gleeful, of course, and dammit, so is Ma.

"This isn't a date," I say. "It's a business meeting in preparation for a *fake* date."

"You go on telling yourself that," Nicole says.

"Wait a minute," I say, remembering our conversation before dinner. "What was your big plan? Did you already know about Friday?" I got the sense Marnie hadn't told her yet, but Nicole's not the kind of person to let that stop her.

"No," she says, shaking her head. "And the big plan is on hold . . . for now. You can question Marnie's ex at the happy hour thing. See if he knows anything useful."

Funny, before she mentioned it, the thought hadn't occurred to me. I'd been thinking about going with Marnie, putting on a big show on her behalf, but that was the extent of it.

I look from Nicole to Damien and back. "No crashing the party on Friday. I can handle this. You know I'm good at getting information out of people."

Women can usually be charmed, men low-key threatened.

"Wouldn't dream of it," Nicole says sweetly.

I know her much too well to take her word for it.

thirteen

MARNIE

NONE OF THIS IS SMART.

In fact, people should be telling cautionary tales about me. Oh, who am I kidding, I'm already the subject of dozens of cautionary tales. *If you don't eat your vegetables, you're going to get left at the altar, and everyone will call you pathetic, and if you don't laugh longer and harder than they do, you'll be called a humorless rhymes-with-witch. Enjoy that!*

What was I saying?

Yes. I'm being dangerously foolish. Then again, I've been feeling a bit on edge since Saturday night. I've vacillated between wanting to show up at the bar and wanting to avoid Griffin entirely, because he affects me in a way that can't be healthy.

The way he looks at me and talks to me says one thing, and the distance he's kept says another. Based on what I saw on Saturday night, he has no problem taking what he wants from other women, or at least he hasn't in the past, yet there was that moment between us outside the bar—the one that would have been perfect for a kiss—and he turned away from me instead. I've spent a lot of time thinking about that moment, and how it might have gone differently. And yes, I've had *several* dirty daydreams.

I sent Sinclair the photos of Griff and me last week, and of course she shared them with my mother. Although my mother hasn't called me directly, it would seem both of them have taken a keen interest in "Mitchell." I'd like to think they're happy for me, but I can't forget the way Sinclair acted during our phone call, like she couldn't believe that a man like Griffin, a leather, would be interested in me. I'll have to explain everything to Drew, of course, but later—he's out of cell phone reception.

I'll admit that I've scrolled through the pictures of us several times myself, studying Griffin's body language and trying to decide whether the interest is all on my side. Whether I've misread his cues because I want to believe he's not just being nice out of sympathy.

To top it off, my day job has been particularly awful.

My boss, Val, called me into his office this afternoon. He stood with his back to me, looking out the window, his gut pressing into the whiteboard just beneath it and erasing whatever had been written on there. When he turned around, he had a dark stain on his shirt that was, I kid you not, in the exact shape of a dick and balls. I stood there trying not to stare at it while he delivered a long-winded speech about how sometimes our greatest challenges can give way to our most startling successes, lovers can become enemies, and enemies can become lovers, and on and on.

I was starting to get nervous about where he was going with the whole thing, and then he came out and told me about the Brock thing. It turns out that Brock's deal with Edgar James is very much on, and the reception on Friday is intended to celebrate their collaboration and the part we're going to play in creating graphics and branding for them. He wants me to show up at Brock's little shindig to drink and look happy so someone can take pictures and circulate them to the press. Just like Andy said, Brock wants to put out the message that there are no hard feelings so he can stop looking like the bad guy.

Which seriously suggests that no one affiliated with him would have circulated that video. It made me look stupid, sure, but it also portrayed him as the kind of asshole who'd leave a woman on her wedding day.

Anyway, I digress.

By the time Val looked at me with an expression he probably hoped conveyed understanding and compassion but which instead made him look like he desperately needed to use the bathroom, I was ready to agree to just about anything to escape his office. But then he added, "I trust you'll be able to hold it together? No outbursts? The man's apologized, and—"

"He hasn't."

He waved a hand around. "Doesn't all of this indicate he's sorry? What does a man need to do? Prostrate himself?"

I had an itch to quit on the spot, but despite what Griffin has said to me, I really don't have a full-blown business yet. Reading Grace's book has given me some ideas about what I might like to do in addition to Sweet Nothings to support myself, but they're not fully formed, and I'm enough of a prey animal to find the prospect of being unemployed, or rather self-employed, terrifying.

So I settled for laughing.

He blanched, as if he were worried I was suffering from some form of hysterical feminine laughter, and then my gaze landed again on the dick-shaped stain on his shirt, and I laughed harder.

Quit, a little voice inside me urged. *Quit*. But I couldn't . . . could I?

My father was such a steady, reliable presence in my life. He wasn't the sort of person to launch businesses or celebrities, and I loved him for it. Did I dare do something he never would have? The money he left me ensured that I could, technically speaking, and yet . . .

"Care to let me in on the joke?" Val finally asked.

"The joke, Val, is that I couldn't care less about Brock. You can rest assured there will be no scene, unless *he* causes one." My thoughts shifted to Griffin peering into my eyes on Saturday night. "I'll be bringing my boyfriend."

"Oh," he said, perking up. "So you *are* seeing someone."

Good God, the men in this office gossiped more than teenage girls at sleepaway camp.

"I am."

"Good for you," he said with a nod, putting his hands on his hips. One of them brushed the head of the ink dick, and I almost burst out laughing again. "You're looking good, Marnie. Keep up the good work."

As if looking good was synonymous with good work. I had a profound urge to tell him he had a dick on his shirt, but I just smiled thinly and left. Let him figure it out.

Back at my desk, I tapped my pen on my chin, debating who to contact first, and landed on Grace and Andy.

Andy was right, although it took longer for the bomb to detonate than I thought. We're working with Brock on his new collaboration with Edgar James AND he wants the whole staff to attend a happy hour at his place on Friday night.

Grace: *Tell me you're not going.*

Andy: *I think she SHOULD go...and punch him in the face. Chet and I will crash so I can catch it on camera. We'll make our own memes.*

So, both of those are interesting ideas, I replied, *but I got pissed off and told Val it wouldn't be an issue because I'm bringing my boyfriend.*

Grace: *The hot bartender is going?!? Have you started talking again?*

They'd stayed at the bar on Saturday night, to "get the lay of the land," Andy said, and apparently Griffin had returned looking dejected. He'd said something to Gwen, who hadn't looked very pleased about it, and she and her friends had left their stools at the bar and gathered around a table in the back. The words "he has a girlfriend" were floated. Hearing that was encouraging, of course, but it didn't make me any less confused.

Andy: *New idea. You bring the hot bartender and rub HIM in Brock's face.*

Grace: *I hope you mean that non-literally.*

Andy: *Literally. Because hopefully HE will punch Brock. Yes, that would make me very happy. Then you'll obviously need to whisk him away so you can thank him properly.*

Me: *Small problem: Griffin doesn't know about any of this yet.*

Andy: *Ticktock.*

Grace: *He'll do it for you. That man has a very real thing for you.*

I could have called Nicole obviously. She would have played go-between or figured out another way to capitalize on the Brock situation, but despite the aforementioned confusion, I wanted an excuse to spend more time with Griffin.

So I went home, paced a lot, and when that didn't offer me any magical solutions, I bit the bullet and called *him.*

That brings us up to the present. I'm standing in my closet, considering what to wear to the bar. I'd like to put on something pretty for him, but I don't want to look like I tried too hard. Somehow those warring impulses translate to me wearing the old Star Wars T-shirt as a joke, layering it over sexy lingerie that will make me feel bold and empowered . . . or at least that's the hope.

When I reach the bar, there's a "closed for cleaning" sign on the door. I try it and find it unlocked. Griffin's standing behind the bar, which makes me smile. It's like the whole place is open just for me. It's cold out, but he has on a short-sleeve shirt with the bar's logo on it. It's not the greatest, a simple pink circle with Summer Nights written over it in neon letters, and I make a mental note to design a new logo for them.

My gaze skates to his arms. The ink I've seen peeking out of his sleeve is part of a larger tattoo—a griffin curling around his arm.

He gestures for me to come in, and I do.

"Did I come at a bad time?" I ask. "I didn't expect to find you in bed."

He laughs, his eyes dancing with it. "You're funny. I like that about you."

At least he's laughing with me and not at me. I think.

I close the door behind me.

"You can lock it."

"Aren't the lights going to confuse people?"

"There's a closed-for-cleaning sign and the blinds are closed," he says, quirking his brow. "What's unclear about that?"

He's not wrong, but people tend to be attached to their misconceptions. When it comes to Griffin, I'm hoping I'm not one of them. "Even so. I'll bet you five dollars someone tries to open it within the hour."

"I'd suggest different stakes," he says, "but I don't like taking losing bets."

I lock the door, enjoying the finality of the click, like Griffin and I are now in one of those lock-ins teens go to so they can use bounce houses and eat ice cream instead of getting wasted. Except we're being locked in with a full bar's worth of booze, so really, it's like I'm getting both.

"Will you make me a drink?" I ask, walking toward him.

"Of course." When I take off my coat and hang it on the back of one of the barstools, he gives me an amused smile. "Nicole didn't get rid of that shirt? I'd wondered."

"She tried. Really hard, actually. But I had Damien as an accomplice."

"I'm glad."

If he's disappointed that I didn't show up in anything sexier, it doesn't show.

If he's noticed that I've been giving him the cold shoulder for the last few days, he doesn't say.

He starts pouring things into a cocktail shaker.

"Aren't you going to ask what I want?" I tease.

He smiles without looking up. "I'm starting to learn what you like. Besides, I've tended bar since I turned twenty-one. If I can't make you something you enjoy, I'm not good at my job."

"And you think you're good?" I ask inanely.

He looks into my eyes, holding my gaze. "I know I am."

Stick a fork in me, because I'm done. *I am done.*

Lowering onto the stool, I say, "You don't have to flirt with me, you know. No one else is here." My gaze skips around. "Not even Reggie. There's no one for us to convince."

Maybe it's a test. Maybe I need to know whether any of this is real.

"I know," he says, adding ice to the shaker and really going at it, his arm flexing in a way that makes my cheeks heat. "I can't seem to help myself."

"You flirt with everyone, then?"

His smile falls flat, and I know we're both thinking of last weekend. Still, he tries to be glib. "Only the fake girlfriends I like."

I'm not sure how to respond. I have the inane urge to apologize.

Griffin exudes charm. It's not his fault if other people take notice, and last weekend he made a point of telling Gwen he was off-limits, even though that's not actually true.

No brilliant turns of phrase enter my mind, so I pull a paper out of my purse and set it down on the bar. "I wrote down some questions people are likely to ask us. You know, the kind of details couples should know about each other and their shared history."

"Hit me," he says, pouring the drink into a glass. He adds one cherry, then another.

"How did you know I like cherries?"

He smiles to himself. "I noticed you eyeing them longingly the other night. I figured I'd get it right this time."

I like the thought of him watching me, trying to figure out what will please me. I like it a little too much.

Clearing my throat, I glance down at the list. "I already know you're originally from Sacramento." He'd told me that much last week. "Do you miss California?"

"No." There's nothing equivocal about his answer. "It may be where I'm from, but Asheville is home."

I nod. "For me too."

"Because Drew is here," he says with a slight smile.

"Don't forget Aunt Helen," I say. "She needs someone around to make sure she doesn't get food poisoning."

His smile widens, making my breath catch.

I glance down at the paper again. It's not very good armor, as such things go. "How should we say we met?"

He slides the drink across the bar to me. "Here at the bar." When I don't say anything, he runs a hand through his hair and says, "Unless you'd prefer for them to think you're dating some high roller, but I figure it's best to stay as close to the truth as possible."

"No, it's not that," I say quickly, not wanting him to get the wrong idea. "I told Sinclair your name is Mitchell. She doesn't have regular chats with Brock, but the story should stay consistent, shouldn't it?"

He's quiet for a second, then he taps his tattoo. "If anyone asks, you can say my name's Mitchell but people call me Griffin. Hell, there aren't many people who'd know it's a lie."

"I was thinking your tattoo was very literal of you," I say. "I like it though."

He shrugs. "I figured it might come in handy if I ever forget my name."

"Or accidentally acquire a new one."

We laugh together, which is a good feeling, and some of the nerves that have been bouncing around in my body take pity on me and settle. Our rapport is starting to feel natural again, like we're shedding some of the awkwardness injected into it on Saturday night.

He motions toward the drink. "Moment of truth?"

I take a shallow sip and glance up at him. "Are you a drink psychic?"

"I'd like to think so," he says with a grin. "I'm glad *you* do."

It tastes like sunshine in a cup. Orange, pineapple, and uncategorized goodness.

"Well, you are. I haven't asked you before." I motion to the bar. "Is this what you'd do if you could do anything?"

"Yeah," he says. "I think maybe it is. I like talking to people and hearing their stories. How about you?" He nods at the card still taped up behind the bar. "Are you going to do your business full time someday?"

"Maybe," I say. "I've been thinking of something else, too. Something I'd enjoy doing."

He lifts his eyebrows. "Care to share with your friendly local bartender? There's only a ten percent chance I'm going to steal your idea and sweep it out from under you."

I give a self-conscious shrug. "It occurred to me while I was reading Grace's book. I think it would be fun to put together teaser graphics for authors. Draw their characters for them. Stuff like that. I looked it up the other night, and some people do that kind of thing for a living. Between that and my Etsy business, I could probably scrape by, although I know it'll take a while for it to build up."

"So why don't you?" he asks, his gaze so intense, I suspect he can see inside of me. My doubts. My dreams. My fears.

"There's security in having a regular job. I guess I'm having a hard time letting that go after . . . everything."

He nods slowly. "You'll be ready soon enough. And when you are, you're going to do great things, Marnie Jones. I'll be able to tell people I knew you way back when."

"You can already tell people that," I say with a snort. "That's another problem—my name has become synonymous with failure."

"People are stupid," he says bluntly. "They also have short attention spans. You don't need to let the court of public opinion decide anything for you."

My gaze takes him in like it's hungry for him, pausing at his broken nose. It strikes me like a blow that for everything Griffin knows about me, I know nearly nothing about him. He's not a man who talks about himself. He's told me stories about Damien and Nicole, his brother, and the bar, but few of those stories directly involve *him*.

"How did that happen?" I blurt, pointing to my own nose.

"No need to do a field sobriety test. You've only had one sip."

I give him an arch look.

For a second, he just studies me, then he pours himself a beer from one of the taps. "I'd rather not tell you."

"Oh," I say, feeling a stab of disappointment. He doesn't trust me. Or maybe he just wants to keep our connection, such as it is, surface deep. "That's okay."

He reaches across the bar and grabs my hand. "I can see what you're thinking, and it's not like that, Marnie."

"So what's it like?" I say, looking at his hand. It's big and broad, and there are a couple of scars across the knuckles. He seems so upbeat, so laid-back, yet it's obvious there's more to him. His past is folded up inside him, like the almond paste in those croissants a week and a half ago, only I sense it's not so sweet.

What happened to him after he left Asheville?

All of our conversations have skirted around it, like it's a black hole in his life, and he's afraid to get too close in case everything's sucked in.

Griffin is such a mystery. Charming but reticent, outgoing but more inclined to spend his time alone with a book than out with other people. God help me, I'd like to know everything about him.

Including his last name.

Shit. How could I not have asked?

"What your last name?" I ask.

"Mountainbottom," he says with a straight face, then gives me a hint of a smile. "Adler. Let's go sit down." He nods to a table across from the bar.

I follow him like those children trailed the Pied Piper. Of course, those kids went missing and were never seen again, weren't they?

Even so, I can't help but lean in a little closer as I sit across from him.

"It's not that I don't want to share things with you," he says, swallowing thickly, "but I don't have pleasant memories from that time in my life, and I try not to relive them. I also don't want to burden you. Some of that shit is heavy."

I almost laugh. "What have I done *but* burden you? You've spent all this time helping me."

He takes my hand again, his touch sending shivers of awareness through me. "It hasn't been a burden. If I can help you in any way, it's my privilege."

My throat clogs with emotion. I'm starting to believe he actually means it.

"I realized I barely know anything about you," I say. "I'd like to, is all."

"For the party," he says, his eyes focused on me.

"No," I say slowly. "I just want to know. Maybe I want to be able to make *you* the perfect drink without asking."

"Don't put pickles in it." One corner of his mouth hitches up. "I hate pickles."

"No pickles." I make a check mark with my hand.

"And I love Star Wars."

"No," I say. "You're teasing me again."

He lifts his free hand in the Vulcan symbol. "Scout's honor."

"I thought that was from Star Trek."

Grinning, he says, "That was a test. I watched the movies with my dad and Gary, back when things were good in my family. Gary was home from college for spring break. Most guys in their twenties wouldn't trouble themselves with a younger stepbrother, but he always treated me like I was his real brother. Anyway. We made a whole day of it, starting with *A New Hope* and ending with *Return of the Jedi*. My stepmom made us themed snacks and everything." His smile drops, and his thumb starts drawing little circles on my hand. Does he realize he's doing it? All I know is that I don't want him to stop.

"Things were good between your dad and your stepmom?"

"Between all of us. It felt like we were really a family. After I left, when I was missing Gary and Ma, I'd watch the movies to feel closer to them." He lifts his free hand. "Only the first three. Don't get me started on Jar Jar Binks."

"Nicole told me your father died," I say, knowing it might make him shut down. Risking it anyway.

"He did. It happened right before I came back to Asheville. But I don't keep him on my mantel. He always loved the water, so I scattered his ashes from a friend's boat in the Pacific Ocean. Now I watch Star Wars whenever I'm missing him too. It reminds me there were some good times. He was a troubled man . . . an addict . . . but there was more to him than his issues."

"Well, damn," I say as his words burrow into me, augmenting the picture I'm forming of him. "I guess I'll have to watch Star Wars after all."

"Really?" he asks, smiling again. He looks almost boyish, despite his close-cut beard, those thick, muscular arms, and the crook in his nose that suggests he's seen violence and maybe dealt it out.

"Yeah," I sigh. "But if you ever meet my brother, do *not* tell him. In fact, don't tell him you're a fan in general unless you want to get sucked into a really long, boring conversation."

"I enjoy getting drawn into long, boring conversations," he says, continuing with those mesmerizing thumb caresses. "He sounds nice."

"He is."

"Did he like Brock?"

I jolt a little. Not because it pains me to hear Brock's name, but because it's a reminder of why we're here. We're supposed to be preparing for Brock's party. I'm not supposed to be mooning over Griffin, forgetting that there ever was someone named Brock and that I, in a fit of insanity that had everything to do with the *very* public proposal he and Sinclair orchestrated, agreed to marry him. Sitting here, feeling Griffin's thumb on me—his thumb, for God's sake—none of it seems to matter much. The doubt and fear that drove me then, that have plagued me for years, seem to have taken the night off.

But Griffin doesn't know why I'm thrown by his question, he only knows that I am, and he pulls back that lovely, large hand of his. "I'm sorry. It's none of my business really."

"It's not like that," I say.

He laughs a little, but there's a shuttered look in his eyes. "Wasn't that my line?"

"You were right, I guess. And so am I. My brother hates Brock. He disliked him from the beginning, but it escalated after the way Brock proposed. He thought Brock backed me into a corner on purpose."

"Yeah, I heard about that," he says softly.

I rub my forehead. "It was so embarrassing," I admit. "Still is."

Not so much that he did it but that I actually accepted. Would I have said yes if there weren't all those eyes on me, in person and on camera? I'll never know. What I do know is that I had doubts from that very first day, deep-seated misgivings that clawed at me. But one minute I was accepting his proposal in front of cameras, and the next Sinclair was telling us, on air, that she was going to pay for us to get married at the Biltmore—in three months, no less—because there had been a last-minute opening. Before I knew it, my fate was sealed, and there was no time to process anything, to talk it through with Drew and Grace and Andy.

I could have put my foot down, of course. I could have stopped the process at any point along the way, but I didn't. I let myself be carried along by the force of other people's convictions.

"No reason for you to be embarrassed," Griffin says. "You're not the one who did it. I agree with your brother though—that's probably the worst way he could have proposed to you. Your sister should have known better."

"Maybe. But Sinclair thrives on that kind of attention. It's hard for her to understand not everyone is cut out for it."

The look on his face suggests he has a less generous interpretation.

"Look," I say with a sigh. "I get that you didn't get the greatest impression of her the other day, but she cares about me in her own way. She paid for my entire wedding, for God's sake."

"Shouldn't she have made sure you wanted to get married first?"

His words are like a blow.

"How do you know I didn't?" I ask, pushing back, trying to escape his orbital pull.

"Shit," he says, leaning back in his chair as if he's trying to awaken himself too. "I shouldn't have said that."

"No, you shouldn't have," I agree. "You barely know me."

But sitting here with him, talking and flirting and touching, it feels like we *do* know each other. It feels like he's exactly the type of person I'd like to get to know better. A little voice whispers that it was like this with Brock in the beginning, that we'd shared a false intimacy that led me to make a terrible mistake, but that voice lacks conviction.

"That's true," Griffin says, repentant, his eyes on mine. There's a plea in their tawny depths, and I feel a pull toward him again. "But I'd like to know you."

My heart starts pounding faster. "Nicole told me the other night that you're not being paid for this. That you volunteered to help me."

He practically growls. "Nicole's much too talkative for her own good."

"But is it true?"

He studies me for a moment before answering. "I volunteer my time to the agency now and then, but this is the only time I've done anything like this. She's asked before. I've refused. This time I'm the one who asked her."

He pauses, as if trying to collect himself, but he must lose that battle, because he reaches up and traces my cheekbone, his hand leaving a burning path on my flesh, like it's branding me.

Then I do what I've been wanting to do again ever since that first day, when he called my sister Scarlett. I lean in and kiss him.

fourteen

GRIFFIN

I'VE BEEN LOOKING at Marnie's lips all night, soft, pink, and inviting, but a voice in my head reminds me that I wouldn't be able to keep her at arm's length . . . that I wouldn't want to. I shouldn't take what I want until I know I'm ready for it.

Goddamn it, though, all my good intentions burn to dust when she leans toward me and presses those luscious lips to mine, making that little almond croissant moan. I weave a hand into her hair and slant her head for better access, plundering her mouth. I want to throw her over my shoulder and carry her upstairs. I want to touch her, to taste her, to *claim* her. It's just a kiss—one that started out soft more than sensual—but I feel my cock stirring, and I'm already imagining where it could lead.

Oh, who am I kidding. I've been very liberal with my imagination for the last week and a half.

So it comes as an unwelcome surprise when a knock lands on the door.

Marnie startles and pulls away, her hair slightly mussed from my fingers in a way that pleases the Cro-Magnon in me. She inclines her head toward the door, her eyes wide. "I told you someone would show up," she says, her voice breathy.

"And I would have been a fool to take you up on that bet," I say. "Because I ordered us pizza."

"*Oh.*"

"I'm definitely feeling some regret," I say, smiling at her.

"No one should ever regret pizza," she says with a small return smile.

Normally I'd agree, but this feels like an exception to the rule. I'd far rather be alone with her so we can continue what it felt like we were starting. Except I can see caution creeping back into her, suggesting my *let's pick up where we left off* plan is fucked.

She has every right to be cautious. I've let down almost every important person in my life. I may have had good intentions, but does it matter?

At the same time . . . Marnie nearly got married three months ago, and she's only starting to shake off the fog that's shrouded her. She's probably not looking for a happy ending. With a history like hers, I'll bet she's only interested in a happy-for-now.

Shaking it off, I head to the door to collect the pizza.

After I send the deliveryman off with a tip, I lock the door and return to Marnie. She's smoothed her hair, more's the pity.

"I shouldn't have done that," she says, glancing up at me.

"Why the fuck not?" I set the pizza down, but my gaze is on her. She's worrying her hands now, and I layer my hand over them. Her eyes seem to get even bigger.

"I wasn't sure you'd want me to. Last weekend—"

I tug her to her feet, letting my hand come to rest on the swell of her hip. My gaze flits to the bar, just behind us, and I back her up to it. "I didn't volunteer to do the whole boyfriend act out of the goodness of my heart. I wanted to kiss you last weekend, and I should have."

"What held you back?" She reaches up to touch my chest, a gentle touch that burns through my shirt as if it were tissue paper.

"I'm an idiot. I want you, Marnie."

All the reasons I've held back don't feel very important anymore.

Her other hand lifts to my chest. "But you obviously . . . I mean, you meet plenty of women doing what you do."

"I don't have any trouble meeting women when I want to," I assent, unwilling to lie to her. Besides, she already knows or has guessed as much. "But I don't want to meet anyone else. I want *you*."

"Griffin," she whispers, and it sounds like a request. Maybe even an entreaty. "I can't be the type of woman you usually . . ." She trails off, at a loss over whatever this is we're doing.

"No," I say. "I can't say I've ever been lucky enough to meet another woman like you. Beautiful, funny, and smart."

"But you . . . you're so—" I can tell she's about to say something self-disparaging, and I won't let her.

"I'm a high school dropout who only co-owns this bar through the grace of my friends," I say with a smirk. Surprise flickers in her eyes for an instant but doesn't stick. If she's less than impressed, I don't hold it against her. She doesn't strike me as the kind of woman who has many or even any friends who took the GED track. No, she's more like a tutor who would have been assigned to me.

"Don't put yourself down," she says, intent.

"I'm not," I say. "I'm not ashamed of who I am . . . just aware of it. Although we probably shouldn't throw that out there on Friday. Something tells me it won't impress Brock and his friends."

"Screw Brock," she says fiercely, showing me another flash of that iron inside her.

I draw her to me and claim those soft pink lips. She kisses me back hard, her mouth opening to me, and our teeth clash in our haste to take more from each other, our tongues twining. My hand returns to its place in her glossy hair, pulling her closer, and her body is so soft and pliant against mine, I'm instantly all-the-way hard. No, fuck that, I'm harder than a rock.

Instead of backing off, she gets closer, her body rubbing against my hard-on in a tease that's going to drive me batshit crazy.

I take more from her, plundering her mouth, slipping my hands under that too-large shirt, which has the delightful bonus of leaving her accessible to my touch, and feeling her soft skin, the swell of her breasts that were teased by that purple nightgown. She's touching me too, her hands slipping inside my shirt and skimming over the muscles of my chest and around to my back, sending flames of heat licking through me. Then she's lifting the edge of my shirt, teasing it up, and I break away long enough to take it off and throw it to the ground.

Her lips are pinker, her eyes sparkling, her hair rumpled. I feel a swell of pride because *I* did that.

"You should never wear a shirt," she says, her gaze appreciative. "Never. It should be illegal for you to wear a shirt."

"I'd say I feel the same, but I don't want anyone else looking at your breasts," I say as I lift the Star Wars shirt over her head.

Electricity coils through me, gathering in my cock, because goddamn it, beneath her borrowed shirt she's wearing a lacy red bra that hugs the swell of her breasts. I trace my hands up her sides, then cup them, feeling her nipples bead against my touch. I lower my head to suck one through her bra before looking back up at her. "Did you wear that for me, Marnie?"

She gives a little nod, her hands already reaching for me, but I take a small step back.

"I want to make you feel good tonight."

"You are," she says. "You *really* are."

"I want to taste your sweet pussy and make you come with my mouth. Do you want that?"

She swears under her breath, then gives a nod.

"Take off your pants."

She steps out of her shoes and socks, then shimmies out of her pants, leaving her in her bra and a pair of matching red lace panties in my empty bar. It's like she stepped straight out of my dreams.

I come forward again and kiss her, needing to feel her bare skin against mine, and the sleekness of it is everything I could have hoped for.

"I read your favorite Ivy Anders romance book this week," I say in a throaty whisper as I let my hands travel down her torso to the swell of her hips. Gripping her, I lift her easily onto the bar, her little gasp of surprise making me even harder. "Seems to me you were telling me what you wanted. I'm going to give it to you."

There's a scene in the book where the hero goes down on the heroine while she's perched on the bar. I've been imagining this ever since, and when I say imagining, I mean I've had to take a lot of cold showers over the past several days.

"Oh my God, Griffin," she says as I run my hands slowly up and down her legs, feathering the insides of her thighs, feeling the soft heat of her flesh and the way she trembles beneath my touch. "Didn't you say they just cleaned the bar?"

"Yeah, so I can't think of a better time to do this," I say, amused that she's focusing on that. My hands skate up her legs again, and this time I let myself touch her panties. She's hot and wet for me, ready for my mouth, and I feel another twitch in my cock, like it's reminding me it would like an MVP role in this game. "But I'll clean it again before we open tomorrow. It'll be a damn shame, though. I'd personally like the taste and smell of you all around me."

"Am I dreaming?" she asks lightly. "Because I could have sworn this happened in my dream last night. It was a *very* good dream."

I slide my fingers into the top of her panties and pull them down, enjoying the sight of them slipping down her legs, giving me what I want, revealing that soft patch of trimmed curls. God, she's gorgeous, perched on my bar, her hair a mess, her breasts cupped in that bra that shows more than it conceals, her legs open to me. Spreading them wider, I lean in to kiss the hot flesh of her thighs, and her little moans shoot through me and settle in my dick.

Then I lower onto my knees on the bar's foot rail, which brings my mouth into the perfect position. It hurts my knees a little, but the slight discomfort only heightens the anticipation burning through me.

I kiss her thighs, making my way to her center, slowly, so slowly, because I don't take for granted that this will happen again, and I want to make every second count. She tenses as I reach my target, and I kiss her there before sucking on her clit, flicking my tongue.

"Griffin," she sighs, weaving a hand into my hair. Her throaty exclamation, my name on her tongue, excites me, and I feast on her the way I've wanted to all night, licking and sucking and reveling in the way her body reacts, the little sounds of pleasure escaping her.

I pull back slightly, and her soft sound of complaint sends more blood down to my straining dick.

"Lie back," I command, and she does. I perched her on the corner of the bar, so there's plenty of room for her to recline on the counter, just like the heroine in that book she likes. She does, her legs spread even wider, and I edge them over my shoulders, one on either side. "You taste delicious, Marnie. Do you like feeling my mouth on you?"

"Yes," she says, her voice shaky. "*Yes.*"

I lick and suck and plunge my tongue between her hot folds. Her body quakes beneath me, her legs trembling. I feel the satisfaction of bringing her close to the edge, but I'm not ready for her to come yet. I let my hands roam up her body as I pleasure her, cupping her breasts through the red bra and then slipping them beneath it, stroking her beaded nipples.

"Oh my God," she says, her body arcing up.

I slide my hands back down and plunge two fingers into her as I continue to give her clit the attention it needs, pulsing them toward where my mouth is licking and sucking.

My cock is so hard it could probably bludgeon someone. I can't remember ever being this turned on or feeling this profound need to possess. To take what I want.

"I'm going to come," she says in a breathy whisper. "Oh my God, I'm going to come."

I want to stand up and plunge my cock into her. I want her to come around me, her walls clenching me and driving me over the edge too. I'm desperate for it, but my desire to give her pleasure is even stronger. I want to give her a memory she can look back on while she touches herself and uses that vibrator she mentioned after our breakfast call with Sinclair.

Hell. I want her to pleasure herself while thinking of me.

"Are you going to ask for permission?" I say.

She must like that I asked, because another quake travels through her body, and she looks down at me, my mouth poised over her, and licks her lips. "No."

Her voice is firm and throaty, and I fucking love that she told me no.

"That's my girl." I'm smiling as I lower my mouth to her again, sucking her clit and circling it with my tongue while I pulse my fingers. I feel her body tensing and releasing as she falls over the edge for me, my name escaping her lips again in a breathy sigh that charges straight to my cock, making that feeling of wanting, needing, almost painful.

I pull back and then stand, my knees aching from kneeling on the railing for so long. I soak in the sight of her arched back on my bar, her eyes nearly shut but filled with a look of bliss, no tension or anxiety left in her. Her breasts cupped in that maddening red lace. She's so beautiful like this, uninhibited, basking in pleasure. I store the image in my mind for later.

Then she's lifting up, sitting on the bar. She reaches for my chest, exploring more freely now. Her fingers tracing the lines of muscle.

"Griffin, I want to make you feel good too. I want—"

"Not tonight," I say harshly, even as my cock is throbbing, urging me to stop being a fucking idiot and bury it inside her already. "Tonight's about you." I hadn't necessarily planned on waiting ten minutes ago—my plans hadn't gone much further than *make Marnie come*—but for some reason it seems like the right thing to do.

"But . . ." She nods to my extremely uncomfortable hard-on.

"Make no mistake," I say. "I want to fuck you, Marnie, but it won't be on this bar. At least not the first time."

With a feat of self-control someone should really give me a medal for, I pick up her shirt and pants and hand them to her. I watch, hungry for even this, as she pulls her shirt over that sexy bra, hiding it from view but not from memory, and then I lift her off the bar and watch as she shimmies into her pants. She stares at me, her lips parted, as I tuck her panties into my pocket.

Her gaze dips to the hard-on straining the front of my pants. It might as well be shouting, *Look at me! Look at me!*

I think deflating thoughts.

"Can I touch it?" she asks in a husky voice.

Her words weave through me, making my cock strain again. "Not right now," I say through gritted teeth. "If you do that, I'm going to lose control."

"Is that a promise?"

"Hell, yes. But not tonight." It seems important for me to stick to that. To prove to myself—and to her—that I have self-restraint, especially after what happened last weekend.

"So, what now?" she asks, looking a little lost.

"We're gonna make an honest woman of you."

MARNIE

I'M in Griffin's apartment above the bar, surrounded by his smell and his things, and somehow I'm more turned on now than when he made me come on top of his bar.

It's a small place, the décor clean and simple, with a leather couch and a recliner that looks like it's been around since the Dark Ages. There's a mantel over a closed-off fireplace, but there are no photos here like there are in Gary and Liza's home. In fact, the apartment barely seems lived in. The only glimmer of personality can be seen in the bookshelves, stuffed with books, and a framed drawing of a griffin hung on the wall. It looks like it was the basis for his tattoo. I'd like to know who drew it.

When I first saw his place, I found myself thinking of Liza, who doesn't seem to trust that Griffin is around for the long haul. Because it looks like the kind of place someone could leave easily, without coming back. Maybe he's just used to living this way, though. Habits can be hard to break.

We're sitting on the couch, his arm wrapped around me like I'm his, while *A New Hope* plays on the TV. Yes, I gave in. How could I not? So much about Griffin is unknown to me, but he went out of his way to tell me this movie is important to him.

It reminds him of a time in his life when things felt perfect, or near enough, and he wanted to share it with me. So I'd watch it even if it were terrible.

It's not, though. To be honest—and I have no intention of telling my brother this—it's kind of fun. Although maybe that's just the magic of being tucked up close to Griffin, knowing my panties are in his pocket and that he was hard enough for me to qualify as a statue. He still is, actually. The man must have the self-control of a monk, because he clearly meant what he said. He's sitting sideways on the couch, with me cradled between his legs. His hands keep dipping onto me, exploring my body as if I'm unchartered territory and he's a cartographer intent on accuracy, but he hasn't broken . . . even though I'd definitely like him to. Being near him, having his arm around me and his hard cock pressed against me, is sweet torture like nothing I've never experienced, especially after what he did to me on the bar.

Thinking about it only worsens my torture. The man gave me the best orgasm I've ever had in my life, and if his mouth and hands can do that, what can his cock do? So, yeah, the proximity's making me feel drunk and needy. It's making me crazy. At the same time, it feels really good. We've sat here, watching the movie, eating cold pizza, both of us commenting on what's happening onscreen, and the whole time my body has had an aching, almost painful awareness of him—of every small movement he makes, of the feeling of his strong arms wrapped around me, his hands drifting up and down my arms and gliding over my stomach, his cock straining against my back.

When the movie ends, I turn to look at him. He's watching me, his eyes as bright as they probably were when he was a kid, watching this movie with his father and Gary.

"It's all wrapped up," I say. "What's going to happen in the eleven billion other Star Wars movies and TV series?"

"Hush," he says through a smile. "I only acknowledge parts three through six."

"Well, Drew would tell you that's a mistake. He has a real boner for the one where everyone dies." My hand flies to my mouth. "Sorry. Spoiler alert."

He laughs. "Sounds like a downer. So . . . what did you think?"

"I sort of liked it," I say. "I especially liked thinking of you watching it when you were a kid, with your dad and Gary."

"Your brother . . . did he watch the movies with your dad?" he asks, tilting his head.

I give a little shrug, embarrassed. "Yeah. My sister always made fun of them. I wanted to be like her when I was a kid, so I did the same. Then, when I was older and Sinclair was gone, it had already become a whole thing. It felt like I couldn't back down."

Drew and Dad were pretty into the movies, to the extent that they frequently had battles with their fake lightsabers. One time when I was little, I borrowed Dad's so I could play with Drew, and Sinclair gave me a withering look and said I'd never land an audition if I wasted time playing with toys.

Yeah, auditions. When we were kids, my mother dragged Sinclair and me to every audition or open call within a hundred miles of Asheville. There weren't too many of them to drag us to, but she was nothing if not determined. We'd be dragged out of bed first thing in the morning, primped and polished, and then piled into the car.

My father never had dreams of grandeur, for himself or for us. He was a CPA, and he only thought about work when he was at work. Weekends were for family. Although he never approved of my mother's fixation, she told him not to stand in the way of our dreams.

They were *her* dreams. Sinclair and I both wanted to impress her back then, though, so we'd cry and beg, and he'd always relent. He'd only ever wanted to make us all happy. But as we got older, I started making excuses to avoid going with Mom and Sinclair: a stomachache, a headache, any old kind of ache. I didn't like being scrutinized and judged. I didn't like being found wanting, or told my hair or eyes were the wrong color, or my body type wasn't quite right. So the auditions and callbacks stopped being an *us* thing and became a *them* thing, and Sinclair and I started to grow apart, long before she landed a spot on a nationally broadcasted talent show when she was sixteen. Everything snowballed from there.

Even then, I had a dogged loyalty to Sinclair, maybe because I felt I'd abandoned her in a way, and it had made me scoff and walk out whenever Dad and Drew put on a Star Wars movie. I regretted that now that my father was gone. I'd never get him back. He'd never know I'd changed my mind.

"It feels pretty stupid now," I mutter, feeling tears well in my eyes. "I wish I could have watched it with my dad too."

"Hey," Griffin says, cupping my cheek, his fingers spearing into my hair. "You're many things, Marnie Jones, but stupid isn't one of them. Not even close."

"How about misguided?"

He pretends to give it thought, then smiles and says, "We can roll with that. After all, you *are* here with me."

I'd say something about that, maybe ask him what he means and why he seemed reluctant to kiss me last Saturday, but his hand tightens a little in my hair, almost to the point of hurting, and he kisses me for the first time since we came upstairs. His lips are firm and demanding but also soft, and the way his whiskers brush against me only adds to the sensation. I want to be closer, to take more from him. His tongue finds mine, and he angles our heads, taking the kiss deeper. It's like he's been holding back throughout the movie, and—

I pull back, panting a little, thinking of my underwear nestled in his pocket. No man has ever affected me like this before. It's like all of the sexual longing I've felt in my life has been packed into this one night. "Can I touch your cock now?"

"Fuck," he says, and I can tell he really, really wants to tell me yes. He looks like it's killing him, actually, and I feel a rush of feminine power. He's such a man, so powerful and handsome, so compelling, and he wants me badly enough that it hurts. But it's obvious something's still holding him back.

"Why is it important to you to wait?"

He doesn't have any trouble picking up women when he wants to, and Gwen serves as evidence that he's used that superpower before. It's obvious from his persistent hard-on that he's attracted to me, or at least attracted enough, so what's the holdup?

"Marnie, I—"

My phone rings, and when I check it, I see it's Grace. She's more of a texter than a caller, and she and Andy know I'm with Griffin. They're under strict instructions not to call me before eleven, although if I don't call or text them by then, they're free to assume I've been murdered and act accordingly. In other words, they wouldn't interrupt us for anything but an emergency.

Blood pounds in my ears, and my mind conjures a million possible disasters. From Drew getting . . . I don't know, eaten by that bear he photographed, to Andy being injured or killed in a car accident. It's catastrophic thinking, and I hate it, but I got a call like that ten months ago, about my dad, and my brain is now wired to expect disasters to be real . . . the kind that can't be undone by asking nicely.

"Is everything okay?" Griffin asks with a frown, exuding his own adrenaline, like he would punch that fictional bear if he could. It's stupid, but his presence calms my racing heart. I may have only known him for less than two weeks, but he's so big and capable, so good to me. If anyone could punch all of my fictional bears, it's him.

"Yeah . . . I just. I need to get this. It's my friend Grace, and she wouldn't call unless—"

"Take it," he says.

I pick up the call, getting to my feet to pace off some of my nerves. "Grace? Is everything okay?"

"I know it's against the rules to call before the cutoff point, but I figured you'd understand. Andy's here too, but I thought I should be the one to call you, because you know how she is about Sinclair, and she's really worked up right now, and—"

"Grace, you're babbling. You only babble when bad shit happens. What's going on?"

"YouTube," she says. "Look up Sinclair's appearance on *Late Night with Mike*."

I press the phone to my chest and convey her directions to Griffin.

His brow lowers into a near glower as he does my bidding, and I know it's because of Sinclair.

He doesn't like her.

It's a first, actually. Every single boyfriend I've ever had has fallen over his feet to impress Sinclair, to charm her, to win her over. I don't know what to do with his obvious dislike. On the one hand, it pleases me that he's one of a very few people who prefers me to her. On the other, I love my sister. I know she's flawed and tone-deaf, sometimes even cruel, but I know her as the girl who used to give me piggyback rides. Who braided my hair into designs so intricate my mom once burst out crying from the effort it took to unweave them. To me she's not some vacant celebrity. She's my *sister*.

In the background of the call, I hear Andy swearing loudly enough to potentially wake up Griffin's neighbors. Yes, *Griffin's* neighbors.

Then it's there on the screen, a clip of Sinclair's appearance on the show. She didn't even tell me she was going on tonight.

"Tell Andy to stop it," I say over the phone. "She's going to give herself an aneurysm. I guess I'll go watch the clip." I feel no enthusiasm over the prospect.

"Do you want us to come over so you don't have to do it alone?"

What could be so bad? Did Sinclair go nuts on the air and murder Mike with a microphone cord? I mean, the guy makes terrible dad jokes and then laughs at them. It's legitimately annoying but hardly the kind of thing to whip someone into a murderous frenzy.

"Marnie? Should we come?"

"Um, no," I say, not wanting to admit I'm at Griffin's place. "I'm in the middle of something."

Or at least it felt like I was. Sinclair's hijacked my evening, however indirectly, and I can't help but feel annoyed by it.

"In the middle of something, or some*one?*" Grace says with renewed interest.

"That's an Andy comment," I say.

"She's busy raging, so I had to make it for her."

I almost smile. "Well, goodbye. I assume I'll be texting some sort of emphatic reaction gif to you."

Hanging up, I turn to look at Griffin. He's still sitting on the couch, his back straight, his mouth in a firm line that suggests he's less than pleased with whatever we're about to watch. I suspect it's a wise attitude.

"I'm sorry about this, Griffin. I can just go home and watch the clip. This is a lot to ask of you."

His jaw clenches. "I want to watch it with you."

I nod slightly, and he motions for me to come to him. I do, lowering into his arms, and he presses play.

Mike, the annoying-dad-jokes host, gives Sinclair a lecherous smile that makes me want to be the one who strangles him with a microphone wire. "So, we've all seen the memes featuring your little sister," he says. "I think I speak for all of us when I say we'd like to know if the old adage is true. You know," he adds with a wink, "how they say the best way to get over someone is to get under someone else?"

He's leaning forward as he says it, giving Clair a look that suggests he'd like to try out his theory with her. Gross.

I glance up at Griffin, and his expression is murderous now. I'd almost be afraid of him if I weren't sure that he's now entered the wants-to-strangle-Mike-with-a-microphone-cord race.

Sinclair's tinkling laugh, the fake one she used to practice with my mother in the car, draws my attention back to the TV.

"Well, Mike, I'm happy to announce that my little sister is seeing someone new, and let me tell you, she seems infatuated."

"Great news!" he says, to a chorus of claps. "What can you tell us about the lucky guy?"

Sinclair looks straight at the camera, grins, and says, "Well, you can imagine I thought the worst when she told me his name was Mitchell Mountainbottom."

"No . . . that's *not* his name," Mike says with an exaggerated gasp.

"It is," she doubles down, pretending to smooth her perfectly glossy hair. "But I have to admit I thought she'd made him up. My mom did too. I mean, can you blame us? That name!" She reaches into her purse and pulls out a phone. "But here they are together."

The whole reaching-for-her-phone act is just that—an act— because suddenly the screen fills with one of the photos Reggie took of Griffin and me.

My first thought is, *Thank God I didn't send her the video with the fake blood.* My second thought is, *We look happy.*

But any happiness I could have had with him has probably been smashed to bits, because I know without asking that Griffin, unlike Brock, doesn't want his face plastered all over people's TV screens. A man like him, with a past he doesn't like to visit, prefers to be left alone.

Sinclair beams at the camera. Her fake smile. "Obviously, I couldn't be happier for my little sis. She deserves nothing but the best."

"There you have it, folks," Mike says. "Mitchell *Mountain- bottom.*" He pulls a face. "Nah. I still think it's a fake name."

He and Sinclair laugh together, that horrible, tinkling laugh.

Then they move on to the more important subject of who her character is about to bone in *Sisters of Sin* as if they hadn't just stirred up shit for me.

Griffin switches the TV off without comment, but his face is stony now, as if the walls that had tumbled within him have been patched back up with concrete, stronger than ever.

"Griffin," I say, grabbing his arm, anxious for him to go back to the Griffin of ten minutes ago. "I'm so sorry. She had no right—"

"It's not your fault, Marnie," he says evenly. "Not even a little." A corner of his mouth lifts. "Except for the name. I guess that part's your fault."

He lifts to his feet and reaches for my hand, pulling me up without any effort after I give it to him. But he keeps hold of my hand, which gives me hope that he doesn't totally regret what happened between us tonight, or, hell, everything that's happened since the Sunday before last.

"Someone might think it's a story worth following up on," he says. "She showed everyone a picture of us at the bar. It won't be hard for people to figure out that's not my real name. I mean . . . even Google won't have much to say about the Swiss Mountainbottoms. We're lucky she hasn't looked before." He tilts his head in thought. "Unless she *has* looked, and this is her way of letting you know."

"Shit," I say. "What do we do?"

"I'll talk to Damien and Nicole," he says.

He obviously doesn't want his real name getting out. He didn't sign up for this. He volunteered to help me, and then he made me come with his mouth, but he didn't ask for his secrets to be blown apart by a celebrity with a thing for discussing her sister's private business on TV.

I've told Sinclair to stop answering questions about the whole mess, but she's always insisted I was the one who was wronged and everyone should know it. And some weak, guilty part of me that remembered she paid for the wedding-that-wasn't kind of felt like Sinclair had a right to have her say. But this? This is wrong. It's exploitative. Before, it felt like she was trying, in a bumbling famous person way, to vindicate me or have my back, but this is different. If Griffin disliked her before, he probably loathes her now. I'm lucky if he doesn't loathe me too.

"I'm sorry," I repeat.

He lifts a hand to my lips and traces the bottom one, his trailing finger giving me the errant desire to take it into my mouth. "And it's still not your fault. Maybe it's better for this to have happened now. People will ask us about it on Friday, and we can tell them you gave Sinclair a fake name because you figured she might talk about me publicly. That's what you should tell people at work too."

That makes sense, but a fresh wave of horror courses through me. He's right—people *will* ask us about this. I'm furious at my sister. *Furious.*

"I need to—"

"Let me bring you home," he says, intuiting that a third or fortieth apology is about to come out of my mouth.

"My car's downstairs."

"Then I'll walk you to it."

My rattled nerves are infecting me from the inside out. Part of me is afraid that if I leave now, like this, we'll go back to being nothing. That this thing that's been spinning between us will turn from spiderwebs, sticky and strong, to old cobwebs so diffuse a good duster will take them down with one swipe. The thought awakens something like panic.

"Griffin, I—"

"You're sorry, I know," he says, lifting my hand and giving it a kiss, sending pleasure to my very pleased core. "I'm *not* sorry. I can still taste you."

No one's ever spoken to me this way before. I feel like I'm going to melt into a puddle of goo that will then melt into a second puddle of goo. I—

I reach onto my toes and kiss him, maybe just to prove to myself that I still can, and he meets me halfway, his mouth hot and commanding, his scruff rubbing against me, reminding me of what it felt like between my legs.

I'm the one who pulls away this time, mostly because I can't think when he's touching me. "I don't really know what's happening between us," I admit. "But this doesn't feel fake."

"Good," he says with a smirk. "If it did, I'd know I was doing something wrong."

"What does it mean?"

"I'm not sure," he says. "But I think we're going to have a fun time finding out. I already have."

My blood may as well have turned to fizzy water in my veins. "Me too."

"Still," he says, reaching up and cupping my cheek. "I think I'd better get you down to your car. I'm guessing you'll want to send your friends that gif you promised them."

His comment might have made me wonder if he was teasing me, before. But I've come to appreciate his teasing. It's not mean-spirited. It's . . . sexy. "Yes, and make a strongly worded phone call to my sister."

"I'd like to listen to that," he says with a slight smile.

Something seems to catch in my throat. "I know you don't like her."

"That's not why," he says, which isn't exactly a denial. "Maybe I'd just like to see you get worked up."

From the way he says it, I'm pretty sure he isn't solely referring to a phone call. "Does this mean I'm going to get to touch your cock next time?"

He groans and swears under his breath. "Marnie, I'd like you to do a whole lot more than touch it. We'll definitely need more time than you're going to have right now."

He holds my hand all the way down to the car, then kisses me in front of everyone walking by, as if we belong to each other.

Back home, my body feels strangely cold. Maybe it's staging a revolt because it wants to be back with Griffin. Ignoring it, I send my friends a cartoon gif of someone with their head blowing up and then start pacing the floor, making passes near the sadly wilting Christmas tree as I call Sinclair on my cell phone. She must have been expecting this, she must have been *waiting* for it, because she actually answers, even though she is presumably still at the show or at an after-party.

Voices blend behind her in a tidal wave of input.

"You saw the show?" she asks, her tone bright. It clearly it hasn't occurred to her that I might be anything other than pleased. Has being around Hollywood types made her immune to common sense?

"Yeah, I saw it," I say, plenty of bite in my voice. "Why would you do that? Gri—Mitchell and I are private people, and we don't want anyone popping up to ask us questions or take pictures of us. Not cool." That doesn't seem strong enough somehow, so I add, "Seriously not cool."

"I helped you," she says, her voice tight. "I could have talked about anything tonight, and I talked about *you*. I made sure everyone knew you weren't moping over Brock anymore. You should be thanking me. I *thought* you'd be thanking me."

"So . . . what . . . you saw me as some pathetic loser, moping over a guy?" I seethed through clenched teeth. It's not a surprise, obviously—I *knew* she thought that—but for some reason I need her to say it.

"Weren't you?"

"It wasn't just about him," I say. "I was *moping* about my face being everywhere. I was *moping* about being a fucking joke. I was *moping* about Dad being gone. What Brock did to me didn't feel good. It felt awful, but thank God he did, because otherwise I'd be married to an asshole. I didn't *want* to marry him."

"Don't you think you should have told me that before I spent forty thousand on your wedding?" Sinclair asks sharply.

"I would have if you'd stopped for half a second and asked. But you were so busy pushing me down the aisle, you didn't. *Drew* asked."

She's quiet for a long moment, and for a second, I think she may have hung up. Even though I'm pissed, livid, angrier than I can remember being for a long, long time, I don't want to leave things on this note. "I thought it would be good for you," she says. "You needed a distraction. We could all see it."

"It *did* distract me," I admit, because for a few months, there was so much to do—invitations, and dresses, and preparations—that I didn't have to think about the quietness of the house, or my regret that we never pushed my father to date again after Mom left him. It had always seemed like there'd be more time . . . until there wasn't.

The busyness of the wedding planning was seductive for a while. The reality of the situation hadn't fully set in until just before the wedding, when I had my talk with Drew.

"It's not your fault," I tell Sinclair. "I let it happen, but I'm done letting things happen to me. I'm trying to be more . . ."

Myself. More assertive. More of a badass bitch, like Nicole. I channeled some of that tonight, calling Griffin, kissing him. Opening my legs to him. Maybe some badass bitch energy is exactly what I need in my life.

"I'm coming to visit you," Sinclair says.

"What?" I blurt, alarm flooding me.

"I'm coming," she says. "I should have come to see you months ago, and now I have another reason. I want to meet Mitchell. I'll bring Mom so she can meet him too."

Well, this certainly isn't good.

sixteen

GRIFFIN

"THIS IS BAD," I say to Damien and Nicole after they settle on the barstools in front of me on Thursday afternoon, a half hour before the bar opens. "Actually, it's a goddamn disaster."

Marnie called me last night to say Sinclair is coming to Asheville next weekend, with their mother, no less. She tried to put them off, but ultimately she couldn't refuse to let them come. They won't be staying with her, and they're adults with their own credit cards. So they're coming, and that's that. And both of them look forward to meeting Mitchell Mountainbottom.

If you ask me, Sinclair is setting me up. She knows my last name isn't Mountainbottom, and last night was about her calling my bluff. She's setting me up. Or setting Marnie up, which comes down to the same thing.

Marnie has a kinder interpretation, but I've concluded that she sees her sister through beer goggles. She looked so goddamn sweet last night, apologizing to me for something that wasn't her fault, and rage had kindled inside of me. I didn't like the way she was being treated. I felt . . . protective of her. I still do, and it's putting my teeth on edge. It's making me skate the limits of my self-control.

If I feel like this after getting a taste of her, what's going to happen to me if I take everything? If I sink my cock deep inside her like I was aching to do last night?

That's the real reason I held back, and I haven't forgotten it. Maybe I should have left things as they were, with Marnie at arm's length, tempting but untouched.

"I don't know about that," Damien says, grinning at Nicole. "You might have gotten lucky. This saves you from Nicole's plan."

She pouts a little. "I liked my plan. You said you did too."

He laughs. "No, I didn't. I said it would be interesting, and it would have been."

In this case, "interesting" doesn't sound very promising.

"What was your plan?" I ask, lifting my eyebrows.

She gives a beleaguered sigh and nods to the bar. "Make me a drink before I tell you."

I have to laugh at that. "What? Do you think I'm going to spit in it?"

"A person can never be too careful."

Rolling my eyes, I pour her a vodka tonic and a beer for Damien, pushing them across the counter.

"Well?" I ask.

Nicole heaves another sigh, as if I've annoyed her with my perfectly reasonable question, and tucks her pink hair behind her ears. "I was going to have you two become fake-engaged so we could reunite everyone from Marnie's side of the original wedding."

I stare at her in disbelief. She stares back, unflinching. Damien laughs.

"That's a stupid fucking plan," I finally say.

"And that," Nicole says, tapping the side of her glass, "is why I asked you to make the drink first."

"You really thought Marnie would want to get fake-engaged to someone after the way her last engagement ended? Why the hell would she want to have two failed engagements in the space of six months?"

"That's the brilliant part," she says, warming to the subject. "I figured she could dump you. I mean, you're way hotter than Brock. And charming!" She nudges Damien. "Didn't we agree he's charming? If she dumps you in the dirt, she's automatically a goddess. Boom. I'm a genius."

"You thought this would make me like your plan more? It makes me like it less." I rub my chest, feeling tightness there. "It might make her look like a goddess, but it wouldn't do great things for my ego."

"Pshaw," she says, reaching across the counter to give me a shove. "The women in this bar would all try to jump you. There'd be a competition over who gets to do it first—the poor hot bartender, abandoned by his fiancée. I feel no pity for you and your imaginary heartbreak."

Only I'm not so sure it would be imaginary. The thought of Marnie moving on and inviting some other guy between her legs makes me want to break the bar into sticks.

"It's still a shit plan."

She shrugs and pops the cherry from her drink into her mouth. "Of course, you could just marry her."

Damien gives a slow shake of his head as he watches her, his eyes shining. "You're some woman."

"So you always tell me."

"I never thought I'd be grateful for a visit from Sinclair Jones," I mutter, annoyed. Running my hand through my hair, I say, "What do we do if someone shows up at the bar asking about the late show?"

Maybe I'm a coward, but I haven't left the building all day. I've dwelled on the possibility that they might be out there, waiting to ask questions, to confront me with truths I don't want to own.

"Oh, there are already a couple of people out there," Nicole says flippantly, waving a hand toward the front window. The blinds are still drawn, so I don't see anyone peering in at us. "On the plus side, they probably work for really shitty blogs and have nothing better to do."

Shit, I thought there'd be more time.

"Did you talk to them?" I ask.

"No comment," Damien says.

"What the hell does that mean?"

"That we told them no comment." He gives me an incisive look. "But people are going to find out who you really are, Griff. It's on all the business documents for the bar, and Marnie's sister shared your photograph. It's only a matter of time, man. You prepared for them to release your name?"

"Do I have a choice?"

"He was being rhetorical," Nicole says. "You know how he likes his inspiring speeches."

I do. But I'm not feeling inspired just now.

Swearing again, I grip the bar. Less than twenty-four hours ago, I made Marnie fall apart on this bar, but the moment couldn't feel farther away.

"We'll tell them Marnie used a fake name for me because she wanted privacy. Maybe no one will look into my background. Besides, my record got expunged."

They'd helped me with that too. Their lawyer friend had gone to law school with someone who practiced in California.

Damien gives me a sympathetic look that says it all. "Nothing goes away without leaving a trace. I'm not saying you should go out there and spill your guts to the reporters, but you should probably tell Marnie soon. It's not a big news week. If someone who's determined enough gets a hold of this, they could cause trouble."

"We know you like her," Nicole says slyly, pausing to take a sip of her drink.

"How do you know that?"

She lifts up her middle finger and points to the card that's still hanging behind the bar. Then she lifts up another. "You volunteered to do this." A third finger goes up. "The instant she called last night, you ran off like someone lit your ass on fire." A fourth finger. "Reggie told me."

"What?"

She laughs, bending over and slapping the bar. "You should see your face. I'll have you know Reggie is a *very* close friend of mine."

Damien grins at her. "By that she means that they have both gotten drunk here an unreasonable number of times."

"He told me about your little photography sesh *and* the blood drinking. He said you always look like you want to maul each other."

"I'm not denying I like her," I say, sliding a few things around on the surface of the bar. They don't need to be centered or fixed, I just feel like pushing something. Plus, I'd rather not see Nicole's look of victory as she turns to Damien for a high five. He gives it to her, obviously.

"I don't know what you're so happy about. This is a fucked-up situation, all around. Her sister's going to find out that I have a fake name *and* a record."

"An expunged record," Nicole corrects.

"Expunged or not, I doubt she'll approve."

"Consider things in a different light," Damien says, popping a pretzel from the bowl on the bar. "She liked the last guy, and look what happened there. Maybe she's learned some humility."

Unlikely.

Leaning against the bar, I study him. "Did you hear anything else from your contacts in California?"

He gives a slow nod. "I did, as it happens, but I don't want you to jump to conclusions."

"What's that mean?" After taking a moment to think about it, I say, "You found out something that doesn't look good for Sinclair."

He makes a rocking motion with his hand. "Sounds like the new director has started spreading rumors about her being difficult on set, and a few people suggested he was doing it in a bid to kill off her character and replace her with another actress."

"Fuck," I say. I remember what he told me before, that this particular director is known for causing trouble for women who aren't inclined to fall into bed with him. I'd feel sorrier for her if she weren't causing Marnie and me so much trouble.

"Fuck," he agrees. "Let's just say the timeline suggests she had plenty of motivation to help Brock with the proposal and pay for the wedding. Talk about good publicity."

Nicole cocks her head. "The post-wedding publicity hasn't hurt her either. She's the protective sister, standing strong for her baby sis. Either way she wins."

"You think she's the one who circulated the video?"

"Like I said," Damien tells me, "no jumping to conclusions. We don't have enough information to throw around baseless accusations. For all you know, Marnie's aware of the situation with the show. See if you can get the ex to talk about Sinclair, though. I'd be interested in what he has to say."

I nod absently, my mind working through it all. Damien's right. Without knowing more, we can't lay the blame at Sinclair's door. Because she wouldn't have *needed* the video. She could have acted the part of the aggrieved big sister without embarrassing Marnie. If she was behind all of this, it wasn't just about pumping up her reputation—it was about punishing Marnie for letting the wedding fall apart.

Protectiveness has my teeth clamping together again.

"You know," Damien says softly, "Nicole didn't need to put forth evidence items one through four. The way you feel is right there, my friend." He points at my face.

"You've tapped that, haven't you?" Nicole says, leaning forward as if I've become an episode of must-see TV. "Tell me you tapped that last night."

"Not yet," Damien says, still scrutinizing me. "But it's going to happen soon."

They don't need to know everything, so I keep my mouth shut, going through the pre-opening preparations.

The last thing I have to do is open the blinds, and sure enough, a couple of strangers are waiting outside, looking a little too eager to get into Summer Nights. I shoot a desperate look at Damien and Nicole, and Nicole says, "We're not going anywhere, and we're very good at trapping people in inane conversations."

"One might even say it's our specialty," Damien adds with an indulgent smile.

"Gary and Liza are coming over as soon as Gary gets off work. We've got your back, boo."

I feel a swell of appreciation for my friends, my *family*, and I give a fatalistic nod and open the door.

The first person to come in, of course, is Reggie.

"Et tu, Brute?" I say.

"I don't know what the fuck that means," he grumbles, "but I'm going to go claim my stool. There are some shifty types waiting out front."

I have to laugh at that . . . and also at the bloggers or reporters, or whoever the hell they are, as they make their way inside tentatively, giving Reggie a look that suggests he might be rabid.

I wait on Reggie before I make my way over to the first probably reporter. He has short-cropped blond hair and eyes so light blue they're almost white. "Drink?"

"Water," he says.

Yup, narc.

I pour it for him anyway.

"You know, it's pretty uncool not to order something if you're hanging out at a bar," Nicole comments.

"That's between me and this gentleman," the guy says, his bluster almost admirable, actually, because Nicole can be fierce when she wants to be.

"Actually," Damien says, his voice pitched low, "we're part owners of the bar, so it's also between you and us."

He lifts his hands, his eyes widening slightly, and tells me, "Sure. I'll have a seltzer."

I grab him a can from under the bar and push it across the counter. "You want to start a tab for that?"

His answer is a headshake, and I can hear my heart start to pound, because eventually he's going to get around to the point.

The other probably reporter is edging in closer, like maybe she hopes she can get the same story without having to say or order anything—not a bad strategy, really.

"You're the guy who's dating Sinclair Jones's sister," the first guy says.

"And you're wearing a purple shirt," I say back, keeping my tone even. "See, I can state facts about you too."

"You're killing this, Griff," Nicole mutters.

"Griff?" The reporter type lifts his eyebrows.

I'd be annoyed at Nicole, but she and Damien are right. Anyone can look up the ownership of the bar. Better to get ahead of this thing than to be left behind in the dust.

"Griffin," I say. "That's my name."

The other reporter type edges closer, as if she smells blood in the water.

"Really?" the first guy says. "I thought Sinclair's sister was dating a fella named Mitchell Mountainbottom."

"I'd prefer for people like you—" I give a nod that encompasses both of them, "—to keep the hell out of my business, so my girl and I told a little white lie. Now pay for the seltzer and get out, because other than that, I've got no comment."

Nicole glares at the guy. "That'll be ten dollars."

"*What?* he cries out, getting to his feet. "That's highway robbery."

"People are always bitching about the prices going up around here," she says, shaking her head slowly. "I'm just getting in on the action."

An hour after we open, Gary and Liza show up with enough takeaway for all of us. It's from a vegetarian/vegan place downtown, but thankfully it's from a *good* vegetarian/vegan place. While I didn't get the dubious pleasure of trying that lasagna last night, Gary tried to bring me some for lunch earlier, and we both about fell down laughing when I opened the container and a stench wafted out from inside. He asked me about Marnie too, and I told him about as much as I've told Nicole and Damien.

Yes, I like her.

No, I don't have the slightest idea what I'm doing.

Another reporter type comes in later, this one way more subtle in her approach, but we have a fairly good system, and my friends alert me to her presence long before she even asks for a drink.

To my surprise, Marnie shows up with her friends, the ones who like reaction gifs. She's not very tall, Marnie, but she looks taller tonight, her eyes alight with righteous indignation, her short hair framing her face. She's wearing a long-sleeved dress that doesn't show much skin but leaves nothing else to the imagination.

That first night, she hung back from the bar, her troubles seeming to press down on her, but tonight she approaches it immediately, her gaze meeting and holding mine. It's like my whole body is leaning forward, wanting to touch her, to kiss her. Wanting to claim that fire in her eyes.

"Let me guess," I say as I start to make her that drink she liked the previous night, "you loved *A New Hope*, and you're back for more. Your personal Star Wars consultant, reporting for duty."

seventeen

MARNIE

"I DIDN'T KNOW I'd hired a Star Wars consultant," I say, grateful he's still looking at me like my sister didn't just pull his privacy out from under him like it was a picnic blanket she wanted for herself.

"Sometimes people don't know what they want until it's right in front of them. I'll always give you what you want," he says, and pushes my sunshine-in-a-cup drink across the counter. I'm tempted to tell him that I wanted his cock yesterday and he wasn't feeling compliant, but I'm too pleased to be surly.

I take the drink, and Griffin nods to Andy and Grace. "What'll it be, ladies?"

They place their orders, and we settle in at the bar to wait. He makes the drinks methodically, his hands doing a mesmerizing dance, and I can't tear my gaze off him until he slides the drinks across the counter.

"On the house," he says with a wink.

I have yet to pay for a drink in this bar. A girl could get used to this kind of treatment.

It's a busy night. I doubt Griffin will be able to talk to us much, but I wanted to come. I wanted to make a show of solidarity. If anyone shows up to bother him tonight, *I* should be bothered too. It's only fair.

"I can't believe he went down on you on the bar," Andy says, much too loudly. "Where was it on the bar?"

Yes. I told them. I mean, he gave me the best sexual experience of my life. How could I not tell them?

"Oh. My. God. Shut up," I say through gritted teeth. "If you're going to talk like that, it completely defeats the purpose of being here."

"I thought you brought us here so you could brag," she says, all innocence, and then bumps me with her shoulder.

Very funny.

"You *should* brag," Grace says wistfully. "It's just like what happened in that Ivy Anders book."

"It is," I say, feeling my cheeks heat, even though I *do* feel like bragging a little. "He read it because I told him it was my favorite romance book . . . other than yours, of course."

"Wait," Andy says, tapping the bar, "he can make a kickass drink *and* follow instructions? This guy's a keeper."

"Shhh," I say as Griffin glances over, sending me a look that zips straight to my vagina. Or maybe it's just muscle memory. I've spent all day thinking about his mouth on me . . . fantasizing about having other parts of him inside of me. I only managed to do a few minutes of work, and even then, I have to admit it wasn't on any of my projects for Val.

"Just calling it like I see it," Andy says.

"Yes, you enjoy doing that," Grace tells her.

Andy's gaze skewers into her next. "Speaking of my outspokenness, have you shown your book to Vera yet?"

"No," Grace says, scrunching her mouth to the side. "I was hoping to fix the ending first, but I'm stuck."

"She might have some ideas," I say, patting her on the back. "Maybe give it to her now in case it takes her a couple of months. But

I can tell you this . . . whether she likes it or not, there are a lot of people who will. Actually, I was hoping you'd let me put together some teaser graphics for you. Maybe make some mock-ups of the characters."

"For real?" she asks with wide eyes. "You'd do that for me?"

"Obviously. Actually, I was thinking it would be fun to try to do that for other authors too . . . like as a freelance graphic designer."

"Does this mean you're finally going to quit?" Andy asks. "Because, if so, I'd like a front-row seat for when you tell Val. I intend to watch his reaction in real time."

"He'd probably assume it's because I'm pregnant with Mitchell Mountainbottom's baby," I say. "He's misogynistic like that."

A guy in a purple shirt sidles up to us. "Did you just say you're pregnant with Mitchell Mountainbottom's baby?"

"No," Andy says. "Is there something wrong with your ears?"

"I've heard Mitchell's real name is Griffin," the man says. "Do you care to comment on that?"

Griffin was on the other side of the bar, making drinks for a large group of women who're either celebrating a bachelorette or are the kind of people who wear tiaras on the daily, but he's suddenly in front of us. "You heard that from me, Purple Shirt," Griffin says. "It's hardly hearsay. I thought you'd left, but I'd be happy to get you another seltzer if you want to hang around."

"I'm good," the guy says, his eyes darting around the bar. They land on Nicole. I hadn't noticed her before, but she, Damien, Liza, and Gary, whom I recognize from photographs, are gathered in a little knot behind the bachelorette party. Nicole points to her eyes, then points both fingers back at Purple Shirt. I know without asking that they're here for the same reason I am, and I feel a swell of gratitude that Griffin has friends and family who have his back.

"Gotta drink if you're gonna stay," Griffin says.

"I'm not buying another ten-dollar seltzer."

Andy guffaws. "You got hosed, Purple Shirt."

The guy gives her a hostile look that becomes much less hostile once he takes in her long, curly hair and curvy figure.

"I'll buy *you* a ten-dollar seltzer."

"No, thanks," she says, lifting her drink. "We got the good stuff, and I have a lover with a ten-inch dick."

Purple Shirt flinches but doesn't retreat.

"Is this guy bothering you ladies?" Griffin says, his gaze on me. There's something gruff and protective about him tonight, and while I feel like preening, I also want to start dealing with my own problems, even if they *are* problems of my sister's making. I'm sick of sitting back and letting other people decide things for me.

"No, he was just leaving," I say to Purple Shirt. "But to set the record straight, my boyfriend's name is Griffin. The other name was my sister's idea of a joke."

It's not until after I said it that I see Griffin's SOS expression. Shit, I just said something wrong, I'm sure of it.

Purple Shirt looks like he won a shiny prize as he turns to Griffin. "You said the two of you made it up because you wanted some privacy."

Griffin's better at thinking on the fly than I am, though, and he cocks his head, his eyes tawny as a lion's—a lion ready to bite—and says, "Yeah, *buddy*, we told Sinclair she couldn't release my real name, and she made up Mountainbottom. What kind of trap do you think you're going to catch us in? There's no mystery here. No big conspiracy to rip wide open. We're just two normal people trying to date in peace."

The guy scowls at him and leaves, muttering about ill treatment and Yelp.

There are about six people trying to flag Griffin down, but he reaches across the bar and takes my hand.

"You okay?" he asks softly.

"Yeah," I say. "You? I'm—"

"Don't you dare say you're sorry," he cuts in, a slow smile spreading across his face.

"Okay, so I'm not sorry. I'm glad that guy tried to tear apart your privacy."

"No need to go that far," he says, his smile stretching wider.

"And I do want to watch *Empire Strikes Back*. You want to do it tonight?"

He scratches the back of his neck, and from the look in his eyes, regret and hesitation, I'm worried this is all too much for him.

"There's something I have to tell you," he says at last.

He glances down the bar, his gaze finding Damien, and without a word exchanged between them, Damien slips behind the counter to take over.

I can feel my friends' scrutiny, and a quick glance reveals that they strongly resemble the mind-exploding gif I sent them last night.

"I'll be back in a bit," I tell them, upbeat. "Enjoy your drinks."

"We're gonna go talk to Nicole," Andy says.

Yeah, I'll bet she is. She wants to gossip about Griffin and me. I can't really hold it against her. For one thing, I'd do the same in her position. For another, none of this would have happened without her, and she deserves to take some ownership of it.

Besides, maybe she and Grace will find out something I haven't. I texted Nicole this morning to fill her in on the Brock situation. She thinks we can use the reception at Brock's house to my advantage, because Griffin can talk to Brock and try to get information from him. I'm almost positive Brock's not behind the video's release, so I'm not sure what she expects Griff to find out, but I didn't try to dissuade her. That's part of the reason he's coming, isn't it? And I really, really want him to be there.

Griffin slips out from behind the bar and comes to me.

"Take your coat," he says, so I do, even though the practical part of me would like to point out that he doesn't have his.

He engulfs my hand with his much larger one. It feels like it's anchoring me. Although we haven't known each other long, I can't deny I feel more of a connection to him than I ever did to Brock. That scares me to my marrow. I made a really big mistake with Brock. Epic. And I might be running toward my next big one with Griffin.

As he leads me out of the bar, I feel eyes on us. Not just our friends. Maybe the people who are watching us saw Sinclair on that show last night, or it's possible the women in that bachelorette party are just jealous as hell that I'm the one who gets to leave with Griffin. I can't blame them; they're right to be jealous.

We wind up the stairs, and I shoot him a curious look as we continue upward past the landing to his apartment.

"We're not going up to your place?"

"No," he says. "I don't trust myself to be in there with you right now."

"Why?"

He pauses on the stairs, his gaze soaking me in. "Because we need to talk, and if you're in my apartment, I won't be able to stop thinking about stripping you out of that dress."

"Oh."

"Oh," he repeats, smiling at me, and then he continues to climb the steps, our hands still linked.

"So where are we going?"

"The roof," he says as we reach the top of the stairs. Sure enough, there's a small, warped wood door at the top. He opens it, and we're on top of the building. A couple of lounge chairs are sitting out, and there's an alarming lack of a railing that has me keeping a good distance between myself and the killing ledge.

"You come up here a lot?" I ask.

"When I need to think," he says, which isn't totally an answer . . . except I can tell he's the kind of man who spends a lot of time reflecting. On the surface, he's not someone who seems like he would—he's confident and handsome and a bit brash, a total leather—but he spends most of his spare time reading, and his inner circle is even smaller than mine.

Still holding my hand, he leads me to the chairs. We sit in them sideways, facing each other, and our clasped hands finally fall away from each other. I'm tempted to ask him if he's cold because it's objectively freezing up here, but it would probably be a stupid question. More heat seems to be coming off him than from the lining of my coat. He might as well be a human furnace.

"What is it?" I ask.

He leans his head into his hands for a moment, his elbows resting on his knees, and then looks up.

"There's something the reporters might find out if they dig deeply enough. I mean . . . I don't see why they would bother, but it's possible."

I'd suspected as much from the fervency of his reaction last night. Does he have a secret family? A literal skeleton in his closet? Maybe it reflects badly on my character, but those sudden fears don't make me lean away.

I place a hand on his knee. "Tell me."

He looks into my eyes, and this time his gaze is tortured. Maybe it's a leap, but my gut suggests that whatever he's hiding has something to do with the California phase of his life.

"I have a criminal conviction," he says. "It got overturned . . . that's something that can happen in California if it wasn't a violent crime and you have a really good lawyer."

"What'd you do?" I sputter.

He places his hand on mine, still layered on top of his knee, but his touch is tentative, like he expects I'll pull back now. Like it's happened before. My heart hurts for him.

"It was a drug charge," he says. "For opioids."

He must feel my jolt, because he lifts his hand from mine. Swearing under his breath, he runs his fingers through his hair. "You don't have any reason to believe me," he says, "but the drugs weren't mine."

"Who'd they belong to, then? The one-armed man?" There's more bite behind the words than I intended, but . . . opioids. I'd listened enough to the D.A.R.E. talks as a kid to be scared shitless by what he'd just told me.

His eyes meet mine again. "They were my father's. I told you. He was an addict. He must've pissed off one of his friends badly enough that they turned him in. Or maybe the cops found out about him from interrogating someone else, and they were hoping he'd name his dealer's dealer, or whatever. But I couldn't let him take the fall. He'd already been to prison on drug charges. Twice. They would have given him a stiffer sentence, probably, and he was sick by then. Liver disease. I couldn't let him go down for it."

His words are like a bucket of ice-cold water to the face. Maybe I'm being naïve, but I believe him.

"You knowingly went to jail for him?" I ask. "For how long?"

"It was only a few months. The judge suspected I was taking the fall for my dad." He looks down at his arm, the tip of his tattoo visible beneath his shirt sleeve.

My eyes widen. "Is that a *prison* tattoo?"

He laughs, and some of the gloom lifts from his eyes. "My friend wouldn't be happy to hear you say that. He's a pretty well-known tattoo artist. Prison tattoos are made with things like safety pins. They're a lot simpler."

"Oh," I say, feeling stupid. Then again, he's the only person I know who's been to prison. How am I supposed to know what a prison tattoo looks like?

He rubs the slightly crooked bridge of his nose.

"Is that where your nose got broken?"

He gives his head a little shake, something flickering in his eyes. "No. Prison wasn't that eventful, believe it or not. Didn't do much besides work out and read."

He's obviously making it sound easier than it was, but I let it go. I'd prefer to believe the fantasyland version of prison as a boring vacation.

"And your father," I ask, "what happened to him while you were in jail?"

His eyes are so sad, I think I might drown in them. "He stopped using again, but it was too late. He died a few months after I got out. Liver failure. They never would have given him a transplant with his history."

"Jesus, I'm sorry." I remember the way he comforted me when he found out about my dad, wrapping me up in his arms, and I lean forward to embrace him, only he stands up just as I'm leaning, and I find myself with my arms around his waist, my head pressed to his . .
.

Holy shit.

Griffin looks down at me, surprised, but the surprise morphs into something else, and I realize that I'm a couple of layers of fabric away from what I wanted last night. From what I've been daydreaming about. My hand shifts to the left, wanting to touch him, to feel him, to *taste* him, and—

The door opens, and a shouted "Holy shit!" shatters the moment to bits.

I jolt back, Griffin steps away, and I shout, "This isn't what it looks like."

My cheeks, which felt frozen a few minutes ago, could probably melt polar ice. Okay, admittedly that's not so difficult anymore, but you catch my drift.

My gaze flies to the door. I'd expected Nicole, or maybe Grace and Andy, but it's Griffin's brother. Who no doubt thinks I was about to give his brother head on the roof of a very short building, within view of dozens of people in higher apartments and commercial buildings.

Great. Now I'll never be able to look Gary in the face

To be honest, I'm more embarrassed because I was actually considering it.

"Um. I didn't mean to interrupt anything," Gary says, his cheeks probably as red as mine.

"You didn't!" I cry, jumping to my feet like a jack-in-the-box. "I was just giving Griffin a hug."

He gives me a dubious look that suggests he knows it's not normal for people to go around hugging other people's dicks, but he doesn't call me on it. Griffin puts an arm around me, and even though I'm the one who set out to hug him, I can't help but draw comfort from it.

I need to apologize to him. And yeah, I know what he'll say if I throw another *I'm sorry* grenade at him, but he doesn't need my sister pulling out all his old baggage. That's probably the last thing he needs after what he's been through.

"What's wrong?" Griffin asks. His gaze darts to the stairwell. "Is someone making trouble downstairs?"

Gary pushes his glasses up the bridge of his nose, blushing again. "Not really. Just Nicole getting salty at the bachelorette party women for hitting on Damien. I . . . Nicole told me you were probably up here telling Marnie about . . ."

He trails off, probably realizing his plan had some major flaws in the event Griffin had brought me up here for roof head.

"I did," Griffin says, cinching me closer. "I just told her about my record."

"Oh, thank God," Gary says, the tension in his shoulders releasing. "I was afraid I'd put my foot in it. Anyway—" His eyes skate back to me and hold, firm and determined. "I just wanted you to know that we have complete confidence in my brother. He would never lie about something like that. I can tell he really likes you, which is kind of a big deal for him, and—"

"Gary," Griffin says softly. "Stop helping." There's a fondness in his tone and in his eyes that suggests a strong attachment to Gary . . .

which is probably why it strikes me that while Gary refers to Griffin as his "brother," Griffin calls Gary his "stepbrother."

There's also a flicker of guilt in Griffin's gaze, a fire that refuses to gutter out.

Add it to the list of Griffin mysteries.

Gary nods, his glasses slipping a little. "I just wanted to make sure. Sometimes you're not great at standing up for yourself."

This catches me off guard. Griffin seems so strong, so confident. He's not someone I would expect to have difficulty with that sort of thing.

"I'm not a teenager anymore," Griffin says with a smirk.

"No one would have trouble noticing that," I murmur. Looking at Gary, I say, "Thank you. I'm glad Griffin has such a wonderful family."

Gary beams. "Just wait until you meet Ma. I bet she'll even give you her sugar cookie recipe."

This is clearly a compliment of sorts, so even though sugar cookies are only a millimeter above cinnamon raisin in my book, I try to seem pleased.

Griffin gives Gary a *please shut up* look, and we all start toward the stairs by mutual silent agreement. When we get down to the bar, it feels like everyone in the place glances up at us . . . probably because they do.

I hate the attention, but I try to pretend I don't. I've learned the only way to get through this sort of thing is by acting like you don't care. Like you can't see that you're being seen.

"I'm going to . . . um, go over there," Gary says in a transparent effort to give us a second alone.

Griffin nods absently, his attention already fixed on me. "We'll talk more later?"

"Yes," I say. He's about to slide behind the bar, but I grab his arm, suddenly desperate, like this might be my only chance to talk to him. To air what I'm thinking. "I'm sorry, Griffin."

I can tell he's about to tell me what I can do with my sorries, but I push ahead, a true champ at making apologies. "I'm sorry Sinclair's causing problems for you. You don't deserve that. If you don't want to be involved in—" at a loss for words, I make a gesture to encompass the whole FUBAR situation, "—I totally get that, and I won't be upset. We can just tell them it was an amicable breakup. A rebound thing."

He's watching me with intensity, his expression unreadable. Then he pulls me to him and kisses me in front of everyone at the bar. I tell myself it's at least partly an act to appease Purple Shirt, if he's still lurking, and anyone else who came here tonight because of Sinclair's TV appearance, but I can't help sinking into the moment and kissing him back. His lips are slightly cold from outside, but there's warmth beneath it. The heat pulses into me and promises of things to come.

When he pulls back, he looks down at me, his eyes meeting mine, and it feels like flames are licking the surface of my skin, playing up and down my body.

"I don't want to be your rebound, Marnie. You're never going to get that sugar cookie recipe as a rebound."

Then he grins at me and slips away, leaving me immensely sexually frustrated.

GRIFFIN

SHE BELIEVES ME.

She fucking believes me.

It's been a while since I've told anyone about my record. Usually the topic doesn't come up, since most people don't have a record, and it's not the kind of thing I'm tempted to roll into casual conversation. *One time, in prison, I saw one guy punch another so hard his tooth flew out.* Yeah, that's a fast way to kill a vibe.

Still, I've confided in a few people over the years, and I'm used to the judgmental, knowing looks. To disbelief. It's hard for people to accept that someone can go to prison for something they didn't do. It's not pretty, believing the justice system can be played. It wasn't pretty for me either, but I don't regret it. It was the last thing I ever did for my father . . . an attempt at redemption that didn't come close to meeting the mark.

I can hear Gary saying, *He would never lie about something like that.*

If only he knew. While the story about my conviction isn't a lie, there are other lies, more deeply buried, and lately I feel them trying to sprout.

I go through the motions, making drinks, throwing out charm, looking at Marnie. Always looking at Marnie. It's like a flower is blooming inside her, and every time I see her, it's fuller and brighter.

Upstairs, before Gary walked in, her head was next to my cock, her sweet lips inches away from it, and even though she obviously didn't mean to do it, I can't get that image out of my head—Marnie peering up at me through her thick lashes while her face is next to my zipper. My mind fast-forwards through what could have happened. Her staring up at me like that while her hand reaches for the button of my jeans . . .

I'm *definitely* in over my head with her, and not just for the obvious reasons of Mitchell Mountainbottom and the press. This woman does things to me.

My gaze flits back to the group sitting at the edge of the bar. Gary and Liza left half an hour ago, Liza saying she needs her beauty sleep, and Andy headed out not long afterward. Marnie and her blond friend, Grace, the writer, are still here with Damien and Nicole. The last time I looked, Damien had them all enraptured with some story he was telling. Although he's only social when he feels like it, he can easily hold the attention of a room.

Only he's not talking anymore. Marnie has a worried look on her face, and she's tapping her phone to her chin.

I finish filling the beer I'm pulling too quickly, leaving it with a head full of foam, and slap it on the bar in front of the man who ordered it.

"Hey," he says, aggrieved. "This is half foam."

"More like a quarter," I say. "But you'll get half off, so there's that."

He thinks about this a second before shrugging, but I'm already headed to the other end of the bar.

"What's wrong?" I ask, leaning over the counter.

"I've gotta go," Marnie says, tucking her hair behind her ear. "I just got a call from Green Oasis."

"Shit. Is your aunt okay?"

Her eyes warm. "You remembered?"

"There's nothing wrong with his retention abilities," Nicole says with a smirk. "His problems lie elsewhere."

I roll my eyes. "I appreciate the vote of confidence. What's wrong with Helen?"

Grace cringes, her already pale skin turning milky. "There's a spider infestation in her apartment. Black widows. They need to fumigate."

"She noticed them a while ago but kept it from everyone," Marnie says with a scowl. "She believes in live and let live, even though they're poisonous."

"Let me guess," Nicole says. "She thought her STD crystals were going to protect her from spider bites?"

Marnie grimaces. "Maybe we should call them anti-STD crystals. Otherwise, it sends the wrong message. But yes. That's the gist of it."

"How'd she get black widows anyway?" I ask. "Aren't they more common in garages and woodpiles? Places that're dark and crowded with things?"

Marnie's grimace deepens. "She doesn't exactly like to throw anything away." She lifts a hand. "She's not a hoarder . . . more of a collector of useless items and food past its sell-by date."

"In other words, a hoarder," Nicole says. "How'd they find out about the spiders anyway?"

"Her friend's the one who alerted them," Marnie says with a deep sigh. She puts her phone in her bag and shrugs into her coat. Looking at me, she says, "Rain check? I need to handle this."

Marnie told me that Helen has a daughter who lives in town, but the people closest to you in blood aren't always the ones you can count on when shit goes sideways. Maybe her daughter can't be reached. Maybe she's an asshole, and she just can't be bothered. It doesn't matter, I guess, because Marnie has clearly decided to make it her business. I have a feeling she'd do that for anyone who matters to her, and again there's that prickle of protectiveness on her behalf.

"I'll take you," I say.

Her blonde friend nearly sags with relief. Two things become obvious, the first being that she hates spiders. The second is that she planned to go with Marnie despite hating spiders, which means she's a good friend. I'm glad for that. Marnie deserves to have steadfast people in her corner.

"But the bar . . ." Marnie sputters.

Nicole winks at me, acting as if I'd announced that Marnie and I are going off to have sex. I seriously wish that were the case. "Damien and I will handle it," she says. "One of our favorite games is pretending we're strangers who meet at a bar."

"Just don't forget there are other customers," I say.

I slide out from behind the bar, and Nicole slides in, the overhead lights playing on her bright hair.

"What if we're not strangers, but you have temporary amnesia?" Damien says with a twinkle in his eyes.

"Oh," Nicole says, brightening. She does a little shimmy. "We can work with that. Let's go with this: I forgot you, and the doctors have all told you that experiencing familiar things will help restore my memory. So you have to seduce me and fuck it into me."

"I think you're missing my point," I say.

"Yes," she says, "purposefully. I'm at a loss as to why you're still here."

"Did I even agree to this?" Marnie asks, but she sounds more amused than annoyed. She seems pleased, actually.

"Do you object?" I ask.

"No," she says, looking into my eyes. "In fact, I'm grateful. *Thank you.*"

"For a second there, I was worried you were going to apologize again."

Her lips tip into a nearly there smile. "It was touch and go for a minute."

Marnie's friend collects her things, and the three of us leave together.

"Marnie told me about your book," I say to Grace as we make our way out. "Congratulations. That's pretty damn awesome."

Blushing, she says, "Thank you. I mean . . . it's just a romance novel. It's not going to change the world or anything."

"That doesn't make it less of an accomplishment," I say. "I know a lot of people who've tried to write books, and most of them don't get past the first page, let alone the first chapter. I'd be impressed if it were a manual about buying and selling used socks."

Marnie puts an arm around Grace's shoulders. "What if your book reaches exactly the right reader for it at exactly the right time? It might change *their* world."

"Oh, you guys," Grace says, waving a hand. But she's clearly pleased. "Let's just hope Vera likes it. That'll be the real litmus test."

I have no clue who Vera is, but Marnie must, because she says, "She'd be a fool not to. See you later, Gracie."

"Do you have a way to get home?" I ask Grace, used to my role as barkeep.

"I live within walking," she says, signaling to the left of the bar.

I send her a salute and then slide my arm around Marnie, liking the feel of her tucked up against me. "Where's your car, Marnie? We'll take it so you don't have to pick it up in the morning."

She turns in my arm to look at me. "But how will you get back here?"

"I could take an Uber," I say. "Let's be honest, though, I'll probably bother Nicole and Damien and make them pick me up."

She laughs, and then sobers. "Thank you for this, Griffin. Here you are, changing your plans for me again. You like taking care of people, don't you?"

Her words burrow into me. She's right, and she's wrong. I don't always like it, but I do always feel inclined to do it. Or to try. "I like taking care of you," I say. "But I'm no saint."

"Good," she says with a wicked smile. "Because a saint wouldn't let me touch his cock."

"Christ, Marnie."

She glances around, then pulls me into the alley between the bar and the building next to it. It's dark, bathed in shadow, and it smells of grime. No one's around. "You deserve an out, Griff. My sister had no right to share that photo of us last night." She bites her lip. "I hate that it might cause problems for you. That purple-shirt guy was really persistent."

He wasn't the only one, but I don't want to tell her that. She already looks so penitent, as if she thinks every problem I've unleashed on my own life is somehow her fault. As if she's the one who personally purchased those pills and stuck them in my father's cabinet.

Guilt spears into me, because Marnie thinks I was upfront with her. She thinks I've told her everything, but I've only revealed the tip of the iceberg lodged inside my gut. What makes me think I deserve a second chance? I don't, but I've seized it with both hands. I've let Damien and Nicole help me. I've let Gary and Ma forgive me. And here I am, letting this woman who is much too good for me offer me things I have no business wanting.

"If I didn't have a fucked-up past, there'd be nothing for them to dig up," I say, reaching up to trace her jaw, giving myself that small pleasure. "I'm the one who should be apologizing to you. I doubt your sister will be pleased if she finds out you're dating a convicted felon."

"The record got expunged," she says.

I huff a laugh. "She won't see it that way. She'll think I'm a liability."

She doesn't deny it, and I feel a little prick of alarm. Marnie cares about what her sister thinks of her. That's the reason for this whole charade, isn't it? What will she do if her sister decides I'm bad for the family image? Sinclair wouldn't be wrong, necessarily. If the director of her show wants her out, it would be easy enough for him to start rumors that she's using drugs and getting them from yours truly.

"I don't care," she says, full of fire and conviction, and I almost believe her. "I'm more worried about your reputation."

She's so lovely, so full of unjustified concern for me, and I find myself moving my fingers from her jaw to her lips.

"Don't be," I say. "No one will give a shit if they find out their bartender spent a few months in prison. I'm not the kind of person who needs to have a good reputation."

"But you *are* a good man," she says more firmly.

Guilt roils through me. "I wouldn't be so sure about that," I say, tracing her lips with my finger. "I want you. I've been thinking about you splayed open on my bar, bared for me. And for the last hour I've been thinking about your mouth half an inch from my cock, and what might have happened if my stepbrother hadn't come upstairs."

If I'd hoped to shock her, I failed.

"I think we both know what might have happened," she says softly, looking into my eyes. Then she shocks me by sucking my finger into her mouth, working her tongue over the top.

I'm instantly hard. I pull my hand back, but only so I can back her into the wall of the alley.

"You're playing with fire, Marnie," I say, my voice harsh to my own ears as I take her hands and pin them over her head. She looks up, her eyes meeting mine.

"Good," she says, her voice slightly shaky. "It's cold out here."

I lower my head and claim her mouth, my need almost a vicious thing. Hers must be too, because she immediately takes our kiss deeper, her mouth opening to me, our tongues twining together. I still have her hands pinned over her head, and she makes a needy sound of protest that charges straight down to my cock, her body pressing against me, demanding to be closer. So I release her hands and grab her by the hips, lifting her up. Her legs wrap around my waist, and I back her into the wall again, my dick trapped between us, her breasts pressing against my chest even though they're out of reach, covered by her bra and dress. Fuck, I want to feel them. I want to taste them.

Marnie rocks against me, trying to get my hardness where she needs it, while our mouths clash together. Her hands reach up and grab the back of my head, pulling me closer, her hot little mouth claiming mine. I suck in her bottom lip and bite it gently, or at least I mean for it to be gentle, and my hand roams up the side of her body, finding the swell of her breast.

She sucks in a breath, and I capture the exhale in my mouth. Her hand tightens in my hair, the grip almost painful, but I revel in it because she wants me the same way I want her. Our mouths keep dueling, claiming each other, but I hear the crunch of gravel under feet, and it's like a cold bucket of water dousing me.

There's at least one reporter with a hard-on for following us. No matter what my dick tells me, I can't drive into her against this alley wall, exposed for anyone walking by to see us. The last thing she needs is for us to get arrested for public indecency.

I pull back and set her down, her mew of protest almost prompting me to say fuck it and take what I want. What I *need*. But I can't. I just can't.

"Your aunt," I pant, struggling to get myself under control. "We need to help her." I tuck a strand of her mussed hair behind her ear. "I don't want you to hold it against me if she gets attacked by a horde of black widow spiders."

To my surprise, I realize I actually want to meet her aunt. It meant something to me, Marnie meeting Gary earlier. Granted, I wish he'd stayed the fuck downstairs, but I liked seeing them together. Listening to Gary talk about Ma's sugar cookie recipe as if it were the holy grail of cookies. So yeah, I want to meet her aunt, and it's not such a bad way to meet someone's relative, doing them a solid.

"My aunt," Marnie agrees sadly.

I carry her back to the car like that, her legs wrapped around my waist, because screw it, we're supposed to be dating anyway, and if Purple Shirt has lurked around to get a picture of us, we'll be giving him what he wants.

In the car, I get into the driver's seat, adjust it so it's no longer set for a short person, and turn toward Marnie. She's looking at me like she's thinking about straddling me on the seat.

"Fuck, Marnie," I say. "You've got to stop looking at me like that."

Her smile lights her up from the inside. "I can't, and it's your fault, so you're just going to have to put up with it."

I laugh a little, try to ignore my incredibly hard cock, and follow her instructions to her aunt's retirement community.

"The situation is under control," Helen insists, giving her white curls a pat. She's a small woman, which is a good thing, since I'm starting to think I might need to drag her bodily out of this place.

Although Marnie was right—I wouldn't call her a hoarder—the situation is a little more touch and go than she let on. There are piles of stuff everywhere, neat but chaotic due to the sheer quantity of them. Piles of magazines and paperbacks, old food containers and pill bottles repurposed into planters, tapestries pinned to the walls. Honestly, I'm surprised it's her first infestation.

"You do not have anything under control," Marnie says, her tone harsher than usual. "There are poisonous spiders in your apartment."

Helen's jaw clenches. "You have poisonous chemicals in your cleaning cabinet, but I'm not dragging you out of your house."

"No, but you did try to sneak all of our cleaning products out the last time you visited. Besides, my 409 is not climbing all over my things. It's not going to weave a web on my face while I'm asleep."

"Look!" Helen says, pointing at a small . . . shrine is the only word that comes to mind. "Black tourmaline. It has immense protection qualities. Nothing can harm me in this apartment while I'm surrounded by black tourmaline. The spiders can live in their place while I live in mine. I sang to them earlier, and they seemed calmed by it."

"Aunt Helen, there's a spider climbing on one of the stones," Marnie hisses through her teeth. "Besides, all of this is irrelevant. You're being told by management that you have to get out while they fumigate. You have no choice."

My phone vibrates with a text, and I check it quickly, turning away. It's Nicole: *Ha! Some jackass just tried the old "the other bartender said I could get my drink half off" trick. Damien turned on Na Na Hey Hey Kiss Him Goodbye, and the guy got all pissy, so he had to bodily remove him from the bar.*

Oops.

I text her back, telling her that I'd actually told him he could get the drink half price.

Ha, she responds. *Somehow that makes it funnier.*

When I turn back to them, Helen is sagging a little. She must have finally realized that Marnie's not the one who's holding the keys to the castle, so to speak.

"They're going to do it no matter what I say?" Helen says.

"Yes. If you want to stay with one of your . . . er . . . gentleman callers," Marnie says, looking so goddamn cute when she's embarrassed, "I guess that's fine, but you need to get out of the apartment for the night."

"Oh, I couldn't do that," Helen says with a dismissive hand gesture. "I don't want to give them the wrong idea."

"The wrong idea?" Marnie says. "Aren't you already *sleeping* with them?"

"Exactly. That's all I want from those particular friends." She pauses, thinking, then adds, "Danielle wouldn't come?"

"I'm sorry," Marnie says, putting a hand on her aunt's arm. "I guess they couldn't get a hold of her."

Marnie told me more about Danielle, Helen's daughter, on the car ride over. Danielle's all right, she explained, just not reliable. Careerwise, she's very successful—she's a judge—but she doesn't own a cell phone because she thinks electronic devices mess with her natural energy.

Helen sighs. "Let me get a few of my things together." Turning to me, she adds, "You'll help me, Griffin?"

We gave her my real name, since Mitchell Mountainbottom has already been revealed as a lie.

"Of course, ma'am," I say. "Just tell me what you need moved."

Apparently packing a few things for the night means something different to me than it does to Helen, because we're there for an hour, collecting everything from a half dozen hairnets to three packages of expired cookies, which she was, and I quote, "thinking of giving Marnie anyway." Marnie and I exchange a look at that, and she bites her lip to keep from laughing.

The last thing to get packed is the crystal shrine. The spider has abandoned the black tourmaline, which Helen takes as evidence of its effectiveness. She suggests sharing said evidence with the building management, but Marnie tells her the night manager does not have a sense of humor or an appreciation for crystal therapy.

"Maybe Griffin can charm her," Helen says hopefully. "She has a weakness for young men. One of the other residents got her to overlook a fire safety issue because her grandson flexed his muscles for her."

"For one thing, that's terrifying," Marnie says. "For another, Griffin's not going to fake-flirt with someone so you can stay in your spider-riddled apartment." She smiles at me, her eyes warm and deep. "He only does that for me."

"There's nothing fake about it," I insist.

Several boxes later, we're on our way back to Marnie's house. Marnie's in the backseat, and Helen's up front next to me. She seems to have gotten over the whole spider episode, although it's obvious she doesn't like the thought of her home being sprayed, even after the night manager assured her, at length, that an eco-friendly solution would be used.

"You know," Helen says, turning in her seat to glance back at Marnie, "you didn't mention a word about your young man on your last visit. I should be vexed with you. I would have given him one of those fruitcakes."

"Aunt Helen, Christmas was several weeks ago. You shouldn't be giving anyone those fruitcakes."

She makes a dismissive gesture. "Oh, you and your sell-by dates. My gentleman callers were more than happy to take my fruitcakes."

There's a dirty joke hidden in there, but I bite it back.

"Thank you, Helen," I say. "I'd be happy to have one another time. Maybe we can even bake something together."

"You bake?" Marnie asks in surprise.

I glance at her in the rearview mirror, taking in her big eyes, her swept-back hair. Her lips look slightly swollen. I like the thought that she'll look in the mirror later and notice. That she'll think about what we did against that wall—and what we could have done if we'd had more privacy.

Would you really have taken her if you could? asks a voice in my head. Maybe it's my cock asking for some clarification about when he can enter the game.

I'm not sure.

I can't remember ever wanting a woman this much, but something's still holding me back. Maybe it's that I know my feelings for her have the potential to grow into something I can't control or compartmentalize. Maybe it's that I still don't think I have it in me to take care of someone the way they deserve, even though I've spent my life practicing.

"Griffin?" Marnie asks, and another glance in the rearview mirror shows me the questioning wrinkle on her brow.

"I know how to bake," I say, even though I'm guessing she's no longer interested in her original question.

Growing up, I had to learn a lot of things most kids didn't. How to make food for myself and my dad when he was too strung out to prepare anything. How to get to school if I missed the bus. How to lie to guidance counselors. But there are better memories with baking, of Ma teaching me that sugar cookie recipe and Gary and I decorating her gingerbread people at Christmas. He was in his twenties by the time I came along, but he still did it with good humor, the way he does everything.

"I'd like that very much," Helen says with satisfaction. She taps my arm and then lets her hand linger. "Goodness. I'd forgotten what a young man feels like."

"Aunt Helen," Marnie exclaims, "stop groping my boyfriend."

It makes me smile to hear her call me that, even if she's just saying it to fit the story we've told, and I can't seem to stop.

nineteen

MARNIE

WHEN WE GET to the house, my aunt glows at the sight of the Christmas tree in the corner. "How jolly!" she exclaims, seeming genuinely pleased. "I've always wanted to leave my tree up all year."

That really makes me think it's time to take it down, Drew's chore or not.

Griffin and I see Aunt Helen up to the guest bedroom, which is where Drew and I store all of our unneeded crap that we haven't yet summoned the energy to sort through. She promptly declares it has bad chi, though, and I have to resettle her in Drew's room, which meets her approval for . . . reasons. He *is* neat, but she isn't, so it's hard to believe that's the motivating factor. Griff and I get her some fresh sheets and leave her to it, because she says she's tired and needs her beauty rest.

We go downstairs with the intention of watching *Empire Strikes Back*, which Griffin claims is the "best" Star Wars movie, but that doesn't end up happening. We sit on the couch together, turned toward each other, my whole body aware of our knees touching, and get to talking about baking, of all things. He tells me about his cookie tradition with his mom and Gary, how they used to help her decorate dozens of gingerbread men as public figures, not because they liked it, but because she got such enjoyment out of figuring out who they were supposed to be. Sometimes Griffin's dad would even take part, back when things were good.

I like imagining Griffin like that, a little boy trying to make his stepmother smile.

"And what about your family's world-famous sugar cookies?" I ask.

He laughs, his eyes twinkling. "They're only world famous in Gary's mind. Ma used to make them for us as a reward—good grades for me, a promotion for him, that kind of thing—and he believes in those cookies like a kid believes in Santa."

"Speaking of Santa," I say, nodding to the tree, "I'm beginning to think this is a problem."

"Why?" he says, clearly amused. "Because your aunt approves?"

"Precisely. That's when you know you've done something problematic."

He gets up and holds out a hand for me. I take it, and he easily lifts me up. "So let's do something to fix it."

Which is how we wind up taking down the Christmas tree together. A part of me had been glad to leave the chore to Drew, because it was, objectively, a depressing one. Not only because it's always less fun to take the tree down than to put it up, but because it had been our first Christmas without our father.

To be honest, I think Drew played the system on the chore wheel. He knew I didn't want to do it, and while I highly doubt he was looking forward to it, he's a good brother. I mean, not good enough to actually take the tree down or clean the fridge before his extended vacation, but I think I'll keep him anyway.

"You know, my dad really loved Christmas," I find myself saying as I wrap ornaments and tuck them into their box. "It made *him* like a kid. He always put our presents under the tree after we were asleep, even after Drew and I were all grown up."

Griffin smiles at me. "That's a nice memory."

"Yeah," I say, my throat clogging with emotion as I wrap up one of Dad's favorite ornaments, a flamingo in a top hat. "It really made things special. I think it made him sad when Clair stopped coming home for Christmas, but she didn't want to leave our mother alone, and she had plenty of other things to do." Parties with famous people. Club openings. Photo shoots.

He just nods and takes down a snowman that has not aged well. Its chipped smile has become a thing of nightmares. Weirdly, I'm still fond of it. Maybe more so.

"Dad and I stopped celebrating after we left Asheville," he says. "It was more of my stepmother's thing."

He sounds sad as he says it, and I remember he was only sixteen when he left. Still a kid, really.

"Does that mean you didn't do the whole Santa thing before they got married?"

"Not really," he says, giving me a half smile. "But you don't have to feel bad about it, Marnie. There's something to be said for getting an early dose of realism. My dad struggled enough to be a parent. He wasn't putting on any red suits. I was lucky if he remembered to buy groceries."

Something twists inside of me. "If you're trying to make me feel better about your lack of Christmas, you're doing a shitty job of it. I feel like dousing you with hot chocolate and cookies immediately. What toy did you want as a child? It was an Easy-Bake Oven, wasn't it? I'm totally getting you one."

"Caught me." Laughing, his eyes bright with amusement, he gestures to the clock. "It's almost ten. Don't you have work in the morning? You don't seem like the kind of woman who's late to work."

I wonder what kind of woman I *do* seem like. The kind who lets her borrowed boyfriend pleasure her on top of a bar? The kind who lies to her sister? I should probably feel ashamed of those things, but strangely I don't. Because I've felt more alive in the last two weeks than I have for months, maybe longer.

"We've already established my job sucks," I say. "Plus, I want to see about this cookie recipe of yours."

"I hate to break it to you," he says, taking down a glass ornament and carefully wrapping it. It's surprising that his hands, so large and strong, can be so gentle. It dawns on me that we've almost finished taking down the ornaments. The task had been looming large in my mind—and Drew's, apparently—but with Griffin, it didn't seem to take any time at all. "But I'm ninety percent sure it's the Pillsbury recipe. Just don't tell my stepbrother."

There it is again. Stepbrother.

"Why do you call him that?" I blurt, too curious for my own good.

"Because he is," he says. "You see, when two people love each other very much, and they get married, and they both have kids already . . ."

It's a joke, but there's no humor in his delivery.

"Very funny." I'm a little hurt, actually. Even though he shared with me tonight, there's still so much I don't know. In comparison, he knows everything. Logic suggests there's less to know, that my life has been . . . boring, for lack of a better word. But I still want to know him, and it feels like he's shutting a door.

He must see it, because he sighs, gently unfastening an ornament from the tree, and says, "I guess I've never felt like I deserve to call him anything different."

"But you love him, and he loves you," I say. Even though I was only with them for a short time today, it was as obvious as seeing rain in the weather report when raindrops are already hitting you in the face. "Isn't that what makes a family?"

"Our parents were only married for five years," he says flatly. "He was alive for twenty years before he even knew I existed."

"Doesn't make you love him any less."

He doesn't deny it. "I left him," he says flatly. "I left him and my stepmother. I didn't reach out or answer any of their messages, and I stayed away long enough that they didn't know if I was alive or dead. I wasn't much of a brother, or much of a son. I don't have any right to claim them, legal or otherwise."

"But you were a kid when that happened," I say, clutching an ornament to my chest. "You were a minor who had limited control over your father's decisions."

"I was perfectly capable of picking up a phone, Marnie. Writing an email."

"Kids make mistakes."

"It was no mistake."

His mood has soured, I can tell. I feel a stab of guilt. I want to know more, but I shouldn't push him. Hasn't he already put himself on the line for me? I don't have a right to this knowledge, just a hunger for it.

"I'm so—"

"Marnie," he says, his expression brooding. "Don't apologize to me."

"How do you know I was going to apologize to you?" I say, trying to lead us toward sturdier ground. "You didn't lie to *me* about my favorite ancestral recipe."

His mouth twitches. "I don't want to break Gary's spirit."

"You're trying to protect him," I say softly. "The same way he protects you. Drew and I are like that too." My smile tips up. "So was my dad. You know . . . he always kept a stash of cash in the house *just in case*, like he was one of those old men who didn't believe in banks even though he worked in one. I think maybe he imagined himself becoming Liam Neeson in *Taken* if anyone ever tried to kidnap us."

He smiles slightly. "I don't think Liam ever paid anyone anything in those movies. Seems like he made sure they were the ones who paid the price."

"Yeah, maybe he wanted to be Liam Neeson without the whole violence thing. My dad was like Aunt Helen. A peacekeeper. Sometimes he was too much of one."

Griffin raises his brows. "Oh?"

I find myself telling him about all of those auditions my mother brought Sinclair and me on. The way she'd made us think it was our idea.

His lips set into a firm line. He doesn't look surprised, though, and I can't help but think of what he said to me last weekend—that I was lucky Mom and Sinclair left for Los Angeles without me. It's obvious he'd like to double down on that, but instead he says, "I'm sorry they made you think you had to do that."

"I didn't know I had a choice," I say. "The thing is . . . Griff. I don't think Sinclair felt like she had a choice either. This is her life now, and obviously it has serious perks, but I don't know how much of a say she's had in any of it." I look away for a second, our shared gaze too intense. "As much as I loved my dad, he didn't protect us from that."

"You don't believe she had anything to do with the video getting out." It's a statement, not a question.

"No. I don't think she'd do that to me." My mouth drifts up a little, an almost smile. "She'd flick me in the back, but she wouldn't stab me. And it goes both ways."

He rubs his jaw. "I should tell you . . . Damien found out she's having trouble with her new director. He says the guy's out to get her. The timing . . . let's just say she got a lot of good press from your engagement, and even more from paying for the wedding."

"Huh," I say. "I hadn't thought of it that way. I know all about that asshole, though."

"Oh?"

"Yeah. I'm not surprised he's giving her shit. He tried to hit on her, and she wasn't interested. He reacted the way most jackasses react to that kind of thing."

He lets his hand drop. "Aren't you worried about how this guy might use the information if he finds out you're involved with a convicted drug user? He could say your sister's been buying drugs from me."

I shake my head. "Sinclair's been calling me a lot since the breakup, but I rarely see her. That would be a stretch."

His mouth hitches up. "The tabloids make up half their stories. They live for stretches."

"I'm not worried about it," I insist.

He seems unappeased, but he says, "You know we can't rule out that your sister spread that video, Marnie. Talking about it in the press has made her look good too. And your mother . . . it sounds like she has a lot invested in Sinclair's career."

"I know," I say resolutely. "But family means something to me."

"And that's exactly what could be blinding you."

Something flickers in his eyes. Maybe I should be pissed at him for making accusations against Sinclair and my mother, but is he really saying anything I haven't considered myself?

I can't resent him or Nicole and Damien for pursuing all of the options. That's what this is all about—pulling my head out of the sand. And if I'm honest, what he's said isn't without merit. Still, I've had enough of a dose of reality for one night, thank you very much. So I take him by the hand and lead him into the kitchen.

"I think we both need some cheering up, so we're going to make *my* ancestral recipe." I take a couple of hot chocolate packets out of the cabinet. "Don't share it with anyone."

He laughs, some of his darkness slipping away, charm welling up in its place. It's strange, but his charm feels like it's as much a part of him as his emotional scars. Griffin is an intoxicating mix of light and darkness, like those cocktails he makes for me.

"I make no promises," he says. He puts his hands on my hips, sending a jolt through me. "I might want to steal it."

I squeal as he lifts me effortlessly onto the kitchen counter.

"You have a thing for putting me on counters," I say, suddenly breathless. It's exhilarating to have him here in my home, his hands on me.

"I do," he admits, shameless, stepping between my legs and crowding me. "I liked the way you had your legs wrapped around me earlier." He tucks hair behind my ear and takes the cocoa packets from me, setting them down. "I keep thinking about the way you taste, Marnie." He leans in, his big hands moving up my sides, setting off sparklers of need that settle in my core. "About seeing you splayed out on my bar. Spread your legs wider for me."

"Why should I?" I demand. "You've been very withholding with your cock."

"You have an obsession with my cock," he says, his lips tipping up. "I think I like it."

"You only think you do?" I reach for the band of his jeans.

He gives a little shake of his head. "Not right now."

Frustration pounds into me, allayed only a little when he reaches between my legs over my thick stockings and instantly finds my clit. His fingers rub around it while he looks at me.

"You're not going to make me forget what I want," I say breathily.

"I know," he says with a little smirk, circling and rubbing me with one hand while the other trails up and down my inner thigh. Then he goes for the band of my stockings, and because I'm all about taking what I can get when it comes to Griffin, I help him.

We've gotten them halfway down when I hear Aunt Helen coming down the stairs.

"Goodness," she says with amusement and absolutely no embarrassment, "have I interrupted something?"

Yes, and please go away.

Only I'd never say that to my aunt, so I settle for, "I got spiderwebs on my stockings. Griffin was helping me take them off."

His expression is downright wicked, and there's a pulsing in my core that says it wants more of him, now please, but it'll have to wait.

"Is everything okay, Aunt Helen?" I add, trying to focus on her.

"Yes, dear, but I find I'm not tired yet. I was thinking of having a snack."

"Yes, a snack sounds good," Griffin says.

Maybe I'm imagining it, because I am apparently a dirty, dirty girl, but I think there's a hint of insinuation in the remark, meant for me.

Dammit.

I expect Griffin to make his excuses and leave, since he probably has things he'd prefer to do than hang out with my septuagenarian aunt, but he doesn't. What happens is far more pleasant.

The three of us make sugar cookies together, using Betty Crocker's famous recipe, and even though we serve them up with the package hot chocolate, they *are* good.

After Griffin leaves, I surprise myself by taking down the rest of the ornaments. Monday is trash day, so in a few days I'll set the tree out on the curb to be hauled away.

It doesn't hurt as much as I thought it would. It feels like something manageable now, because we did most of the work together.

I'm starting to feel more like myself.

My mind is gooey and sluggish the next morning, my thoughts focused on Griffin. I should be worrying about what will inevitably be a dysfunctional night spent having drinks with my ex-boyfriend and my fake . . . well, sort-of fake . . . boyfriend. Instead, I find myself working on a new logo for Summer Nights. It should be simple, because the bar is simple—the kind of local dive that has permanent residents, like Reggie—but it should also be inviting enough to prompt interest in passersby *before* they see the sexy as sin man working behind the bar.

I end up going for a simple logo, a wave enclosed by a circle with a patch of yellow sand at the bottom and a single pink conch shell on top of it. The colors are bright and appealing—a promise of summer in what has every appearance of being a long winter. If it looks vaguely sexual, that's because I'm extremely sexually frustrated.

I'm working on the typography when my phone starts vibrating. It keeps it up like a vibrator that won't turn off, the number "unidentified." Personal calls are forbidden in the office, so much so that the HR guy actually disposed of one woman's phone after she took a personal call, although on second thought, maybe the perv was just looking for nude photos. Still, after a brief look around, I answer it.

Maybe it's Griffin.

"I can't fucking believe you," Sinclair seethes.

"Well, hello to you too," I say, even though my mind and heart are racing. Shit. I didn't give her a heads-up that Mitchell is actually Griffin. Good old Purple Shirt must have written something about it . . . but what? Did he reveal Griffin's secret?

"You and this *Griffin* have been playing me for a fool," Sinclair hisses. "I don't like being played for a fool."

It's on the edge of my tongue to tell her that no one particularly likes being played for a fool, and also that she's the one who offered up details about my personal life to a TV personality who has over three hundred bow ties in his wardrobe and frequently brags about that fact. But I don't. Because I'm too busy googling "Mitchell Mountainbottom and Sinclair Jones."

Air gushes out of me. There's nothing about Griffin's record in the blog article. It's a boring piece of clickbait for a site that has willingly named itself *C+ Celeb News*. The headline is no better— "Should Sinclair Jones Change Her Name to Sinc-Liar?"

The gist of it is that Griffin and I are both rude, Summer Nights charges exorbitant rates and is ungracious to their clientele, and Sinclair knowingly lied to poor, impressionable Mike Dickson because we asked her to. There's also a not-so-subtle implication that she's stupid for coming up with the name Mitchell Mountainbottom.

"Are you even listening to me?" she asks in my ear.

The answer is obviously no, but she won't like that anymore than she likes the rest of this situation.

"Yes, sorry," I say. Then I remember what Griffin told me about my constant apologies, and I'd like to reel it back in like a fish I've decided I'd like to fry and eat. "Actually . . . this guy never would have shown up at Griffin's bar if you hadn't shared that picture on broadcast television. I mean, according to the byline this blogger lives in Charlotte. He must have driven two hours to get this scoop. If you're looking for someone to blame, you can blame yourself."

"Excuse me?" she says.

She's pissed, but I am too, so I snap, "You're excused."

"This Griffin guy isn't a good influence on you. He's really a bartender?"

Her tone sets my teeth on edge, like there's something lewd about tending bar. I feel a surge of protectiveness toward Griffin, something I've felt for my friends and family but never for a man. "Yes."

"What the hell, Marnie? You have a degree from Vanderbilt."

"What the hell does that have to do with anything?" I ask, anger blooming inside of me—no, raging like a fire someone doused with alcohol. "Are you implying he's not my equal because he didn't go to college?"

"He didn't go to college?" she asks with a horror that's misplaced given she didn't go to college either. Maybe she thinks her millions make up for it. Maybe she hasn't yet figured out that plenty of people who've pursued higher education are ignorant and bad at their jobs, and it's no great signifier of a person's worth.

I glance around to check for eavesdroppers, then hiss furiously into my phone, "You've become such an elitist asshole since moving to LA. I'll have you know he's *extremely* smart. I'll bet he's read more books in the last week than you have in a year."

"You don't need to insult me to prop up your boyfriend," she says, which only feeds my fire, because isn't she insulting him to prop up herself? "You usually go for ambitious men. Men who have a very clear career trajectory. This guy isn't your type."

"Maybe that's a good thing." Also, while she's right in a sense, I have to wonder how much of that was my parents' influence—my father with his steady job, my mother with her high-handed beliefs about which endeavors were worth pursuing.

"And maybe not. Besides, this isn't a class thing. He's encouraging you to lie, and—"

"He did no such thing," I say, off the cuff. "It was *my* idea. Turns out I was sick of you sharing details of my life with complete strangers. Lo and behold, I was right to lie. It would have been smarter to tell you nothing at all."

She's quiet for a long moment, and the silence lances my heart like a needle. I went too far. I actually hurt her. It's not easy to hurt Sinclair. She was raised with a thick skin. My father didn't know this, but when we were girls, on the way to an audition, my mother used to pummel us with the kind of insults we'd likely be confronted with—reality checks, she called them—so we'd learn not to react. It didn't work in my case, but it *did* work for my sister. She learned to wear a mask, and sometimes she forgets to take it off. That's not to say there's not a real, living, breathing person behind it.

"I'm so—" I say on instinct, stopping myself halfway through.

"I don't like that you feel that way," she says in a small voice, her anger fizzled or buried. "If you didn't want me to talk about all of this . . . you should have said so."

I had. I'd told her directly and indirectly, and Andy, in a fit of pique, had suggested that maybe Grace should render the message in needlepoint to really hammer it home. But it wouldn't do any good to say so.

"I'm glad I'm coming to visit," Sinclair says after a beat.

I'm not, to be honest. But I don't actually want to hurt her, so I just say, "I'm glad too."

"You really like this guy, don't you?"

"Yes, I really do."

And the messed-up thing is that I mean it.

She sighs and says, "You should probably call Mom. She's upset you haven't directly told her anything about Griffin. I swear, she's just as eager as I am to meet him."

Maybe it's petty of me, but I feel like I shouldn't always have to be the one to reach out to *my* mother. She hasn't called or texted me since Christmas, when Drew and I had an awkward, listless video call with her and Sinclair that lasted all of three minutes. They spent the whole time talking about all the things they had to do, from social engagements with famous people to a joint spray tan appointment Sinclair had booked for them as a Christmas gift. Their Christmas present to us was a gift basket packed with expensive, gourmet food that didn't taste as good as it looked. As soon as they hung up, we exchanged a knowing look. I gestured to the bottle of wine in the basket and asked, "Mulled wine?"

"Fuck, yes," he said. Then he got up and grabbed the big pot from the cabinet and poured the entire bottle into it.

It was eleven in the morning.

"Well," my sister says, impatient. "Will you call her?"

"We'll see." The person I should really call is Drew, to tell him that we're about to get a visit. He'll be home on Sunday, though, and it'll be so much easier to explain all of this in person. Besides, I'm fairly sure his cell phone battery is dead by now, despite the battery packs and portable chargers he always brings, and probably out of range.

Sinclair sighs as if I've disappointed her in some fundamental way, again, and I feel guilty for inexplicable reasons.

As I hang up, I look up and jump at the sight of Val standing in front of my desk. Slow moving as he is, he probably overheard a good bit of our conversation.

"Personal call?" he asks, furrowing his brow.

"Yes," I say, because what the hell, if he fires me, at least I won't have to work up the nerve to quit. I can practically hear Andy in my head, singing, *and severance!*

"Your boyfriend?" he asks.

"My sister."

"She coming to visit anytime soon?" he asks, eyeing the phone hopefully.

"No," I lie.

His scowl suggests he doesn't believe me, or that he heard enough to know it's not true.

His gaze dips to the logo on my desktop. "That something you're mocking up for Tilton?" His brow furrows as he studies it. "It's good, but it'll never work. They're stepping away from white water rafting and fishing. Get this. Edgar James, the man Brock's teaming up with, is afraid of water. The man can fight a bear or live for months on the side of a mountain, but he almost drowned once, and now he's allergic to water."

He lifts a hand to his jaw, the action so slow I wonder if his brain misfired, like a malfunctioning robot. Finally, it meets his mark, and he says, "Make sure you don't mention any watersports tonight. Edgar is touchy. Brock's doing business with this guy, and we're looking to do business with both of them. Bygones and all that."

Everything he just said is absurd, from the implication that I might casually bring up watersports to a stranger to his supposition that I should forgive and forget already because it'll make everyone more comfortable.

"No watersports," I say with a nod, angling to get him out and away so I can send the article to Griffin and Nicole and Damien. And Andy and Grace, obviously.

"I'm counting on you to make tonight a success," he says, giving me a shallow nod.

"I brought cookies," I say with forced cheer. "They're in the break room."

They're not the ones from last night. No way would I give Val my sugar cookies. No, these are from Aunt Helen's stash, and I'm almost positive they're stale.

This is going to be the longest day of my life, without question.

Except I can't deny there's a part of me that doesn't much mind, because I'm going to see Griffin. Because I'm going to get to pretend, to everyone else, and a little bit to myself, that I really am his girlfriend.

GRIFFIN

"YOU'VE GOT to be fucking kidding me," I say, even though it's obvious from Damien's expression that he is not, in fact, fucking kidding me.

It's the afternoon before what's sure to be the shittiest happy hour I've ever attended, and I'm about to turn the place over to him and Nicole before opening.

He shrugs and leans forward on his stool, propping his elbows on the wood planks of the bar. "That's what I heard."

"Mighhhhty suspicious, wouldn't you say?" Nicole says.

Yes, it is pretty goddamn suspicious.

They finally met with Brock's former assistant earlier. Turns out Brock asked her to make a large cash deposit into his personal account the day after the wedding-that-wasn't. It was the only time he'd ever asked her to do that kind of thing. The business doesn't usually deal with cash, unless it's in the form of tips, and that money typically goes to the tour operators, not the director's personal piggy bank.

"Smells like a bribe," Damien says. "See what you can find out tonight. It's possible someone paid him to leave Marnie."

Goddamn. I mean, obviously I'm relieved she's not married, but

203

if the same person convinced Brock to leave her *and* distributed that video . . . it's diabolical. It suggests there's someone who has been actively working to destroy her. I can't imagine why anyone would want to do such a thing. Maybe they're jealous. Maybe they look at her and see what I do—a strong woman with the potential to do and be whatever the fuck she wants.

My mind skips to her sister, to the way she manipulates Marnie, but I can't make it square. Why go through the effort of paying for a wedding only to sabotage it? It's not outside the range of possibility—Sinclair came out looking good, regardless—but it seems unlikely.

So who else would have done it?

I groan and run a hand through my hair. "We need more suspects."

"We're still in the *everyone's a suspect* phase," Damien says. "But her brother gets home on Sunday, and the sister and mother are coming for a visit next week. We need to talk to all of them, obviously. We're going to have Marnie throw a party while Sinclair's visiting and invite as many of the people who came to the wedding as possible."

"I think we can safely eliminate Aunt Helen from the suspect list," Nicole says. Lifting a finger, she adds, "Which means we should probably recruit her to our cause. I could see her being a Mata Hari type." Her eyes light up with the thought. She's been acting like Helen is some kind of deity ever since she saw those sex videos on her phone.

Damien considers this for a second and then gives a slight nod.

"She's not going to be there tonight," I say.

"Yes, that's factual," Nicole says. She leans forward and pats my arm. "See if you can find out about the maybe-bribe."

I scoff at the suggestion. "Why the hell would Brock tell her boyfriend he took a bribe to leave her?"

"You raise a good point," Damien says. "That's going to be a hard sell."

"Luckily you could sell sand to someone who lives in a desert," Nicole says.

"Actually, fuck getting information from him. I'm not so sure I can talk to him without punching him. I saw that video. He has a very punchable face."

Not to mention he took advantage of Marnie by proposing like he did, then proceeded to hurt her in front of most of the people she knows. The thought makes me grit my teeth and flex my hands. It makes me remember that prison wasn't just a long stream of reading and working out like I told Marnie. Some people only respond to violence.

"Beats me," Nicole says brightly, seeming to derive too much amusement from this whole thing. "But we're counting on you, Obi-Wan. *You're our only hope.* Just don't get into a lightsaber measuring contest. He'd obviously lose, and men get pissy about that sort of thing."

I roll my eyes. She kept poking at me about what Marnie and I did the other night, and I insisted that all we did was watch Star Wars. So she's taken to quoting the movies around me, usually incorrectly. Her teasing is mildly amusing, but I refuse to let on.

I glance up at the clock and slide out from behind the bar. "Don't do anything I wouldn't do."

Damien salutes me. "Don't beat up Marnie's ex-fiancé. He's the sort to press charges."

They both pat me on the back as I leave the bar, acting like I'm a player being sent out onto the field. I suppose I am.

"I can still help you figure out what to wear," Nicole calls after me.

I give her the finger as I walk away.

"You love me," she shouts.

"Debatable."

It's not, really. I *do* love them. But the people you love can fuck you over better than anyone else.

I feel stupidly nervous when I pull into the driveway of Marnie's house, like I'm a kid picking up his prom date. It strikes me that I've only known Marnie for two weeks, yet I can't remember the last time I felt this close to a woman. It gives me an uneasy feeling, like the other shoe is about to drop on my head.

Trying to shake it off, I get out and head to the door.

It flies open, revealing Helen in a red muumuu. "Oh, it's you, handsome boy," she says, grabbing my arms and ushering me inside. "I thought it was one of my gentleman callers."

"Who says it's not?" I say with a smile. Nicole's not the only one who finds Helen amusing.

She laughs long and loud. "Bertrand said he would collect me after management finishes with my apartment."

Her expression slips, and I know she's worrying about whatever they're doing in there.

"I'm sorry you had to leave," I say.

"It's not that," she says, tapping her lips. "It's those poor spiders. We were getting along just fine."

It's on the edge of my tongue to tell her there's no peacefully coexisting with creatures that could kill you the second they get pissed off or scared. Something tells me we're not going to see eye to eye, though, and the situation is being resolved.

Besides, Marnie walks out of the bathroom wearing a glossy green dress with golden buttons up the middle and high-heeled leather boots. She's gorgeous, and I get that prom feeling again, even though, hell, I never *did* go to senior prom. We'd moved away by then, and although I went to school for a while, I dropped out before senior year to work. School became a memory of my other life, the one that had skated toward normal but never stuck the landing.

"Oh, you're staring at her like Bogart stared at Bacall," Helen says delightedly.

I'm shocked to feel my ears burning, mostly because there shouldn't be any blood left in my head. Just from looking at Marnie, I'm fighting a hard-on, but maybe that's because I haven't buried myself inside her yet. I've been thinking about it, though. Holy shit, have I been thinking about it.

I should be worrying about Purple Shirt trying to dig up dirt on me, Marnie's sister supplying him with the shovel. I should be thinking about what's going to happen when Sinclair and her mother roll into town. Because I'll need to walk a fine line with them—to wheedle information out of them without pissing off Marnie.

Because I don't want to piss her off.

I want to make her moan with pleasure. I want to make her body writhe with it, the way it did on my bar, but I don't want to piss her off. No, I want her to be happy.

"I have no idea who those people are, Aunt Helen," Marnie says, self-consciously tucking hair behind her ear.

"You look gorgeous," I tell her.

"So do you," she blurts. "I mean . . . you look really handsome."

"Yes, he does," Helen agrees. She circles around me as if examining a quarter horse.

Marnie gives her a look that's at once chiding and fond, then shifts her gaze to me. "Let's get out of here."

I grab her coat from the tree by the door and help her shrug it on. Then, because I want to, I take her hand.

"Do everything I would do!" Helen croons, waving at us as we leave.

Marnie mutters under her breath, "God forbid." Then she calls out, "If you invite Bertrand in, please take it upstairs. Drew has a black light, and he is *not* afraid to use it."

Helen laughs as if she told a merry joke, then shuts the door.

Marnie turns to me, a smile playing on her lips. "We're definitely going to come back to her and Bertrand doing it on the couch, aren't we?"

"I hope not," I say.

Mostly because I'm hoping to take Marnie home with me tonight.

We're mostly silent on the drive. I know I need to tell her about Brock and the cash deposit. She may know who'd be in a position to offer him a sizeable payoff. But she's nervous as hell on the way to the party, and I don't want to make it worse. It makes me fume inside, to see what her ex is doing to her, even now. So I pull over on the side of the road several blocks away from his house.

"I think you can find closer parking," she says, waving to the open stretch of road in front of us. "He has a really long driveway, actually. All the cars will probably fit."

"I'm not getting stuck in that asshole's driveway," I say. "But I pulled over because you're nervous. You don't want to walk in there looking nervous."

Her brow lifts. "Shit, really? I thought I was doing a good job of hiding it."

"Here's the thing about pretending," I say, my mouth hitching up a little. "You have to believe in what you're selling, at least a little."

She shifts in her seat so she's facing me. "Like with us?"

"No, Marnie," I say, touching her arm. "I've never pretended with you. We just put on a little performance for your sister. Same as we're going to do tonight."

There's still some uncertainty in her eyes, so I lean between our seats and kiss her gently, then tuck her hair behind her ear. "Let's go show these assholes what you're made of."

She surprises me by taking my hand and squeezing it. "I couldn't do this without you."

"Yes, you could," I rebut, because it's true, and I can't have her thinking that she needs me. "You're a lot stronger than you give yourself credit for."

"I'm trying to be."

Something steels in her, and it occurs to me that I shouldn't be treating her like someone who needs to be protected, like someone who's not perfectly capable of making decisions on her own.

"Marnie, Damien told me something I should tell you before we go in there."

"Oh?" She peers at me, her expression shifting. "I'm not going to like this, am I?"

"I'm afraid not. He found out that Brock asked his ex-assistant to make a substantial cash deposit into his personal account the day after the wedding was cancelled."

She gapes at me. "Does that mean . . . ?"

"Maybe," I say, rubbing circles into her hand. "It's definitely odd."

I expected her to be upset, but her reaction surprises me.

"That asshole accepted money not to marry me?" she asks, pulling her hand away.

She's not sad, she's *angry*. Her eyes tell the story, and I can't help but smile.

That's my girl.

"I was worried it would upset you."

"Oh, I'm upset all right. I want to walk in there, kick him in the balls in front of all of his sycophants, and leave."

"I'd like to see that," I admit. "It would be sexy as hell. But you can't do that. You'd get fired, for one, and for another, we wouldn't find out about the possible payout."

"Nicole and Damien asked you to talk to him," she says.

"They did." I run a hand over my beard. "I'd be lying if I said I was looking forward to it."

"But you'll do it for me," she says, looking into my eyes. "Thank you for that."

"Is there anyone you can think of who might have given him that money, Marnie?" She starts shaking her head, then stops. Something flickers across her face. She glances out the window before looking back at me. "Maybe," she admits. "But I'd rather not say until you've talked to Brock, okay?"

I'm disappointed. I want to know what's going on in her head, but I have too many secrets of my own to go mining for hers.

"Okay. Ready?"

She regards me for a second, then leans over and gives me a quick kiss, energy zipping between us even from that simple contact. "Now I am."

Who can blame me if I'm smiling as I make the rest of the drive?

I park on the street outside the house. When I come around to her side of the car, I help her out and take her hand.

"I can get out by myself, you know," she says, though her tone is teasing.

"Like I said, we're putting on a show."

She glances around and says, "No one's watching us."

"I didn't say who it was for." I point to a cardinal in a nearby tree. "I think we impressed the fuck out of that bird."

I get a smile from her, and though it's a weak smile, it's still a damn fine sight.

We pass the tall trees bordering the property, Marnie's small hand tucked in mine as she makes purposeful steps beside me, no sign of nerves in her now. I feel a surge of pride.

We snake up the driveaway, and I have to bite my tongue, because holy shit, this guy has money. Why would someone whose driveway is this long need a cash bribe?

Of course, most rich people aren't like Damien and Nicole. For most of them, there's no such thing as too rich.

The long driveway is already full of cars, and the land behind the tree hedge, which is obviously there to shield Brock from the prying eyes of his less fortunate neighbors, is carefully sculpted, with plants, currently leafless, studding the manicured lawn. Something tells me Brock didn't plant them himself.

The house, when it comes into view, is one of those modern constructions that have been springing up across town. Lots of windows and angles, not a lot of the personality I love in the old bungalows and arts and crafts homes like Marnie's.

I sneak a glance at her. If this is what she wanted a few months ago, I can't imagine why she'd be interested in a man like me. Then again, she's asked about my cock at least half a dozen times in the last forty-eight hours. Maybe it's obvious what she wants.

I'm no prude. Usually, she'd only need to ask once for it to be a done deal, but it's different with Marnie . . .

I don't have time to chase that thought to its natural conclusion, because we're approaching the door.

"Remember," I say. "No kicking him in the balls. Or at least wait until we're ready to leave. It could be a good note to go out on."

Her smile is less tentative this time, and I feel the glow of having done something right.

The door opens before we can knock, and I'd know the tall, pale man who opened it was Brock even if I hadn't looked him up online. It's the proprietary way he looks at her, like she's a snack he set aside for later. It makes me bristle before he even says a word, and I release her hand and wrap an arm around her back. The guy's wearing a charcoal gray suit, which seems like a poor showing for a so-called outdoorsman, not to mention an overly formal choice for a reception being held at his own house.

"Brock," she says, her tone conveying how unimpressed she is.

I'm glad I told her about the money. Her anger seems to have restored something to her.

Brock reaches forward as if he wants to hug her or maybe kiss her cheek, but she rocks back, leaning into my arm. I wrap it more tightly around her.

"Marnie, I'm so glad you could make it," he says, recovering quickly. "I've been hoping we could talk."

"Which is why you invited me to this little gathering through Val? Most people would have texted."

"Some conversations are better had in person," he says, his gaze flicking to me. His eyes are pale blue, like tinted glass. I instantly dislike him. Actually, fuck it, I disliked him the moment I saw that video.

"Hi," I say. "I'm Marnie's boyfriend, Griffin."

His eyes pinch as he takes in my leather jacket and button-down shirt and finds me lacking. "Yes, I saw the article this morning."

"Oh? Do you have a Google alert on her or something?" I ask, raising an eyebrow. "That's weird."

"Of course not," he says, taking a slight step back as if he feels physically threatened. "No hard feelings, man." His gaze slides to Marnie. "I meant what I said to Val. I want to let bygones be bygones."

As if *he* has anything to forgive.

"Of course not," I say, borrowing his phrase. "If anything, I should be thanking *you*. If you'd made wiser decisions, I never would have met Marnie. Now, we heard there'd be drinks?"

His lip curls with dislike, but he nods toward the interior of the house, where several people are gathered in little knots in a cavernous great room with a ceiling that goes up a story. A bar is set up in back. I would have been more comfortable behind it. "Marnie knows where the coatroom is."

A coatroom. Fuck.

It's a room as large as my bedroom, it turns out, lined with rails and hangers. We deposit our coats without comment, and I lead Marnie back out into the great room.

My gaze catches on a couple standing near the back fireplace, which looks like it's never once hosted a fire. "You've got to be fucking kidding me."

But once again, they're not. It's Nicole and Damien, sipping on cocktails. She's wearing a slinky black dress that probably cost as much as my couch. Let's be real, it probably cost many times more than my couch. He's wearing a suit. Was there a dress code memo that I missed?

twenty-one

MARNIE

I'M ANGRY. And God, it feels *good.*

Someone offered money to Brock to do this to me, and he took it? Even if the person who offered it is who I suspect, and even if they did it for the reason I suspect, it paints a pretty clear picture of the mistake I almost made. Marrying that man would have been a catastrophe. Dating him was bad enough, and the fact that I showed up at the altar speaks volumes about what I was going through at the time.

Then there's the way he greeted us, acting as if he wanted to pull out his dick to start a measuring contest with Griffin. The nerve!

I'm boiling with all of it as Griffin hustles me toward Nicole and Damien. Maybe my first reaction to seeing them should have been panic. After all, they're definitely loose cannons, and my boss is here, eating canapes by the food set up next to the picture windows. But they're undoubtedly on Team Marnie, and I'm happy to have as many Team Marnie friends as I can get.

"What are you doing here?" Griffin asks them in a pissed-off undertone as we get closer.

"We were invited guests," Nicole says with a grin. "Didn't I mention? Turns out Brock's looking for investors for his new collaboration with the mountain man."

She nods toward a man standing in a group at the other side of the room. It's Edgar James. I recognize him from all the fan-boying Brock used to do. In a room of suits, he's the only one wearing hiking boots. He looks like he fits in about as well as . . . well, Griffin.

"There's no way you got randomly invited," Griff says tightly.

"No, but Damien *does* know how to make the right comments to the right people." She gives him a suggestive look, and he snaps his teeth together to mime biting her.

Griffin glances back and forth between them. His arm is still around my back, and he makes no move to remove it. Neither do I. "You said you were leaving this to me."

"And we are," Damien says. "But you may need a distraction. We're the distraction. Well, part of it."

"DeeDee's coming later too," Nicole says brightly. I'd correct her, but I'm assuming she's just given Andy a nickname at this point.

"Who's tending bar?" Griff asks.

"Leah came in," she answers. "She brought a friend to help out."

"I don't like this," he says.

"Me neither," I offer. "Any of it. Let's get some drinks to dull the pain."

There's a stormy look on his face, and some of my own anger trickles away at the sight. I'd like to smooth his face. I'd like to make cookies with him again and laugh and forget about the stupid video. I'd like to take him back to his apartment and finish what we've started. But we're here for a reason, several of them actually, and it's time for me to finish the other things I've started too.

We get a couple of old-fashioneds at the bar, but Val waylays us on our way back to Nicole and Damien's table.

Worse, he's with Purple Shirt, the reporter from the bar yesterday, although today he's had the nerve to wear a blue button-down, thus impinging our nickname for him. His presence can mean nothing good, especially since he lives in Charlotte. Does he believe in pursuing our story so much he shelled out for an expensive hotel room?

"I want to introduce you to my friend, Marnie," Val says in his best Godfather voice.

"We've met," I say crisply.

"Not officially," says the man formerly known as Purple Shirt. "I'm Jim." He reaches a hand out for a shake. When I don't reciprocate, he slowly lowers it at his side. From the look on his face, I expect this happens often.

Val gives me a dark look. "Jim here is going to be writing a piece about the party."

"Interesting," Griffin says. He looks downright intimidating right now, his eyes hooded, his handsome face in a glower, and if Jim aka Purple Shirt were a smarter man, he'd retreat right out of the room. "I figured he just wrote puff pieces about celebrities."

"Well, Edgar James *is* here," I say.

Jim sniffs. "You said there were no hard feelings, Val."

"No hard feelings for Brock," I say. "You? You're a different story. You upset my sister."

For a second Jim looks surprised, but then he laughs with what appears to be genuine amusement. "Who do you think invited me?"

The implication is that *she* did. But I don't believe it. She's good at pretending, sure, but she's never been the sort to prostrate herself before men. He called her "Sinc-Liar." He's not the guy who's going to get her exclusives.

"Nicole and Damien," I guess.

"Got it in one," Jim says, playfully enough, but his expression is a little sulky. He clearly hoped he could get one over on me.

"They thought you might want to write about Brock's new collaboration?" I ask. "Edgar James *is* a big name."

It's true, but my gut tells me Nicole and Damien had a different reason for inviting him. Something's going to go down, and they want *him* to write about it. Why they chose someone who seems inclined to dislike us, I'll never know, but so be it.

"Something like that," he says. Angling his head to study me, he asks, "What's it like to be here, Marnie? To be back in the house that would have been yours?"

I feel Griffin stiffen beside me, as if he's preparing to act in some way, and I wrap an arm around his waist, keeping him put.

"How do you know we weren't going to move into my place?" I tell Jim, leaving the *you asshole* part silent.

He looks around, soaking in the immense picture windows and vaulted ceilings, the gorgeous wood floors. "Were you?" he asks, lifting his eyebrows. "I heard you live in your childhood home."

"You've heard a lot of things," Griffin says in a seething undertone.

I can *feel* his rage. It's rumbling through his chest, his whole body, and it's not just directed toward Jim. He's pissed at Nicole and Damien. They didn't let him in on this for some reason. Maybe because they knew he wouldn't like it.

Griffin snarls, "You—"

"Hey, it's my buddy Purple Shirt," Nicole calls out, her voice merry as she pushes her way to the bar. Literally. "Get me a soda water for this guy. I know what he likes."

Jim smiles at her like a sycophant, suggesting he's somehow learned that she has both money and connections, but I can detect the annoyance buried beneath it. He's probably still sore about the ten-dollar seltzer from the bar. Or maybe it's the nickname he doesn't care for. "Your friends are certainly interesting," he comments.

It's Val's turn to look surprised. "You know Nicole and Damien?"

"They're close, personal friends of ours," I say, tightening my grip on Griffin.

Val cogitates on what I told him, probably trying to figure out how my connection to them can benefit him. He still hasn't figured out a way to capitalize on Sinclair, though, so he probably shouldn't hold his breath. "And this is your boyfriend?" he asks, nodding to Griffin.

Griffin puts his free arm around me, possibly to avoid giving Val a shake, so now we're standing like two high school kids with their hands in each other's back pockets. "Yes," he says. "I'm Griffin."

"How'd you two meet?"

Griffin glances at me. I take a long sip of my drink, leaving him to answer the question. Smirking a little, he says, "We have a mutual passion for the original Star Wars trilogy. We met at a fan convention."

A laugh nearly escapes me, and I choke a little.

"Really, Marnie," Val says, tilting his head slightly. "I had no idea you were such a big fan. Which of the movies is your favorite?"

"*The Empire Strikes Back*," I reply, stealing a look at Griffin. His lips twitch tellingly.

"My nickname for her is Padawan," he says. I'm stuck between admiring his improvisational skills and being annoyed.

Nicole slings an arm around Jim's shoulders. No doubt he wants to shake her off, but instead he thanks her for the soda water he almost certainly didn't want.

Damien approaches them with a drink in his hand. Lifting an eyebrow, he says, "Making a move on my girl?"

Jim nearly drops his soda water in his haste to duck away from her.

"Just joking, buddy," Damien says, clapping him on the back, a smile transforming his face. "Good to see you again. We love seeing our patrons out in the open."

"Yes. Such a privilege to see you. So you're interested in investing in Brock's project with Edgar James?" Jim asks.

"Why else would we be here?" Nicole asks him blankly, and I have to fight a smile.

Someone rings a bell at the other end of the room, and we all swivel to look. It's Brock, and I feel a moment of pure gratitude that I didn't marry him, however nice it would be to move into a house with windows that aren't a hundred years old.

I mean, a bell? For God's sake . . .

"Did he used to ring that to summon you to the bedroom?" Nicole asks in a whisper that at least half a dozen people hear.

Griffin tenses again. I finish my drink and set the empty cup on a nearby high-top table.

His drink is still full, but he sets it down next to mine.

"It's okay," I tell him in an undertone. "It's . . . all of this is okay, Griff."

I'm surprised by how much I mean it. The anger I felt when we arrived has largely seeped away, and my heart doesn't feel raw or even tender. If anything, being here has proven to me how awful it would have been if the wedding had gone off as planned. Still, Griffin gives me a look that suggests I must be at a different reception than the one he's attending.

Brock clears his throat dramatically, then says, "Thank you all for being here this evening. I'm so excited to begin this new chapter with Edgar James."

He motions toward the guy in hiking boots, who seems a little displeased at being singled out. He looks like he's not quite sure how he wandered in here, among these suited people who look like they belong at some sort of black-tie benefit rather than a casual afterwork gathering. He's tan and muscular, with dark hair, almost black, and eyes to match.

"All of you know how much I value our—"

There's a knock at the door, and Brock frowns at it as if it offended him.

Another knock lands.

He holds up a finger to us and goes to open it, letting in Andy. She's wearing a black coat over a red dress that makes her look like an actual goddess, her hair down and loose. There's no sign of Chet.

Brock's frown deepens, possibly because Andy has no real excuse to be here solo, but he must be worried about pissing me off because he motions for her to come in. Her eyes light up when she notices Griffin and me, and she dispenses of her coat and makes her way to us.

"Where's Chet?" I whisper as she gets close.

"We broke up," she tells me with a shrug. "I intended to stick it out until after this party, but he did something so utterly douchey he left me with no choice. I figured there was no reason I should let being single stop me."

I'd like to ask more questions, but there's no chance.

"Sorry for the interruption," Brock says with conspicuous passive-aggression. "I just wanted to say that I'm pleased to be part of this collaboration, even more so because Val and his team will be working with us. As many of you know, Marnie and I ended our engagement quite suddenly . . ."

"Is that what you call it?" Andy calls out.

Griffin's posture has tensed further, as if every muscle in his body is tightly wound. I rub his back, and he looks down at me, the rage in his eyes softening. I feel a pull of wanting, and I'm again hit with the knowledge that this man means more to me than Brock, a man I agreed to marry, ever did.

Brock's face flushes. "It wasn't my finest moment," he says, "but we've made amends. I'm grateful she's here this evening with her new partner." He nods toward us. "There's no one I'd trust more to help us with the branding for my joint venture with Edgar."

"Are the white water rafting excursions cancelled?" someone calls out.

"Yes," Brock says, gesturing toward Edgar James. "We're moving in a different direction, one I couldn't be happier with. Our focus is going to be on hiking excursions and extreme camping."

There's a smattering of grumbles, and one guy calls out, "I'm a river raft guide. Does this mean I'm fired?"

Brock's gaze cuts through the crowd toward the speaker. From his slight wince, it's obvious the answer's yes, but he gives a feeble shrug. "We're going to be moving some staff around, but the objective is to grow, not to shrink. Edgar, will you say a few words?"

Edgar moves to the front of the room.

"Nature is our friend until it's our enemy," he says, his tone bleak. "Four months ago, I almost drowned on a white water rafting expedition. I'll never forget what it felt like when the water tried to suck me under. It was like an old friend had turned against me. The only person who can fully understand an experience like that is someone who's been through it too." He indicates Brock with a nod. "Which is why I'm so grateful to have met Brock. After my accident, he reached out to me with a kind gift and a note revealing that he'd recently been through the same experience. He said he could no longer imagine running white water tours and river expeditions. It was a sentiment I shared, one hundred percent, and our partnership grew from there."

He pats Brock on the back, and apparently he's every bit as powerful as he looks, because Brock lurches forward a bit. I notice it in a kind of haze because my brain is stuck on WTF. I mean . . . *that didn't happen*. Like, not even a little. Brock and I were together back then, and he's the kind of person who complains for twenty minutes about a hangnail.

If he'd almost drowned, I would've heard about it at least a thousand times.

twenty-two

MARNIE

BROCK'S FACE is pale as he smiles at Edgar James. He obviously didn't expect the whole story to pour out of the other man.

"I didn't tell many people about my near drowning," he says with the solemnity of a man who's afraid he's been caught in a lie.

"Of course not," Edgar says, oblivious. "It's hard for an outdoorsman to admit to a thing like that." His gaze catches on Brock's suit, though, and a little furrow forms in his brow. It isn't entirely lost on him that Brock doesn't look like much of an outdoorsman.

I want to shout out, "Bullshit!" but I'm very aware that both Jim and my boss are present. The last thing I need is a follow-up article that paints me as a bitter ex. An unsupportive liar. Because that's what Brock and Val would say I am.

Maybe the truth would eventually come out, and maybe it wouldn't. Sinclair's director got another actress fired, according to her, for rejecting him like she did. Sometimes being on the side of truth doesn't matter the way it should.

My hand drops away from Griffin, forming a fist, and I can feel him watching me.

"You okay?" he asks, turning me toward him. He reaches for

222

one of my fists, and just like that, my hand relaxes. Instead of releasing it, he weaves his fingers with mine, his touch anchoring me.

I take a deep breath, hold it, then let it out in a heavy exhale. "Five minutes ago, I was perfectly fine."

"What changed that?" he asks, his brow arching. "And who should I fuck up for you?"

Andy's expression is exactly the same as it was in second grade after a little boy pulled my pigtail during recess. "I'll tell you what just happened. Brock is *gaslighting* Edgar James. Just like he gaslit Marnie into almost marrying him."

I glance around, making sure Jim isn't eavesdropping, waiting for us to say something he can twist into a delicious pretzel of a story. Luckily, Damien has already roped him into conversation. Jim seems totally entranced and not at all aware of the drama unfolding around him.

Val is equally distracted. He's making his way over to Brock, who's talking to Edgar James, their heads tilted together. Knowing Brock, he's probably asking him to keep the whole near-drowning incident on the DL. He'll say something like *I'm a private man,* or *I don't want my employees to realize I'm not Aquaman.* It'll all sound perfectly reasonable.

"He made up the whole near-drowning thing," I hiss to Griffin. "There's no way that happened. He would have issued half a dozen media blasts."

He scowls and scrubs a hand through his hair. "I didn't need another reason to dislike that asshole."

"You're here to talk to that asshole, if you'll recall," says Nicole, sidling up to us from wherever she was lurking. "Presuming you're talking about Brock."

I give a tight nod. "Yep. That's the one."

"Why would he tell me anything?" Griffin says in a near growl. "When we came in, he acted like he was worried I'd mug him."

"Fear is a great motivator," Nicole says. "Plus, you're Eskimo brothers. You've been in the same igloo."

I squawk and Andy snorts, which is obviously a betrayal.

"Too far, Nicole," Griff says.

Nicole lifts a hand in capitulation. "Okay, okay. I get it. You don't want to think about that guy being in Marnie's igloo. But trust me. He's going to break like a piñata. After I get him drunk, obviously. Then you can charm him or intimidate him, and he'll spill everything. He looks like an easy mark."

"That plan might need to be put on pause." I dart another glance at Brock and Edgar James, who are still engaged in a tête-à-tête. "Brock lied to Edgar to secure this deal. There was no near-drowning incident. No fear of water. If I say anything, I'll be painted as the vindictive ex, but we can't let him get away with this shit."

I might not know Edgar James, but I feel protective of him, or rather the situation he's in.

"Oh, I know all about that," Nicole says with a toothy smile. "Damien and I found out earlier today. Why do you think we're here?"

For a second, I just stare at her, flummoxed. I figured they were here to watch me and Griffin potentially make fools of ourselves, but it seems I underestimated them. They are P.I.s, and it would seem they've been P.I.ing.

"Why didn't you say anything?" I ask.

"Yes, Nicole," Griffin says through his teeth. "Why didn't you say anything?"

"Because we were busy dealing with it," she says with a flippant wave of her hand. "Brock is going to answer for his actions, Marnie. That was *always* going to happen. But first we need to find out what he knows."

I suspect my mouth resembles a fish's.

"I knew I liked you," Andy says with a grin. "I'm so glad I crashed this party."

"Good," Nicole says, "because I need *you* to get Edgar away from Brock."

"She's not some femme fatale," I chide. "She's here as my friend."

"Excuse you," Andy says, bumping my shoulder with hers. "I could absolutely be a femme fatale. Besides, as your friend, I want to help you get revenge on your douchebag ex." She glances at Edgar James and adds, "Besides, I'm not going to complain about talking to that hottie with a body."

Griffin smiles in amusement. "I don't think I've ever heard anyone call a man that."

"Trust me, someone's definitely called you that behind your back," Andy says.

"I do it all the time," Nicole confirms.

Griff inclines his head. "I thought you said I was only an eight and a half."

"I have *very* high standards."

"Ugh. Okay," I say, then turn to Andy and add, "Off with you. Go flirt with the hot outdoorsman."

"You don't have to tell me twice." She takes off toward the front of the room with a swish of red fabric.

I check on Jim, who's still reeled in by Damien's story. And Val, who's joined the Brock-Edgar James huddle. The situation, such as it is, is under control.

I turn toward Nicole. "Your plan sounds like it needs some time. I assume Griffin and I can take off for a few minutes?"

There's something I need to tell Griffin, and it suddenly feels like it can't wait.

She studies me for a second, then nods. "You want to have revenge sex with Griffin in Brock's house. I get it."

"Nicole," Griffin grits out, although there's no real heat behind it, just the kind of habitual annoyance exchanged between two people who spend a lot of time together.

"I can't deny that I would enjoy that," I say, feeling Griffin's gaze as he shifts it to me, "but it's not what I had in mind."

Ignoring Nicole, I turn toward Griffin. He looks a little unsure of himself, like that boy I saw in the photo on Liza and Gary's mantel, and achingly handsome, from his tawny eyes to his slightly off-kilter nose. I take him by the hand and lead him out of the room, to a small office that's rarely used.

Once we're inside, he shuts the door and turns to me, the space rendered small by his presence.

"You're tense," I say, rubbing his arms. A sliver of his tattoo comes into view on his right arm. His arms are so firm and defined I feel a spark of wanting. That's never far when I'm with him, though. It's not just his charm and his looks, or even his loyalty to the people who are lucky enough to earn it, it's the brokenness I sense beneath all of that, because someone who's been hurt will always recognize it in others.

I pull away. "You're as wound up as I was in the car."

"Fuck," he says, rubbing his nose. "I was hoping you couldn't tell."

"That was my line," I say with a small smile. "I need to say something."

He lifts his eyebrows. "Please tell me you haven't had second thoughts about Brock."

"You're wondering why I told him yes."

He swears under his breath, then meets my eyes. "No. That's not my place. Besides, your friend's right. He's good at backing people into corners, and it's obvious he backed you into one. I'm glad Nicole and Damien have a plan. Otherwise, I would have had to come up with one."

"Or me," I say.

"Or you," he agrees, taking a step closer. "You're more than capable of standing up for yourself, Marnie."

"Thank you," I say in an undertone, feeling an aching awareness of him. "You're a pretty liar."

He smirks at my choice of words, but it fades quickly. "I'm not lying about that."

That. It's confirmation of what I already know—there's a part of his history, of his story, he won't talk about with anyone. He should, I think. Talking to him is healing me, and I'd like to offer him the same grace. But it's not the time or the place to push him.

"Thank you for that," I say. "Thank you for believing in me. You need to know that I don't have any feelings for Brock." I scrunch my mouth to the side. "Well, that's not quite true. I think I might legitimately hate him. I don't know if I'd try to save him from a burning building." I sigh. "Okay, I'd probably still try, but I'd feel really put out about it."

"Is that what you brought me in here to say?" he asks. "That Brock's low on your to-be-saved-from-a-burning-building list?" He reaches out a hand and catches mine, a simple touch that sends a jolt through me.

"Not just that." I pause, considering, then decide to go for it. "I'm pretty sure I know who paid Brock that money after the wedding."

He looks me in the eye. "You weren't ready to tell me earlier."

"I'm not positive, and I don't want you to think badly of both of my siblings."

"Your brother," he says, his eyes flashing. "You said your father left both of you cash."

I nod, still holding his hand because right now it's grounding me. "The night before the wedding, Drew tried to talk me out of going through with it. He told me it was too much, too soon, and he didn't think Brock was right for me. I . . . I told him I'd think about it, and I did. He was right, Griff. I *knew* he was. But everything was already in motion, and I couldn't bring myself to disappoint so many people. I told myself it was just nerves, and . . . you know the rest. All this time, I think the person I've been the most disappointed in is myself. For going through with it even though I knew better."

"Dammit, Marnie," he says, pulling away. If he was tense earlier, now he's pissed enough to punch a wall. "You almost married that douchebag because you were worried about disappointing other people? What about what *you* want? No one's going to see the real you if you keep them in the dark."

Maybe I've done it intentionally. Maybe I'm afraid they won't like what they see. Or that they'll realize I'm just a pale reflection of the person they'd rather be looking at.

He's looking down at me so intently, as if all of this is of great importance to him.

"Why does it matter so much to you?"

"Isn't it obvious?" he says, running his hands through his hair. The action leaves it sexy and mussed. "You drive me crazy."

I huff a laugh. "That's not what I was hoping you'd say."

"There you go again, driving me crazy," he says with a quirk of his lips. There's fondness in his eyes. An answering wave of affection washes through me. "The people I like best are the ones who drive me crazy."

"I want you, Griffin," I say, feeling bold.

He swears. "I'm not sure I can be a rebound for you," he says, his expression regretful. "You make me want more than that."

"Good," I say, catching his gaze, "because so do I."

I get a wild thought, the kind I'd usually ignore, but I'm feeling a little impulsive, like maybe all of the things that have held me back for so long don't matter. Like maybe he's right, and I'm the only one who's been holding me back.

I take a step toward him, then lower onto my knees.

"What are you doing?" he asks, his voice strained. It's obvious he already knows.

"You told me I should take what I want," I say, reaching for the button of his jeans. "What does it look like I'm doing?"

"Marnie," he says, but his hand weaves into my hair, and he doesn't try to pull me away. With something like wonder, I see that all he needed was the insinuation of a blow job to get hard. His cock is outlined by the denim of his pants, straining to be free, and I run my fingers over it, reveling in the feel of him.

"I want to make you feel good, Griffin."

"You want my cock?" he says, with a thread of humor in his voice, because surely he remembers the many times I've asked. But his voice is husky too, and his eyes are hooded. His hand grips my hair, not hard enough to hurt, but enough to ignite the nerve endings in my scalp.

"I want your cock," I affirm.

"So we can agree it's better than a vibrator?"

"Let's see." I slowly lower his zipper. His erection springs out of his jeans, barely contained by his boxer briefs, and I feel a swell of satisfaction, because this beautiful man wants me. Maybe it's against his better judgment, but he wants me all the same.

I push down his boxer briefs and take him in my hand, savoring his harsh intake of breath and the flexing of his fingers in my hair. I pump my hand up and down once, learning the shape of him, thick and so very hard. He closes his eyes for a second, his lips drawn tightly together.

"Yes," I say. "Felix is very good at what he does, but he has nothing on you. Or at least his shape doesn't. I'll need to see the goods in action before I can fully decide."

"Fuck," he breathes out as I give him another stroke with my hand. "You named your vibrator?"

"It seemed too impersonal not to."

There's a small smile on his lips as he looks at me, his eyes gleaming. "You're delightfully weird."

"Thank you," I say, giving him another stroke.

"You know," he says, his eyes still closed. "I've been thinking about you wrapping your soft lips around my cock ever since last night on the roof."

"Only since yesterday?" I ask, feeling a surge of power.

"I've been thinking about it a lot," he says in a low, husky voice, opening his eyes again. Watching me with some emotion I can't decipher.

I keep my eyes on him as I lower down and swirl my tongue over the head of his cock and then take him in my mouth. He releases a guttural groan, leaning into me, his hand still in my hair, gripping a little, sending waves of pleasure between my legs. His eyes are molten, his lips parted. I love seeing the way I affect him.

Sucking and swirling my tongue, I move up and down, taking my time, then let him pop out of my mouth for a moment so I can kiss the side of his shaft and then lick around the head again, teasing him.

"*Marnie*."

Smiling coyly, feeling a thrilling rush, I look up into his eyes as I suck him in, taking him in deeper this time. His hand flexes in my hair, and he swears under his breath. Out then in, again and again, sucking and licking and learning him. Basking in the sensation of his hand in my hair, which is making my nerve endings prickle to attention, and the look he's giving me.

It's not just pleasure. There's something like awe in his eyes, something like—

"Oh, holy shit," a familiar voice says from the door.

It takes me only half a second to place it. Andy.

I was already flushed, although now I'm red all over for a different reason. I've never been caught in the act before. *Never*. Up until now, the closest I'd come was Griffin's brother walking in on my accidental dick hug. As previously mentioned, Brock is extremely vanilla, and even if he weren't, he never would've spun me up so much that I'd feel inclined to go down on him in the middle of a party full of people. Griffin makes me lose control. He makes me feel like I can do anything. That's probably dangerous, but it also feels really good, like eating the first chocolate chip cookie after they come out of the oven.

Griffin pulls me up and turns me away from the door, although not before I catch a glimpse of my friend with Edgar James.

"Carry on!" Andy says cheerfully. I suspect she'd give me a high five if she could.

The door closes, but Griffin's already tucked himself away.

I feel a pang of disappointment that's pretty ridiculous considering my best friend since childhood just walked in on me giving a blow job to my . . .

I don't even know what he is. Fake boyfriend isn't quite right, because this thing between us is real. I just don't know what it means, and it's clear he's struggling with the same thing. All I know is that I want him. I want all of him, his story *and* his cock, although not necessarily in that order.

"Let's get out of here," Griffin says as he starts for the door.

"Please tell me we can finish what we started," I say, tugging his hand.

"No," he says, turning back and cupping my cheek. "No, when I finish, I want to be inside of you."

twenty-three

GRIFFIN

I DIDN'T REALIZE how deeply Marnie had sunk under my skin until we walked into this house. Maybe that makes me a dumbass, because I've thought about her every minute I haven't spent with her for the past couple of weeks, but I'd prefer to think I'm just delusional.

It's dangerous, feeling this way, and goddamn uncomfortable. Ever since we stepped into this house, there's been something tight in my chest.

Being hung up on a woman shouldn't cause you chest pains, should it?

It's just . . . it kills me to act civil to all of these people who have been complicit in screwing her over, ignoring her, or using her. There's Jim, the reporter who's apparently made nice with my friends. Val, who's made it abundantly clear he's not in Marnie's corner. And Brock, who makes me want to punch the wall—or preferably his face—until my hand's bloody. Maybe the only person I'm not pissed at is Marnie's brother, because even if he shouldn't have gone behind her back to offer Brock a payoff, I understand the impulse. I would've done the same to protect someone who matters to me.

I *have* done the same.

This situation has all the marks of a grenade ticking toward an explosive countdown, the kind of thing I'd usually avoid like a pretzel that's spent two months trapped under the bar, but my willpower has the consistency of swiss cheese. I don't want to step away from Marnie. I don't want to go back to the way things were two weeks ago, doing nothing but working and reading. Books can bring you to a different place, but when you finish reading them, you're still alone with yourself. Spending time with this woman has changed my world for the better. It's made me realize all the things my life has been lacking—all the things *she* could bring to it.

If I let her.

Still, I'm aware I'm in over my head. Edgar James's little speech earlier slid under my skin, because I understand that kind of fear—the fear that arises after the thing you covet has turned against you.

"Should you go out there like that?" Marnie says, pressing a hand to my chest.

She nods down to my cock pressing against the front of my jeans like it might find a hole to poke through if it tries hard enough.

"No, probably not. If Jim writes a blog post about Mitchell Mountainbottom's public hard-on, it might earn us another mention on Mike's show."

She cringes. "You're right. At least Damien seems to have charmed him stupid." She pauses, eyeing my pants. "Do you want me to . . . take care of it?"

Air hisses out of me.

Fuck, yes, I want her to take care of it. I want her to wrap her hand around my dick again, eagerly exploring it. I want her mouth to envelop me, sucking, teasing. And, more than anything, I want to pin her against the wall and sink my cock into her. I want to claim her, even more so in *his* house.

But I'm not so far gone that I don't realize it's a stupid impulse.

"Give me a minute," I say. "Why don't you go talk to your friend?"

"You're right," she says, her brow furrowing. "I want to find out more about Nicole's plan."

It occurs to me that it may not be necessary for me to put the screws on Brock if Marnie already knows who paid that bribe. Confirmation would be good, obviously, but if she tells her brother what she knows, I'm sure he'll confess.

Like you did?

There's that tight feeling in my chest again, and I rub against it.

At least my hard-on is wilting.

"I'll be right out," I say.

She gives me one of her Bambi looks, like she's worried about *me*, but she nods and leaves the room. I barely restrain the urge to slam a fist into the wall.

I spend several minutes pacing, then a few minutes more trying to patch up the holes in my willpower. I leave the room, ready to . . .

Actually, I don't know what I plan on doing, let alone what I *should* be doing, only that I'm sick of being in this house.

I take two steps, then slam into someone. "Shit. I'm sorry, man," I say, before realizing it's Brock.

I couldn't care less about having potentially hurt him, but I still stop to make sure he's okay. I'm a leave-no-one-behind type. Even though, like Marnie, I'd resent saving this asshole from a burning building.

"I'm fine," he grumbles, but he doesn't look fine. He's pale, and he smells like he's been going drink for drink with Nicole, a losing proposition for anyone. People have tried it at the bar since we took over. Most of them get nothing to show for it but a raging hangover.

"You been hitting the sauce?" I ask.

"I just need a minute," he says, stumbling past me toward the room I just left.

I follow him.

He doesn't look particularly happy about it, but it's obvious he's not in any shape to do anything about it. Less from the alcohol, which hasn't had much of a chance to kick in, than from his lie almost being dragged into light.

"What do you want?" he asks. "You already got my girl."

I laugh, although it's not funny. "You left her."

He scrubs a hand across his close-shaven jaw. "I fucked up."

"You did," I agree. "Why?"

"Why should I tell you?" he says with a choked sound that vaguely resembles laughter.

I shut the door behind us, and his eyes widen. Lifting my hands, I say, "I'm not going to come for you, man. I'm not that kind of person anymore."

"But you were?" he asks, taking a step back. His eyes are beady with fear, like a rat caught in a no-kill traps. He's not happy to be in here with me.

No shit, Brock. Neither am I.

"I've made mistakes," I say, raising my brows.

There's an implicit threat that I might make more mistakes if he pushes me far enough. I'm mostly sure I won't hit him, no matter what he says, but he doesn't have to know that.

"What do you want?"

"I want you to tell me why you left Marnie at the altar after practically forcing her into an engagement."

"I didn't force her to do anything," he sneers. "She was grateful for the attention."

Rage licks at me. He saw her vulnerability, her fear that she would never measure up to her famous sister, and he took advantage of it. I fist my hand, wanting him to see it. "Be careful. You don't want to shove me toward another mistake, *friend.*"

"You want to get arrested?" he says, although his voice lacks conviction. He realizes that while he could get me arrested, it wouldn't unpunch his face.

"It's been a while," I deadpan. "Why not?"

He cringes, but he's not talking, and I need him to talk. So I throw another coal in the fire.

"There's another reason you should listen to me. Edgar James probably won't be thrilled to discover you lied to him. He doesn't strike me as a forgiving man."

Might as well use what I know as leverage.

"Marnie lied to you," he insists. "You can't believe anything she says. She's a liar."

I just give him a look. "Why don't you impress me with your truthfulness by telling me why you left her at the altar."

He swears and paces back and forth a few times in the tight space, stumbling over his feet as the booze settles in. I won't lie—it brings me pleasure to know that Marnie sucked my cock in this very room less than half an hour ago.

"Her brother," he finally says, stopping to look at me. "He offered me fifty grand to call it off."

Fifty thousand dollars. Shit. Did her father leave them that much cash? It's hard to believe. Then again, people bury gold in their back-yards. It's not the strangest thing I've ever heard.

"You don't seem like you're hurting for money," I say, gesturing to the walls around us.

He frowns. "I had a cash flow issue. It happens when you expand a business."

He says it as if I'm incapable of understanding any concepts related to business.

"It happens if you expand too fast," I say. "Hence your need for Edgar James."

He shrugs and takes a step toward the door. "Guess you've got it all figured out."

"Not so fast. Why did you say you regret your decision?" Something tells me it's not out of any love for Marnie. I've seen his kind before. He's a narcissist, willing to do anything to get what he wants, whoever it hurts.

"She's Sinclair Jones's sister," he scoffs. "What's fifty grand compared to that? I let a short-term problem get in the way of my long-term success." His gaze bores into me, and even though he's tipsy and headed toward drunk, it's shrewd. "But you've thought of that too. Everyone who's ever asked her out has thought of it . . . same as everyone who'll come after you. Only thing better would be to hit it with the golden goddess herself."

If I were going to hit him, I'd do it then. I *want* to. I want to annihilate him. The rage inside of me demands a release, ideally one that would lead to him clutching his bloodied face. But he's right. He could get me arrested, and then I'd have another record, one that wouldn't get expunged.

Marnie wouldn't thank me for that.

No one would thank me for that.

"What do you know about the video?" I growl.

He laughs at that, although the sound verges on unhinged. Maybe he's already realized he won't get away with his lies. He's spun too many of them. "I don't know shit. If I did, I'd go after whoever did it. It's brought me nothing but trouble."

Which is an interesting point, because it's possible someone did it to undermine him, not Marnie. The theory doesn't gel, though. Whoever did it was almost certainly on Marnie's side of the church.

I let Brock stumble out of the room, taking no small pleasure from his stumbling. It's not a good look for him to roll out in front of his employees, and Edgar James doesn't strike me as the kind of man who'd be impressed by public displays of drunkenness.

I also have the satisfaction of knowing I'm sending him out to whatever fate Nicole has in store for him. I have a feeling it won't be kind.

Even so. There's no denying I feel more ill at ease than I did before.

It's just . . . this thing with Marnie's brother is bringing back a lot of memories I'd prefer to keep buried, memories I'd hoped to send off to sea with my father when I scattered his ashes all those years ago.

I suck in a deep breath, trying to settle myself. It doesn't work, but I leave the room anyway, shutting the door behind me.

Marnie's waiting for me at the end of the hall, her hip propped against the wall, and it sets my teeth on edge to imagine Brock shuffling past her a few minutes ago. She's alone, no sign of the others. She's gorgeous, and I have the urge to pick her up and carry her the fuck out of here before that grenade I mentioned goes off.

Did Brock say anything to her?

"There you are," she says, taking my hand as if it's natural. It shouldn't be, but it is.

"Here I am," I agree. "Did Brock—"

"A couple of minutes ago," she confirms. "Did everything go okay?"

I squeeze her hand, thinking about that fifty-thousand-dollar payoff . . . about Brock saying, *Only thing better would be to hit it with the golden goddess herself.*

Fuck, I still want to hit him.

I'm not going to tell Marnie the comment about her sister. There's no reason to. It'll only hurt her. I do, however, need to tell her about the payoff. Not now, though. Not here. "Yeah. He told me some stuff."

Her brows pinch together. "And?"

"Nothing too surprising," I say, wrapping an arm around her. I feel a powerful need to reassure myself that she's okay—that being in proximity to Brock hasn't magically restored whatever hold he had on her. "I'll tell you after we leave."

She thinks this through before nodding slowly and leaning into my embrace. "Okay. I'll give you a temporary reprieve."

"What happened when Brock came out? Did he say anything to you?" I don't want him near her. I'd prefer for him to be in a different country, actually, although a different house would do. It's not because I don't think she's strong enough to deal with him on her own. It's that I want to protect her.

You've never been very good at that, a voice reminds me.

Marnie makes a face. "He seemed really drunk. Before he headed back there, Nicole challenged him to do shots with her. He must really want their investment, because he downed, like, six of them. Nicole seems fine."

She probably swapped out some of her drinks. Or dumped them in a plant or something. Even if she drank them, though, it wouldn't have affected her the way it did him.

"Where's your friend?"

"Talking to Edgar James," she says, a hint of curiosity in her eyes. "They're over there."

She points to the side of the room. Sure enough, Andy and Edgar are sitting on a love seat, deep in conversation. Although they're close together, nearly touching, it doesn't seem flirtatious. There's a different kind of energy zinging between them. Brock's lurking about fifteen feet away, eyeing them with growing agitation.

He's right to be agitated. There's an intense look on Edgar's face, and Andy's doing most of the talking.

Has she revealed that Brock's a liar, or is she telling him what happened with Marnie?

Either way, it's not good for Brock. I'm surprised he hasn't interrupted them, although maybe he's self-aware enough to realize he'd make a terrible impression now, stinking of alcohol and stumbling.

"This is about to get good," Nicole says.

Marnie and I both jolt as she steps into view.

For someone whose hair is practically neon, Nicole can sneak around with the best of them. Or maybe I'm just off my game tonight. I *feel* off my game. I feel like my nerves, usually tucked safely out of sight, are raw and exposed.

"How, exactly, is it going to get good?" I ask.

She cocks an eyebrow. "Did you find out what you need to know?"

She's avoiding the question, but I steal a quick glance at Marnie and then nod. "We'll tell you later. But I'm positive Brock isn't the one who spread the video. He's enough of an asshole that it's possible someone might have done it to ruin his reputation, but it seems like they'd try something more direct."

"Good," Nicole says, taking out her phone and glancing at the screen. "Because Brock's present is almost here."

"Why are we getting him presents?" Marnie asks as she props a hand on her hip. "I'm pretty sure we don't like him. I definitely don't like him."

Nicole winks at Marnie, which I don't much like. "Not all presents are good. Gary gets everyone socks."

"Socks are practical," I say. "Where's Damien?"

"Still talking to that reporter," she says with a grin. "I think Jimbo's tried to escape at least once, but Damien knows how to make someone a captive audience. Every time our blue-shirted friend tries to step away, Damien throws him some bait about this-or-that famous person he met one time. He's a master at the art of manipulation." She says this like it gets her hot and bothered, and I suppose it probably does. At another time I might have teased her, but right now, my mind's set on getting out of here.

"Where's Marnie's boss?" I ask.

"He's with Damien too."

A knock lands on the door. Our eyes fly to it, and Nicole's smile widens.

"Is someone going to get that?" she calls out.

My gaze sweeps to Brock, who's still lingering behind that love seat. It's obvious he'd love to ignore both Nicole and the knocking, but whoever's behind the door is not giving up. It would look bad, or at least weird, if he didn't answer it, and no one else is likely to step up—it's his house.

Brock inches his way to the door, glancing back at the party as if we're in a grown-up game of red light, green light and he's worried we're going to rush him the moment his back's turned.

"Another guest, I'm sure," he says, carefully enunciating the words.

He opens the door to a dark-haired woman with high cheekbones and dark brown eyes. She's wearing a faux fur coat over an emerald-green pantsuit.

Her face is familiar, but it takes me a second to place her. Patrice. She's friendly with Damien and Nicole.

She's also an actress at the local theater.

What the hell are they up to?

I don't have long to wonder, though, because Patrice is already pushing past Brock, who looks understandably confused.

"You didn't invite me to your little party?" she accuses, her voice carrying through the room. Conversations trickle to a stop. Eyes dart to the front of the room. Like Damien, Patrice is naturally good at commanding attention. "I had to hear about it from social media, Brock. Honestly. You sweep me away for a snorkeling trip over Christmas, and suddenly you have no use for me? We made love in the ocean, Brock. In the ocean!"

He gapes like a fish. For all the lies he's told, it's obvious no one's ever lied about *him* before. Still, I'm not amused. This isn't cute or funny.

I take out my phone and text Nicole. *WTF? An actress? What if he traces this woman back to Marnie?*

I give her a hard look. She rolls her eyes but takes out her phone and checks the message, immediately typing a response: *Not a problem. He DID actually go snorkeling with a woman over Christmas. His former assistant, in fact. She wasn't into making a scene, but if anyone fact-checks, they'll find out it's true. BOOM. Besides, who's going to believe his ex-fiancée hired a couple of P.I.s, who then hired an actress to pretend to be his ex-lover? People believe what's right in front of them*

Not your risk to take, I respond, although I'm slightly pacified.

I glance at Marnie, who's watching the scene with rapt attention. If she's upset, it doesn't show. Not that she'd have any reason to be. She's made it clear she's over Brock, and if he went away with someone for Christmas, it was months after they broke up.

Edgar James has swiveled on the love seat. He doesn't appear amused, which is probably the point of this whole farce. Andy watches him with a look of satisfaction as he gets to his feet.

"I've never met you in my life," Brock sputters. "You're a person I don't know. A *stranger*." He says this last word as if patting himself on the back for remembering it.

"Liar! You're lying to everyone," she says passionately.

Edgar James takes several steps toward them, his expression stony. "You say you went snorkeling with this man a few weeks ago?" he asks Patrice.

She nods, her gaze fixed on Brock.

Goddamn. There are real tears in her eyes. If I didn't know better, *I'd* believe her.

Val and Jim, aka Purple Shirt, pop up on the periphery of the scene like a couple of poisonous mushrooms. Damien's with them, smiling at them like an indulgent father. Maybe because they're doing exactly what he might have hoped: Jim looks borderline ecstatic, and Val has clearly realized he backed the wrong horse.

"In Cozumel," Patrice says. "It was the most romantic experience of my life. We spent every day in the ocean." She gives Brock a murderous glare. "I'll never forgive you."

Then she whisks herself away with enough flair that I'll bet Jim just sprang a bad-news boner.

Edgar's already shaking his head, his eyes glowing like embers. "You lied to me, Tilton?"

Brock looks like he wants to run away, just like Marnie did from that wedding service. It would be satisfying if he did, even more so because we're in *his* house, but he stays put. More's the pity.

"I don't know that woman," Brock insists, clinging to the one thing that's true.

From the expression on Edgar's face, it's clear he doesn't buy it. Good. He may have been fooled into this agreement, but he obviously has some sense. "I suppose you can prove you didn't go snorkeling over Christmas?"

Brock opens and then shuts his mouth without letting any sound escape.

Edgar paces a few steps forward and then back, looking like a pissed-off mountain lion. "I should have known you were full of shit the second I walked in here and saw everyone in suits. You're no outdoorsman."

"We have a deal," Brock hisses. "There's a contract involved. You can't just walk away from that."

"Seems you have no problem walking away from your commitments," Edgar snaps, gesturing back to Marnie. "Your ex-fiancée's friend painted a pretty damning picture. Deal's off, Tilton. If I can find a way to bury you, I *will*."

"I don't like the water," Brock practically screams. He points toward the door. "She insisted. I did it for her."

Edgar's mouth forms a tight line. "I thought you didn't know her," he says coldly.

"I don't!" Turning, he glares at me and Marnie. "*You* did this."

I bristle, feeling that urge again—that need to pick her up and take her away from here. But she's a grown woman who can stand on her own two feet, and she's learning to like it. I'm not going to take that away from her.

"She didn't do anything," I say, injecting a threat into it. "You did it to yourself, man. None of this would have happened if you hadn't lied."

What about your lies?

Brock lunges and grabs Marnie's arm before I can stop him. "Time for you to get out."

"So much for bygones being bygones," Marnie says, but her flinch is unmistakable. He's hurting her.

My blood catches fire, the heat so intense it feels like it's blistering my skin. "You get your fucking hands off her," I snarl, reaching for him. "Now."

He gives me a scathing look as he releases her, and I notice the white marks where his fingers dug in. My grasp on self-control is straining like an old rubber band. He's too stupid to realize it and get out of my way. Or maybe he's too tipsy.

"You think you've got a shot at the sister?" Brock sneers. "She's classier than Marnie. She won't go for white trash."

I'd planned to protect Marnie from the knowledge of what a total shithead this man is, and I've failed even at that.

That rubber band snaps, and I shove him.

BROCK CRASHES into the floor and yelps. For a second, I'm worried that I'll have to help him, but he gets to his feet, making a real production out of it, and stares daggers at Griffin. "You assaulted me! I'm going to have you arrested."

"Are you kidding me?" I say, stepping in front of Griff. He gently moves me to the side, but instead of stepping in front of me, he stands beside me. I don't like the look in his eyes. It's . . . blank. Like he shut off his feed.

"You're the one who did *this* to me," I tell Brock. I lift up my arm, pointing to the tender spots where he grabbed me. My mind plays catch-up, rewinding to what he said to set Griffin off. "You have a thing for my *sister*?"

It shouldn't be a surprise—he was always so solicitous of her attention—but it's the poisoned cherry on top of a shit sundae.

"I'm calling the police!" Brock squeals.

"Don't make an even bigger ass out of yourself. We all saw what happened," Edgar James says with a grunt. "No judge alive would condemn him."

Fear pricks into me, because I'm not so convinced that's true. What if the judge found out about Griffin's expunged record? Or . . .

there are other things from his past, other haunts attached to him. I don't know what they are, but it's possible they could get him into trouble.

"Now, Edgar," Val says, stroking the straining buttons of his shirt. "I imagine there must have been some kind of misunderstanding. Brock isn't a dishonest man. Some men can nearly drown one day and go snorkeling the next. Others aren't so lucky."

Edgar James fixes him with a look that cuts. "He told me he hasn't been able to get within twenty feet of a natural body of water since his 'accident.' If he tries to go after that guy—" he nods to Griffin, "—he'll have my lawyers to deal with. Where I'm from, you don't grab ladies. He's lucky he only got pushed."

Val doesn't instantly respond, but when he does, it's instantly dissatisfactory. "Be that as it may. This could be a lucrative deal for all parties. Business is business."

Instead of realizing Brock's a bad bet, he's trying to resuscitate a dead horse. He has no scruples, no line that can't be crossed. Why have I put up with it for so long? Why did I agree to come here, to the house of a man who publicly humiliated me, so I could keep a job I dislike?

If this is what security feels like, I'd prefer to do without it.

"Consider this my two weeks' notice," I say. "I quit."

I can feel Griffin looking at me, but he doesn't say or do anything. He doesn't try to stuff the words back into me, and I don't attempt it either. I don't regret them.

"If you go freelance, I'll hire you," Edgar James says. "Tilton showed me your designs. I'm the one who wanted to bring you on."

His words surprise me. I'd figured Brock was the one behind it—not because he valued me but because he wanted to prove he wasn't a bad guy. It hadn't occurred to me that I'd earned it. I feel warmth gathering in my eyes as I nod and say, "I'd like that. Thank you."

Andy's already sidling up to him, saying she'll give him my information.

"You'd throw away your career?" Val says, his eyes bulging. He looks like a father who can't believe his child has defied him.

"I'm not throwing away my career," I respond, my voice surprisingly firm. "I'm starting it."

"If you're abandoning us, don't bother showing up on Monday. I don't want another two weeks from someone who'll be phoning it in."

"That's convenient," Nicole says. "I was going to convince her not to give you two weeks."

Val sputters something about younger generations, as if there are decades separating us and not something like fifteen years, but I don't pay him any attention. Instead, I take Griffin's hand and pull him toward the door, grabbing our coats from the cavernous coatroom along the way.

I glance back before heading out the door. Nicole and Damien salute me. Andy's busy relaying all of my pertinent life information to Edgar James. Brock's in a huddle with Val, who's probably soothing his bruised ego. Brock's employees look like they're planning to drink as much free booze as they can for as long as they can.

If Jim is in there somewhere, and I'm sure he is, he's probably typing on his phone as fast as his fingers can move. This is the kind of story he probably dreams about while he types up puff pieces so diaphanous they could float away on the wind.

Then we're outside, the cold air at once biting and refreshing. It seems to whisk away the taint of having been in that house for so long. I turn to Griffin, but he still has a shuttered look in his eyes, and he hasn't put on his coat.

"Your coat," I say.

He shakes his head slightly. "Let's get you to the car."

He's not himself, though. Either he's beating himself up for what happened back there, or he's wishing he didn't volunteer for the loaner boyfriend gig.

That thought creates a sinkhole in my stomach, like everything inside of me is going to come spilling out.

He opens my door for me. After I get in, he throws his coat in the back, as if he wants to freeze as some sort of penance, and silently starts driving me home.

"I made a new logo for Summer Nights," I blurt out, wanting to distract him. "I mean. You don't have to use it if you don't want to, but—"

"You didn't have to do that." His tone suggests he wishes I hadn't, which stings.

"Obviously not. I wanted to."

"Thank you," he says without asking any follow-up questions.

"Maybe we should go to your place," I say, taking a different tack. "Give my aunt some space."

"I don't think that's a good idea, Marnie," he says gruffly, his gaze not even flickering my way.

"Why not?"

"I told you I'm not good for you. Case in point, everything went to shit back there. It was my fault for losing control."

I raise my eyebrows, although the dramatic effect must be lost on him—he's focused on the road ahead. "I just quit my shitty job, like everyone—including you—has been encouraging me to do. Why's that a bad thing?"

"You shouldn't have been cornered into it," he says, his voice flat.

"I wasn't," I say. "But look at you taking credit for everything. You didn't even know what Nicole and Damien were planning tonight."

He flexes his hands on the wheel. "I shouldn't have laid my hands on Brock. I wasn't going to push him."

"You barely did," I say, frustrated. "Why are you beating yourself up for protecting me?"

"I don't make good decisions, Marnie." He still hasn't even glanced at me, as if looking at me would tear him open.

"And I do?" I ask, laughing. "You just met my ex-fiancée, who apparently has a thing for my sister."

He doesn't say anything, but his mood darkens until he has the air of that kid who never bathed in the *Peanuts* cartoons.

"That's not on you. He pushed you to accept his proposal."

"Sure, but no one forced me to say yes, Griffin," I say. "We all make bad decisions. I'm capable of owning mine."

There's an implicit *are you?* in there that I'm not sure I meant to include.

His jaw clenches, but he doesn't say anything for a few minutes. When he does speak, he says, "You were right. Your brother gave him the money."

Deep inside, I knew it, but it feels different to get confirmation. "How much?"

"Fifty grand."

Shock roils through me. "*Seriously?*"

He does look at me then, briefly. "You thought it would be less."

"When I said my father left us some cash, I meant, like, five thousand bucks each."

Of course, we did get other resources from him. The house, for one, and Dad also split his retirement accounts between Drew and me, since Sinclair doesn't need the money. It's just . . . unexpected.

We sit in silence the rest of the way to the house, but it's not the comfortable silence we've enjoyed in the past. It's a shitty silence, barbed and brutal.

Finally, he parks the car in my driveway. For a second, I think he's just going to wait until I get out and then drive away, but he circles around to open my door. Unnecessary, but right now, I'll take any point of connection I can get.

"Are you angry with him?" he asks, startling me.

It takes me a second to register what he's asking. He's not the kind of person who talks about himself in third person, thank God, so he's talking about Drew.

"A little," I admit, "but not for doing it. I'm upset he didn't tell me."

Something darkens in his eyes, and his hand squeezes the top of the door before he shuts it with a little more force than necessary.

"I'll forgive him though." Taking a leap, I add, "Your brother would forgive you for whatever you did."

"You don't know what the fuck you're talking about," he says, shaking his head. Then, chagrined, he touches his close-cut beard and says, "I'm sorry, Marnie. I'm not myself right now. I should just go home. We'll talk later."

Except I don't think that's true. This darkness is as much a part of him as the charming, teasing Griffin I've gotten to know . . . and it's eating away at him.

"No," I say. "Come inside."

He looks like he's going to walk away anyway. Like he's suddenly desperate to escape this conversation and where it might take us, but I reach out and grip his arm. It's the one with the griffin tattooed on it.

"Who drew that picture?" I ask. "The one in your apartment that this is based on."

He peers down at it, as if he needs to see it to remember. "Gary."

Why would a man get a tattoo, especially one this large, devoted to a brother he'd lost touch with? It suggests a kind of longing that doesn't jibe with the story I've been told.

"Come inside, Griffin." I nudge his arm.

"Not right now." He swears under his breath, his whole countenance as mercurial as the sky before a storm rolls in. "I shouldn't be with you right now. I don't have much control over myself today."

"Good."

"Not good," he says with a mirthful twist of his mouth. "I let you suck my cock in a room with an unlocked door."

"Oh, you *let* me do it?" I ask, getting a little pissed off by his attitude. "There you go again. Am I not an active participant in my own life?"

"That's not what I meant," he says. His hands are fisted at his sides. His whole body is full of seething energy, as if bees are swarming beneath his flesh. "I lost control, Marnie. I completely lost it. I almost pounded your asshole ex into the ground. I might have only pushed him, Marnie, but I wanted to do more." There's a dark energy pulsing in him right now. I believe him.

"Control isn't always a good thing, Griff," I say, reaching out to touch one of his hands. It flattens into a palm, but he doesn't take my hand. "I stayed in that horrible job for years because I was afraid to take a bet on myself . . . I almost married Brock, for Christ's sake, because I worried what people would say if I didn't." I let out a humorless laugh. "And guess what? They talked anyway."

Except I think I understand why he's upset. His father wasn't able to control his behaviors, at least not permanently, and Griffin grew up suffering the consequences.

He takes a step away from me. "You asked me about my nose," he says. "My father broke it. I could have gone to a clinic to get it set, I guess, but he never offered, and I never went. Because I wanted to remember."

Emotion strangles me. I want to go to him, to hold him, to show him how much he means to me, but I can tell he wouldn't let me right now.

"Come inside the house," I say, trying to choke back what I'm feeling. I don't want him to misinterpret my mood and think I pity him. I know what pity feels like, the cloying sweetness that somehow still tastes sour. "We need to talk."

"That's not a good idea right now," he repeats.

"Because you might tell me things? I *want* to know about you. It's not good for you to carry all of this around. I feel so much better because you've helped me share my burdens. I want to do the same for you."

"I . . . can't. Goodbye, Marnie. We'll talk later."

From the look on his face, I wonder if he's saying goodbye for good. If this is the last I'll ever see of him. It's a stupid thought, because Nicole and Damien aren't done working their dastardly magic, and he works with them, except . . .

He's run before, hasn't he?

What if he runs again?

What if this is the last time I'll ever see him?

He starts walking around to the driver's side of the car.

"*Griffin*," I say, not liking the edge of desperation in my voice. But he doesn't turn to look at me.

I step back, because I can't stop him if he's this intent on leaving, or if I did, he wouldn't thank me for it.

I watch him drive away, wondering if it's forever, and then make my way to the porch. I'm stumbling a little, and it's not until I struggle to read the note attached to the door that I realize I'm crying.

It's written on a used Post-it. The information that was on it is crossed out, and Aunt Helen's cursive scrawl is beneath it. I can practically hear her saying, *Waste not, want not.*

Bertrand has spirited me away. Don't wait up. My apartment must not be returned to for twenty-four hours, but he's offered to put me up for the night. xx Helen.

If Griffin were here, he'd probably crack a joke, and we'd laugh. But he's not. He's angry and upset, and I hope to God he doesn't leave town.

It strikes me with something like wonder that I'm more upset by Griffin driving away than I was by Brock leaving me at the altar. If my father were here, he'd wrap me up in his arms and say, *It's no big thing, Marnie. People come and they go, but family is forever.*

Only family isn't always forever, and watching Griffin drive away *felt* like a big thing.

The house feels unbearably empty, and I find myself heading to the mantel. I press my hand against the side of the urn, and I cry and I cry and I cry.

GRIFFIN

I DIDN'T MEAN to tell her that.

I didn't mean to tell anyone that, ever. I'd hoped the truth would go to the grave with me, the way it did with my father. He wouldn't have wanted anyone knowing either. He was remorseful about my nose. Not that first day, when we left the house we'd shared with Ma, with only a couple of suitcases each, my face bruised and bleeding, but a couple of years later. After he got clean again.

For a while.

Blood is pounding in my ears, my mind a storm of thoughts and memories and anger. So much fucking anger. Most of it is at myself. I lost control back there, and I *hate* losing control. It makes me feel as if everything is slipping away, as if I'm gripping this new life of mine with fingers covered in grease.

It feels like Marnie's been pressing *her* fingers into the seams of my being, trying to tear it apart. I know she wants to help, but that doesn't make the sensation any less excruciating.

I intended to go back to the bar, because it's my home, my safe haven, but I find myself driving to Gary's house. I feel a strange need for him right now.

I pull into the drive and sit there for a second, stewing in the feelings that are tearing at me, the anger, the remorse, the deep sadness.

I shouldn't be here right now.

I shouldn't be here, feeling like this. All of my secrets might come tumbling out.

I have no idea how long I've been sitting there when the front door opens and Gary pops his head out, eyeing me with confusion and no small amount of concern. "What are you doing sitting in your car, Griff?" he calls. "You've been out there for at least five minutes."

I get out, because that's what a normal person would do, and I go inside with him wordlessly.

Liza's sitting at the kitchen table, and they have some Monopoly Deal cards out. It's a homey scene, from the fruit basket next to them to the cups of tea in front of them. I never had that sort of thing in my life until Dad and I moved in with Gary and Ma. Domesticity didn't come naturally to him. No one had seen fit to give him any, so he didn't know how to give it to other people.

Liza takes one look at me, and her eyes widen. "I'm going to go fold some laundry." She stands to leave. "I'll leave you boys to talk."

"You don't have to do that." I collapse into a chair more than sit. "I didn't mean to ruin your night."

"You haven't," she says. Then she surprises me by patting my shoulder before she leaves the room.

Gary gives me a sharp look. "What happened, man? Is this about your girl?"

"I think I fucked up," I say. Although I'm still not sure how I did it . . . by losing control at the party? By leaving her at her house?

By nearly telling her everything?

"Care to elucidate that remark? Despite what Liza thinks when she's pissed off, I'm no mind reader."

I consider him, my mind flashing back to another moment, to the day I returned to Asheville. They didn't live in this house, then. They lived in an apartment. I'd shown up without warning, maybe because I wanted to give myself the option to chicken out. I stood outside his door for a solid two minutes before I could bring myself to knock. It had been ten years. Ten years without a single word from me.

The look in his eyes when he opened that door . . .

I wanted him to hit me.

I wanted him to yell at me.

Instead, he was grateful that I'd come back.

That was when I really knew I'd fucked up.

"I've made a lot of mistakes, Gary," I say now.

"Join the club," he says, adjusting his glasses with a sigh. "I spent forty-five minutes on TikTok this morning. There are some messed-up people out there."

"Not those kinds of mistakes," I say with a small smile.

"I know." He studies me for a long moment. I notice, with some disquiet, that I can see my reflection in his glasses. "You really like this woman, don't you?"

Like is a small word for what I feel. Talking to her, laughing with her, feels like a revelation. And call me shallow, but watching Marnie suck my cock while she looked up at me, holding my gaze, is probably the best thing that's ever happened to me. I want more of her. I want *all* of her.

But to get what I want, I know I have to give her more of myself.

I heave a sigh. "She makes me lose control, man. That's dangerous."

Gary cocks his head. "I don't know how to break it to you, but any woman you want that much is going to make you lose control."

"I almost punched someone today," I say, flexing my hand. "You know what that would mean."

"Marnie's ex," he says with a nod.

"It would have gotten me into trouble. *And* her. That's the last thing I want."

"You didn't do it, though."

"How do you know?" I ask, inclining my head.

"Because I know *you*. Besides, Nicole would have sent me a video of it if you had."

"Probably," I say with a huff. "Still. I wanted to hit him."

"Of course you did." He laughs. "Do you think you're the only one who's ever wanted to hit someone? I have news for you. People want to hit each other all the time. Granted, if I hit someone, the most damage I'd do would be to my fist, but even so. It's natural to feel like that around someone who's hurt your woman."

"Were you like that with Liza?" I ask. "Did she make you crazy?"

He laughs. "I'm still like that with Liza. When I first met her, some asshole had cheated on her. His loss was my gain. But you think I didn't want to hit *him*?" He leans forward. "You can't expect to get everything unless you risk something."

"It's just . . ." I'm not sure how to finish that statement, but Gary knows me enough to do it for me.

"You're worried you'll lose control like your dad did."

I don't say anything. We both know he's right.

"You're not Frank."

"No. But he's part of me."

It's on the edge of my tongue to tell him everything. I've almost told him a hundred different times and ways. Maybe a thousand. But I've never gotten past the *almost* stage.

I should have gotten it over with the first day I came back. It would have been easier then, like ripping off a Band-Aid, but time kept passing, and the longer it took me to tell him, the harder it became, until it had been long enough that I thought maybe I didn't have to.

"He wasn't all bad, Griff," Gary says, gazing at me with obvious sympathy. "He could be funny and charming and smart. You're like him in those ways. You don't have to be all the way like him. We're not our parents." He gives me a wry look. "My father is a piece of shit. Do you look at me and see him?"

"No, obviously not," I say. "But—"

"But nothing. You're not your father any more than I am mine."

"Sure," I say, only half believing him. "But Marnie's got a lot of shit to figure out. She just lost her father, and she's trying to figure out her career. She doesn't need my shit piled on top of hers."

"Maybe that's not your call to make," he says, raising his eyebrows. His words remind me of what Marnie said to me earlier, that she was capable of making her own decisions, and I can't deny they're both right. "Now, what else did you do?"

I rub my chest, recalling the way Marnie looked at me before I took off in my car. She looked so sad. *Devastated*.

"I left her," I say. "I left her just like that asshole Brock did."

"I wouldn't say it was exactly like that," he says. "Unless you're keeping a big part of your evening out of your story, but yeah . . . you might want to go back there and apologize."

"I should leave," I say, getting to my feet. "I didn't mean to—" I gesture to the half-played game.

"I was losing anyway," he says. "I always lose. Liza's a shark."

He stands too and claps me on the back. "I love you, man. Don't forget it."

Emotion makes my throat thick, and I hug him. "Thank you. I . . ."

I'll tell you someday. I'll find a way.

"I know."

twenty-six

MARNIE

"AND HE LEFT?" Grace asks.

"Yes," I say, my voice still hoarse from crying. "I messed up. I shouldn't have pushed him so hard, Gracie. I could tell he was upset."

I'd called her and not Andy for two reasons. One, it's possible Andy is still with Nicole and Damien, and I don't necessarily want them to know what's going on with Griffin. Not if he doesn't want to tell them himself. Two, Gracie is the soft touch, and that's what I need right now.

"No," she says intently. "Maybe this is good. Maybe he just needs some time to process how he feels. I saw you guys together last night—he is *definitely* into you. It's not every day a man will offer to be your fake boyfriend to help you . . . and then go down on you on a bar. I mean. That's a forever kind of connection."

"Please don't write this into a book someday," I say, laughing a little despite myself.

"No promises. But if I do, it will be heavily fictionalized."

There's a knock on the door, and I wipe at my face. My whole body comes to attention, as if I'm a golden retriever who's been offered a treat. I tell myself it's probably just a neighbor come to ask about the weird howling sounds, or an intrepid Jehovah's Witness who ignored our "no soliciting" sign.

But I peer through the spyhole and see him.

"It's him," I hiss. "He's *here*."

"Well, go," she says, sounding a little too excited. "He processed everything even faster than I could have hoped."

I hope to God she's right, and he's not just here because he accidentally left a tin of breath mints or something. I hang up the phone and set it on the table in the foyer.

I take a deep breath and open the door.

He swears under his breath when he sees me, then lifts his hand to touch my cheek. "You've been crying. Because of me."

I don't deny it. I just pull him inside with one hand and close the door with the other, not wanting to release him. He's still not wearing his coat, and his skin is cool to the touch. I trace the bottom of his tattoo, the griffin based on Gary's drawing.

"*Griffin*. Where'd you go?"

"I . . . I went to talk to my stepbrother. You took down the rest of the tree," he says. "I didn't notice earlier."

"I did. I felt stronger because you helped me do most of it."

It's an entreaty. I want him to let me in, and yes, part of it's for me—because I want to understand him—but mostly it's for him. I think he needs this.

Maybe he realizes it too, and that's why he came back.

I lift onto my toes and kiss him gently, showing him that it's not him I'm upset with . . . not really. Then I reach up and trace the line of his nose.

"You want to know the rest," he says flatly. "About when I left Asheville."

"Did you tell Gary?" I ask. "Is that why you went over there?"

He shakes his head. "He doesn't know. What I told you about my dad . . . he doesn't even know that much."

"The past is weighing on you, Griff. I think it probably has been for a long time. I can't make you tell me, and I wouldn't if I could. But I want to listen."

He takes a jagged breath, considering, and for a moment I'm certain he'll drive off again, this time for good. But he stays put, his legs like trees rooted to my floor, and meets my gaze. "I found out my father was using again, Marnie. I could tell from the way he was acting. I'd seen the signs before, more than once. Then I found his stash."

My heart is already broken for him.

I'm desperate to soothe him, but this is a delicate moment, one that could crack open like an egg. So instead, I stroke his forearm, the colorful edges of his tattoo peeking out, and I look up at him. Waiting.

"I knew what would happen," he says, his eyes glistening. "Ma is the kindest person I've ever met. She would have asked him to stop, obviously, but she wouldn't have thrown him out if he couldn't quit it. And he wouldn't have. He never did until something terrible happened. So she would have tolerated it. She would have let him spend her money and run her into the ground with worry, Gary with her. She would have let him get her into legal trouble, though she hasn't broken a damn rule in her life."

"So you forced him to leave," I say softly.

"He was fucking around too," he says, a touch of defensiveness in his voice. "He was like that whenever he used. It was like he stopped caring about any of the things he was supposed to do . . . or maybe he just *couldn't* care about them anymore. I couldn't let him do that to her, Marnie."

I keep stroking his arm with my fingers. My heart is quailing for the boy he was, the boy who's still locked inside of him.

"I told him I'd turn him in to the cops if he didn't leave with me."

"And that's when he punched you?"

"He didn't want to go." His eyes are glassy, his entire being tense. "In his own way, he loved her."

"Why'd you go with him, Griff? Gary and your mother . . . they would have wanted you to stay. You were old enough that you would have been given a say."

His smile is bitter. "I didn't want him to bring them down, but I couldn't let him destroy himself alone. I had to at least try."

And he had. For years. He'd gone to prison for it.

Maybe he'd thought he was making up for the wrong he believed he'd done.

Maybe he just couldn't bear for his father to potentially die behind bars.

I hate that his father let him do that. That he hurt him, literally and in so many deeper ways, but I can't say that to him. It's clear he still loves the man. I know better than most that love is complicated. You can feel it toward someone who isn't always good to you.

I slide a hand up to his face, letting the other hand join it. Looking into his eyes, glassy with tears I doubt he'll allow to fall, I say, "Thank you for telling me. Thank you for trusting me." I pause, letting my words sink in. "Are you going to tell them too?"

"Ma loved him," Griffin says, shaking his head slightly, his hair brushing against my fingers. "I'm not sure she'll forgive me. I'm not sure she *should*." He inhales a deep breath. "It hurt them that I stayed away. It wasn't until I came back that I realized how much. I destroyed everyone . . . and for what? I didn't spare them any pain, and he died anyway."

I can tell his soul is thirsty for their forgiveness. Without it, he won't truly forgive himself. This must be part of the reason he's isolated himself. Why he's held back with me. He doesn't forgive himself for what he did, or at least not the way he did it. He thinks he let all of them down, and that if he lets anyone else in, he'll let them down too.

"You protected the people you love," I say. "You tried to protect *all* of them, and I think you're probably the person who suffered the most."

The look on his face tells me he doesn't agree with my interpretation, just like I don't agree with his take on *The Alchemist*.

"They love you," I say, letting my hands fall. I'm about to give him some tough love, and I don't expect he'll like it. "I mean, I haven't met your mother, obviously, but I've met Gary, and he *loves* you. Like a lot." I firm up my gaze, peering at him intently. "Look at what you did for the people you love. Do you think so little of your brother that you don't think he'd do the same?"

Brother. Mother. I'm using those words purposefully. Because he needs to accept they are his family, that he has a right to them. That's what will help him heal.

There's something a little wild about Griffin as he pulls away from me and starts pacing. His eyes are full of dark fire.

"What's the point?" he asks, running his hands through his hair, making it unkempt. "What's the point in digging all of this shit up again? Isn't it better to remember the good things and throw the rest away?"

Maybe the nice thing to do would be to pretend to agree, to allow him the justification, but he doesn't need me to be nice. He needs me to be strong. "Liza thinks you've kept one foot out the door because you're going to run again." I pause. "She probably thinks that because Gary thinks it too."

"I wouldn't," he says, stopping and turning toward me. Intensity ripples from him, but it's threaded through with that aching vulnerability. "I wouldn't fucking *do* that."

I take a step toward him. Then another. "So prove it to him," I say, touching his arms again. Needing to anchor myself to him right now, and sensing he might need that too.

"Maybe you're right." He looks at me for a long moment, his gaze seeping into me, and then wraps his hands around my waist. "Do you want me to prove it to *you*, Marnie?"

I feel them down to my toes.

When I look up at him, his eyes are burning with a different kind of intensity. I know what it means without asking. "Yes. *Yes*."

twenty-seven

GRIFFIN

I'D PLANNED everything out that day. I'd bought Ma movie tickets as a late birthday present, for her and a friend, and I'd confronted my father with the bottles I'd found. I'd hidden a few others, I told him, and I could make sure they were found if he didn't comply with my demands.

Of course, plans are for suckers.

By then, I'd already known *The Alchemist* was full of shit, without having even known there was such a book. Because what I'd wanted more than anything in the world was for my father to stay clean. Even though he stopped using more than once, sometimes for years, it never stuck. The universe never aligned to make it happen, and no one smarter or older stepped in to fix things. I was the one who had to do that. Or at least my teenage logic had told me so. In the end, I hadn't fixed shit. I'd just broken more things.

I haven't fixed anything for Marnie either. If anything, I've made life more complicated for her. Will she feel compelled to tell her mother and sister the truth about how we met? What about her brother? If he's protective enough to pay Brock Tilton fifty thousand dollars not to marry her, what will he do to get an ex-con bartender away from his sister? *Especially* an ex-con bartender she met the way she did.

I should tell her all of that. I should warn her away from me, but I can tell she's not a woman who takes warnings, and right now my willpower is less 'swiss cheese than a colander.

I want her so badly I can't stand it, and she's holding my arms and looking up at me with those Bambi eyes, even though I know she's no helpless woodland animal. I've wanted her since that first night when she flashed me the finger. But it got harder to take what I wanted as I got to know her, as I came to realize it would never be casual with her. She's not the kind of woman I can take upstairs one night and see with someone else a week later.

The rage I felt earlier, when that asshole dared to touch her, was proof enough of that.

Looking down at her now, her dark hair slightly mussed around her face, her lips pink and begging to be kissed, I feel something lurch inside of me. Something deeper than wanting, and even though it's terrifying, it's also intoxicating. I don't want to keep her at a distance anymore. I can't. I need something good.

I need *her*.

I lean in and kiss her. I meant for it to be a gentle kiss, but I'm not feeling gentle right now, and it shows. A little hum of pleasure or surprise escapes her, and I swallow it. My tongue finds hers, and she kisses me back with equal intensity, our lips and tongues moving as they seek the magic angle that will somehow be enough.

I wrap my hands around her hips and hoist her up, the way I did in that alley, and back her into the wall, still kissing her as she straddles my hips. Her sweet heat is maddeningly close and still too far away, buried under the layers of clothes between us.

I'm already hard for her. Honestly, I've spent most of the past couple of weeks hard for her. Being around Marnie is sweet torture.

She rocks against my cock, and I reach down, still kissing her, and start to unbutton her dress. The silky fabric pools, revealing a lacy red bra that cups her breasts like they're a present for me to unwrap. It's almost a shame to push the lacy fabric down, but I feel no remorse as I lean in, breaking our kiss, and capture her small, beaded nipple with my mouth.

"Griff." She breathes out my name on a sigh as she rocks against me.

"Let me guess," I say, lifting my head to look at her. My mind is still a mess, but I can't help but tease her. "You want my cock?"

"Yes," she says in a breathy voice. "Obviously."

"Don't worry. I'm going to give it to you," I say and then move on to the other breast, pushing down her bra to claim her nipple with my mouth. "In fact, I'm going to fuck you against this wall."

She dips her head back into the wall, pushing her chest into my mouth. "I like your plan, but I think we're wearing too many clothes."

Her words unleash something in me. I pull away and tear at the dress, brutal in my haste, and the buttons ping against the floor. Her eyes go wide, but there's no fear in them as she shrugs off the top part of the dress. I pull the rest away and let it fall at my feet.

"That's one way to solve the problem," she says.

She's still wearing opaque black stockings, though, and underwear beneath them, and I won't be ripping those away, so I set her on her feet.

"Take off the rest," I say, my voice hoarse.

"And you?" she asks. "Will you take off your clothes?"

I'm already stepping out of my shoes. I take off my socks and start unbuttoning my shirt, watching her pull the stockings off, my mouth dry. Her panties are red, and I know without asking that she wore this set for me, just like the lingerie from earlier in the week. I watch as she eases them down her legs, bending and showing off her perfectly rounded ass. My cock would get harder if it could, but it already feels like granite. My shirt's only half unbuttoned, so I rip it, just like I did with her dress, and throw it on the ground.

She comes to me. When she reaches for the button of my jeans, I let her, enjoying the view of her freeing my cock and the way she strokes it with her hand as she lowers my jeans and then my boxer briefs. It feels impossibly good, like a revelation, as if she hadn't just touched me like this a couple of hours ago.

I'm not sure how long I'll last inside her, so I need to make sure she comes first. I want her to come long and hard, and often.

"Where's Felix?" I say.

She releases my cock, her mouth parting in a look of surprise so adorable that I lean forward and kiss it.

"You want to make this a threesome?"

"Only with your vibrator," I say. "I won't share you with anyone. You should know that."

"Good." She reaches down and runs her hand over my cock, her featherlight touch a fucking tease and she knows it. "Because I don't share either. The next time anyone hits on you in front of me, I reserve the right to tell them to leave you alone."

"I'd like to see that."

She takes a step toward the back of the house, her bedroom probably. "Are you coming with me?"

"I promised to fuck you against this wall, and I intend to do it," I say. "We'll use your bedroom later."

She fans herself with her hand, and I watch as she retreats into the house, her peach-shaped ass flexing, her small, perfectly shaped breasts bobbing.

I stroke my cock once, up and down, and try to think taming thoughts, but she's back in less than half a minute, a purple vibrator in her hand.

"This is what you use to fuck yourself?" I ask, taking it from her.

"Yes," she says, her gaze lifting from the vibrator in my hand to my face, pausing for several seconds on my chest. "Is this really happening? It seems an awful lot like a dream I had the night after you came over for the first time. Maybe you should pinch me."

I reach down and pinch her ass, and she gives a little jump that makes me laugh. Then I look down at the vibrator in my hand. "Felix, you're one lucky bastard."

"I guess that makes you a lucky bastard too."

"I guess it does." I trail my free hand over the swell of her hip, tracing the side of her body and then arcing over to cup her breast. "You're gorgeous, Marnie."

"You make me feel gorgeous," she says, reaching for my chest. Her fingers trail across my pecs, her fingernails creating a pleasing friction, and then she traces the griffin tattoo down my arm until she reaches my fingers.

"Then at least I'm doing something right." I lower my head to her breast again, sucking her nipple, and then trail kisses up her neck. The way she writhes against me tells me she likes that spot, so I settle in behind her ear for a moment, kissing and sucking, and her hands slide from my chest to the muscles of my back. I reach down between her legs, tracing around her clit and then thrusting two fingers into her, hooking them and rubbing the area above her clit. She's so wet for me, I feel another surge of blood to my cock, reminding me that I've kept it waiting too long.

"I'm going to fuck you with Felix now," I say into her ear. "Then I'm going to fuck you with my cock. I think that's the only fair competition, don't you?"

"Oh. My. God," she says. "You keep talking like that, and I think we'll find a new way you can make me come with your mouth."

"Stand against the wall and clasp your hands above your head," I say. "I want to watch you."

She does what I asked, edging back against the wall, her hands lifted above her head. I position the vibrator up between her legs, slowly easing it into her, watching the way her face changes as I do. Then I turn it on, aiming the vibrating head at her clit. Her head tips back into the wall as I fuck her with the vibrator, thrusting it in and out, making sure she's getting plenty of vibration where she needs it.

Her hands fist together where they touch the wall, but she doesn't let them fall.

"Good girl." I lean in and kiss her throat, then behind her ear, where I know she likes it. I kiss her lips and suck down her little moans of pleasure as I continue to move the vibrator, then I lean back and soak in the sight of her as I keep using the toy. Her breasts bob a little with her small movements, and her head is thrown back against the wall, her hair mussed and her eyes dewy with pleasure. She looks wild and uninhibited, and I can't get enough of it. My cock is more statue than flesh by now, but I'm a determined man when I want to be. And with intense determination, I reach up to touch her breasts, to trace the delicate line of her throat with my fingers and then run my tongue down her neck.

I can feel when she's close. Her whole body starts to stiffen, and I lean back again, to look into her eyes as it happens. To watch her as she tumbles over the edge.

"*Griffin*," she says. "I'm close."

"Come for me."

"Not like this," she says through pants as I hold the vibrator inside her. "I want your cock."

I don't have it in me to deny her, or myself, anymore.

I take out the vibrator and set it down, and reach for my pants.

"You're not getting dressed, are you?" Marnie asks with such genuine horror that I would have laughed if I weren't so desperate for her.

"No, I'm getting a condom."

"I'm on birth control," she says, lowering her arms from where she was holding them to the wall. "Are you—"

Is she saying what I think she is? "I was clean at my last checkup, and I've always used a condom."

Always. I've had offers before, but I've always refused. But with Marnie . . .

I guess my cock *could* get harder after all.

"Then I need you to get inside me *right now*. I mean . . . as long as you're okay with it, obviously."

"I'm more than okay with it. I like it when you're bossy," I say, stalking toward her.

I lift her by her waist, and she wraps her arms around my neck and her legs around my hips. It feels like all the blood in my body has settled in my cock. I lean her back against the wall to line myself up, and I finally thrust into her, my hands cradling her ass as I drive in deep. Sensation throbs through me as I feel her stretching around me, accommodating me in her slick heat until I'm fully seated, and there's the wild urge to thrust into her again and again until we both come, but I also want this to last.

"Don't hold back," she says, her tone leaving no doubt she means it. Her ankles tighten above my ass and she threads a hand through my hair. "Don't you dare hold back on me, Griff. I want everything you can give me."

I kiss her as I slowly pull out and then thrust in hard, laying claim to her. Again and again, her back hitting the wall. My senses are all engulfed by Marnie—her breasts pressed against my chest, her hand in my hair, and my cock buried deep inside her, nothing between us. I haven't lived my life as a monk, but the sensations are like nothing I've ever experienced. It drives me to go harder, faster, to take more of her. To give her more of myself too.

I've never wanted to give myself to a woman until I met her. With her, I've been tempted from the beginning. It's what held me back, but I could hold back no longer.

"You feel so good," I say, thrusting in again, pushing her ass toward me so I get a deeper angle.

"So do you," she says. "You . . . have officially . . . won the contest against . . . Fe—" A moan releases from her lips, and I kiss her deeply as I move inside her, trying to push her over the edge. I feel her body quiver and stiffen against me. Arching back, I look into her eyes as I keep thrusting.

"I want to watch you come around my cock."

"*Griffin.*" Her eyes narrow, and she clenches around my cock, the sensations sending me over the edge as she says my name again.

I'm left seeing stars . . . and knowing that nothing will ever be the same.

With my one last moment of clarity, I decide that's a good thing.

twenty-eight

MARNIE

I'M on the couch with Griffin, watching *The Empire Strikes Back*. This is a vastly different viewing experience from the first movie. Then, I was sexually frustrated, painfully aware of his hard cock hidden away in his pants. Now, we're both naked, nestled together beneath a blanket. Actually, I'm still sexually frustrated, because even though he left me *very* sated earlier, I want him again, and he's trailing his hands over me in a way that makes me want him *now*. At least I know his cock is going to be mine again as soon as the movie's over.

He promised.

"What do you think?" he asks.

He's talking about the movie, probably, but I'll be damned if I have the slightest idea what's going on. It would take a stronger woman than me to pay attention to a space opera while nestled up to him.

"Nicole's full of shit," I answer glibly. "You're definitely a ten. Maybe an eleven."

He puts the movie on pause, then rolls me on top of him, which doesn't do much to change the direction of my thoughts. "I own my eight and a half."

"Too bad. You're an eleven."

"I guess we should talk about what happens now," he says.

My heart starts racing in my chest. "It sounds like you're talking about something other than me riding your cock."

The corners of his mouth hitch up, and he's so freaking beautiful, I can hardly stand it. I still can't believe that he's really mine, if only for right now. Then again, I guess that's what this talk is about.

He reaches up and tucks my hair behind my ear. "You can ride my cock while we talk, but it might get in the way of the logical flow of conversation. We should probably wait until afterward."

Which hopefully means he isn't going to utter the word "mistake" . . . not that I thought he would. You can't have that kind of sex without wanting to repeat it, preferably at every moment of consciousness, but a small part of me worried. We're both working things out, Griffin and me, and my sister hasn't stopped being a problem between us.

"I really like you, Marnie," he says, peering up at me, his eyes shadowy in the dark. His hair is mussed, and his chest is a thing of beauty.

"I should hope so. Otherwise this would be awkward." His smile widens, and I add, "Also, I really like *you*. Like a dangerous amount."

"Good. I've avoided relationships in the past, but I want to try. I know I have a lot of shit to work out."

"I want that too," I say softly. I'm tempted to ask if he's going to talk to Gary and his mother, but I don't want to push him. Telling me was a big deal for him. Telling them, even more so.

He pulls me down to him for a kiss, our bodies pressed together beneath the blanket. We're in our own warm world while outside it's chilly and cold and dark, and I feel a moment of pure happiness. It's a gentle kiss, until he sucks on my lower lip, the sensation shooting through my body and welling between my legs.

He pulls away, damn him, and asks, "What are we going to tell your family about how we met? Will you want them to know the truth?"

I consider it for a moment, but I already know the answer. "Drew knows about Nicole and Damien. I'll tell him but not my mother and my sister."

I don't like lying, but I also don't see the point in telling them everything. Now that the truth about Mitchell Mountainbottom is out, the story they know is mostly true. Griffin and I *did* meet at the bar.

He nods slowly. "He isn't going to like me."

"Drew? Of course he will," I say, surprised. I figured he'd be worried about Sinclair and my mother. Then again, neither of them plays a large role in my daily life, and it's pretty clear that Griffin doesn't think highly of my sister. Drew's my roommate and, in some ways, my closest friend. "He's not like them," I add. "He doesn't care about . . ."

I trail off, and he fills in the blanks, his mouth tipping into a small smile. "Which part? My expunged record? My addict father? My GED?"

I open my mouth to protest, but he speaks first.

"It's okay, Marnie. I meant what I said the other day. I'm not ashamed of those things. But I know how it'll look. He'll think I'm using you. Same way Brock did."

"Look on the bright side," I say. "Maybe he'll offer you fifty thousand dollars to dump me."

I still can't believe Drew did that. As soon as he gets home on Sunday, we're due for a lengthy conversation. Then I register the look Griffin's giving me. I was joking, but it's obvious the suggestion infuriated him.

"I'd never take money from someone to stay away from you," he says. "The only person who could keep me away from you is you."

"Hey, I was kidding." I reach up and smooth his furrowed brow. "Thank you, though. I guess maybe I needed to hear that."

He pulls me down for a kiss, and I become achingly aware of the fact that I'm on top of him and his hard cock is trapped under me. I grind against him a little as our tongues move together, and he makes a growl that I capture in our kiss.

Pulling away slightly, I say, "We don't need to wait until the movie is over, do we?"

The sound he makes is too pained to be a laugh. "Are you begging to fuck me?"

"Maybe," I say.

"There's no need to beg, Marnie. You can ride my cock anytime you have the inclination."

"Good."

I line him up where I want him—*need* him—and take him in slowly, enjoying the delicious way he stretches me and the sound of pleasure he makes as he reaches up to caress my breasts. Then he settles a hand on my ass, contributing to my rhythm. It turns out he's a little bossy in the bedroom . . . er . . . living room.

I wake up to the sound of the door opening.

Oh shit. Is that Aunt Helen? I may have accidentally watched some *excessively* revealing footage of her, but that doesn't mean I want her to see me splayed out with Griffin on the couch, naked under our blanket. We must have fallen asleep out here after our second abandoned attempt to watch the movie. Our clothes are still scattered everywhere, and—

"Marnie?" Drew calls out. Then I hear him murmur under his breath, "Huh. She took down the tree."

I *glance* around wildly, making calculations about whether we'd fit under any of the furniture. Maybe I would, but Griffin wouldn't, and it would be worse for Drew to walk in to find a hot, naked man on our couch, alone. I could pull the blanket over both of our heads, but Drew's not stupid. He'd figure it out. Likewise, he'd see us if we made a dash for it, and Griffin's only now starting to stir—he's not in dashing form.

"What the hell?" Drew says, and I can just imagine him stooping down to look at . . . what? My torn dress? Griffin's torn shirt? Oh my God. *What did we do with Felix?*

The thought of my brother finding my vibrator in the middle of the floor is what breaks me.

"Get out!" I shout, and Griffin startles all the way awake.

"Is there an intruder?" he asks, already alert and rising up from the sofa. Except he's naked.

This is *not* good.

"Who the fuck are you?" Drew shouts. "Did you break in here, and . . ."

The words trail off, because he's obviously unsure of how the tableau he walked in on could possibly be explained by a break-in.

I really do not want to do this, but there's no choice. I wrap the blanket around my body and stand up beside Griffin, flinging out one end of the fabric with my arm like a crossing guard would use a flag to hide his nudity.

"Hi, Drew," I say brightly. "You're back early, huh? I wasn't expecting you until tomorrow."

"*Marnie?*"

Honestly, does he need to sound so surprised?

"Can you go up to your room and give us a minute?"

"Not until you tell me what's going on," Drew says stubbornly. He looks grimy and tired, a natural result of having spent two weeks in the woods. This probably wasn't how he imagined his homecoming.

I swallow the *isn't it obvious?* and say, "This is my—"

"Boyfriend," Griffin finishes, and I feel warmth settle in my chest because it's no longer a lie. "I'm Griffin. I'm sorry we had to meet this way."

Drew's gaze swivels to me, accusatory. "I'm gone two weeks and now you have a boyfriend?"

"Surprise . . . ?"

"Five minutes," he says, swallowing. "I'll be down in five minutes."

He stomps up to his room, and it occurs to me belatedly that I probably should have told him that Aunt Helen's been staying in there. God knows what she left for him to find. His scarring might be complete.

"You missed your calling as a crossing guard." Griffin's giving me a wry look, but I don't miss the disquiet beneath it. He was worried Drew wouldn't like him, and we obviously haven't made the best first impression.

"Never say never. I *am* technically unemployed."

He frowns a little but starts gathering up his clothes and getting dressed. The shirt's a lost cause, but he does his best, buttoning up the part that still has buttons, and then hands me Felix, who *was* resting on the floor, dammit. From his expression, I can tell he'd think it was almost funny if not for the probable impact on Drew's psyche. This is *not* good.

I know my dress isn't much better off than Griff's shirt, and we've already scarred my brother enough for one day, so I bring Felix into the downstairs bathroom, hide him beneath the sink, and pull on a huge bathrobe that belongs to Drew, tying it up tight, reassured by the knowledge that everything is covered.

When I return to the living room, Griff is pacing a little, looking adorably nervous. He pauses at the sight of me, smiling a little at the oversized man's robe. "He's not going to be pissed you stole his robe?"

"I steal his clothes all the time. It's a whole thing. He doesn't do laundry, and I retaliate by grudgingly doing it for him and taking the things I like."

I lead him over to the couch and we sit, but his foot is tapping with nervous energy.

"Should I leave?" he asks, worry etched into his brow as he looks at me. "Would that be better?"

"Not yet. Stick around for a few minutes. Show him you're not a psychopath."

The corners of his mouth twitch. "Uh-oh. Now, by the power of unconscious suggestion, I'm going to act like a psychopath."

There's vulnerability threaded into the joke, though, and I take his hand and squeeze it. "He's going to like you. It just might take a little time to get over . . . everything."

Drew reemerges then, taking stock of us on the couch, his gaze absorbing the fact that Griffin's shirt is busted.

"Why are there crystals under my pillow?" he asks accusatorily. "Did you do . . . something in my room?"

"No!" I say.

But I can't honestly promise him that no one did something in his room, because it's quite possible Bertrand did some wooing before he took Aunt Helen home with him. My aunt thinks her crystals protect her from STDs, so for all I know that was the reason she had them tucked under her pillow.

Cringing, I add, "But you might want to clean the sheets. Aunt Helen stayed in your room the other night because her apartment was infested by black widows. It's possible those are her STD-avoiding crystals."

Drew looks shell-shocked. "I was gone for two weeks," he groans, lowering into the chair across from us. "We were only out of cell reception for the last week and a half." His gaze settles on Griffin, and Griffin's foot starts tapping faster. "Sinclair told me you had a boyfriend."

"Seriously?" Sinclair and Drew don't talk, or at least I didn't think they did. They've never really gotten along, and after Clair left with my mother, any attempts at pretending were forsaken.

"She sent me a text," he says, scrubbing a hand over his beard. "I didn't get it until last night."

Was this why he'd come home early?

"Did she also happen to mention that she and Mom are coming for a visit next weekend? Surprise!"

He groans. "Yes, she did. They're not staying here, are they? It's one thing to find someone else's sex crystals in your bed, and another to have people sticking cameras in your windows because they want to have sex with your sister." Then he glances at Griffin and dryly adds, "Another one of your sisters."

"I'm not going to stay," Griffin says. He squeezes my hand and then gets up. "I just wanted to apologize, man. We fell asleep on the couch last night." He scratches the back of his neck, the movement making the bottom of his shirt gape, showing off a few of the muscular ridges of his chest. He notices and lowers his hand quickly. "We wouldn't have left the place such a mess, especially if we'd known you would be back this morning."

Drew's mouth is a firm line, but he gives a slight nod.

"And hey, you can do the same thing if I'm ever away for the weekend!" I blab, which is a stupid thing to say.

Drew's expression sours into a scowl.

"I think that's my cue to leave," Griff says. "But I'd like to get to know you, Drew. Marnie's told me a lot about you."

"I can't say the same," my brother says tightly. "I didn't know you existed until last night."

"Like you said, it's been a busy two weeks. Maybe you two can swing by the bar later?"

This last question was directed at me, and I give him a slight nod.

Griff flashes the Vulcan symbol at me, making me grin like an idiot, nods to Drew, and then leaves, shutting the door behind him.

"Marnie," Drew says on a groan. "You've just sentenced me to years of therapy. That's the only way I'm going to get over this. I almost tripped over your vibrator. I don't even want to know. I don't."

I can actually feel myself blushing, as if all the blood in my body, which was very happily settled down south last night, has rushed to my cheeks.

"I won't deny that's unfortunate," I say. "But I'm really happy. It's not just Griffin, I feel . . ."

Like I was sleeping and someone woke me up.

Like I'm not as worried about what other people might think.

Like I'm finally stepping out of Sinclair's shadow.

"You cut your hair," he says. "It looks good." He pauses, as if reaching for which of his eleventy billion questions to ask me first. So it surprises me when he says, "Thank you for taking down the tree. I wasn't looking forward to it, but I didn't want you to have to do it by yourself."

"I didn't," I say. "Griffin did it with me."

"Huh," he says, his expression shifting. "Maybe he's not so bad after all."

It's good that he thinks so now, because I'm about to tell him everything.

Okay, maybe not everything. He doesn't need to know anything else about Felix.

twenty-nine

GRIFFIN

"THAT. Was. Incredible. Like, chef's kiss to us," Nicole says to Damien.

"I'm glad you're so pleased with yourselves," I say dryly. But I feel a creeping awareness of Gary, sitting across from me. We took him out for coffee, Nicole's suggestion, to fill him in on everything that had happened, something I'd failed to do in my heightened state last night.

I texted him before we met up, telling him that I'd worked everything out with Marnie but would prefer not to get into the details around Nicole and Damien. Despite giving me many significant looks, he has complied.

An article came out this morning on *C+ Celeb News* about the downfall of one Brock Tilton. It was a brutal takedown, even for Purple Shirt, and it made Edgar James look like a god among men. Marnie and I were barely mentioned, except as further proof that Brock is a worthless piece of shit. Nicole and Damien look far too pleased with themselves. From the state of them, it's obvious they stayed up late having self-congratulatory sex.

Not that I can talk.

My mind keeps skating back to Marnie.

Marnie standing naked against that wall, waiting for me to make her come.

Marnie writhing over me on the couch, a still frame of Jabba the Hutt on the screen that did nothing to put me off.

Marnie curled up next to me, her head tucked under mine.

Marnie . . . who is even now alone with her brother, telling him things that will probably make him want to black-bag me to some desert.

Or maybe he'll hire a P.I. to investigate every last mistake I've ever made.

It occurs to me, with some amusement, that he might accidentally hire Damien and Nicole, if Marnie hasn't already given him their names.

Then there's my other, larger, source of disquiet.

It's time to tell Gary the truth about my dad. Now that I've spoken of it to Marnie, I no longer have any excuse to stay quiet. It's simple enough: if I'm not taking my secret to the grave, he needs to be one of the people who knows. I have to tell him.

Ma deserves to know too, of course, but I've decided I'll talk to Gary first.

"Why wouldn't we be pleased with ourselves? Not only did we help Marnie get revenge on her ex-fiancé, but we also found her a new man to get under," she says, making eyes at me. "We're really knocking this one out of the park."

My brother gives me another of his significant looks.

"Nicole," I chide.

"What?" Damien asks. "Do you deny it? You left the party together, and you stopped answering your phone for hours. The facts speak for themselves."

Nicole leans her shoulder against his in a sign of solidarity. "Plus, you look *much* less blue-balled than you have for the last two weeks."

"Can a person look blue-balled?" Gary asks with what seems like genuine curiosity. He takes a sip of his coffee, which he prefers with cream and sugar but which has only been doctored with oat milk, and makes a face. "This is supposed to be a treat?"

"You were told to cut back on caffeine too," Damien comments blandly. "The coffee itself is the treat."

"And a person can absolutely look blue-balled," Nicole says. "You *definitely* did that time you pissed off Mom by using her hair scissors to cut your pubes."

"What? No. That didn't happen." Gary glances from me to Damien and back. "You guys, that didn't happen."

"Uh-huh, sure," Damien says. "Now that I know where Liza's scissors have been, I'm never letting her cut my hair again."

"You're such a dick."

At least the attention has shifted off me. Temporarily.

"Well?" Damien says, giving me a pointed look to say he, at least, hasn't forgotten what we were talking about. "*Do* you deny it?"

"Do I always answer my phone that quickly?"

"Yes, you have no life. It's very sad. We talk about it often."

I glance between him and Nicole, then at Gary, who gives a half-hearted shrug. It's obvious he wants me to crack already so he can ask the dozens of questions he probably has stored up.

"I see you assholes all the time. Doesn't that count?"

"Not really," Damien says. "We're family. And before you say it, it doesn't count that you talk to people at the bar, either. That's literally your job."

"I'm doing just fine, thank you," I say. But I can't stay pissed, because I'm caught on how casually he said it—*we're family*. None of them share my blood. None of them have any obligation, legal or otherwise, to be in my life. But he's right. They are family in every way that matters . . . if I let myself accept that it's true. In my head I can hear Marnie telling me that Gary's my brother, Ma my mother. I rub my nose. "Actually. I'm doing better than fine."

"Thank God," Gary says brightly. "I was having trouble staying silent."

"What the hell?" Nicole says, glowering at me. "You knew before we did?"

"I did." It's obvious from his tone that he's pleased to have gotten one over her. It doesn't happen often. "But I knew something was going on before he confirmed it." Turning to me, he adds, "I really sensed some energy firing between you two."

Nicole snorts. "Because you saw her hugging his dick on the roof of the bar."

"You told them about that?" I ask, temporarily affronted.

"Sorry, man," he says, his cheeks slightly pink. "Nicole asks really pointed questions."

"It's okay," I say. "But that was kind of an accident. Marnie didn't know I was about to get up, and—"

They all exchange an *uh-huh, sure* look, and I roll my eyes. "Anyway. Yeah. We like each other. We're going to give it a try."

"Boo-yah!" Nicole says, and she and Damien turn toward each other for a high five. It's such a seamless action, I have to wonder if they choreographed it.

"Don't congratulate yourselves too much yet," I say. "We still haven't figured out who circulated that video."

"What's your gut opinion?" Damien asks. He studies me for a moment, as if my expression can reveal my thoughts, and maybe it does, because he says, "You still like the sister for it."

"Yes," I say. "Honestly, I don't know who else it could be. It fits."

"But Marnie clearly doesn't think she did it," Nicole says. I don't get the sense that she agrees with Marnie, necessarily, just that she's playing devil's advocate. It's a role she plays well.

"So who else could it be?" I ask.

"We spoke with Brock's old assistant, obviously," Damien says.

"The one he was banging," Nicole helpfully supplies. "She also deposited the cash for him. I didn't get the sense it was so much money, so I'm guessing he had a check and some cash."

"Is she a suspect?" Gary asks, despite not knowing the whole story. "Sounds like she'd have a reason to put off the wedding."

"But Marnie's brother's the one who put off the wedding," I say, frustrated. "Whoever circulated the video either wanted to embarrass Marnie or to make her into a victim."

"The assistant might have wanted to embarrass her," Nicole says, nodding. "But for some unconscionable reason she wanted to get some dick from Brock. It wouldn't be to her benefit to make him look like an asshat."

"Possible, yes," Damien says. "Likely, no."

"Someone did it," I say. "My vote's on Sinclair. She had the most to gain, and she's been talking to the press, willingly, for months. Do you like her for it too?"

"I told you, bud. I'm withholding judgment until I meet Sinclair and the mother."

It takes a second for the implication to hit me. "Shit. You think her mother could have done it."

Maybe it's stupid, but I hadn't even considered her as a serious possibility. Maybe because the only mother I've ever known is Ma, and she'd die before doing something to hurt Gary or me. But Marnie's mother isn't like that. I don't know much about her, but it's obvious she's ruthless. She brought her daughters to audition after audition even though at least one of them didn't want to go.

"I'm not saying it's her," Damien says, lifting his hands. "But it's a possibility."

"Even though Marnie doesn't want to believe it," Nicole says, "it's also possible one of her friends did it to embarrass Brock, and the situation got out of hand. Let's not forget the video came from Grace's phone. That girl always seems nervous as hell. This could be why." She pauses. "For that matter, it could even have been Marnie's brother, trying to get payback on Brock by taking a jab at his reputation. Again, we don't know why the original video was released."

"Shit," Gary says, looking at us with wonder. "Should we have a murder board? Because it sounds like we should have a murder board."

I laugh, but there's a tight feeling in my chest. I don't like this. I can't see a way this situation can come to a natural conclusion that isn't FUBAR. Either way, Marnie's going to have to face the reality that someone close to her betrayed her.

Unless it really was the assistant.

"So what's your plan? You're going to convince her to throw some sort of reception for Sinclair?"

"I was thinking of a cocktail party," Nicole says, a little more excited than the situation merits.

"She wants it to be like one of those murder mystery dinners," Damien says with no small amount of amusement. "She asked me to dress up."

Nicole scowls at him. "Like you don't enjoy dressing up."

He gives a small shrug, his lip curling as he regards her. "When the situation calls for it."

"Gross," Gary gripes.

"You obviously can't convince Brock's former assistant to attend a dinner party at Marnie's house," I say.

"No," Nicole concedes, "but we already agreed that it's most likely Marnie's sister, her mother, one of her friends, or her brother. We can make sure all of those people are there."

"And what's your excuse for being there?"

Damien grins at me as he lifts his coffee cup for a sip. "Like I said. We're family."

"Oh, you beautiful bastard," I say, shaking my head slightly.

But I love it.

My gaze shifts to Gary, who has a huge grin on his face. I know how happy it makes him that I fell in with his friends like I have. That we've become a family.

I have to tell him. I have to.

Maybe tomorrow.

"You're nervous," Reggie says, and I snap my head up, surprised.

We just opened five minutes ago, and sure enough, he was the first one to come in. There are a few other people at the bar now, but he's in his usual spot, which should probably have a plaque of some sort. Maybe I'll talk to Nicole and Damien about acquiring one. They're coming in later tonight, because Marnie will indeed be in here with her brother. Leah's going to mostly take over in an hour or two, when the night crowd starts trickling in, and Nicole or Damien will help her if it's busy.

God help me. This is not going to go well.

Marnie told Drew everything, and in her own words he's "not pleased" and would like to have a talk with me.

I think that translates to *fucking pissed* and *wants me to stay the hell away from his sister.*

On the plus side, she's down for the whole cocktail party idea.

Reggie clears his throat, drawing my attention back to him.

"Why do you say that?" I ask.

"You've been cleaning that same spot on the bar for five minutes. Trouble in paradise, son? This about your girl?"

"Sort of," I say, slinging the towel over my shoulder and stepping over to stand in front of him. "Her brother doesn't like me much. He's coming by the bar tonight." I scratch the bridge of my nose, feeling the old misalignment.

Reggie chortles, his Santa Claus beard bobbing. "Don't worry, young friend. I'll help you make a good impression."

"Um . . ." I start, not really sure where to go from here.

I don't want to think about what he'd do to help Drew form a good impression of me—there are any number of ways it could go wrong—but there's no time to press him because a big group of suits comes in. They're all cheering the good fortune of the guy in the middle, who landed some big contract and is feeling pretty fly because of it. I only half listen to the whole story, though, because it's boring, for one, and also because my mind is stuck on Marnie and her brother.

On my brother too. I feel like a coward for not pulling him aside earlier, but last night was . . .

I've never felt so many emotions at once. I've never felt . . .

Well, shit. I feel like my whole being is a raw wound, and if I talk to Gary right now, it'll be like poking it.

Leah shows up to help, and not long afterward, I catch sight of Marnie at the door. My heart and my dick both respond to her, like she's my homing beacon. I expected her to show up with just her brother, but she comes in with a small group—Andy, Grace, and Drew, who looks like he'd rather stick his dick in a blender than step foot in my bar. Maybe she figured he'd have less opportunity to interrogate me if she brought her friends along.

Fine by me.

They take a seat at one of the tables, and then Marnie heads toward the bar.

"Hey, you," she says. There's a troubled look in her eyes that suggests talking to Drew wasn't a good time. Even though Drew might be watching, I lean across the bar and kiss her.

"Hey, yourself," I say.

Her hand lifts to touch her lower lip, and a look of lust has displaced whatever trouble lurked in her eyes. Good.

"I suppose it's out of the question for me to sneak you upstairs?"

"Probably," she says, smiling coyly. "But I'll take you up on that later. We never did finish that movie."

"And we probably never will," I say. "There are other things I'd rather do with you."

"Tease."

I sigh. I don't want to be a tease. I'd rather be inside her, but that's clearly going to have to wait. "So it's time for me to get my talking-to?"

"He'll behave with Andy and Grace around. They've both already vouched for you."

My gaze flies to the table. I expected to see Drew shooting eye daggers at me, but to my surprise it's Grace who's staring at the bar—not at me, though. Her gaze is locked on the suit, the guy who made a big deal.

She knows him, and not in a casual way.

She is *not* happy to see him.

"Marnie," I say slowly. "Grace seems upset about something."

Marnie swivels to look as her friend gets unsteadily to her feet, says something to Andy and Drew, and then heads toward the door. They seem concerned, but neither of them tries to stop her.

"Grace," Marnie calls out, and like clockwork, the suit turns to look, his entire expression and demeanor shifting when he sees Grace halfway to the door.

"Grace Parker?" he asks, getting off his stool and taking a couple of steps toward her. He looks surprised but not shocked. The shock is all on her side.

"I'd pretend to be happy to see you, Enoch, but we both know that would be a lie. Leave me alone." Then she leaves, pausing only to wave to us.

"*Enoch*," Marnie repeats with interest.

"You know that guy?" I ask, watching to see if he tries to go after her. If he does, I'll have to stop him, but he only makes it to the door before pausing.

"I know *of* him," she says. "He screwed Grace over in business school. They were . . . interested in each other, I guess, but he used her to get an internship with her father. I have no idea what he's doing here. I thought he lived in Charlotte."

"What kind of internship?" I ask. "Isn't she an author who works for another author?"

Maybe I'm stereotyping, but the suit doesn't look like a would-be novelist, or at least not the type who'd write romance novels. He looks more like someone who got lost on the way home from Wall Street. He walks back toward his group, but the wind has gone out of his sails. He's no longer puffed up by his success.

"She is now," Marnie says. "But her dad is this big-time business guy, and he wanted her to follow in his footsteps." She aims a worried look at the door. "I should go after her."

But she doesn't have the chance, because the suit walks right past his party and down the bar toward us. He pauses in front of Marnie. His throat bobs with a nervous swallow, and he reaches up to straighten his perfectly straight tie. "You know Grace?"

I hadn't noticed them getting up, but Andy and Drew appear at his side, and Andy answers the guy with heaps of attitude. "Yeah, we do. We know *all* about Grace."

The implication is that she knows about him too, and doesn't much like what she knows.

To his credit, he's smart enough to pick up on it.

"That's good," he says, ruffled. "It's just . . ." He taps the bar and then pulls out his wallet and retrieves a business card. He surveys the four of us and then hands it, wisely, to Marnie. "Give this to her, will you? I'd like to talk to her."

"I wouldn't hold my breath," Andy says.

"Yeah," he says. "I can take a hint. But give it to her anyway, will you?"

Marnie inclines her head slightly, a halfhearted yes, and he taps the bar once more and turns away. I figured he'd go back to join the little celebration but instead he stalks off without even saying goodbye to his buddies. Their gazes follow him as if he's Bieber skipping the agreed-upon meet-and-greet.

Enough time has passed that I'm confident he won't be running into Grace. She's probably already home by now. So I let him go without issuing a challenge.

"That was unexpected," Andy says. "Should we follow her?"

Marnie casts a worried look at me, probably concerned about leaving me with her brother, and I give her a slight nod.

I don't want an inquisition, but Drew would have found a way to get me alone anyway, and I might as well face the firing squad willingly.

Marnie reaches for my hand, squeezes it, and then turns to leave with Andy. My gaze follows her sashaying ass as she walks away, and when I glance back at her brother, it's obvious he noticed.

"Drink?" I ask him.

"Bourbon."

I pour him one, and then one for myself.

"You drink on the job?" he asks, lifting his eyebrows. He looks a little like Marnie, despite the beard. Same coloring. Similar eyes, except right now they're narrowed at me.

"Not typically. I told Leah I'd be taking an extended break once you all showed up, and Nicole and Damien are coming in soon to help out. I suppose Marnie told you about them."

"I suppose she did. She also told me that you were supposed to be her fake boyfriend, and yet . . ."

He makes a hand gesture that summons the scene he walked in on this morning, Marnie and I intertwined on the couch, our clothes and Felix strewn across the floor. I'd laugh if I didn't have so much on the line.

"Nicole and Damien are my friends and business partners," I say. "I help them out with their P.I. work from time to time, and I volunteered to help Marnie because I like her. I got lucky, because it turns out she likes me too."

"You can understand my concern. This whole situation is . . . abnormal."

I take a sip of my bourbon, needing the warm burn of it. "I do. And I even appreciate it. I can also appreciate why you sent Tilton packing."

He lifts his brows again. "Are you hoping for a payoff?"

"No, man," I say, giving him a look that shows I mean business. "And I wouldn't repeat that again if you know what's good for you. Your sister means a lot to me."

If he's pissed by the implicit threat, he doesn't let it show. If anything, something settles in him, and he takes a sip of the drink. "I saw the article today. Your friends made short work of Tilton."

"He dug his own grave. They just gave him a push."

He smiles a little. "I never liked that smarmy bastard."

"Obviously not. Now you're one of many." I extend my glass for a cheers, and he clinks his against it.

Hell. If Purple Shirt were around, I'd give him a seltzer on the house.

"Are Nicole and Damien going to figure out who circulated that video of Marnie?" Drew asks, studying me. I study him back, looking for any signs of guilt. Nicole suggested that he could have done it without realizing what the fallout would be. But there's no sign of guilt on his face. He seems to want the responsible party to crash and burn, just like Tilton.

"They're going to try," I confirm. "When they show up, they're going to petition you to hold a cocktail party at your house while your sister and mom are visiting. They think the best way to find out who did this is to gather together a bunch of the people from the wedding in one place."

"I'll do whatever it takes," he says, and I believe him. His mouth lifts into a slight smile. "Is it true you got Marnie to watch Star Wars?"

"I did," I say. "We stalled halfway through the second movie, but I have high hopes."

He opens his mouth to say something. Shit. I hope he didn't see the paused movie on the screen in the living room.

That's when Reggie ambles over, his half-full beer in hand. He's had this one since we opened, so it probably went flat about two hours ago.

He stands much too close to Drew, their elbows practically bumping.

"What's up, Reggie?" I ask. "You need a refill, bud?"

I'm hoping he'll take the hint that I don't need his help, but apparently he misses the signal, because he tells Drew, "You don't have any reason to be intimidated by Griffin, son."

"I'm not," Drew says, his tone slightly defensive as he clinks his glass down onto the bar.

"No shame in it at all," Reggie says as if he hadn't spoken. "He's a hard-looking man. He could probably knock you flat with a single punch." He lifts a hand. "Not that he would, mind. I've only seen him throw troublemakers out on their asses. He'd only punch you if you deserved it."

"Thanks," I say dryly.

Undaunted, he continues, "You know, I saw this man and your sister drink each other's blood just this last week. There's no question the two of them are in love. You don't drink the blood of a woman you only tolerate."

Drew looks at me in disgust. "You did *what*?"

MARNIE

"IT'S NO BIG DEAL," Grace insists. "I knew there was a chance I'd run into him eventually."

But if it were no big deal, she wouldn't have immediately left the bar after seeing him. Or thrown his business card into the trash with all the affection of a fishmonger disposing of guts. I was interested to note the name of his company, Parker Brand Management. It suggests he still works for Grace's dad. She doesn't use that last name anymore—she goes by her mother's maiden name, Donnelly—but she shared it with Andy and me.

"Grace," I ask softly. "Is Enoch the guy the hero in your book is based on?"

"What gave you that idea?" she asks, her voice unnaturally loud.

Andy sits down at the tiny kitchen table. Grace's apartment is a small loft, and although it's far from spacious, it's more than what anyone could afford on an author's assistant's salary. Although she doesn't take money from her father, she has a small trust fund from her mother.

"Well?" Grace asks.

"Let's see," Andy says, crossing her legs. "There's the whole enemies-to-lovers, will-they-or-won't-they thing. Plus, your hero and heroine are in business school together, like you were with Enoch. It's a solid conjecture, honestly. I'm fond of it."

"You guys have been talking about this behind my back?" Grace accuses, glancing back and forth between us.

"A little," I admit.

She lets out a sigh and lowers into the chair next to Andy. I'm full of nervous energy, like ants are crawling inside of me. I want to be fully present for Grace, but at the same time, I'm painfully aware that Griffin and Drew are alone together, something I was actively trying to avoid.

Drew was unimpressed by the whole Mitchell Mountainbottom snafu. I responded that *I* was unimpressed that he'd bribed my ex-fiancé with an exorbitant amount of money to *leave me at the altar*.

"I don't want to sound ungrateful, but five minutes earlier would have really done the trick."

"I *didn't* tell him to do it at the altar," he said, pacing, which he basically hadn't stopped doing since Griffin left. "In fact, I specifically told him not to. It's not my fault he has a flair for the dramatic."

"You could have told me," I said pointedly.

"I was going to," he said, finally stilling. "Marnie, I *was*. Then someone started circulating that video, and it became a meme, and I felt so goddamn guilty . . ."

"I can't believe you spent all that money on him." I shook my head.

"I . . . I kind of felt like Dad would have wanted me to. No offense, but he would have said Brock was twenty pounds of shit in a two-pound bag."

We both started laughing a little, even though I had tears in my eyes, because we both knew he was right.

"I feel like I should be mad at you for going behind my back, and I sort of am, but I'm mostly grateful. I wasn't seeing things properly. I was worried about the wedding, when I should have been more worried about what came after it," I said. Still. I gave him a little push for good measure. "You're an asshole, though. You should have told me."

"Yeah, I should have," he agreed, and we hugged it out.

I told him more about Griffin, and even though it was obvious he wasn't a fan—he *did* get an eyeful of him naked—he heard me out and promised to keep an open mind.

Even so, I'm not so positive that open mind will stick if it's just the two of them hanging out in the bar. Or if he learns about Griffin's time in prison. I didn't tell Drew about that because it's Griffin's personal information, only to be shared if he chooses.

My mind conjures an image of him from yesterday. Of the raw torment on his face as he told me about his father.

A feeling of misgiving settles on me. Maybe I shouldn't have left the bar.

Grace is having a crisis, though, regardless of whether she'll admit to it. She stuck to my side like glue during my various crises, so I'm not about to leave her now. Even so, my thoughts won't let me sit down.

"It's just . . . it seems like you still have some baggage to work through about all of this, Grace," I say. "Maybe you shouldn't throw his card away. It could give you some closure to talk to him."

Maybe it'll also help her distance herself enough from the situation to write a different ending to her book.

"Or you can talk to us," Andy says. "Seriously. Is the book really based on you and Enoch? Did the Chapter Fifteen scene in the library actually happen? I've been dying to know." She leans forward a little in her eagerness to get the scoop.

I have to admit I'm curious myself. Grace is reserved in some ways. I hadn't realized she had Chapter Fifteen in her. But oh, boy . .
.

"In my imagination," Grace says, her cheeks going pink. "I mean . . . yeah . . . I guess the hero is based on him a little, but only because it's a good setup for a story. It wasn't like that between me and

Enoch." She starts picking at the drawstring of her pants, avoiding eye contact with us. "He's an *asshole*."

Andy and I exchange a look. I don't think I've ever heard Grace call anyone that with such vehemence.

"It's immaterial though. He doesn't live here, and there's little chance we'll run into each other again. If we did, I'd walk out."

"Or throw a drink in his face?" Andy asks hopefully.

"I'd walk out," Grace repeats. "Because he's not worth wasting a drink on. If it had been up to me, I never would have seen him again."

I'm not convinced. The way they looked at each other . . . there's still plenty of feeling on both sides, although whether it's hatred or lust or something in between, I can't tell.

"It *is* a good story," Andy agrees. "Has Vera read it yet?"

She makes a face. "She's busy. She has a new muse, it seems, and she's been doing lots of word sprints."

"With a hot twenty-year-old doing jumping jacks in front of her typewriter?" I guess.

I've heard stories. They're *very* entertaining.

"No. Believe it or not, I haven't met this one yet. Anyway, she says she'll get to it 'in due time.'"

Andy scowls. "In due time could mean anything. It could mean five years. Or ten. You're not working for Dragon Lady for another ten years."

"Don't call her that," Grace says, but it's a rote response, and there's no heat to it. Her gaze turns to me, and she tilts her head. "You said you'd tell us more about what happened with Griffin as soon as we were alone together. We're alone together."

"You're deflecting," I accuse.

"I'll allow it," Andy says.

I lift my eyebrows. "When did you become a judge?"

I can feel their scrutiny, and even though I'm still worried about

Grace, I don't fight the smile wrestling to take over my features. "I like him. A lot."

"And his cock?" Andy says, laughing. She mimes giving a blow job, exaggerating all her motions. "You seemed to like that a lot too."

"I can't believe Andy walked in on you," Grace says.

I don't feign surprise. I mean, if I'd been in Andy's position, I would 100% have told Grace too.

"It was unfortunate," I admit, "but yes, I like his cock too. *A lot.*"

"This is such a dream," Grace says. "I mean, it's truly like a fairy tale."

Andy snorts. "Having one of your best friends walk in on you giving your guy a blowie in your ex-fiancé's house?"

"No, you ingrate," Grace says, kicking one of the feet of Andy's chair. "Everyone talks about fake relationships becoming real, but how often do people even pretend they're in a relationship in real life? It's amazing that this has actually happened to you."

She said my whirlwind engagement with Brock was "like a fairy tale" too, but I don't feel inclined to bring it up. Being with Griffin *feels* like a fairy tale. Except for the part where people keep walking in on us in compromising situations. Which reminds me . . .

"What about you and Edgar James?" I ask Andy. "He had a hot alpha outdoorsy thing going on, and he seemed into you."

Andy shrugs, her curly hair spilling down her shoulder. "I was mostly just talking about Brock being a dick. Edgar's a nice guy, but he's not really my type."

I can't see why not. But I don't push her on it, because Drew and Griffin have had plenty of time alone for a lengthy interrogation. I'm worried something will go wrong and I won't be there to fix it. I mean, I'm not sure what I'd do to fix it, beyond pulling out one of the greeting card templates I have in my bag and presenting it to one or the other as a peace offering, but at least I'd feel less helpless.

"I've got to go check on Griff," I say.

"Do you want me to come with you?" Grace asks.

I can tell she really would come if I wanted her to, although it's obvious she'd rather stay home and eat her feelings. She'd already changed into pajama pants by the time we got to her apartment, and was eating directly from a tub of cookie dough ice cream.

"No, Gracie. You stay at home. I can tell you need some me time."

"I'm coming," Andy says, then glances at Grace. "If that's okay."

She nods. "Marnie's right. I could use some quality time with my ice cream."

My thoughts shift to the business card in the trash can. I wonder if she'll fish it out after we leave. I wonder if she'll look Enoch up online to convince herself he's still a dick, or maybe he's not quite as hot as she remembers.

He probably is, though.

Getting up from her chair, Andy nudges me with her shoulder. "I'll distract your brother so you can sneak upstairs with the hot bartender."

"You know his name."

She smiles. "Sure I do, but now it's tied to images of you giving him head."

"Shuddup."

I'm not sure what I expected to find. Maybe Drew in a headlock, because let's be honest, he's not the one who'd come out ahead if he instigated a fight, but instead, *The Empire Strikes Back* is playing on the one big screen in the bar. Leah and Damien are behind the bar, serving customers, and Griffin and Drew are sitting with Reggie and Nicole, watching the movie, I guess.

Christ, how long were we gone?

I can't help but be pleased by the tableau. It reminds me of what Griff told me about watching the movies with his dad and Gary, his mother making them thematic snacks. Star Wars is a shared love language for them, and this is Griffin's attempt to bond with Drew, even though my brother probably went in hard.

Griffin's the first one who notices us, and he sits up straighter, his gaze taking me in like I'm a hot fudge sundae he'd like to swallow whole. An answering wash of heat fills my body.

"Drew is such a nerd," Andy says with a slight smile. "He's succeeded in making Griffin a nerd by proximity. It's like it radiates from him and infects other people."

"Oh, they both like it." Just like she loves poking fun at Drew, and has since we were kids.

"I think Drew likes it more," she says. "This is basically his wet dream."

"Ugh," I say, making a face. "You're talking about my brother."

"And you gave both of us eyefuls we didn't ask for," she says, giving me a wicked smile. "So here we are."

Griffin rises to greet me, surprising me by sweeping me off my feet and twirling me around in a circle before giving me a soft kiss.

Fairy tale.

He leads me over to the mostly empty corner of the bar. Drew waves from the table where he's sitting but doesn't attempt to get up as Andy lowers down beside him. Nicole salutes me halfheartedly with her swizzle stick.

"We decided to make it a Star Wars theme night," he says in an undertone, keeping one hand on the small of my back. "Drinks too. Turns out Reggie's also a fan. He claims he was one of the set photographers."

"You don't believe him?" I ask.

"Do you?" Amusement sparkles in his eyes.

"No, not really. Not unless it was a porn parody of the movie. Everything go all right?"

He makes a face. "There was a slight misunderstanding about the whole blood-drinking incident, but we've moved past it."

I wince. "Reggie?"

"Reggie. I explained the joke. It's possible your brother finds it funny too, or he might have just pretended because Reggie implied I could beat him to a bloody pulp." He lifts his hands. "Not that I would, obviously. How's Grace?"

"Pretending she doesn't care about Enoch, but pretending a little too hard."

He nods slightly. "His buddies didn't stick around once they figured out he wasn't coming back."

"Too bad. Nicole and Damien could have interrogated them."

"Maybe next time. If there is a next time. Your brother is down for the cocktail party, by the way," he says. "We're going to finish this thing, Marnie. We're going to find out who did this so you can move on."

What about you? I want to say. *Are you going to let yourself move on?*

I know without asking that he still hasn't told Gary his secret. His baggage is heavy and painful, and he's been carrying it by himself for so long. He wouldn't be smiling and making themed drinks if he'd spent all day dealing with it.

I remind myself that he needs to make the decision for himself. It doesn't fully ease my mind, but seeing him smiling like this, finding some common ground with my brother . . . it's a nice moment, and I let myself soak it in.

Andy's shoving Drew's arm, probably making some snarky comment about his Star Wars addiction, and Nicole's rolling her eyes at both of them, paying more attention to her phone than to what's going on around her. Damien's glancing at her from behind the bar, a secret smile on his face, and Griffin . . .

Griffin's arm is still around me, his gaze locked on him.

Two weeks ago, I thought the hot bartender might be a good rebound fling . . . if only I had the courage to hit on him.

Now . . .

I'm falling for him, a quick plunge off a steep cliff.

That's terrifying, especially considering what happened the last time I rushed into a relationship. Logically, I know it's an unsound approach, but being with Griffin feels exhilarating, like going down a hill on a roller coaster after the terrifying buildup.

Which suggests it can't last, a voice in my head warns.

But I ignore the voice, which is kind of a Debbie Downer, and I lift up on my toes and whisper, "Do you want me to dress up like a Star Wars character for you sometime?"

"Is that a serious question?"

I answer him with a wide grin, and he responds by pulling me tightly to his chest. I take that as a yes.

"Good. Because I can tell you're vibing C-3PO."

THE LAST WEEK has been fucking bliss. No other word for it. Marnie's come around every night I've had to work, reading a book at the bar or talking to Reggie, her presence a soothing balm. She's been busy too, building up Sweet Nothings and seeking work as a freelance graphic designer. Part of her portfolio? The new logo she designed for Summer Nights. Nicole even ordered a new sign for us, and we installed it the other day, Reggie looking on and critiquing the angle, even though we used a level to ensure it was straight.

We helped Aunt Helen further clean out her apartment to avoid new troves of black widows, and in so doing, found a stash of pictures that have further scarred Marnie's psyche. And on Monday, my evening off, we watched *Empire Strikes Back* and *Return of the Jedi* in their entirety with her brother, which is probably the only way we could sit through an entire movie right now without getting distracted.

Marnie can wear her stolen *Empire* shirt proudly.

Or she could if she didn't despair, loudly, over the ending.

"It's *supposed* to seem hopeless," Drew said with all the fervency of a true believer. "That's the whole point. Don't all of the romance books you read end with teasers for the next one?"

"Teasers are different than cliff-hangers. Could you imagine if you watched it in the theater and had to wait a whole year to get the ending? I mean, what a tease." Her gaze shifted to me, a playful glint in her eyes. "No wonder *you* like it."

"Wasn't much of a tease last night, was I?" I said, lifting my eyebrows.

"This conversation has just gotten very uncomfortable for me," Drew said with a groan.

"Good," I said. "So let's cut it short and watch the next one to put Marnie out of her misery."

So we did.

Ma's angling for me to invite her over to dinner with her and Gary and Liza, but I told her it was too soon. It doesn't *feel* too soon, but I want to have my talk with Gary and Ma before I bring Marnie to them. Marnie's been hinting in a fashion as subtle as a sledge-hammer that I need to talk to them—and I know she's right. So I won't let myself take that step until I do.

Part of me wonders if I'm also waiting for the party with Sinclair and Marnie's mother. It's happening tomorrow night, in less than twenty-four hours.

It's a given that neither Sinclair nor her mother will like me, and I'm at peace with that. It was Drew I wanted to impress, and despite having greeted him naked in his own house, his sister splayed out naked beneath me, I seem to have muddled my way through. It helps that our priorities are in line: both of us want Marnie to be happy. Still, I can't shake the worry that Marnie cares about what her sister thinks. She cares so much that she agreed to marry Brock on national TV because Sinclair played a role in the proposal. Yes, that's reductive, but there's at least a seed of truth buried in it— Sinclair's opinion matters, and there's no question she's going to tell Marnie to stay away from me. I'm bad for business, or at least I could be.

Maybe it just feels like it's all going to go to shit because it's always been in my happiest moments, the ones where I'm not on my guard, when everything *does* go to shit.

A pretzel hits my forehead. "Earth to Broody McBartender."

"Yes, Nicole," I say before looking up.

Sure enough, she's regarding me with the same look of satisfaction she's had on her face for the past week. It would be unendurable if she weren't responsible for bringing Marnie into my life. Her pink hair is shorter than it was last night.

"You braved your mother's tainted scissors, huh? Pun intended."

She barks out a laugh. "You know we were just teasing Gary."

I give a small nod as I toss the pretzel missile into the trash can beneath the bar. "So what's up?"

I glance around but don't see anyone else we know other than Reggie, of course, at his usual seat. Marnie hasn't shown up yet, as she's busy with preparations for dinner tomorrow night, and there's no sign of Damien.

She nods to the other end of the bar. "Damien's outside with Purple Shirt. We found him lurking. I think maybe he caught on about Sinclair coming to town."

Fan-fucking-tastic.

"You aren't the ones who told him?"

"Nope," she says. "Our use for him ended at the party last week."

But not his use for us, apparently.

I grip the edge of the bar. "You don't think he found out about my record, do you?"

I don't need another disadvantage going into this dinner.

"I don't know, Griff," she says, "but if he did, I give Damien fifty-fifty odds of convincing him to shut the hell up."

"If anyone can do it, it's him," I agree.

She levels a look at me and says something surprising. "Try not to worry. She's crazy about you. Marnie, I mean. Her sister probably thinks you're shit on her shoe." A pleased smile stretches across her face. "You know, when you go in, you go all in, Griff. I was hoping you and Marnie would get down and dirty, but I didn't realize you were going to fall in love."

"I'm not . . ." I say automatically, but the rest of the words won't come out, because . . .

Shit, I am, aren't I?

I'm in love with her.

Nicole's expression takes on greater satisfaction. "I'm starting to think I really *am* a fairy godmother. I gave her a makeover, I got her the guy, *and* I made the putz realize how he feels. I'm unstoppable. That dinner party won't know what hit it."

"You're incorrigible," I say, rubbing my chest.

You're in love with her.

I am.

I'm not particularly good at loving people. I loved my father, and despite everything I did to save him, I lost him anyway. I love Gary and Ma, and I broke their hearts. So this Nicole-induced revelation is not entirely a welcome one. But there's no room for doubt.

The rest of the night passes in a blur, until Marnie finally comes in, wearing a sweater and jeans that hug her ass as if they appreciate it as much as I do.

There was something defeated in her when we first met—like life had thrown her in the grinder, and only sheer will had prevented her from succumbing to it.

Not anymore.

She looks like a woman who's facing up to her shit and owning it.

She deserves to be with a man who's doing the same.

Determination builds inside me, and I know that the next time I have an opportunity to talk to my brother—really talk to him—I'm going to do it. I'm going to own my shit too.

It's gotten busier at the bar, and Leah's not coming in tonight, but Nicole gives me a wink. "Go on, lover boy," she says, slipping behind the bar and giving me a smack on the ass for good measure. "I got this covered."

"I saw that," Damien says, lifting an eyebrow at her. It's the one with a scar forking across it, reminding me that Damien has his demons too.

"I don't know what you mean, stranger at the bar," Nicole says, "but say, you're very handsome. Have you ever considered having a one-night stand?"

Reggie, who's sitting next to him, says, "If you don't accept her, I will."

He's really come out of his shell, Reggie. All it took was three years and the presence of Marnie.

Marnie, who's walking up to the bar.

I don't ask questions or make comments—I just go to her.

"Hey," she says, her face lighting up, her eyes full of warmth. It's for me, and this time I don't try to quell the urge. I hoist her up and sling her over my shoulder. "We have places to be."

A laugh bursts out of her, and she slaps a warm palm against my back, holding it there. "Come on, you're not really going to carry me like this."

"I am," I say, taking a few steps before stopping. "Unless you want me to stop."

"No, proceed," she says. "I'm getting used to making a spectacle of myself."

So I carry her upstairs and into my room, feeling like a caveman, or maybe a god, because I really am one lucky bastard. By the time I toss her onto my bed, I'm so hard there's probably no blood left anywhere else in my body. I lean down and kiss her, laughing into her mouth as she wraps her legs around me.

When I eventually untangle myself, because she's not nearly naked enough, I look down at her, soaking in the sight of her lying on my bed.

"You're mine," I say, surprised by the possessiveness of my voice.

"Yes, but only if you're mine too." She rises up on her elbows. Her eyes are searching, her hair ruffled. I hope she leaves it like that when she goes back downstairs so there can be no doubt how we've been spending our time.

"Oh, I'm definitely yours," I say, taking off her shoes and socks and then helping her shimmy out of her jeans. It's as I say it that I realize how much I've longed for this—to belong to someone, to have someone who belongs to me. It's like being incredibly thirsty but not realizing it until you chug down two liters of water.

"Now that you have me, what *are* you going to do to me?" Marnie asks as I pull off her sweater, leaving her naked but for her underwear and bra. They're clinging to her hot flesh in all the places I'd like to touch, the lace a pretty tease.

I smile, tracing the line of her panties before slipping my fingers under the band and dipping them downward. She's slick for me. "I'm going to make you scream my name so everyone downstairs knows whose tongue is in your wet pussy."

Her eyes widen a little. For a second I think I pushed her too far, but then she says, "No time like the present. But you need to get undressed first. I want to enjoy the view."

I take my promises seriously, and apparently so does she because I barely work her with my mouth and fingers for a minute before she's gripping my hair and shouting my name.

"Inside me. Now," she orders.

I lift up and then prop myself over her on my elbows, kissing her as I slowly thrust inside, giving her sweet taste back to her. Even though I'm feverish for her, I make each stroke slow and deep, because I want it to last. I'm worried about what will happen tomorrow, and the next day, and the next, and *I've never felt like this before.*

Afterward, while we're lying next to each other on the bed, I turn to face her. I touch the curve of her cheek, tracing it, and I let the words spill out. "I'm in love with you, Marnie."

She flinches, which isn't the response you want when you've told the first woman you've ever loved how you feel, but maybe I was a dick to lay it on her like that. It's only been three weeks, and a few months ago, she was supposed to marry someone else. She's probably wondering if I'm going to end up being the next mistake she grimaces over three months from now. But there's no doubt in my mind. I wanted her to know that, especially since this started as an act, a gimmick to get her sister to leave her alone.

"Griffin," she says at last, her voice thick. "I . . . I have really strong feelings for you too. I just—"

"It's okay, Padawan," I say, stroking her hair. "I wanted you to know how I feel. This isn't a social media follow party. You don't need to say it back. I'm here for you, no matter what happens tomorrow. We'll deal with it together."

She kisses me, hard, and in her kiss I feel what she's not saying. She's right there with me, or close enough.

"Thank you."

"You don't need to thank me," I say, wrapping an arm around her. "I'm going to talk to my brother too." I play my fingers down her side. "I want to be a man you can respect."

She pulls back. "I *do* respect you, Griffin. You had everything lined up against you, and you still became . . . *you*. That's a miracle." She gives me a significant look. "That's the universe conspiring to do something right."

I give a small shake of my head, but I can't begrudge her a small smile. "What I meant is that I told you to stop hiding, and I was doing it myself. You helped me realize that."

"I guess we helped each other realize a lot of things," she says, sitting up.

I do the same, but even though my dick should be satiated, I take notice of the curve of her breasts and her long, sweeping neck.

"Nicole told me she thinks one of the people who's coming to dinner tomorrow night circulated the video. I guess she still hasn't ruled out that it could be Grace or Andy or Drew. She says they might have done it to get back at Brock, not realizing what it would become." Her gaze is incisive as she asks, "What do you think? You know all of them better than she does."

"None of them would have done it without talking to you first . . . or saying something to you since."

She nods resolutely, her mouth tipping up a little. "Agreed."

She's studying me, and I don't need to be a mind reader to know what she's thinking.

"It could still be Brock's assistant," I say.

"It could," she agrees.

"Who do you think did it?" I ask.

She makes a face. "I kind of wish we never started this . . . but if we hadn't, I never would have met you."

It's a deflection, but I understand why she doesn't want to share her views on the topic.

"Oh, I don't know about that. You could have stumbled in here in your extra-large Star Wars shirt any day of the week, and I would have felt compelled to hit on you."

"Oh, yeah?" she asks, smiling.

"Definitely. It's not every girl who can mix up Star Trek and Star Wars with such aplomb."

"It's not every gorgeous, tattooed hunk who uses words like 'aplomb.'"

I laugh. "Nicole thinks I have no life. I suppose she must be right if I've read my way into a big vocabulary."

"And a *remarkably* vivid imagination about how to pleasure your woman," she says.

Yes, there is that.

"Shall we practice a little more?" I ask.

Sinclair is landing in about twenty minutes, and Marnie's going to meet her at the airport. She offered to bring me with her, but I wanted to talk to Gary first. I didn't want to put it off any longer. If I did, it would be easy to put it off some more.

Gary said I could come over after he got off work because Liza's going to a happy hour with some friends. So here we are, both of us sitting down with some seltzer water that would make Purple Shirt get a nut off. It feels excruciating to sit with all this energy running through me, making me want to run or fight—although who I'd fight is anyone's guess, since my father is dead, and I never really wanted to fight him anyway.

"There's something I need to say to you, man," I blurt.

"What's up?" Gary asks. Then the color leaches out of his face. "Shit. You found them, didn't you? Look, man. Everyone needs vices. It's pretty harmless, and there's no need for you to tell Liza. I mean. She probably assumes I'm doing it."

"Wait . . . what?" I say, temporarily sidetracked. "Are you watching porn on the sly or something?"

"Oh," he says, shifting his mouth to the side. "Never mind."

"Um. No. Now I absolutely have to know what you were talking about."

He sighs heavily. "She's going to find out anyway. I have a few party-size boxes of pretzel goldfish hidden around the house that she hasn't found yet. This heart-healthy diet is going to kill me before my blood pressure or diabetes does, Griff."

The guilt sitting inside my chest suddenly becomes a few pounds heavier. Great. What if I give my brother a heart attack?

But he's told me so much, even about his secret stash of snack food, for Christ's sake, and I owe him.

"Not what I was talking about, bud," I say. He gives me a sharp look, like he's just caught on that this conversation isn't about pretzel goldfish. Something shifts in his expression, but he doesn't speak, just nods.

I want to look away. I want to look anywhere but at his earnest gaze, but he's my brother, my *brother*, and I owe it to him. He never gave up on me. Never. I didn't deserve it, but when I came back, he and Ma were waiting for me. They still wanted me, after all those years of nothing.

So I hold his gaze, and I say, "I need to talk to you about when I left home, Gary. There are some things I have to say."

"You can tell me anything," he says, staring fiercely back at me.

I hope to hell he means it.

thirty-two

MARNIE

"YOUR HAIR," my mother says, making a big production of it.

This is not a good "your hair," not that I'm surprised. My mother likes to find at least six things to criticize about me within moments of seeing me. She's always considered short hair "unfeminine," so I basically gave her a freebie.

"I like it," Sinclair says. It's impossible to tell whether she means it, but I appreciate the gesture all the same. Despite having flown here from New York, where she was staying after the Late Night with Mike appearance, she looks flawless, like she spent the entire flight with cucumber slices on her eyes and her hair in curlers. Actually, I've flown first class a couple of times, courtesy of my sister, and they *do* give you hot cookies and champagne. I suppose anything's possible.

She has a pair of oversized sunglasses on, presumably to mask her identity, but if anything, they make her look more like a movie star, and I've already caught a few people pointing at her.

"Let's get out of here," I say. "Did you guys check bags?"

"Of course," my mother scoffs. "It's a three-day trip."

"Drew went camping for two weeks with just a backpack."

"Is he camping now?" she asks, pointedly looking at the blank space next to me.

"No," I say. "He had to work late."

"And *Griffin?*" Sinclair says.

"He'll be at dinner tonight," I say. "He wanted to leave us to our reunion."

My mother makes a sound that is presumably disapproval, or the result of ingesting bad cheese, and then steps in front of us to lead the way to baggage claim.

Either she's gotten worse, or I've become less tolerant of it. My father might have been the nicest man alive, too good for this world, or so about a dozen people told me at his memorial service, but I'm half my mother too. I'm tired of putting up with people's shit.

Sinclair casts me a *that's just Mom being Mom* look, but it feels like an old refrain that was never particularly catchy in the first place.

"Is that asshole director still giving you trouble?" I ask her.

"We'll talk later," she says.

Not twenty seconds afterward, a woman runs up and asks for an autograph. Only she doesn't have any paper, so she asks Sinclair to sign her T-shirt. She does, smiling as if she enjoys signing other people's sweaty shirts.

Sinclair was always better at pretending than me.

About half a dozen autographs later, we're finally on our way to the car. It occurs to me partway through that my mother must have wanted this for some reason. There are work-arounds for celebrities —back exits, special treatment. She's good at demanding what she wants, so for some reason she wanted Sinclair to be seen here.

So she'll look like a good sister, I can hear Griffin saying.

Except he doesn't understand that Sinclair isn't nearly as obsessed with her image as my mother always has been.

I've suspected for a while.

Maybe that's why these last months have been so awful. It's bad enough for a man to convince you to marry him, steamrolling past any reluctance, and then leave you at the altar. If I'm right, my own mother made a joke of me to ensure that my sister kept getting good press off of my misfortunes. How fucked up is that?

It could still be someone else, I suppose, but I know. *I know.* I lost my father last year, and now I'm losing my mother . . . except a voice inside my head suggests I lost her a long time ago.

The only thing left to resolve is whether I still have a sister.

I hope to God Sinclair didn't know.

There's something Griffin doesn't understand about us . . . beneath it all, Sinclair and I have always loved each other. We're different, very different, but there was a bond formed between us on all of those auditions. Sinclair used to hold me while I cried, after some commercial director said I had buck teeth. And she'd spend hours braiding my hair and telling me what we'd do when—not if— we finally made it.

It's different now, obviously.

It changed the moment I stopped going on those auditions—it was like I was shifting teams, joining Dad and Drew and leaving the Mom Squad. But for me, at least, there's still an undercurrent of love tying us together.

I hope she feels it too.

While I accept that she probably tried to throw me at Brock because she thought it would be good for her image, she probably thought she was doing me a favor—in her defense, she hadn't met him in person yet. I struggle to think she'd do something so cruel to me for an uncertain benefit to herself.

She was my defender, once. I'd like to think we can still defend each other, when it comes down to it.

My thoughts turn to Griffin.

He was going to have his talk with Gary today. Did he go through with it?

I wish I'd told him how I felt last night. He tore his chest open and told me something that couldn't be easy for him. I love him too, but I'm not so far gone that I don't realize it's crazy to feel this way about someone I've only known three weeks. It doesn't *feel* crazy, but I'm still learning to trust my instincts.

Griffin doesn't believe in the message of *The Alchemist*—in the possibility of wishing for something hard enough that the universe manifests it—but I'm not so sure anymore. The universe has come through for me. Knowing Nicole, she'd probably say she's the one I should be thanking, not the universe, and maybe she'd have a point. She might not be a pleasantly round woman with a magic wand—or at least not the kind of magic wand they'd feature in a kid's movie— but she is a pretty damn good fairy godmother.

Finally, we get packed up in the car, and I ferry Mom and Sinclair to their hotel. Mom sits in the backseat, Sinclair in the front.

They're staying in the Grove Park Inn, an old, sprawling hotel that looks more like a gingerbread house than a hotel, which is a bit on the nose, since they just finished holding their yearly gingerbread house competition. It's one of the most prestigious hotels in the city, and J.Lo has even been photographed near the fireplace.

I'm not surprised they're staying here.

I'm even less surprised when, after they freshen up in their room, Mom bribes a couple of staff members ("tips," she corrects me) to clear the fireplace so Sinclair can take some pictures in one of the iconic rocking chairs.

I take the opportunity to check my phone for news from Griffin.

There's only one text, sent half an hour ago.

I told him. I hope your family got in okay.

It's not much of an explanation, but I know in my gut that if it had gone great, no fallout to speak of, he'd have said so.

I send back: *You don't have to come tonight. xx. We can meet up with them later if you need some time.*

He immediately texts back: *Not up for negotiation, Padawan. I'll see you soon.*

My mind is running through every possible thing he didn't say as we prepare to leave the hotel. There are more autographs, a shouted proposal, and then I'm ferrying them to my house, where we all used to live together what feels like several lifetimes ago.

"You were going to tell me about your director?" I ask my sister.

She makes a face, but her nose doesn't scrunch the way it used to, suggesting that she and Mom got some other cosmetic treatments along with their spray tans on their Christmas spa day. I asked her why she got Botox treatments once, and she gave me a look that suggested my maturity hadn't progressed past a toddler's.

I play a twenty-year-old, Marnie. I'm thirty-two. You do the math.

"I'd rather not talk about him," Sinclair says. "Why don't you tell us more about Griffin . . . or your new friends?"

"Griffin is—"

Suddenly I'm at a loss for words, not because I can't think of any, but because so many have come to mind. He's sexy, charming, funny, smart, *loyal*, and so deeply wounded. I'm much more concerned with how his talk with his brother went than I am with this dumpster fire of a cocktail party.

I mean, I don't even know how to make cocktails, although Nicole suggested that Griffin could play bartender.

"Everyone always talks to the bartender," she said with a wink.

I'm not sure why I agreed to this charade, except that I don't know how to handle this situation. Maybe I just want my friends and family around me when I finally confront my mother. Their presence will, I hope, bolster me.

"I always forget how small this house is," Mom sniffs as I pull into the driveway of my two-story house.

"It's plenty big enough for Drew and me," I say tightly. She's insulting Dad in that passive-aggressive way of hers, saying he wasn't enough, didn't do enough.

"I have good memories here," Sinclair interjects, which is frankly surprising.

"Me too," I say, catching her eye. There's something different about her, but I can't put my finger on it. Other than the fresh Botox, that is.

"You were telling us about Griffin?" my mother presses. "I must say I'm a little hurt that you didn't call me about these new developments. I don't like relying on your sister for secondhand information."

"He's . . . here," I end up saying, because the door just opened, and Drew and Griffin are standing in the frame. Griff's mouth is a tight line, and his postures radiates none of its usual ease. Worry eats at me. No, his talk with Gary clearly didn't go well. To be honest, Drew doesn't look much better, but then again, he's always preferred to pretend the Hollywood contingent of our family doesn't exist.

"Is that *him*?" my mother says primly.

"He's hotter in person," Sinclair says, glancing at me.

I'm not sure whether she means it as a compliment.

"He's amazing," I say, getting out of the car.

They come out to greet us, Drew going to our mother and sister and Griff coming to me. I put my arms around him and squeeze, feeling a sudden urge to hasten him away and hide him . . . I don't know where, there's not a ton of foliage in our neighborhood, but I'd make do. He squeezes me back, like maybe he wants to carry me away too.

"Are you okay?" I ask.

"Definitely not," he says, kissing the top of my head, "but I feel better being with you."

I'm desperate to ask him what happened, but the last people he should share his life story in front of are my mother and sister. I try to convey this through silent conversation with uncertain success, but he puts an arm around me, as if he understands.

I introduce them, and Griffin is exquisitely polite. Not even my mother could find fault with him, although I'm sure she'll try.

We're still exchanging pleasantries when a bright red Chevrolet parks at the curb near the house, and Aunt Helen gets out, accompanied by a man with a shock of white hair, a spotted red bow tie, and suspenders.

"Oh, you must be Bertrand," I say, greeting him enthusiastically. I mean, if ever there were a person who looked like a Bertrand . . .

"Uh, no," the man says in confusion, "my name is Paul." He glances to the left and right as if he might find a Bertrand walking around the neighborhood.

Oops. I guess Bertrand's a different lover.

"Oh, you *are* funny," Aunt Helen tells me. "Bertrand was the friend who took me home the other night."

If Paul's thrown by this news of other gentleman callers, it doesn't show. Then again, my aunt has never been dishonest or cruel. Presumably he knows the drill.

"Helen," my mother says stiffly. "I didn't know you'd be coming."

"So wonderful to see you," Aunt Helen says, and since she's Aunt Helen, she probably means it. She draws my mother into a warm hug, which is pretty comical since my mother is as unyielding as an iron bar.

"Why don't we all go inside?" I say.

"Dear God, yes," Drew mutters, scratching the back of his neck as if he has an allergy to our mother. "Griffin said he'd make us drinks."

So we all go inside together, and Griff makes us drinks in the kitchen.

To my surprise, Grace and Andy show up before Nicole and Damien do. Grace looks like she hasn't been sleeping, and I can't help wondering if it has something to do with Enoch. I'd like to know if she ever fished his card out of the trash.

She hasn't mentioned him since last weekend, and Andy and I haven't pressed. She obviously doesn't want to talk about it. If he lived in town, I'd be more persistent, but it's unlikely their paths will cross again anytime soon. She's stressed out enough knowing her manuscript is sitting unread on Vera's kindle. Yes, despite forcing Grace to transcribe all the manuscripts she types on her typewriter, Vera Valence does indeed use a kindle. I suppose we're all hypocrites in some way.

I still want to get Griffin alone. I need to. But he's making Andy her drink, Grace lingering next to her like she doesn't much want to circulate with everyone else. Understandable, although I have to wonder if that's partly because her mind is otherwise engaged.

"How's work going?" Sinclair asks from beside me, and I jolt hard enough to nearly drop my drink—one of the concoctions Griffin, Damien, and Drew put together last weekend for their Star Wars night at the bar.

"Oh, I thought I told you I quit," I say.

I *did* tell her . . . I sort of had to because of Purple Shirt's article about Brock and Edgar James. Speaking of whom, Griffin told me he was hanging out outside the bar last night. I guess he talked to Damien, but if he knows something about Sinclair's visit or Griffin's past, he wasn't giving anything away. But it's unlikely the man came to Asheville because he fancied a joy ride. He has a reason for being here, which adds to my overall state of anxiety.

"No, I'm talking about Sweet Nothings," Sinclair says, nodding to the fireplace. There are a few cards arranged there still, next to our father's ashes.

Sweet Nothings next to the man who was everything to me.

Her gaze settles on the urn. It occurs to me that my father's relationship with Sinclair wasn't as simple as mine. For the first time, I wonder if she felt abandoned by him . . . the same way I felt abandoned by her and my mother. He'd always let Mom have her way when it came to Sinclair's auditions and then her job offers. He'd never tried to put his foot down, even when my mother declared they were leaving for Los Angeles so Sinclair could work on a teen TV series.

It wasn't his way, just like Aunt Helen would never consider killing or even evicting a spider, but maybe it should have been.

I swallow down a surge of emotion. "It's good," I say. "It's actually really good."

I'd finally had time to update my Etsy shop and come up with more designs to have printed. Plus, it turns out Edgar James wasn't kidding. He really does want to hire me to do work for his company. They're a huge client for someone like me, and I don't take that lightly. I'm going to design the shit out of the materials I prepare for them.

I tell Sinclair as much, and she cocks her head a little at the mention of his name. "You mean the guy Brock tried to gaslight?"

"Oh, he definitely gaslit him," Andy says, sidling up next to me. She's dressed in red again, her favorite color. Grace and Griff are with her, Griffin's eyes on me. "He gaslit the shit out of him."

"Do you know him?" I ask, surprised by Sinclair's interest. Then again, Edgar James had his own show for a while. Although he didn't strike me as the sort of person who'd court fame, he *did* agree to be on TV. Presumably he wasn't totally disinterested in the attention.

"Not personally, no," she says, "but I've seen a couple of episodes of his show."

"You think he's hot, don't you?" Andy says conversationally. "He's even better-looking in person. But he's kind of intense."

"Is that a bad thing?" Grace asks.

"Not a bad thing," Andy says, making a face. "Just. You know, I have trouble imagining the guy laughing. The inability to laugh is a definite demerit in my book."

"Maybe because he was too busy getting gaslit," I say. "That tends to douse a person's sense of humor."

"True," Andy says.

"I liked him," Griffin offers. "He was the only person at that party of supposed outdoorsmen who looked like he would spend more than five minutes outside voluntarily."

"What about me?" I say playfully. "I like camping."

"Don't believe a word she says," Drew supplies, joining us. "She's never outside for more than a few minutes before complaining about mosquitoes. The way she tells it, they all have a taste for her DNA."

"Wouldn't that mean they also have a taste for yours?"

It's a nice moment, all of us bantering like there's no underlying tension in the room. Like this whole gathering isn't about revealing someone who's betrayed me. It's nice to forget for a moment, but there's no forgetting the tension in Griff's features, and while Andy and Drew continue bantering about the great outdoors—she's also Team No Mosquitoes—I set down my drink and pull Griffin into my dad's old office. I haven't changed much in here. It still has his old desk, weighed down with books, and his desktop computer. There are framed photographs of Drew and Sinclair and Dad and me on the wall, and his collection of records stowed in the back cabinet.

"This was your dad's office," Griff says.

"It was," I say, wrapping my arms around his waist. "Drew thinks I should make it into my home office now that I'm working from home."

"He's right," he says, hugging me back. "It would be a good space for you. Plus, I'll bet your dad would like it."

I look up at him. "I'm going to do it, but I still haven't gathered the strength to go through his things. I don't want to put them away."

"I get it," he says as he smooths a hand over my hair. "If you want, I'll help you. Maybe we can save some of the things you love about this room but still make it your own."

Look at him saying the exact right thing at the right time.

Look at him thinking about me, when his world has clearly been rocked on its axis.

"What happened with Gary?" I ask.

Raw pain flashes through his eyes. He lets his hold on me drop, and my flesh feels cold where he was touching it, as if he were the only thing keeping me warm.

"He says he needs time to process everything." He scrubs a hand over his head, making his hair wild. "He's disappointed in me for not confiding in him about Dad's relapse. He said we could have figured something out together. That a lot of pain could have been avoided for all of us if I'd just trusted him." His mouth hitches up on one side in a humorless smile. "The last thing I ever wanted was to disappoint him, but I did a pretty damn good job of it."

"He'll come around, Griff," I say, believing it. "You were a kid when you made that call, and plenty of adults in your life had given you reasons not to trust them. You and your brother love each other. You'll find a way to get past it. Are you going to tell your mom?"

"We're going to tell her together," he says. "He offered to do it, but avoidance hasn't worked out well for me, all things considered." He manages a half smile. "He's going to let me know when he's ready."

"That's good," I say, running my hands up his arms, one of them naturally settling on the griffin tattoo. "It's going to be okay. You love each other, and that's what matters. That's what's going to carry you through." I look up into his eyes then, and they're burning with ferocity. With love. With devotion. With wanting. An answering fire roars to life inside of me. I need to let him know how much he means to me . . .

I open my mouth to tell him, but the door bursts open, and in walk Nicole and Damien with all of their usual decorum. I.e., they plow in without a how do you do and slam the door behind them, giving me only a glimpse of my mother's disapproving face behind them.

"Quit your canoodling," Nicole says. "We have trouble."

thirty-three

GRIFFIN

SEEING Nicole and Damien walk in like that is like getting doused with a bucket of cold water. With vinegar in it. Even before they say anything, I know what brand of fuckery is coming next.

"This is about Purple Shirt, isn't it?"

"I knew you were smart," Nicole says, nudging Damien. "Didn't I tell you he was more than a pretty face?"

"What did Jim do?" Marnie says pointedly, and I almost smile at the way she slices through Nicole's bullshit.

"He knows about your record, man," Damien says with a slight nod.

"He's going to write about it," I say, feeling my heart beating double time in my chest. For so long, my past was buried deep, a poisoned well with a sealed lid, but it never went away, and now the poison is finally seeping out, reminding me it was always there.

A logical voice inside of me suggests that the only way to empty a well is to open it, but I'm still not feeling very logical. The way Gary looked at me earlier . . .

"Do you know what it was like for us, Griffin?" he said. "We didn't know what happened to you. For *years*. I thought you might have died. When Damien told me he was a private investigator, I wanted to ask him to find you. I thought about it for months. *Years*. But I didn't, because I figured the only way you'd ice us out like that was if you were dead."

"Why'd you take me back?" I asked, scratching the back of my neck. I felt itchy all over while we talked, like my skin was covered in hives. "Why'd you take me back without asking any questions?"

He laughed then, without the slightest bit of humor. "Because we love you, you idiot. And we were afraid asking you too many questions would have you running off again."

"You didn't believe my story?"

He gave me a level look, one that told me I was still his little brother, and always would be, no matter that I was a man of thirty-one. "I might be naïve, Griffin, but I'm not an idiot. I knew there was more to it. I hoped you'd trust me with it someday. I wish you'd trusted me with the truth before all of this happened."

There wasn't much I could say in response to that. He was right. I should have trusted him. But I was sixteen years old and scared, and other than Gary and Ma, every single adult in my life had failed me.

Talking to him had made me realize something else too. Taking my dad away wasn't just about protecting Gary and Ma . . . I was trying to protect myself. It was easier to walk away from them by choice than to watch them turn their backs on me. They wouldn't have done that, obviously, but I didn't know that yet. What I knew was that Dad had dated other women who'd bought me presents and asked about school, women who'd helped me with assignments and acted as if they gave a shit. Then he'd do something stupid, and they'd leave both of us. There were teachers who'd cared too, ones who'd tried to encourage me, but then I'd move to another grade or another school, and they'd be gone too, sucked back into their own lives.

I know Marnie is right. Ultimately, Gary will get over this. He'll forgive me, because that's who he is—the kind of person who forgives people, who gives them second and third and even fourth chances. It's one of his defining features as a person. And, being who he is, he'll probably also take it upon himself to help me forgive myself.

I already know that Marnie's made that one of *her* special causes. I'm goddamn lucky to have her in my life. Part of me feels like I should do her a favor and stay away, but I tried that before, with two people I love dearly, and they didn't thank me for it. I know the harm it can cause to walk out on someone, to make important decisions for them and act like they're incapable of making those decisions for themselves. She's shown me she's more than capable. She's a force to be reckoned with.

I meant what I said to her last week. She could send me away with a word—but only she can, no one else.

Still, I feel the need to say, "This could be harmful for your sister, Marnie. Remember what I said the other day."

"I remember," she says, her lips closing in a firm line. "But she's the one who talked about you on television. If it bites her in the ass, then neither of us are to blame. You didn't agree to live in the public eye."

I wrap an arm around her, letting my hand settle on the small of her back.

"Let's not get ahead of ourselves," Damien says, lifting up a finger. "Purple Shirt *might* write about it. The operative word is 'might.'"

"Unless we give him a better story," Nicole finishes, her eyes sparkling. "Which we're obviously going to do. This is it, kids. Buckle up. We're going to figure out who circulated that video, and they're going to be Purple Shirt's next victim. We're gonna pass that buck right along."

"I don't like this plan," I say, glancing at Marnie. She's watching Nicole with an inscrutable expression. "In fact, your plans seem to keep getting worse. They have a real downward trajectory."

Because we've essentially narrowed down the list of perpetrators to two: Sinclair and Marnie's mother.

Marnie has spent the last several months unwillingly in the spotlight because footage of one of her worst moments went viral. The last thing she needs is for everyone to be talking about her for a new reason. She hated the pity, the teasing, the lingering looks. I won't be a part of continuing her torture.

"Let him write about my jail time," I add. "It's true. I'll give him my side of the story if he asks."

"He did ask for your take," Damien says. "I'll give him that. Even if it was just professional courtesy because we got him the scoop on Brock and Edgar James."

"There you go," I say. "It's fine. I'll talk to him about my father." The thought makes me want to punch a wall, but I'll do it. I'll do it for her.

Marnie turns and claims the hand that was touching her back. "No, Griffin. I won't let you do that. You've been through enough."

"Funny," I say tightly, "I feel the same way about you. You don't need any more of your private life made public."

Nicole sighs as if she's disappointed in my stubbornness, and I'm tempted to tell her to get in line, but then she says, "Some Henry guy wrote a story about two lovers making sacrifices for each other, you know. The woman ends up bald, and the dude has a chain for a watch he doesn't own anymore. And it's not even the fun kind of chain."

Marnie tilts her head to the side in curiosity. "There's a fun—"

But I'm already shaking my head. "Don't ask."

"My point is that you can't *both* be selfless. It's boring. And unproductive. And you might end up bald for no reason. There *is* a bad guy here, and even though you both have made *very* questionable decisions in my professional opinion, including with that dress, Marnie—did I buy you that?"

"Getting off track," Damien smirks.

"Anyway. Yes. My point is that neither of you deserve to take the fall here. Someone did Marnie dirty, and they deserve to pay for it. Yes, Marnie might get pulled into that in a collateral way, but it's not ultimately going to reflect badly on her."

"I don't like this," I repeat, seeking eye contact with Marnie. She gives it to me, but I can already tell she's going to deny my next request. She has that stubborn look to her. "Let me talk to the reporter."

"No," Marnie says, her expression firm. I wouldn't be surprised if she stamped her foot. "That's not happening. What *is* happening is that we're going to go out there and enjoy this horrible cocktail party."

"You know who did it," Nicole says with an approving smile. "I thought you did."

"Do *you*?" I ask Nicole, taken aback. "If you do, why'd you make such a big deal about rounding up all of the potential suspects?"

She makes a dismissive gesture. "I thought we could all use a party."

But Nicole's not as shallow as she pretends to be. Maybe she thought Marnie could use an audience, a group of supportive friends around her while she faces up to the truth.

"It wasn't Sinclair," I say slowly, looking at Marnie.

She nods.

Fuck. I know what that means.

"Are you sure about this?"

"Positive," she says. "What was it you said about not burying my head in the sand?"

"I was being hasty," I say. "If you did that, you'd be bent over in a very pleasing position."

I surprise a laugh out of her, which was what I was aiming for.

"Shall we?" Damien asks, taking Nicole's arm.

"Yes, let's do this thing." Looking back, Nicole adds, "You guys coming?"

"Yes," Marnie says, staring up at me. "We'll be right there. Distract everyone for a minute, will you?"

"With pleasure," Nicole says. "You're going to bone in here, aren't you?"

"Not right now," Marnie says. Which, I'll be honest, is a disappointment. When she's looking at me like that, like she wants to consume me, there's only one thing on my mind.

They leave, shutting the door behind them.

I'm about to tell Marnie it's probably a bad idea to let Nicole off her leash, but she reaches up with purpose and lowers my head to hers, kissing me like I'm the solution instead of the problem. There's an edge of determination to her tonight that's sexy as hell. I'm the one who breaks away, panting, already half hard.

"If you don't want to fuck in here, we should probably stop," I say with a half smile to tell her I'm teasing. Sort of. "I already have enough things working against me. I probably shouldn't walk out there with a boner."

She smiles at me, and it's the most beautiful sight I've ever seen. Her lips are pink from our kiss, her eyes warm and deep, fringed by lashes that only add to the Bambi effect. Her whole body is tilted toward me like a flower toward light. And in that moment I feel like we can take on the world together. Certainly a shitty party and a reporter who only writes fluff pieces.

"I love you," she says simply. "I needed to tell you that before we go out there. I got scared last night, but I don't want to be afraid of how I feel. When I'm with you, I never am. There's this voice in my head that says it's too quick, and we're crazy, but I've never felt this way before, about anyone, and you deserve to know that."

"I love you too," I say. "I'm only afraid that I'll let you down."

"You will," she says. "And I'll certainly let you down, like by admitting that *Empire*'s an okay movie, but not in my top five or ten. But that's okay, because I think what we have is strong enough to get us past all of that. I think we're strong enough to help each other get through all of this."

"So do I." I reach up to stroke her cheek. "Let's go out there and raise hell."

"I thought you'd never ask," she says.

She lifts up on her toes and kisses me again, a quick kiss, a just-because-I-can kiss, and despite all the shit that's happened today, I know I'm smiling like an idiot. Right now, riding the high of knowing Marnie loves me, I can believe in anything—I can believe that my brother will forgive me and my mother won't forsake me.

I can believe that maybe the universe doesn't have it out for me after all.

thirty-four

MARNIE

WHEN WE EMERGE from the office, Nicole and Damien are speaking with Sinclair, and my mother has been cornered by Aunt Helen and her beau, much to my amusement. My mother is the queen of passive-aggression. Honestly, if there were a group venerating passive-aggression, she'd have all the medals, although everyone would be too circumspect to officially award them to her. Aunt Helen, on the other hand, is the kind of nice where she either doesn't understand or persists in ignoring passive-aggression. They could keep on talking for hours, probably to the satisfaction of neither. My mother has no pressing interest in black widows, crystals, or the questionable chi of our guest room, and if there's one person who undoubtedly couldn't care less about celebrities, it's my aunt. She regularly gets the name of *Sisters of Sin* wrong.

Drew is in a little knot with my friends, which isn't surprising. He's known Andy for as long as I have, and they love giving each other shit. While they verbally spar, Grace is looking off into space. I feel another prick of worry for her. Seeing Enoch really threw her for a loop.

Griffin takes my hand. "Where to? This is your show, Padawan."

"You're going to call me that even more now that you know I'm not a Star Wars nut, aren't you?"

He grins at me. "It wouldn't be as fun if you were."

I suppose he has a point.

I look around the room, my mind and heart racing. We could go talk to Sinclair, but why prolong the inevitable?

There's something I need to do tonight, and I might as well roll out my inner bad bitch and do it now.

So I clap my hands and say, "Let's go sit in the dining room with our drinks. There's something I need to announce to all of you."

Well, not Paul, obviously, but it would seem rude to single him out.

My mother looks like she's going to have an aneurysm. "You're not . . . you're not *marrying* that boy, are you?"

"Not that kind of an announcement," I say through my teeth.

Everyone complies with my request, and there's a great air of mystery about the goings-on, as if this truly is the live-action Clue party Nicole was imagining.

"Now, really," my mother says, once we're seated with our drinks. "What is this about? This is most unusual."

"There are appetizers," Paul says, trying to be helpful or stay relevant.

He's right. Drew set out the things we prepared (i.e., purchased) yesterday, plates of spanakopita and mixed nuts and little cakes we acquired from Bear's Buns, a little bakery downtown.

"Yes, please help yourself," I say. Adrenaline is flooding me, and the only thing keeping me grounded is Griffin's hand, which he's planted on my thigh. I absorb his warmth and steadiness and take a deep breath.

Then I let it out in a whoosh and say, "Nicole and Damien are private investigators. They've been helping me look into who circulated that video of me."

Apparently my mother's face can move enough to indicate surprise, because she seems completely thrown by this. Admittedly, they don't *look* like private investigators. They look like the kind of people who can show you a good time. It just so happens they're both things.

"How exciting!" Aunt Helen says at the same time my mother crows, "What? Why would you invite *strangers* into your private affairs?"

"They're not strangers, Mother. They're my friends." I can feel Griffin next to me, watching me and rooting for me, and hell, it's actually helping. I suck in a deep breath, release it, and layer my hand on top of his on my leg. "I've been really depressed, but I'm finally coming out of it. I needed someone to give me a push. Between losing Dad and that video getting out . . ."

"Marnie," my brother says, giving me a look so gentle I almost get up and hug him. But I'm not done.

"The thing is. I think part of me always knew who did it."

"Time for the ole sucker punch," Nicole says, winking at me.

"It was *you*, Mom," I say, feeling like Darth Vader telling Luke he's his father . . . except it's all in reverse, obviously. "You're the one who spread that video."

There are a couple of gasps, including a very dramatic one from my mother. I'm relieved to see that my sister looks genuinely surprised. Then again, she *is* an actress. It's possible she could be pretending.

Nicole is either scrolling on her phone or filming us. I'm guessing she's filming us. Far be it from me to stop her.

"Why'd you do it?" I ask.

"It wasn't—"

"Can we please skip past the part where you lie and say it wasn't you? I *know* it was you. It's like I said, Nicole and Damien are private investigators. They helped me figure out the source of the video. It came from Grace's phone."

My mother gestures to Grace with a self-satisfied expression. "There you have it. Your friend was jealous and decided to take it out on you." Grace looks taken aback, her eyes startled behind her glasses; Andy looks ready to jump my mother. "Why are you accusing *me?*"

"You were sitting next to her. Sinclair's director's been going hard at her. He wants to take her down, doesn't he?"

My sister's face has blanched under her perfect spray tan. She's watching our mother closely. "You did this?" she asks.

"I guess you figured it would be a good look for Sinclair if she went on a bunch of shows and talked about her jilted sister. You've always been good at publicity, I'll give you that. You knew how to make the gif and those memes go viral, and I'm guessing they took on a life of their own."

"He was going to leave you anyway," my mother says tightly. "I saw him pacing in the breakfast room, and I pulled him aside. He told me that he couldn't go through with it."

So apparently she doesn't know about Drew's role in everything that went down. I won't be the one to enlighten her.

"And?" I say tightly.

"You convinced him to leave her at the altar," Griff says, his gaze narrowing on her. I can feel him bristling next to me. His righteous indignation on my behalf is like a balm to my wounds.

"Was he the one who told you that?" she says acidly. "He signed an NDA."

"No one told us, Mother," I say. "You're the only one who had motivation. But you did just confirm it."

My mother worries her bottom lip as her gaze skips from me to Sinclair and back before settling on my sister. "I did it for you girls," she says. "Everyone's been rooting for Marnie, wanting her to do well. Look how much interest there's been in—" She waves a hand at Griffin as if she can't bring herself to say his name, or maybe she just doesn't remember it. "And yes, it's helped you too, Sinclair. Consider how many interviews you've booked in the last few months! All of the press has been favorable. It's worked out in everyone's best interest."

I think of all those months I spent in a fugue, somewhere in between awake or asleep, always aware of people whispering behind my back.

I can tell Griffin wants to physically remove my mother from the premises. And from the way Drew's face is contorting, I suspect he'd help him. Actually . . .

My gaze pans the dining room table. I'm confident most of us would be on board with that plan, aside from Aunt Helen, Paul, and Sinclair—Aunt Helen because she's a pacifist, Paul because he's a complete stranger, and Sinclair because my mother is her manager. The curator of her image. The one person who will walk over anyone and everything that stands between Sinclair and her goals.

But none of them say or do anything. They're waiting on me. They respect me, which is more than I can say for my mother. To her, I've only ever been a means to an end. When I was a child, I was a possible star, but when my star dimmed and Sinclair's rose, I stopped having any importance to her except as fuel to make Sinclair rocket even higher.

"I thought you might say that." I pause, looking at Griffin, who turns his hand to squeeze mine. *Go on*, he seems to say. *You can do it. Do what I couldn't.* "Mom, it's time for you to leave. You're not welcome back, and I'd appreciate it if you didn't try to contact me again."

"I'm just going to cut in to say ditto," Drew interjects.

"We'd *both* appreciate it if you didn't try to contact us again," I say with a nod to him.

Silence hangs over the table for a moment, broken when Sinclair says, "Make that all three of us. I've always known you were a ruthless bitch. I thought it was part of what made you a good manager, but Marnie's your daughter. My *sister*. You humiliated her after pushing her to marry that asshole, and then you sent me out on national TV to talk about it. We're through."

"Pushing me . . . ?" I ask, my gaze pinging between my mother and sister. My mother looks like she's already working through half a dozen contingency plans to turn this to her advantage. I doubt she'll manage it, though. My sister looks furious, angrier than I've ever seen her.

"Brock contacted me about setting up the proposal. I told him I thought it was a horrible idea, not at all suited to you, but Mom insisted it would track well for the cameras. We called you . . . and you seemed happy. So I went along with it. I'm sorry, Marnie."

"This may be the most exciting thing I've ever recorded on camera," Nicole says gleefully.

"Turn that off this instant," my mother snaps, getting to her feet.

Damien rises to his feet too, standing up next to Nicole. "Did you get lost, ma'am?" he asks my mother, his tone bland but firm. "The door's in the other direction."

"I know very well where the door is, young man. This is *my* house."

"*Was* your house," I say, standing. Griffin rises with me, and we're followed by everyone else. "But it stopped belonging to you a long time ago."

Mom leaves eventually, but it's obvious she hasn't given up. She spent her whole life trying to make one of her children into somebody. While she's probably not too put out by the thought of calling it quits with Drew and me, Sinclair would be a real loss for her.

She's at a point in her career where she could easily find another star to manage, but it wouldn't be *her* star.

As Sinclair and I watch her walk out the door, Drew comes up and wraps his arms around us. The three of us hug silently for a long moment, drawing strength from each other as we watch our one remaining parent walk away from us.

Sinclair is the one who finally breaks away. "I can't believe you just willingly instigated a group hug," she tells Drew.

"I can't believe you willingly sent away your minion," he says, but with a ghost of a smile. "I honestly don't remember the last time I saw you without her being within six feet of you at all times."

She makes a face. "I think I've been *her* minion." Her gaze seeks out mine. "But I didn't mean to be. You need to know that I wouldn't have encouraged Brock's proposal if I didn't think it was what you wanted. You were just so sad after Dad died, and then you met him, and you seemed happy. I figured . . . I thought I was doing the right thing."

"I believe you," I say. Because I do. Maybe I need to, if only to hang on to what family I have left.

"He's such an asshole," Drew says. "Also, I think this means you owe me fifty thousand dollars, Clair."

She gives him a weird look. I start laughing.

"I missed a group hug?" Nicole says from behind us.

"Are they really P.I.s?" Sinclair asks doubtfully. We all turn to look at Nicole and Damien, Drew pausing only to close the front door. Griffin is standing behind them, giving us our moment, but I know he'd be by my side in a moment if I wanted him.

I want him.

"Oh yes," I say, gesturing for him to come closer. "Among other things. They don't like to be put in boxes."

"You know, neither do I," Sinclair says with a laugh. Her smile is genuine, and it tweaks something inside of me to see it. "Turns out I'm pretty sick of it."

"Are you sick of being in college too?" Drew asks. "According to that show of yours, you've been in college for seven years."

"Fuck, yes," she says, "but it helps that everyone else is also in their thirties."

We all laugh, and she shares a story about one of her equally aged costars throwing out his back when he tried to move a case of beer.

Aunt Helen and Paul leave soon afterward. "I'm not exactly sure what happened," Paul says, pumping my hand a few times too many, "but it all seemed very exciting."

On mutual agreement, the rest of us make our way to Summer Nights. Griffin made the suggestion to get out of the house, and it's a good one.

The house feels too burdened by memories right now. Sinclair didn't want to get recognized, and frankly, I don't feel like being flocked by her fans either, so she's put on a blond wig Nicole "just happened to have" in her car and wrapped one of my scarfs around her head. I'm wearing the oversized Star Wars shirt for old time's sake.

When we arrive at the bar, it's crowded, but Nicole shouts, "Everyone out! We're closed for the evening."

It takes a while for the patrons to take her seriously. She *is* serious, though, and Nicole's the kind of person who doesn't back down for anything or anyone. It's one of the things I like best about her.

Even Leah leaves, after giving Griffin a fist bump and waving to the rest of us. There's only one person who doesn't heed her command.

Purple Shirt, who's had the courtesy to actually wear a different purple shirt tonight. I take hold of Griffin's arm the moment I recognize him, as if I can physically prevent him from talking to the guy.

"What do you have for me?" Jim asks Damien as the last of the other patrons trickle out, grumbling about the inconvenience.

None of them recognize Sinclair, thankfully.

"You wanted a different story, huh?" Nicole says loudly. "A

different story so you can avoid sharing something that might be embarrassing and painful for Griffin and Marnie?"

Subtle she's not.

Griffin gently removes my fingers from his hand. "It's okay, Marnie," he says in an undertone. "I don't mind talking to him. I think it would be best."

I grab him with my other hand.

"Really painful and *embarrassing*," Nicole repeats, her voice louder.

Sinclair sighs and takes off the scarf.

"It's you," Purple Shirt says with all the awe of a famewhore in the presence of Netflix greatness. "It's really *you*."

"I have a story for you," she says, giving me a glance that tells me we'll be talking about this later. "I'm getting a new manager."

The two of them sit down at the bar, and Andy salutes me from where she and Grace have gathered with Drew. That leaves me and Griffin and Nicole and Damien standing in a small huddle.

"Well, it looks like our business has concluded," Nicole says to me, her smile extremely self-satisfied. "What rating are you going to give us?"

"Seriously? You want me to give you, like, a Yelp rating?"

"See," Nicole says to Damien, her smile spreading wider. "*Marnie* uses Yelp. Damien keeps telling me it's dead."

"I mean, I don't actually use it," I say. "I was sort of being glib."

"Well, you can use it this time. We only have two Yelp scores for the agency, and one of them was from an incredibly dissatisfied customer."

My gaze moves to Griffin, who's looking at me like I'm the only woman in the world. I find myself remembering a different night, weeks ago, when I didn't believe in myself enough to flirt with a beautiful man who'd caught my attention.

"I'd rate you an eight and a half," I say, grinning at him. "Griffin is the only ten." I start to tug on his arm, leading him toward the stairs. "We'll see you guys later. We have business to attend to."

"Important Force business," Griffin adds with a wicked smile. "You understand."

"Oh, you two crazy kids," Nicole says. "All grown-up and running off to have sex."

"They get that from you," Damien adds.

But I'm not really paying attention to them anymore, because Griffin and I are a few steps away from the back exit. We head up the stairs, but he surprises me by leading me past his apartment and up to the roof.

"Are you hoping for a rooftop blowjob?" I ask. "Because I was at least fifty percent kidding about that."

He gives me a look with a raised eyebrow.

"Okay, thirty percent kidding."

"No," he says, "I figured this is one of the places where we have deep conversations, so it might be a good place to come now. How are you? That was . . ." His hand fists and releases. "That was brutal. If I could have saved you from that I would have."

"But you did save me," I say, reaching up to grab the collar of his leather coat. He leans down to me, weaving a hand into my hair, and the nerve endings in my scalp shoot awareness to every other part of me. "You stayed by my side through all of it, and you let me handle the part I needed to handle by myself. You did everything right, Griff."

"But your sister. She's talking to that—"

"My sister," I interject, "is just as crafty as my mother in her own way. She'll tell him that it's time to move on, but she's not going to tell him why. She's making damn sure our mother won't be able to weasel back into her good graces. That's it, though. She won't say a word about the rest of it because it wouldn't look good for her, and she knows I don't want the attention."

"You know, I'm a little intimidated by you Jones women right now," he says, his eyes hooded as he studies me.

"That's probably wise."

"I'd probably feel a lot better if I could make you scream my name again."

I lift up on my toes and kiss him, savoring the needy press of his lips and the brush of his whiskers against my flesh. "Yes," I say, pulling away, "you'd better get working on that."

GRIFFIN

"IS EVERYTHING READY?" Marnie asks nervously.

"Yes," I say, grabbing her by the waist and twirling her around. "This is going to be the best college graduation party a thirty-two-year-old woman ever had."

"Shh," she says, glancing around, "don't say that where people can hear you."

"What? That we're holding a college graduation party at a bar? Most college students are over twenty-one. We won't get shut down."

"That she's thirty-two," she says with sparkling eyes. "Purple Shirt might be lurking. Besides, Drew's going to show up with Sinclair any minute, and she might faint if she hears you."

Ah yes, one of the lovely expectations of fame is that you're never supposed to acknowledge your actual age. That said, Sinclair's making the first move toward admitting she's not really twenty. Turns out the big scoop she gave Purple Shirt a few weeks ago wasn't just about firing her momager.

Sinclair quit *Sisters of Sin.*

Part of her decision was because the director is a sexist dick, no sugarcoating that, but she also got tired of playing a college student in the constant throes of some drama or other, never growing more than a few months older between seasons despite the fact that the filming had gone on for years. She doesn't have a new project lined up yet, but she told Marnie she doesn't mind. She feels like she's finally free for the first time in years.

There's still some healing that needs to happen between the Jones siblings. Marnie and Sinclair had a long talk after the cocktail party at Marnie's house, and I guess there's been some jealousy on both sides. While Marnie doesn't want to be famous, thank God, being the sister of a celebrity isn't for the faint of heart, and although Sinclair *does* like being famous, she's always been envious of Marnie's freedom, particularly her freedom from their shitty mother.

Sinclair is going to be staying in Asheville for a few months to take what she calls her first vacation in ten years. Still. She hasn't had a total personality transplant. She's staying at a high-end rental downtown, not her old room in Marnie's house.

Gary and I have a lot of healing to do too, but we've made progress.

He and I spoke with Ma last weekend. It was awful, *awful*, to see her cry and to know I was the cause, but she forgave me with a grace I struggle to believe I deserve. She also told me something that made my heart quake. She'd known my father was cheating, at the end, and she hadn't stayed with him only out of love and devotion. She hadn't wanted to lose me.

"You're my son," she said, tears running down her face. "You're my boy. I loved you every day you were with me, in my house, and I loved you every moment you were gone. I prayed for you to return. The day you came back home was the best day of my life."

I'm not ashamed to admit that I cried too.

I brought Marnie over to Ma's house for dinner last night, with Liza and Gary, and Ma treated her like *she* was the celebrity. She'd even framed one of Marnie's cards—a thank-you note Marnie had written her for making her a batch of sugar cookies a couple of weeks back—and hung it on the wall in the dining room. It would have been embarrassing if I weren't so stupidly grateful. Surprisingly, Liza actually hugged me at the end of the night. "I'm glad you're here," she said, and even though it was a cryptic comment, since I've been back in Asheville for a good five years, we both knew what she meant.

The graduation party was Marnie's idea.

Like me, Sinclair never finished high school or college, which means she never had a celebration to go with it. Now that she's officially graduating from fake college, Marnie thought it would be fun to give her one.

We hung up cheesy signs everywhere, and there will be a keg, obviously, which I fully suspect Marnie's sister won't touch with a ten-foot pole.

"Was this a dumb idea?" Marnie asks, surveying the decorations at the bar.

"Absolutely." I laugh when she pokes me in the chest. "But it's also amazing. I think she's going to like it, and if she doesn't, the rest of us will enjoy it enough to make up for it."

She pulls down the front of my shirt and kisses me, her mouth hot and demanding.

I really am one lucky fucker.

"Rude," Nicole says, entering the front door with Damien. The door bangs shut behind them. "Ha! This place looks incredible."

"I don't know," Damien says. "Am I the only one who doesn't remember college fondly?"

"Says the hot guy who got tons of ass," Nicole says.

"Excuse me," I say, reluctantly pulling away from Marnie, "we were having a moment here."

"You have a lot of moments," Damien says. "We're demanding this one. We need to talk to Marnie."

"What's up?" Marnie asks.

They settle onto a couple of barstools. "Remember the one

condition of accepting our help?" she says. "You need to nominate our next victim. I mean client."

"Like now?" Marnie asks in disbelief. "You want me to name my least fortunate friend right this minute?"

"Tick. Tock," Nicole says, moving her pointer finger back and forth.

"Oh, come on." I throw a pretzel at her, which she catches. She shrugs and eats it. "You don't need an answer from her right now," I protest. "We're about to have a party. Lighten up."

"Look at you being salty," Nicole says. "You were much more accommodating of our whims before you had a girlfriend. I shouldn't have encouraged you so much." But I know her better than to think she regrets it.

There's a knock on the door, and Andy comes in, Reggie following her. He takes a seat in his usual spot, and even though none of us invited him, and it *does* say Private Event on the door, none of us tries to send him away. It's like we all recognize he's almost as much a part of this place as we are.

"Grace isn't here?" Andy says, glancing around like she thinks Grace might be hiding behind one of the mannequins dressed in caps and gowns. Yes, they're terrifying. No, I didn't try to talk Marnie out of it. The party is kitsch on purpose, she said. I'm not entirely sure what that means, but I'd do anything for my girl.

"Not yet," Marnie says, immediately worried. "What's wrong?"

Andy twists her hair away from her face, a nervous gesture for a woman who almost never seems unsure of herself. "We were supposed to come over together, but she said she'd meet me here. I could tell something was wrong. She sounded upset."

Nicole directs a look at Damien, her interest piqued.

"Should we go get her?" Marnie asks.

Suddenly the door swings open without any kind of knock preceding it, and Grace herself bursts in. Something clearly *has* happened, but she doesn't look sad. She looks furious.

"Gracie?" Marnie says, and she and Andy both hurry toward her.

"You won't believe it," she says. "*I* don't believe it."

I start fixing her a drink. If anyone needed one, it's her, at this moment.

"It's Enoch."

"Who's a eunuch?" Nicole asks.

"I *wish* he were a eunuch," Grace says with a harsh laugh. "That *asshole.*"

I finish her drink and slide it across the bar to her as she approaches it. She spares me a quick smile. "Thanks, Griffin."

"Where's my drink?" Reggie asks in a huff, tugging on the bottom of his beard.

Since I don't have much to add to this conversation, I pour him a drink, listening all the while.

"What did he do?" Marnie asks tightly. "Did you call him? I was wondering if you'd kept his card."

Grace makes a sound of disbelief. "I didn't call him. I saw him at work. He's her new muse. He's her *new muse!*"

Okay, so their conversation is more interesting than I figured. I fumble with the beer, giving it too much of a head, but I bring it over to Reggie anyway.

He gives me a bland look. "Love has changed you."

"Sorry, man. We're having a party for Marnie's sister, but feel free to stay."

"Her sister's a kid?" he asks, looking around at the décor.

"No, but she likes to play pretend."

If he has follow-up questions, he doesn't ask them, so I tap the bar and circle around to stand next to Marnie. She leans into me.

"Enoch's having a fling with the dragon lady?" Andy asks in obvious disbelief, or maybe awe. "How did this happen?"

"No," Grace says, her frantic energy practically sparking off her. "Maybe. I don't know. She hired my dad's company to be her brand managers. He fucking moved here to manage her account. He *lives* here now."

"Who exactly is this guy?" Nicole asks, a spark of interest lighting in her eyes.

"He's the guy who made nice with her in business school so he could get an internship with her dad," Marnie explains in an undertone.

"He more than made nice with me," Grace says, her gaze fierce. She looks like a Viking warrior, not Marnie's friend who writes romances and is afraid of spiders. Shit. The suit better watch his back. "He took my V-card."

Andy looks like someone just smacked her in the face with a dead fish. "What the hell? Seriously?"

"Why didn't you tell us?" Marnie asks.

"I don't know," Grace says. She groans and pulls at the ends of her short blond hair. "It's embarrassing. You're right. I wrote him into my book, and now I'm stuck with him in my life *and* my book, and if he finds out, I'm just going to die."

"Marnie, you do quick work," Nicole says with a slight nod. "We appreciate fast results."

I've known Nicole long enough to make the connection, but Marnie tilts her head, no doubt sifting through our conversation with them. Her eyes light up. "You're going to be her fairy godmothers."

"Yes," Damien says. "Might as well keep it in the family. But I'd really appreciate if you didn't call us that."

"Welcome to the rest of your life, Grace," Nicole says, much happier than the situation warrants, or at least much happier than it would warrant from Grace's perspective. "We're going to make that son of a bitch regret he was ever born."

ANGELA CASELLA is a romcom fanatic. Writing them, reading them, watching them—she's greedy, and she does it all. She writes the Fairy Godmother Agency series solo, and she's lucky enough to collaborate with Denise Grover Swank on multiple series.

She lives in Asheville, NC. Her hobbies include herding her daughter toward less dangerous activities, the aforementioned romcom addiction, and dreaming of having someone else clean her house.

Visit her website at www.angelacasella.com or Angela Denise's website at www.arcdgs.com.

9 781963 896039